YOVO

YOVO

Stephen F. Dexter Jr.

Yovo
A Peace Corps Writers Book
An imprint of Peace Corps Worldwide
Copyright © 2017 Stephen F. Dexter. Jr.
All rights reserved.
Printed in the United States of America
by Peace Corps Writers of Oakland, California.
No part of this book may be used or reproduced in any manner whatsoever without
written permission except in the case of brief quotations contained in critical articles
or reviews.
For more information, contact peacecorpsworldwide@gmail.com.
Peace Corps Writers and the Peace Corps Writers colophon are trademarks of
PeaceCorpsWorldwide.org.
ISBN: 1935925571
ISBN-13: 9781935925576
Library of Congress Control Number: 2017934263
First Peace Corps Writers Edition, February 2017

"For Stephanie, Ian and Zöe,
Inspiration for my life's work

To my fellow Togo RCPVs (1988-91).

To the family of Kadjina Badasso of Tchamba, Togo.

To the former Hearts and Stars writing group from Canton, MA, especially Cindy Zelman for her amazing feedback and friendship.

To Kris Wilton for her first draft edits.

To my first writing coach and author Kate Flora for her patience and insights on the story.

To John Coyne, Marian Haley Beil and Peace Corps Writers for having faith in my work and the patience to see it through.

To Mary Sullivan Walsh and Nedda Chaplin, my final editors for their professionalism, honest feedback and optimism to bring it into the finish line.

To Deborah Luxenberg, Steven Johnson, Beckham and Tina Dickerson for their faith and support.

To brothers Christian and Jonathan and Dawn and Stephen Dexter, Sr. for supporting my dream to live overseas.

For Stephanie, who patiently supported me over hundreds of hours of vacation and family time to write.

To George Killeen for his inspiring cover design.

To Ted LaCrone and Paul Brouwer who were there at the start and never gave up.

CHAPTER 1

ALLER REVENIR

—◆—

SUMMER, 1992

"OLY," THE SHIRTLESS MAN WHISPERED with an inflection that landed some-where between a question and a statement. He changed his grip on a rusty machete and wiped his brow. The machete raised and lowered in his tight fist in rhythm with his heavy breathing. Without looking up, Oly finished the remnants of a calabash of *tchouk*, the sweat dripping into his bowl as he gestured for the man to sit. The man ignored the invitation. Several seconds passed before he responded.

"I've been sent here to kill you."

"I know," Oly said. There was a commotion outside of the hut as word had spread to the village that a stranger had walked in with a ma-chete. A crowd began to gather.

"They need to go away," the man said, barely tilting his head to the right without moving his glare. He shifted his grip.

"*Laissez-nous*," Oly said, finally lifting his head and raising an arm to an opening where several heads peered in. The man slowly lifted the machete, gripping the handle tighter as his muscles tensed. Oly gazed directly into the man's eyes when he felt a shove, as if a wind were sucking him out of the hut. The machete swooped past his head and missed. The man disappeared. A blurry mouth came into focus followed by sound.

"Meesta, meesta Oly. *Allez! Le bus! Allez!* You must go! Wake up meesta Oly!"

Oly popped up, confused and drenched in sweat. A man, so black he could just make out his white eyes, stood over him and shook Oly with a strong arm. The stench of body odor and cheap cologne completed his shock back to consciousness. Chalim.

"Meesta Oly. You miss plane! Today you say get you! Come on, meesta Oly!"

Oly's head throbbed as the physical force of nausea pushed vomit to his lips. Before Chalim could react, Oly covered him with the remains of his last night in Togo. Chalim cursed in Kotokoli and let go of Oly, standing up to avoid another barrage. *"Mon Dieu!"* he cried.

Oly apologized, wiping his mouth and pointed to a pile of clothes in the corner. Chalim changed into one of Oly's t-shirts that he bought in the local market. On the front was a large arrow with the phrase 'I'm with stupid' printed in the middle. Oly pointed at it, trying to lift himself out of the bed without vomiting again. *"C'est moi."* He had little time to make sense of the terrifying nightmare as he pulled on a pair of clean boxers and his favorite Fan Milk shirt. The shirt (not for sale at the time but co-opted with a combination of white privilege and a day's wages) was a reminder to Oly of his entire relationship with Togo: wanting to belong but looking painfully out of place in doing so. It came to him (as Chalim scurried from room to room, closing the shutters over Oly's custom-screened windows ... another symbol of white privilege) that the nightmare symbolized his deepest fears about forcing himself on another people. Although the Peace Corps was officially welcome in Togo, that was a government decision. The people in his assigned village had no idea why he was there. When he had built up enough social capital after several months at post and asked around, he heard everything from 'sent by the Gods to build us a bridge,' to 'CIA spy' (a common theme with Peace Corps Volunteers). Everyone had made up their own minds why the only white man in a village of over 10,000 people would leave the richest country on Earth to come to one of the poorest. To be truly accepted (or as accepted as a white man could be) he would have to relinquish control, the same sacrifice that the Togolese had been making for centuries. *Homme Propose, Dieu Dispose* was a popular expression that he had scoffed at. It ran antithetical to the can-do spirit of the Peace Corps. The distaste for what he considered passive acceptance created a divide between Oly and Togo that strained his relationships and blocked his ability to integrate. He hadn't learned until it was almost too late that making peace with the discomfort was as close as he would get to being Togolese, or killed by a machete.

The familiar rumble of a Peugeot 504 became audible as it turned the final stretch toward Oly's house. He jumped out of bed in a panic, nearly falling over from the nausea.

"Oh shit," he said aloud, pulling on a worn pair of red Converse All Stars.

Chalim grabbed Oly's hockey bag, stuffed with his belongings for the final return flight to Boston.

"*C'est tout?*" he asked, lifting the bag with one hand, his triceps muscles bulging as he grabbed his assault rifle with the other.

"*Oui, c'est tout.*" Oly said, not caring if it was true or not.

The car stopped in front with a loud metallic squeal. A giant cloud of dust that was following the car caught up and settled over it and everything within ten feet. Bawendi waited for the dust to settle and then stepped out from the passenger seat in a purple *boubou* that featured a pattern of palm trees, paisley, and images of the current Togolese president. He wore a pair of wrap-around shades and had a serious look on his face. The chauffeur stayed put, looking bored while the white woman remained in the back seat, unmoving, looking straight ahead. A small group of children started to gather, keeping their distance and staring at the scene. Cars rarely came to this side of Tchamba and always attracted an audience. Oly could hear the local dialect accented with *yovo,* the local word for white man. He stood in the doorway next to Chalim, with the stupid arrow pointing at him. Samantha, the white woman, looked over the top of her sunglasses and shook her head. He had some explaining to do.

Oly gave a big sweaty hug to Chalim after loading the hockey bag in the trunk of the Peugeot and took one last look at what had been his home for over two years. He regretted that the nausea clouded his nostalgia. He knew there'd be a price for trying to numb the goodbye. Chalim and Bawendi exchanged salutations, each putting hands over heart while doing the rhythmic grunts according to kotokoli custom. Before getting in the car, Oly reached into his bag and pulled out his rain jacket and Swiss Army knife, handing both to Chalim. "I visit you in America," Chalim said, holding the gifts in one hand. Oly couldn't tell if it was sweat or tears that started running down Chalim's face when he got in the back seat next to Samantha.

Bawendi took off his glasses when he got in the car and glared at Oly. *"Tu es malade,"* he said.

There was no talking for the first twenty minutes of the ride to Lomé. Oly focused on not vomiting, which was not easy as the chauffeur drove at a high speed, swerving around potholes and panicked chickens.

"I'm sorry about everything," Oly said, when they approached one of the many checkpoints on the *route nationale.*

"Everything? Really?" Samantha said without looking at him.

"You think your hangover apology is going to do it? Tell me what you're sorry about and I'll decide whether or not you deserve it."

Silence.

"Okay, I'll just be quiet."

"Good idea."

There was no more talking for the remainder of the six-hour drive to Togo's capital. After a quiet dinner of *foufou* and guinea fowl, Oly went to bed early, pretending to be fast asleep when Samantha joined him two hours later. "I know you're awake," she said. "And I'm not really that angry. I was just hoping that we'd spend our last night together rather than you doing *sotoubee* shots with your animal-slaughtering friends and acting like an idiot."

Oly rolled over. "Was I that bad?"

"Yes," she said. "But there is a way you can make it up to me," she smiled, removing her t-shirt. The sense of urgency that they may not see one another again added intensity to their lovemaking. Both were thinking it could be the last time but neither would say it. Afterwards, they fell into a deep sleep.

"*Merde!*" Oly yelled several hours later when a laser beam of sunlight spilled into the room through a crack in the curtains. Like most things in Africa, the sun was extreme. It was bright and hot by 7am. He jumped up to throw his pants on, happy that the nausea was finally gone.

Samantha rolled over. "What are you doing?" she said, brushing her disheveled hair aside. Oly thought she always looked her best like this, first thing in the morning.

"I'm late for my checkout appointment with the director. She already hates me."

"Huh? Why? Come back to bed," she said, reaching out for his arm. "I don't hate you."

"*Arrête,*" he said, moving his arm out of reach. "You know I'll miss my plane and my visa's about to expire." He put his hand under her chin, just as he did the night he kissed her for the first time, over a year ago. In many ways, Samantha was the anecdote to everyone he had ever dated. She didn't fuss about her looks (long brown hair, full lips, a lanky volleyball player's build, a girl-next-door smile) but had a natural beauty that matched her confident personality. It was hard enough to be a volunteer alone in a village, let alone a female. But Samantha was different. She was fluent not only in the national language (French) but had also picked up on some of the local dialect (kotokoli). A Women's Studies major at Wellesley, she had connected quickly with the influential 'mamas' in the market and supported several villages with business cooperatives. In short, she knew what she wanted.

"I'd make it worth your while, Oly."

"I know you would. And you will again, I promise," he said, looking her straight in the eye. It was the closest thing to a long-distance commitment since they started saying goodbye a week ago. He kissed her slowly, the warmth of her mouth disarming his need to leave. She put his arm around him and tried to pull him back to the bed. "C'mon," he said, pulling away. "I can't."

She let go, folding her arms across her bare chest and pouting. "Well, actually you can," she said, pointing at his erection. He was going to be late.

Thirty minutes later, when Samantha fell into a slumber, Oly jumped up in a panic, realizing that there was a good chance he may miss his flight. He scribbled a note for her to meet him at the airport with Bawendi and flew out the door, skipping the steps in twos and threes.

He ran the mile down sandy streets to the Peace Corps office, catching the attention of a group of street children who started chanting the yovo song. "*Yovoyovobonsoirçavabienmerci*," they chanted faster and faster as he ran by.

Just outside the gates of the building that housed Peace Corps Togo, a man was cooking meat over an open fire. Oly knew it would probably be a mistake, but he was starving. The spice-covered object resembled shish kebab, but turned out to be a half-cooked goat intestine threaded on a stick-like ribbon. The gastronomic gaffe symbolized Oly's two years in the Republic of Togo: optimism turned stomachache. Before he could finish the ribbon kabob, he vomited next to the stand beneath the Peace Corps sign. One woman passing with a bundle of sticks on her head made a clucking noise and mumbled something with the word yovo in it. He threw the remaining meat on the ground.

"*Ce n'est pas la viande, mon ami*," Oly said.

The man held out his hand. "*Je sais.*"

"*Un franc.*"

The former headquarters of Togo's information minister was a prime piece of real estate, only blocks from the Bay of Benin, purchased by the U.S. government in the early 1980s when the military moved all of its officials to a new compound. Susan Cornick, the recently appointed Peace Corps country director, was sitting behind a gigantic teak desk left by the former Togolese official, when Oly walked in, panting loudly and apologizing for his tardiness. "*Je suis désolé,*" he said, in a Togolese accent. "*L'heure Africain.*"

Cornick, a former official with the U.S. Department of Agriculture, was not amused. Oly's dossier was spread out in front of her. Next to it was his plane ticket home. He contemplated grabbing it and running for the door. She stared at him like a disapproving mother and spent the next hour poring over his file, questioning everything from the 100,000 CFA spent on *gri-gri* for the bridge project to the whereabouts of his motorcycle keys. An air conditioner rattled in the corner, barely able to fight off the persistent humidity outside. Oly started feeling nauseous again, picturing himself vomiting on the desk and his file, trying to miss the ticket.

When she was done, she held up a piece of paper with an official-looking insignia on it. "There's one piece of good news for you, Mr. Olymeyer. It appears you have friends in high places. The director general du T.P.P. has submitted a congratulatory letter on your behalf, thanking you for the bridge that, frankly, I thought you'd never finish. Well done," she concluded, holding out his ticket and directing him to sign the final release form.

"That's it?" he said.

"*C'est tout,*" she said, half smiling and holding out her hand. "Now you can go back to reality."

Reality. It had become a loaded term for Oly. *Whose reality?* he thought to himself as he bounced down the stairs from Cornick's air-conditioned office into the sweltering climate that had been his *realité* for the past two years. She didn't know what reality was, he thought to himself, as a khaki-clad security guard opened the gate for him.

"*Akpe,*" he thanked the guard, surprising him not only with the local language but the correct dialect, as Oly had pegged him for Ewe. *That's reality.* Of course, he knew what she meant. *Her reality.* Yovo reality. He was no longer on the government 'dole,' deciding when to work and when not to (usually when he was hung-over, which was often), shaving, wearing a tie, and all the trappings of being a responsible college grad in America. He remembered joking with the recruiter in Boston (in an interview that now seemed a lifetime ago), that he wanted to join the Peace Corps to 'escape reality.' Now, as he jumped into a taxi with a missing door and windshield, his entire understanding of the word had shifted.

Malnourished bellies and watching as the local butcher slaughtered his dinner, as blood dripped on the dirt, had become reality. Meeting with local chiefs and listening to their translated stories of death and *gri-gri* had become reality.

Gnassingbe Eyadema International Airport, a heavily guarded terminal built in the 1960s during the height of French investment in the region, stood on the edge of the city. As in many West African cities, there was one congested road in and one out. Oly spent several extra francs on a 'taxi express,' which meant that it didn't make the usual five stops on the way to the airport. Oly didn't have a watch and kept asking the driver for the time.

"*Mon ami,*" he kept saying. "*L'heure d'arriver c'est l'heure d'arriver.*" Over an hour later, they finally made it past the heavily guarded entrance, greeted by armed soldiers standing in the oppressive heat next to armed personnel carriers. One of them noticed the white man in the back of the taxi and waved them through, a final reminder to Oly that, at times, his skin color did expedite things.

Samantha stood next to Bawendi in the main terminal, waving to Oly as he walked in. She shook her head at Oly and laughed. "You're a mess," she said, giving him a kiss on the cheek. Bawendi pointed down at Oly's hockey bag, smiling.

"My friend, I have to pay fifty francs to get this one past security. And they take your leather sandals."

"Did Cornick give you a hard time?" Samantha asked.

"Depends what you define as hard time. I got my ticket and that's all that matters, right?"

"*Monsieur, c'est l'heure,*" Bawendi's chauffeur pointed out, looking at the flight information posted in the lobby above them.

Oly and Samantha hugged one final time. "I'll be waiting for you," he whispered in her ear. When she looked up at him, her eyes were a deep green from welling up with tears. It was one of the first times he had confirmed their relationship as something more than a Peace Corps romance, the kind that usually ended at the airport. Throughout their time together, Samantha had fluctuated between independent aid worker change agent and college girlfriend. She left her on-again-off-again boyfriend from California to pursue this dream and hadn't expected (nor wanted) to get into another relationship. Oly snuck up on her. His lack of pretention refreshed her (she'd had enough of that in her Wellesley dating circles) and something about his wanderlust and idealism turned her on. He was good in the sack, too, which didn't hurt.

"I know you will," she smiled. "I didn't know it was going to be so hard." Before she was ready to let go, Oly had to push away from her to relieve the pressure on his gut.

"What is it?" she asked.

"You don't want to know."

He rushed through the goodbyes with Bawendi and his chauffeur, grabbing his bags and running to the departure gate. Across from the check-in desk, his eyes fixed on the small, dark silhouette of a man painted on a door near the boarding gate. Oly excused himself from the line as soon as he checked in and sprinted across the lobby as his flight was announced. Two startled soldiers trained their Ribeyrolle carbine rifles on Oly as he darted past them to the nearest *lavatoire*, throwing caution, and everything else, to the wind. The toilets were Turkish and he prayed fervently for death as his stomach churned and tears flowed during the longest two minutes of his life.

When he came out, he was in a full panic at the possibility of missing the last flight of the day to Paris. Two soldiers were patiently waiting outside the toilet and wanted to have a few words. *"Patron,"* he pleaded, *"Excusez, mais mon avion, ça part!"* They were not impressed. *L'heure Africain* also meant that for any reason at any time you could be stopped. The concept of hurry was literally foreign. Oly could see the gleaming white 747 with the crisp, blue lettering of Sabena Airlines beckoning him through the large glass windows. The soldiers blocked his path, sentries to the first world in faded, threadbare uniforms two sizes too small. He knew that Togolese soldiers often carried unloaded weapons, but this was the airport and things might be different. His experience over the past two years with Togolese roadblocks and armed guards usually ended with an exchange of money, a laugh, and sometimes even a drink. Once, an inebriated sergeant had handed him his bolt-action carbine, a heavy artifact with a wooden stock, an exercise that ended only in a 'click' after Oly aimed it at a palm tree, followed by more laughter and spilled drink. Travelers looked over at the scene in the airport terminal, especially since it involved a yovo, but kept walking. The scars on the soldiers' cheeks gave them away: Kabye, the Republican Guard. In Togo, as in most nations ruled by dictators, the ethnic group of the leader was the same as those most trusted to guard them. And their guns were usually loaded. The one with the deepest scars and the newest uniform stepped forward. Oly thought of Chalim and how quickly he would have gotten him out of the mess. Oly reached into the money belt beneath his shirt and pulled out a hundred CFA note.

"Patron," the soldier announced, looking over his shoulder. *"Ce n'est pas comme ça. Viens avec moi."* When they reached a quiet area outside the glare of passing travelers, the soldier put his hand out. *"Passport, s'il vous plait."*

Oly heard the final boarding call for his flight. *"Patron, c'est à moi,"* Oly pleaded, pointing in the distance. He considered a break. He could see an attractive Dutch woman wearing the distinctive Sabena powder blue and white colors move toward the microphone to make a final announcement. Oly folded the CFA into his blue passport before handing it over.

The soldier ignored Oly's action and stared at the Peace Corps seal on the passport cover. "*Corps de la Paix? Vraiment? Petit frère, pour quoi tu n'as rien dit? Bon voyage!*" He took the note out of the passport and grinned, handing it back. "George Bush," he said, saluting Oly.

"Yeah, George Bush," Oly answered back, sprinting by the soldiers toward the attendant who was getting ready to close the gate door. She gave him a disapproving glare as he pleaded with her and pointed at the soldiers. She waved him past and closed the door behind him.

When he entered the plane, everything seemed to slow down around him. The chaos. The panic. The anxiety. It all slowed down with the fresh smells of the plane accompanied by soft background music. His stomach made a gruesome audible noise that caused him to look up at the toilet sign just in case. His bowels lurched again when he clicked the seatbelt and the attendants welcomed everyone. The sweat began to dry on his brow when it hit him for the first time that he may never see Samantha, Chalim, or even Bawendi again. He hit the call button while one of the flight attendants walked by to do a final check.

"*Oui, monsieur?*" she asked, somewhat annoyed as they prepared for takeoff.

"*Oh, non, c'est rien,*" he responded.

"Actually," he said, as she started walking away. "*Un vodka?*"

She laughed, glancing forward at the cabin crew making final preparations. "Are you nervous?" she said, in perfect English. She leaned over him, turning his call button off with perfectly manicured fingers and a scent of perfume that was intoxicating.

"Not until takeoff. You're American, are you?" she said. "You look like you need a drink. I'll see what I can do. *À bientôt.*"

The lump in his throat grew as the plane left the tarmac. It was real. He was actually leaving Africa. As soon as the plane leveled off, the flight attendant walked toward him with a small bottle and a glass. He was looking out the window. "Here you go," she said. "You leave someone behind?"

"Yes. How did you know?"

"We see that look all the time," she said, handing him the bottle.

When the alcohol started having its effect, even calming his stomach a bit, Oly felt like a rescued shipwreck survivor returning to civilization after decades on a Pacific atoll. The freshness of air conditioning gently kissed his cheek, triggering sensations of the efficient, reliable industrialized world. The magazines on the plane looked clean and busy, splashed with unfamiliar celebrities and products that hadn't existed when he left two years ago. Shiny automobiles and cleaning products whose purpose he did not comprehend filled the pages with a culture he had left behind and no longer understood. It was like emerging from a coma. A third-world coma.

When Oly started drifting off to sleep, the man sitting next to him shifted in his seat. The man smelled like Ivory soap and was draped in a tent-sized, baby-blue *boubou*. "You are Peace Corpse?" Oly did not correct the mispronunciation. The man reached over with sausage fingers that sparkled with gold rings. He introduced himself with a smile that revealed gold teeth. "Kossi Nbosi, my American friend." His hand enveloped Oly's like a soft baseball mitt.

"How did you know I was American?" Oly said, releasing his grip.

"You're wearing African cloth. French and Germans never do that. Only Americans. You want to be liked."

Oly looked self-consciously at the brightly colored shirt that was made for him in Tchamba before he left. Two years ago, Oly would have had stared at the evacuation instructions in the seat pouch, wondering how anyone could emit such a fragrant smell. On this day, he offered Kossi Nbosi some crackers and talked for two hours about everything from New York to the reasons why Africans never seemed to have any trash.

"The Big Apple, so many countries on one island," Kossi said, as he pulled out pictures of his two-family duplex in Queens and brochures for his popcorn vending machine business. "Big Apple, big money," he laughed. "Madison Square Garden. Movie houses. Lots of popcorn. Lots and lots of popcorn." Oly counted four gold teeth during one of Kossi's baritone laughs. "My children go to NYU and Fordham. All popcorn." He laughed again, James Earl Jones-style. "Yes. Big Apple."

"Why can't you do that in Africa?" Oly asked. "Why does everyone have to leave Africa to be successful?"

Kossi pulled a fold of the boubou on his lap. He smiled. "Ah yes, time. How do you say? Time is money? What is the African way? Can I change that? Did I see you near the gate making friends with some of my brothers? In Africa, the sun rises and the sun sets. That is the only thing you can count on. In America, you don't accept this fate. And when the sun goes down, you turn the light on. Thomas Edison." Kossi leaned over, his scent mesmerizing Oly. "But the one thing you have wrong is that you always want to leave behind where you are. That's why you miss the roses."

"The roses?"

"You know, smell the roses."

Oly laughed at the poetic reference and wondered where he had picked it up. Probably some card out of a Korean-run gift shop in Queens. It reminded him of the expressions painted all over the buses in Togo—sayings like 'Tomorrow is today's promise' and 'God is great.'

"That all sounds nice," Oly said. "But how much rose sniffing did you do while you were building your popcorn empire in my country?"

Kossi smiled. "That's why I return to my country. I am a business-man. I go to the Big Apple to get money, not smell roses. Just like you go to Africa to help people and feel better. Why didn't you do that in America?" Oly didn't have an answer. Kossi was very satisfied. He rested his sausage fingers in his lap and closed his eyes. "Big Apple," he smiled, like an African Confucius.

The image of Samantha's tear-streaked face and her hand pressed on the glass at the airport next to Bawendi's filled Oly's head as Kossi's words circled the space in front of him. He flipped through a magazine, reprogramming himself for the commercialism and life that awaited him back home. He had no plan. When Cornick shook his hand for the last time, handing him a wad of cash, she seemed almost concerned when she told him not to spend the 'readjustment allowance' all in one place. Readjustment allowance. As if an allowance could readjust him. He had been cut off from the world he left behind for over two years. He only spoke to his parents once (over a static landline at the post office), lived without the usual electricity or running water, spoke virtually no English as French was the national language, and was now expected to be 'normal' again. He gulped down the remainder of his vodka. All the ambition of journalism and politics that Oly had left college with had been turned on its head. Ambition, in the career sense of the word, had been beaten out of him. He didn't know what he was going home to. He'd hardly heard from his brothers. His parents sent packages and letters but they were few and far between, often several weeks away from birthdays and holidays, like flotsam from a shipwreck. What he did know is that shit happened when you thought you were making plans. He tried not to think of Samantha as another thing in Africa that didn't work out, but it didn't work. He started to flip through his copy of *Anna Karenina*, a dog-eared remnant from an Atakpamé volunteer that he borrowed shortly before leaving. One thing common to a lot of volunteers was that they brought loads of unread literature from college with the lofty expectation that they'd catch up with all of it during their two-year tenure. Oly looked over at Kossi's content face, snoring with visions of popcorn machines dancing in his head and thought how much better the Africans he knew dealt with uncertain fate than Americans. He looked over his seat for the flight attendant, catching her eye_and tilting the bottle upside down in a mocking gesture of its emptiness.

As Oly stared at the pages of his book, unable to focus, he smiled as the attendant put another bottle of vodka in front of him and tapped him on the shoulder. "Take it easy," she whispered. *The American leaves streets paved with gold for the unpaved streets of Africa and the African passes him on the way to the yellow-bricked roads.* Oly remembers being astonished the first time he had heard a Togolese ask him if there were streets paved with gold in America. It was an urban myth that he had learned about in high school history class: European immigrants landed at Ellis Island in New York seeking their fortunes. The only gold Oly had to his name was a pocket full of cash to 'readjust' to the life he'd left behind. Readjust. The word haunted him. It was like turning the cap on a ketchup bottle. Just 'readjust' it and it'll fit. Just like he was supposed to.

Samantha was the only white person within fifty miles of Tchamba. There was a running joke on the Peace Corps' grapevine that he met her at a fictitious 'white night' event in town. Their actual meeting took place several months into Oly's first year, when he planned a visit to her to coincide with the weekly *marché*. Oly looked out the plane window onto the darkening skies as he thought of her. A soft Carolina accent that translated French and Kotokoli into pleasing phrases that made people listen. The self-assuredness complemented by a muscular physique and contagious laugh that made her one of the more sought-after Peace Corps females. Her height intimidated Oly at first (she nearly looked him in the eye), and when they first made love she took complete control - an experience he'd never had with a woman.

Kossi's words clouded Oly's brain as he fought off sleep. "You Americans are never content with where you are." He was right. At the end of his tenure he'd had enough of the chaos, the things that didn't work, the inefficiencies that made no sense and stood in the way of progress. Now he was on a plane, where everything worked, even 36,000 feet above sea level…
    And he wanted to go back.

Over the intercom, the flight attendant who brought him the vodka informed them, in sultry French, of the weather, the length of the flight, and her willingness to assist. Oly turned to Kossi, who was dead asleep. "Did you hear that, Kossi?" he said with a little too much enthusiasm from the alcohol. "She knows when we will arrive! I haven't heard that in over two years! Don't you love the beauty of being on time? Doesn't it feel good? Don't you get sick of waiting for everything?" He was hoping that Kossi's response would convince him that it was okay to return home, where everything was going to be alright.

Kossi waited several seconds to respond and furrowed his brow with annoyance at being woken up. "Yes, my inquisitive friend. It feels good. God willing."

Except that it didn't feel good and Kossi went to sleep, leaving Oly unsatisfied. He shoved the thick copy of *Anna Karenina* into the pouch in front of him and closed his eyes, terrified of facing the life waiting for him, even with its appealing efficiency.

It felt good, *God willing.*

He remembered how idealistic he was when he arrived in Tchamba and how contemptuous he was of the perceived backwardness of everything around him. The farming techniques. The shitting out in the open. The basic misunderstandings of nutrition. It made him mad. But as time went by and he tried to force things to change or get better, the opposite seemed to happen. Only when he gave himself up to his 'fate' towards the end of his second year did things start to fall into place. He wondered if that was something that could apply to Samantha.

Kossi was right about American dissatisfaction. While he lay there, sleeping all fat and contented, Oly was getting worked up about his re-entry to the land of opportunity. It was what made America great, after all. Manifest Destiny. The mother of invention and all. The moon. He looked towards the flight attendant, but knew that would be a mistake. Alcohol was a comfort he had found himself taking solace in too many times. He remembered a volunteer telling him what it meant to be 'alco-vaced' (a play on medevac'd). "There was this guy from Idaho a few years back who was literally the town drunk. He was wandering around the village, falling into people's houses looking for food, bottle in hand. It was bad. The men in the white suits came and got him eventually when word trickled down to Lomé."

It wasn't the noble savage thing that won him over. Too many volunteers fell into that trap. The simple life. Passive acceptance still annoyed him and he knew for a fact that all of Togo would move to New York if given the chance. It was that acceptance had attained balance with denial. Americans resisted so much. Building walls around cities below sea level. Researching cures for cancer. Pulling yourself up by the bootstraps. Fighting communism. It was tiresome.

It wasn't that the Togolese were content, blissfully ignorant or, God forbid, 'noble savages,' but they seemed more in touch with reality. Maybe they didn't have a choice. Maybe it was the proximity to nature, death, and the struggle just to get through the day. He was returning to the land of no excuses. Work hard and you'll succeed. The Gods have nothing to do with it. Never say never. You'll overcome. He had come full circle and it terrified him.

CHAPTER 2
CORPS DE LA PAIX

———◆———

SUMMER, 1990

EVERYONE THOUGHT OLY WAS NUTS to join the Peace Corps. The movie Wall Street had declared that greed was good, prompting millions of young Americans to ignore JFK's call to serve others, instead asking how they could serve themselves. Why get AIDS when you can get an Audi?

The editor of Oly's hometown paper (an octogenarian who had given him an internship in high school) was willing to work his Rolodex to give the young man a start. His efforts produced two leads: a low-paying position with *The Saratoga Springs Gazette* in upstate New York or one writing obituaries for *The Salem Evening News*. Neither one was appealing. One afternoon, Oly wrote his own obituary on a yellow legal pad:

Richard G. Olymeyer. Age 21. Beloved son of Peter and Rebecca Olymeyer of Essex, siblings Andrew and Brett. A late bloomer, Richard (known as Oly to his friends) often spoke of his love for travel and his hatred for the mundane. Referred to by friends as a "postmodern Jack Kerouac," he could often be spotted in local cafés, writing busily or quaffing espresso during intense discussions with locals. Writer, humanitarian, and Red Sox fan, Richard graduated from University of British Columbia in 1989, hoping to leave the world a better place by joining the Peace Corps. He was last seen alive swimming naked in the surf off Gloucester's Good Harbor Beach. Contributions in his name may be made to the United Nations' Small Projects Fund, a development organization dedicated to his Peace Corps service.

Yovo

The Boston Peace Corps recruiting office, located downtown in the JFK Federal Building, was squeezed like an afterthought into a wing of the Internal Revenue Service. Oly waited on a brown plaid couch next to an unshaven man clutching a manila folder and wearing a clip-on tie. His ill-fitting white shirt was stained around the collar as if he dug it out for the first time since he'd entered college four years prior.

A man with a bad case of bedhead and a tight army-green wool sweater with elbow patches came out to greet him. He wasn't wearing a tie.

"Hi, you must be Richard. I'm Josh. I'll be conducting your initial interview for the Peace Corps. Come on in."

"Please call me Oly. How'd you know it was me?" Oly said.

"The other guy waiting is my sister's boyfriend. I did the math. And he's wearing my shirt," he smiled.

Josh led Oly down a dingy hallway that smelled of burning popcorn. They passed several vintage recruiting posters that pictured robust volunteers smiling as they leaned on dirt-covered shovels for the "toughest job they'd ever love."

"Better than 'Nam, is what it should say," Oly said, regretting the comment the minute the words left his mouth.

"What was that?" Josh said, as he reached the office door. "Oh, you mean the posters? Yeah, I wish my uncle took that advice. He died at the Tet Offensive.

Oly looked behind him and wondered if it was too late to turn back.

Josh read his face. "It's okay, buddy, no offense. We're the Peace Corps, not IBM. They should put that on a poster, eh?" he laughed, patting Oly on the shoulder as he opened the office door. "So, what got you interested in wanting to join the Corps?" Josh asked, before Oly was able to sit in a wooden chair with a missing armrest. While Josh looked for a pen and lifted several files off an old stool to sit on, Oly began the answer he'd rehearsed on his way into the city.

"Well, after I graduated from college, I realized I wanted to serve others, and I believe the Peace Corps is one of the best ways to do that."

19

Still distracted with the unsuccessful pen search, Josh picked up a broken pencil and stuck it in a sharpener mounted on the wall, drowning out the end of Oly's answer. "I'm sorry, the best way to do what?"

"Oh, that was it … just that I wanted to serve others."

Josh smiled at the answer he'd heard so many times he'd lost count. He contemplated asking him why not join the army, but decided he liked Oly enough to give him a chance. "So, why don't you just do that here? Why do you have to go overseas?"

Oly recalled a conversation he had with a returned volunteer who informed him that the recruiters try to weed out the half-hearted dreamers by testing their resolve to leave America for two years. "Well, I've thought about that," he responded, shifting on the uncomfortable chair. "And I have served at home. I've worked with inner-city children on urban gardening projects, assisted immigrant families when I was in college, and I feel I'm ready to transfer these skills to another culture." Oly smiled to himself, while Josh nodded, scribbling his response down on the legal pad.

"So, you have gardening experience?"

"Well, sort of. I worked with gardeners to show city kids how to plant tomatoes." Oly thought of the sweaty volunteer in the poster leaning on the tractor. He pictured himself behind the wheel wearing a straw hat and chewing on a grass blade as hundreds of native children from some remote country ran behind him, cheering and singing his praises.

Josh looked up. "So, what else? Any languages, other skills?"

"I took French in high school and college. And I worked some construction in college."

"Good."

Oly watched him write the words 'fluent' and 'carpenter.' "Well, I'm not exactly a carpenter, but…"

"Did you pick up a hammer?"

"Yes."

"Carpenter."

"Are you in any relationships?"

"What?"

"A relationship. Do you have a girlfriend?"

Oly wasn't expecting the question, but quickly suspected Josh's intent, especially as it was the first time during the interview that he had looked up from his pad of paper. It made him reflect on how long it had been. Not since graduation, when Charlotte went back to Quebec. "I'm sorry. What does that have to do with…"

"Well, if you're going to be overseas, part of that is that you won't be able to take your loved ones. Some people don't think that through, and they end up leaving after a few weeks. We try to keep that from happening. Did you know it costs over twenty-thousand dollars just to train a volunteer?"

"No, I didn't," Oly replied, feeling the sweat starting to build on his neck. He stared down at the floor, listening to Josh tap his pencil on the table while he waited for an answer. "Oh, sorry, I don't have any loved ones. I mean, I do, but not like you mean. I'm all set."

Josh smiled. "You're all set," he said, as he wrote on the pad.

"Are you writing that down?" Oly asked.

"Not those exact words, no, but I am noting that you are not in a relationship. Is that okay?" Oly didn't know why the question made him so uncomfortable. But it was the first time in his life that inadequacy worked to his advantage.

"I don't have a girlfriend," he had meant as a thought that came out as a whisper.

"That's okay, dude, neither do I. It'll help your application. Trust me, there's actually women in other countries." He smiled and wrote something else on the form. "And, finally, when can you leave, and which countries did you have in mind?"

"What?"

"When can you leave?"

Oly hadn't expected this. The directness of the question made him feel as though he should have brought his luggage to the interview. "I didn't think it was going to be so fast. Umm, well, I've always been interested in India."

"There's no Peace Corps in India. I won't write that down," he smiled. "How about Africa? We have a group leaving in four weeks."

"Four weeks?" Oly responded, unable to contain his surprise.

"Better than 'Nam!" Josh said, chuckling at Oly's discomfort. "Look, you're going to love it. Don't worry. It flies by. Besides, if I sign you I don't have to sign my sister's boyfriend up. You'll be serving your country and doing me a favor. What's not to love?" He chuckled again and held out a form that he grabbed from the desk. "Here, sign this and I'll forward your dossier to D.C. As soon as your medical clears, we'll be in touch."

CHAPTER 3
LE DÉPART

—————◆—————

"YOU DID WHAT?" OLY'S MOTHER, Rebecca, hadn't expected her son to come home from an interview with a departure date.

"Mom, I had to. He said he couldn't guarantee my spot if I didn't commit."

"They always say that, Richard. Haven't you ever bought airline tickets? Oh my God," she kept repeating, burying her head in her hands. "You're leaving me to go to Africa." The way she said it actually scared him, like he was going to war.

Rebecca Olymeyer, a disease specialist at Mass General, had supported her son's altruism until she considered the real possibility that her son could die of one of the things that gave her a paycheck, none of which had a cure.

Oly's father, Albert, an entrepreneur who marketed, among other things, a pulley system for lobster boats, showed his support by not showing it. "Richard, you're old enough to make your own decisions." When Albert wanted to express his personal feelings, he spoke in the third person, using Rebecca as a foil. "Richard, your mother is having a hard time with this, even though she supports you."

"Yeah, Dad, I'll miss you, too." Oly hugged him for the first time since bedtime stories on Wampatuck Street. His father's eyes watered for the first time since he told Oly his grandfather had died. His two brothers, Andy and Brett, skipped the hugs and fought over his room.

The weeks went by like minutes leading up to Oly's final preparations. It seemed like every day a packet of information had arrived from Washington, D.C. with additional information about what to bring, what to expect, and what forms to fill out. Andy and Brett took Oly out one last time to The Rack in Boston, forcing Oly to wear a 'bra' over his shirt made of half coconut shells, and a straw hat. They even managed to find a cowrie shell necklace. "My brother's joining the Corps" was how Brett introduced him to every pretty girl who looked his way.

The last day together included a family dinner at Legal Seafood. His family sat in awkward silence while Oly pored over the menu, trying to absorb everything at once that he knew he'd miss for two years. "I can't say I've ever seen you guys unable to speak," Oly said to his brothers, finally breaking the silence.

"I was just wondering what to do with your room," Brett said, not looking up from his menu.

"So, how many shots do you need to get at the training?" Rebecca asked. "Did you have yellow fever yet? Typhoid? Hepatitis?"

"Yes, Mom, I had most of those. The rest I get when I'm there." His mother's eyes started welling up again. Oly lost his appetite for fried clams and felt guilty for wishing he was already on the plane.

Oly wasn't sure he'd made the right decision when he crossed Logan Airport's newly refurbished international terminal with a hockey bag filled with everything from eight packages of underwear to a Celtics bottle opener. As his brothers play fought over who would carry the bag, Oly stared off into the distance, wondering why he was a sucker for constantly making himself uncomfortable. Even in his high school days, when everyone else played it safe by going to college in nearby Boston, Oly passed and went to the University of British Columbia on the opposite coast. It was the first official time he broke his mother's heart. People thought he was brave at the time - "courageous" they'd say. But he didn't feel that way. He loved Vancouver, but the initial loneliness, the rootlessness, and being the stranger was a high price. Now, just when he was starting to get familiar again with home, he pulled the roots up. It made him wonder if he fitted in anywhere - not exactly the frame of mind he was hoping for as he headed off to an African village.

The one-way ticket to San Antonio started to feel more like a sentence than an opportunity. He remembered a professor at school once telling him that life was about learning from experience, and that these lessons would keep happening until we learned from them. *Like I didn't learn from being away the last time?* He started to get upset, feeling the distance growing between him and his family even though he hadn't left yet.

"C'mon dude," Brett said, tugging on one strap while Andy held the other. "You're spacing out. You're doing a good thing, man," Brett said, clutching Oly's shoulder. "Watch yourself, though," he added, moving closer to Oly out of Rebecca's earshot. "Don't bring back any excess baggage, if you know what I mean."

CHAPTER 4
ARRIVÉE

MIDSUMMER, 1990

SAN ANTONIO, TEXAS, BLAZING IN the still heat of midsummer, was the site of the regional orientation for Peace Corps *stagiaires* headed to Africa. The dozen or so young men and women from Oly's cohort were put up in a hotel with a view of the Alamo and treated to meal vouchers, papers to sign, and cross-cultural games in a windowless banquet hall with stale air and stained carpets. Oly's roommate, Jeff Pelozey, who arrived after one in the morning and had to be woken up by him the next day, had a shockingly small amount of baggage. He missed most of the morning meetings of the first day, and Oly found himself making excuses to the concerned Peace Corps trainers, an act he would become accustomed to over the years to come.

On the afternoon of the second day, after filling out several release forms related to death in a foreign country, Oly's group was introduced to the Peace Corps brass from the Lomé office. The most notable was Philip Rollings, the Assistant Peace Corps Director (APCD) for Togo. A crabby bureaucrat originally from Pennsylvania, Rollings loved air-conditioning and hated Africa. He was one of those expats who had a little slice of life carved out for himself and would kill anyone who stood in his way. A former Wal-Mart manager, Rollings had stumbled upon the dirty little secret that losers in America could achieve great wealth and status overseas. He had somehow moved quickly up the government chain, turning mid-level paper pushing into a sweet overseas post.

He wore bad Hawaiian shirts, socks with sandals, and floppy hats. He hated to sweat and loved Bombay Sapphire (cold with a twist of lime). He wore flip-up shades over prescription glasses. He was rarely spotted outside of the Peace Corps office or his Toyota Land Cruiser. His claim to fame was terminating early more volunteers than anyone in the Peace Corps. He was loathed, despised, and ridiculed. And he wasn't going anywhere.

"I'm sure by now," he began, looking down at his notes and adjusting his glasses, "that you're wondering what all this stuff has to do with saving the world." He smirked. "Well, I'll tell you. Does anyone know the mission of the Peace Corps? (One hand went up, but Rollings ignored it.)

"Hmm, seems like some of us have some homework to do. Well, that's where it all starts. But before we can even get to that, you have to be prepared. Yes, prepared. How many of you brought toilet paper?" All hands went up. He snickered. "You see? You don't need it. It's cheap in the marketplaces, and the Peace Corps provides it. Did you know that?" The hands slowly went down. "That's what I'm talking about. Being prepared. Last year, 150 volunteers worldwide had to be medically evacuated from their posts because they were not prepared. Now, how can you save the world if you're on a plane back to Paducah?" Jeff's hand went up.

"That was a rhetorical question, but yes, Mr..."

"Pelozey."

"Yes sir, how can I help you?"

The entire room looked at Jeff, eager for the exchange. Wearing a cowrie shell necklace and his long hair back in a bun, Jeff looked more like a volunteer than anyone else in the group, most of whom wore Izod polo shirts and plain cotton blouses. His Adam's apple protruded as he spoke and he had the beginnings of a scraggly beard. It was as if he'd already been at post for a year.

"Yes, I was wondering something. I heard about something called 'alco-vac' from a guy I knew in the Corps. Is that part of the 150 that you're talking about, or is that different?"

Rollings glared at the Peace Corps admissions director who stood like a frightened rabbit at the door. The rep actually shrugged and looked obediently at his clipboard as if to verify whether Pelozey belonged there. The room exploded in laughter until Rollings glared everyone back into silence. Rollings licked his upper lip with a twitch of his tongue and looked next to the podium, his fingers gripping the sides a bit tighter. "It's very interesting that you refer to the Peace Corps as the Corps. My grandfather was in 'the Corps.' And believe me, son, it was and is nothing like the United States Peace Corps. Nothing at all."

Pelozey didn't flinch. "Oh no, sir, no disrespect intended at all. It's just something I heard," he responded, sitting up straight as an arrow, eager to continue the exchange.

"You may refer to it as THE Peace Corps, or the United States Peace Corps, if you please."

"Sir, yes, sir!" Pelozey barked in a clipped, militaristic style. The room burst out laughing again and was thoroughly enjoying the challenge. When the room settled into awkward silence for the second time, Rollings spoke, looking directly at Jeff who did not break his gaze.

"Of the 3,000 United States Peace Corps Volunteers who are accepted each year, over fifty percent, let me repeat, *fifty percent* either do not complete their service or never even finish the training stage of their assignment. The reasons for this range from medical to administrative separation to *death*," he said, raising his voice on the last word. Rollings' brow was speckled with sweat and his face turned beet red. He looked at the nervous recruiter and left the podium and the room to halted applause.

Jeff Pelozey had a childhood combined with moderate entitlement and low-level parenting; the end result being that he managed to find an easy way out of just about everything he did. He conned his way through Montessori school (his creative process, he argued, involved lots of play) and barely graduated from the college where his father was a mathematics professor at the University of Wisconsin/Madison (the two credits he was short of somehow appeared a week before graduation).

Half an hour after the encounter with Rollings, Jeff attempted to up-grade a government-issued economy room to a presidential suite. Using his Peace Corps–issued hotel voucher as collateral, Jeff tried to convince the desk clerk that as U.S. Deputy Director of Housing and Urban Development, it would benefit Ramada if his report looked favorably on the up-and-coming city. The stoic receptionist looked through Jeff, patiently staring at him as he asked her for her name and if she knew who he was. "I'm going to speak to Washington," he concluded. After several minutes of discourse, Jeff earned a discount coupon at the hotel grill and a 'go away' smile from Jilleanne Faltaldo, assistant manager.

Oly marched up to Jeff as he walked away from the reception with his vouchers in hand and a big smile on his face. "Hey man, what the hell are you doing? You're not going to make it out of the country at this rate."

"Which country you talking about?" Jeff laughed, waving the vouchers. Jeff's curly hair framed a face filled with restlessness, a characteristic that would range in degrees of severity over the two years that Oly was in Africa.

"Oh, I get it," Oly surmised. "You want to get thrown out."

"What? What the hell makes you think that? I want to sweat my balls off in a mud hut for two years."

Oly felt himself getting angry. Another sensation induced by Jeff that would become familiar. "Well, you're not bringing me down with you, roomie. That act in front of Rollings was not cool. I overheard him telling the admissions people to keep a close eye on you. If you want out, walk over there and tell them."

Jeff laughed. "Dude, you must admit that Rollings clown is a freak. I was just the only one who had the balls to say anything. Why do you think our government is so fucked up? It's filled with idiots like that. You need a drink. C'mon over and say hello to the captain."

Over two hours at the hotel bar, the two recruits drank six beers and a bottle of Captain Morgan rum, but were cut off by the manager before they could order more. The intensity of Jeff's speech, fueled with alcohol and accompanied by his hand gestures made the room swirl like a merry-go-round. He went on about college, the scams that paid his rent, girls, and, of course, travel. He had crossed the Mojave—on a bet—by dune buggy, hiked the Canadian Rockies, and rafted the Rio Grande, getting picked up by border patrol. He had lived in several cities for varying periods of time and claimed to be one of the first people in America to bungee jump.

As the chemical impairment dissuaded Oly from questioning Jeff's tales, the tonic of adventure washed over him. It seemed ironic to Oly that Rollings could not handle the rebellious type that seemed attracted to the Peace Corps. People like Jeff seemed to have a much better chance at surviving than the girl from Cincinnati who kept asking the trainers if they could ship her extra allergy medication once she arrived in the country.

Jeff poured the last of the rum into his glass without asking Oly if he wanted any more, and gulped it down. He then stood up, jacked his pants up, and starting stumbling towards the door. When Oly decided to follow, the bartender stopped them by the elevator, reminding them they had forgotten to pay. Jeff pressed the button on the elevator and dismissed the man, who had the tired expression of having chased many drunks for payment over his career. When the door opened, the bartender put his arm in the door, not allowing it to close. "Sorry sir, but your reservation does not allow room charges. I already checked. And if you don't pay now, I'll have to call security and notify the leader of your group, sir," he finished with a definitive flair. Oly blinked first and reached for his credit card while Jeff leaned against the door of the elevator, trying to maintain his balance.

The next day they left for Togo.

The duffels, backpacks, and assorted carry-ons were scattered about the lobby like the flotsam of a Wal-Mart going under. Inside them contained every consumer good, medicine, textile, and personal effect that each *stagiaire* felt they simply could not live without. In spite of Peace

Corps warnings that most items could be purchased in local markets, just about everyone (with the exception of Jeff) over packed. Oly looked around at his cohort and wondered how many of them would actually go the full distance of two years and which ones would become his friends. He unzipped his bag one last time before the porters came to load the hotel van and immediately came across a framed picture of his family. He tried to hide it so that the guy next to him, wearing a crisp white t-shirt and repacking his nine-inch Rambo survival knife with serrated edge, wouldn't notice. "Just in case," he said, admiring the blade in a way that was unsettling. He held the knife up and smiled. "Never know what you're gonna run into in the Congo; know what I mean?"

"I don't think we're going to the ... oh, yeah, I know what you mean," Oly said, deciding the correction was fruitless. His name was Chip. He was from Kentucky, had never left the United States before, and would be home again for good in three weeks after a botfly raised a family of maggots in his left inner thigh. Oly never did learn what happened to the knife.

Jeff came fast walking with his one bag over his shoulder just as the van was getting ready to pull away. Rollings stood by the driver's side door, looking disappointed as Jeff squeezed into the passenger cabin. "Sorry to let you down by showing up," Jeff joked. *"L'heure Africain,"* he said, shrugging as he pointed to an imaginary watch on his wrist.

Rollings peered through the open window of the van, silencing the laughter that had followed Jeff's comment. "You have no idea what you're getting into, buddy," Rollings hissed as he tapped the door for the van to leave.

A uneventful connection at Paris' CDG airport to an Air Afrique flight brought the group to Gnassingbe Eyadema International Airport in Lomé, Togo, West Africa, eighteen hours after they left the hotel in San Antonio. The plane banked abruptly to one side on its final approach, offering Oly a clear view of the coastline of France's former colony. It was hard for him to imagine merchant ships from America arriving here for human cargo. The inky blackness of Boston's inner harbor had become a distant memory as the pale-green Bay of Benin, lined with white sand and swaying palm trees, came into view. Oly looked around the plane at the mostly black faces, spotting several white persons in his group with expressions similar to his own. The calm and relative serenity that Jeff had experienced on the transatlantic flight had been replaced by the chaos of the exit on Air Afrique.

They stumbled into blinding sunlight that bounced off the tarmac. Passengers jostled Oly with the extra baggage they had stuffed on the plane and pushed him aside as they competed for the swarming bush taxis that drove at them. A hot breeze assaulted his face, as a man with bulging eyeballs ran up to him. "*Corps de la Paix? Corps de la Paix? Américan?*"

The smell of burning hair assaulted Oly's nose as women with piles of sticks and what appeared to be lumps of coal walked past. A woman standing next to Oly answered the man back. "*Oui, c'est Corps de la Paix.*" The man grabbed Oly's bag out of his hand and headed to a white Toyota van with a red, white, and blue Peace Corps sticker on the door. He was completely disoriented and followed the crowd.

"*Moi aussi,*" Oly managed, speaking French for the first time in his life outside the United States. He was surprised when the man understood his words. He squeezed together in the van with several of the other recruits, including Jeff, who didn't look as confident as he appeared in San Antonio. Jeff stared out the window and didn't say a word, his Adam's apple protruding even more than normal as he took everything in. The realness of their first venture into the third world was startling. Even for Jeff, knowing that all of the safeties of American life were being stripped away was intimidating. Anything could happen now, and they were all at the mercy of their environment.

The driver flew down sandy streets, sending scrawny chickens and bony-legged children scattering for cover. One of the passengers, a skinny Bryn Mawr graduate named Julie, screamed. The driver's bulging white eyes appeared in the rearview mirror as he let out a gigantic laugh. After a pause, the rest of the group joined in his laughter (except for

Julie who had put her head between her legs in the airplane crash position and started moaning).

"U-S-A! U-S-A!" the driver screamed. "America number one! Number one!" he yelled, pumping his fist and beeping the horn at women trying to cross the street with bundles of sticks on their heads. Julie wretched, spewing a trail of yellowish liquid that smelled horrible and made several others start to dry heave.

"Pull over, pull over!" Oly yelled as the driver tried to steer around the last of the women crossing the road. The driver jerked the steering wheel over to the right and pulled over, hitting the brakes too hard, causing everyone to lurch forward. Jeff opened the side door and leaped out of the van, leading the rest of the group onto the sandy street to escape the smell.

A small crowd of curious children and market-goers gathered around the van to see what the white people were doing. Julie wasn't able to get out of the van and instead continued retching from her position on the floor of the van, her head bobbing out the door as long drools of yellowish liquid hung from her mouth. She was in a semi-state of consciousness as Oly grabbed a water bottle from the van and tried to pour it on her face. The rest of the group stood in shock alongside the curious children who chattered in Ewe at the sick woman, some pointing and laughing, others covering their noses from the stench. "She's not gonna make it, dude," Jeff said to Oly, as he twisted off the cap and dribbled water on her face.

She moaned softly. The driver grabbed a portable radio that was stored in a box between the seats and said something rapidly in Ewe. A few seconds later came a response, followed by static. "We must go," he said in broken English, sounding slightly impatient as he waved his arms for everyone to get back in the van.

Several minutes later, the van came to a screeching halt at the rusty gates of the *Hotel Californie*, a four-story crumbling peach-colored building across from the German embassy in the crowded borough of Kodjoviakope, just outside downtown Lomé. The driver leaned on the horn as a thin man in a stained khaki outfit jogged to open the gate. Like most compounds that served expats, the swaying palms and green grass inside the gate were in stunning contrast to the rutted dirt roads and third-world poverty outside. As soon as the van came to a stop, everyone piled out to escape the horrible smell, with several of the volunteers leaning over with hands on their knees trying to hold off from vomiting themselves. Two of the khaki men helped Julie from the van as Oly, Jeff and the rest of the group were shepherded over to a large *paillote* where they could hear the chorus from the hotel's namesake song playing on an old tape deck. At first, the music seemed quaint, a comforting tribute to Americans out of their comfort zone. It wouldn't be until the third day when it became clear that it was the only song the bar played, that the once-welcome tune completely lost its charm. "This could be heaven or this could be hell," Jeff whispered into Oly's ear.

The Americans had checked in, but were not allowed to leave the place for several days as they completed the final booster rounds of vaccinations needed to protect their frail bodies from the likes of yellow fever, typhoid, malaria, and hepatitis. Julie, who had been brought to the infirmary at the U.S. Embassy, was not heard from again after the first day. As much as Rollings had wished, Jeff was not the first early termination of the Togo *stagiaires* in the summer of 1990.

CHAPTER 5

À CÔTÉ DE LA MER

FALL, 1990

BAMWE AKUNDÉ, THE STOUT, IMPOSSIBLY black director of operations, wore a blue polyester *fonctionnaire* suit and greeted the recruits like Mister Rourke from the '70s television show 'Fantasy Island.' In flawless English, he instructed them to drink bottled water, stay out of the sun, and rest. His skin shimmered in the afternoon sun, emanating with the overpowering scent of flowery cologne. It was intoxicating.

After days of idleness, shots, and endless paperwork, the group was divided for preliminary French tests. Word was that anyone not proficient in French after twelve weeks of training would be 'early terminated' in Peace Corps-speak and sent back to America. Oly did not recall that threat in the orientation.

Jeff ended up with *les papillons*, a barely passable group comprised of skinny Erin, a guy who kept showing people a picture of himself next to Ronald Reagan, and a physics professor who insisted on giving everyone—men and women—a shoulder rub whenever the occasion presented itself, which meant all the time. Thanks to Charlotte, a Quebecois girl from college who had schooled him in three things—drinking heavily, poutine, and French—Oly was placed with *les lions*, a sophisticated cadre of trainees that included Patrick, the son of a Belgian banker; Louise, who studied French literature at Vassar; and Michelle, a bohemian hottie with a nose ring whose last residence was somewhere in Singapore. She smiled at Oly like a woman who never took no for an answer. Oly tried to wink back, but ended up closing both eyes instead of just one. He turned red as she laughed out loud, covering her mouth.

After the first week of training, when American Labor Day passed without a mention, Oly tried to distract his homesickness over a lunch of fried plantains and fruit. While he ate, the Peace Corps Togo staff filtered through the group like a pack of hyenas, acting nonchalant but sensing fear in the sick and weak. Oly ignored the gurgling in his bowels and pulled his stomach in. It was obvious to him and the other recruits that the time to back out was now, before faith and resources had been wasted on sending them to post. The *Californie* was rife with tales of lesser-thans: ghost stories of volunteers who'd cracked. The guy from Michigan found in a fetal position underneath his kitchen table. The Rutgers grad that abandoned her post and was found six months pregnant in a remote village. Oly imagined Peace Corps personnel wrestling her into the back of a Chevy Suburban, with mud huts and curious villagers as a backdrop.

Jeff took Oly aside. "Dude, I don't think I'm gonna make it. You gotta help me. These people are freaks. That Louise chick is crying all the time for her mommy, and Jim keeps trying to massage my shoulders. I swear I'm going to pop him if he tries it again. Hey, who's the babe with the nose ring?"

"I'm not going to make it," he rambled on. "I'm not. This whole thing's a sham. I thought it was for me, but I just don't know, man. I was up all night puking my brains out from that spicy goat-anus shit they served last night. I barely got in as it is. My French sucks. I don't think I'll pass the test. But I don't want to get sent home. I can't go home, man. I can't. This is all I got. I really need to stay here."

Oly looked down at Jeff's fingers on his sleeve and felt them digging in. Oly was a little lower on the desperation scale, but he could relate. *I can't go home man, I can't.* Although the other recruits seemed nice enough, Oly had yet to find a kindred spirit: someone who didn't have a plan to go into international development or public health, blah blah

blah. He was running away, not towards something, and so was Jeff. It was too late to back out now.

Oly reached down and removed Jeff's hand. "C'mon man, you're hurting me. You have to get a hold of yourself."

"Sorry, I really am, Oly. I'm sorry." Oly could see tears welling up in Jeff's eyes. Jeff stood up. "I'm going to end this whole thing right now. I can't continue. I know I'm going to get kicked out anyway, so I might as well save everyone the time." Oly stared at Jeff's Adam's apple floating up and down as he tried to catch his breath. Sweat dripped from Jeff's forehead. Oly looked at him with a combination of disappointment and sympathy. The cowrie shell-wearing cool dude from San Antonio was fading. Fortunately for Jeff, there was no one else in the group with whom Oly even felt a remote connection. It was one of the few times that Oly would be in control of their relationship, and he enjoyed the power.

"Well, well, well," Oly said, putting a patronizing arm around Jeff. "You telling me you're going to give up and hand Rollings the satisfaction? No way that's going to happen. *Le lion* will take you into his pride."

"Why the hell do you care?" Jeff said, looking at the ground.

"I don't really. It's just that when I look around the room, you're the only one who's not puking or talking to himself. And, for some strange reason that I hope I come up with someday, I think we need each other." They both laughed and Oly lifted his arm from Jeff's shoulders, tapping him on the side of the head. The confident look that Jeff had left back at the hotel in San Antonio started to come back. Oly closed his eyes and sat down on a broken wicker chair in earshot of the now officially annoying endless Eagles hit. "Goddamnit. I can't think with that song always playing," Oly said, rubbing his temples. "I want to stab that stereo with a *steely knife*."

"Hey, man," Jeff added. "Check out anytime you want!" They both roared with laughter, restoring equilibrium and cementing their relationship.

"You know that girl Michelle?" Oly asked, after they stopped wiping tears from laughing.

"Yeah man, she's hot. "You want to bang her?"

"Yes, but that's not my point. I think she's up for some hijinks. I've seen the way Bamwe looks at her."

"What do you mean?" Jeff said, leaning forward to hear the plan.

"I mean that she can help us out on exam day. You need to pass that to stay in country, right?"

"Yeah," Jeff said. "But I don't get it. She's going to take my test?"

"Not quite. But she's going to test someone else. I think she'll pass." Jeff loved the intrigue and started rubbing his hands together, his Adam's apple bouncing as he swallowed with anticipation. He then changed his expression and looked serious.

"What?" Oly asked, noticing the change.

"You can't do this, man. You'll get thrown out if you get caught. It's not worth it."

"Bullshit," Oly said. "I have to. I don't know why, but I can't do this thing alone, especially with the weirdoes in our group. I won't make it, either. So, we either both make it or both go home. Got it?"

"Fuck Rollings," Jeff said, his eyes full of confidence and wide open at Oly's conviction. He took the cowrie shell hanging from his necklace and kissed it.

Ten minutes later they had a plan. It took no time to convince Michelle, especially when Oly walked up to her and blinked both eyes. She was game for anything that involved danger and probably shared his sentiment towards the rest of the *stagiaires*. During Jeff's final exam that afternoon, Michelle barged into the *paillote* where Jeff was sitting and pleaded with Bamwe to help her remove a scorpion from her room. When he left, Oly helped Jeff complete the written section. Bamwe and Michelle took more than half an hour to return. When they came back, Bamwe had an unusual look on his face and she was smiling. Michelle winked at Oly with both eyes. He felt a bulge in his pants just imagining how she distracted him for that long.

Jeff barely scraped by on the oral part, but his high score on the written brought up his overall result and gave him a passing grade. He was in. Oly felt guilty when he found out that Louise failed and was *separated early,* one of the cold bureaucratic terms Peace Corps used to describe events when things didn't work out. He rationalized the cheating by hoping that Jeff would make a difference once he was actually in the field, but knew deep down it was a decision he made out of pure self-interest and his own lack of confidence in being able to make it alone. It was a rationalization that would cause him much angst.

Following several interminable weeks of intensive training on everything from water filtering to managing grant budgets, bending rebar, and, of course, conjugating French verbs, the *stagiaires* were ready to become converted into *volontaires.*

Jeff and Oly waited in the Grande Paillote for their final site placements. They noticed the Togolese staff moving about with a greater sense of urgency than usual. Bamwe, in particular, was sweating profusely, checking and re-checking a list that he carried with him and looking at his watch. "What is he waiting for?" Jeff said. "The president?"

Right before he had a chance to respond, two of the khaki-clad guardsmen scurried over to the front gate just as Don Henley reminded everyone from the bar for the umpteenth time that they could *check out anytime they liked but could never leave.* An official-looking white Peace Corps car pulled in, the answer to Bamwe's anxiety. The vehicle rolled up slowly to where the group was waiting and came to a complete stop. The windows were tinted, so it was difficult to see who was inside, but Jeff and Oly already knew, and they both started to feel ill. Like a spectacled dictator from a banana republic, Rollings did not exit the car until one of the khaki guardsmen ran to open the door for him. He emerged slowly, a large grin on his face that caused his cheeks to push his thick, prescription sunglasses up on his face. He lived for moments like this: a powerful dictator in his element with no one to question him. Jeff's Adam's apple began jumping uncontrollably.

"He found out about the test," Jeff hissed to Oly. "I knew we shouldn't have done that."

"Shut up," Oly answered. "He didn't find out. This is the shit he lives for. He's probably been rehearsing how he's going to post us in the Sahara. Get ready for your prison sentence."

Rollings (accompanied by Bamwe, nervously checking his list and wiping sweat from his brow) walked slowly to the Grande Paillote and looked straight ahead. One by one, the volunteers entered and emerged several minutes later, most of them with big smiles on their faces. When Oly looked around at the group, he was impressed. Even though they looked awful in local clothes (like tourists in Hawaiian shirts), they were trying. Against the odds, they made it. There was a confidence that permeated the group as they chit chatted in mediocre French and laughed together. Some even wore the sandals made out of old car tires that the local farmers liked to wear. They had shed their skins and integrated the best they could. Now, everyone waited to see where he or she would be living for the next two years.

Aneho, the ancient capital along the coast, was one of the most desirable, with its cool ocean breezes, quaint eateries, and startling views. Bafilo, an ancient village with beautiful countryside and an ancient baobab in its center, was also high on the list as was Dapaong, considered the true 'outback' of Togo where only the hardcore dared to go. Michelle, of course, ended up with an ocean-view apartment in Aneho. The physics masseuse ended up with a decent post in Atakpamé, a popular mountain town.

Jeff and Oly were called last. Jeff went first. "See you in hell," he said, tapping Oly on the knee as he stood up. When he emerged, he looked like he was going to hell. His sentence was to a remote, dusty border town called Kjadoge, which translated as 'the forgotten place.' It was a relatively new post that the Togolese government added, as there were no government agencies within fifty kilometers of the town. No Peace Corps Volunteer lasted over a year at Kjadoge. The last one nearly died from a monkey bite, and the one before him nearly perished when his house was washed away in a flash flood. Jeff had a look of shock on his face when he emerged from the meeting with Rollings.

"That was way too fun for him," Jeff said. "He knows I'm going to die there, and I think he's happy about it. He asked me if my family affairs are in order. No joke. Your turn."

"Did he mention the test?" Oly asked.

"No. That doesn't mean he doesn't know. He looked really evil when he told me."

Oly stood up. He felt lightheaded and couldn't manage to make his feet move toward the Grande Paillote. He was the last *stagiare* in the entire cohort to receive a post and there was only one post left. That could only mean Tchamba, 'village of the old man,' a ramshackle Muslim town forty kilometers from Sokodé, the nearest city. "Come on dude, it's not the electric chair," Jeff said. "It's more like a sentence to hard labor. You'll have a lot of time to think about your indiscretions."

"Have a seat," Rollings said to Oly when he finally shuffled in. Rollings sat back in his chair, sweat pouring down his face, and smiled. "Well, here we are, at last. I had a nice conversation with your friend. And now you. You know one thing I don't understand, Olymeyer? I don't understand why a reasonable guy like you is caught up with, excuse my French, shit-for-brains out there."

Oly stared back. "Well, what are my options right now? I disavow him and you put me in an air-conditioned condo in Lomé?"

Rollings looked down at his papers and smiled. "I actually like the sound of that. Well, it seems like there's only one post left, as I'm sure you know. And I'm also sure that you know that Prince Charming is going to hell, whereas you, my friend, are actually going to a place that has some redeeming qualities."

"Am I supposed to thank you?" Oly said.

"Well, you can if you want. It's one of the oldest Muslim villages in Togo and actually has a fantastic traditional market, a reputation as a voodoo mecca and, get this, a Catholic church built by the French on the edge of town. And you'll be living in a relatively new house on the edge of town. What's not to love?"

"Right. Not to love. Thanks so much, Mr. Rollings. I will do my best to make Peace Corps proud." Oly stood up to shake Rollings' hand, a gesture that was not returned.

"That will be all, Mr. Olymeyer," he finished, without looking up from the list.

Oly and Jeff drank heavily that evening, befriending two Danish doctors with *Medecins Sans Frontiers* at the bar. It wasn't until Akunde came down from his room (long after midnight), and scolded the barkeeper that the two called it a night.

A loud pounding, harmonious with the sound in his head, pulled Oly back into consciousness as he came to early the next morning. "*Monsieur Oly, on y va*," the voice outside his door insisted. Oly groaned as he slowly regained his senses and understood what that meant. Village of the Old Man. His mouth was cotton dry and he hadn't packed. He threw everything he owned—dirty t-shirts, books, a can opener, sneakers, boxes of water purification tablets into the hockey bag and hustled for the door, banging his shin on the corner of Jeff's bed.

"Goddamnit!" he hissed.

Jeff pulled the sheet over his head and groaned. "Where are you going, man?" he moaned.

"Village of the dead man. Or old man. Or no man's land. What the fuck, it's the end of the earth."

"Call me when you get in, sweetheart," Jeff responded, pulling a pillow over his pounding head. "I think I'm going to puke," he added before turning over. Oly looked at the back of Jeff's head, wondering if he was ever going to see him again and opened the door into the blazing sun of an African morning.

CHAPTER 6
EN BROUSSE

———————

LATE FALL, 1990

FOR THE ENTIRE BUMPY, SIX-HOUR ride from Lomé to Tchamba, Oly fought off his own urge to vomit and tried to sleep in the back seat while the driver played an Alpha Blondy cassette on full volume. When he asked for it to be turned down, the driver pointed to a hole where the volume knob was supposed to be. Oly laid his head against his bag and fought off competing urges to puke and cry. He wanted to go home and pictured Jeff snoozing in the air-conditioned comfort of the hotel room. *He'll be in his own version of hell before he knows it,* Oly thought to himself. He wanted to get back on the airplane. It was fun for a while, but now that it was real, he didn't want it anymore. All the excitement was wearing off. He tried to sit up, repressing the urge to throw up, and scanned the passing landscape. Crumbling mud structures with tin roofs. Shirtless young men with sinewy muscles making their way to distant yam fields. Women in colorful *panyas* carrying large bowls on their heads, babies strapped to them like backpacks.

At the final turn off the route nationale, the chauffeur yelled over the blaring cassette (which was on its fourth or fifth repeat … Oly had lost count),"*Prochain arret, Tchamba!*" Oly flashed back to drives home from little league in the Olymeyer wagon, his mother scolding him from the front, as Dad drove impassively, trying to remain neutral. Cement buildings, the symbol of third-world progress, flitted by like frames in a picture show, becoming increasingly outnumbered by ancient mud structures the closer they got to Tchamba. The farther they drove, the wider the distance between clustered houses became, with rows of sagging palm trees in between.

A rusty metal sign, half detached from its post with only the 'tcha' legible, was the only indicator that they had arrived. "*Voila!*" the chauffeur yelled with excitement. "Tchamba!" he pointed at the sign. He made a sharp turn off the main road and headed directly towards a crowded marketplace, sending a flock of chickens scattering for their lives. The driver pulled over next to a man dressed in a full-length yellow bou bou and ejected the cassette so that he could ask a question. The man, surprised to see a yovo in the back seat, approached the open driver's window with an eye on Oly as though he were expecting an attack. After several exchanges interspersed by pointing and repeated 'yovos', the driver thanked the man and parked next to a woman sleeping at a stall selling cans of tomato paste stacked up like a pyramid.

"*Ou?*" Oly asked in French, still feeling self-conscious about the use of a foreign language.

"*Ici!*" the driver answered, pointing down at the ground.

"What?" Oly said to himself. "Yeah, I know Tchamba. I'm not going to live in the market." The driver scurried around to the back of the van, grabbed Oly's hockey bag and a white foam mattress (standard Peace Corps issue) and placed them on the ground.

"Someone come," he said, gesturing beyond the crowded market.

"What? Someone come. What does that mean?" Oly asked. The driver closed the tailgate and hustled back to the driver's side door, pointing at his watch.

"Lomé!" he said. "No lights," he insisted, pointing at the headlights. "No lights," he said again, pointing up at the sun. Oly started to get angry.

"I don't care if you don't have lights. You can't just leave me here!"

The driver looked confused, not understanding. "Sorry," the driver replied. "Sorry." He jumped into the vehicle looking straight ahead and roared the engine. Oly watched in stunned silence as the vehicle sped off, a plume of dust in its wake, leaving him on the side of the road with a government-issued mattress and an oversized hockey bag stuffed with t-shirts.

Oly started to feel nauseous. People at the *marché* no longer kept their distance now that the van had left and crowd of curious children began to form around him. The pungent smells of cooking fires and rotting garbage assaulted his nose as the shoeless kids, all wearing khaki school clothes, stopped and stared from a cautious distance. His throat burned with thirst and he began to sweat. The sun was relentless and pierced every space not blocked by either corrugated tin or palm fronds. He unzipped the bag and fumbled around for a pair of cheap sunglasses that bought him a little space from the glare of sun and eyes. There was hardly any sound or movement around him, thanks to the heat. Even a small group of nearby goats stood still, waiting for evening.

A young boy approached him from a group of staring onlookers. "Yovo?" he questioned, as if asking Oly to confirm that he was real. It was the first confirmation in the "village of the old man" that he was a stranger, an oddity whose movements and actions would be monitored, discussed and observed for the next two years. Those volunteers who had visions of being famous someday quickly overcame their desires after their yovo experience. Oly would learn that no matter what he did, how many local dialects he spoke, what food he ate, what local threads he wore, even local women he slept with, he would always be separated by his status as yovo. He'd heard from veteran volunteers during training that it meant anything from white devil to peeled banana. He wracked his brain for some phrase in French to respond, but could not come up with anything. He started to feel slightly panicked at the prospect of sleeping outside for the night, surrounded by people chanting 'yovo' at him until the wee hours.

"What did you say?" he answered back in English.

The boy paused, confused. "Yovo?" he said again, this time joined by several other children wearing similar khaki clothes. "Yovo? Yovo?"

"*Fama bié. Donnez-moi cinq francs.*"

"*Yovo, bonzoo!*"

The crowd of schoolchildren grew exponentially as the word quickly spread in the market and Oly found himself surrounded. "*Yovo, yovo bonsoirçavabienmerci!*" they started to chant in unison, growing with confidence in numbers. Adults on the outside of the circle began to watch, some giggling at the entertainment, but doing nothing. Oly stepped back, slightly panicked at the size of the growing crowd, looking in all directions for help as the chanting reached a fever pitch.

"*YOVOYOVOBONSOIRÇAVABIENMERCI!YOVOYOVOBONSOIRÇ AVABIENMERCI!*" picking up in tempo. It had officially become a celebration and there was no end in sight. Sweat dripped into his eyes and stung. His shirt clung to his back and he clutched the hockey bag. He tried to 'shoo' the now large group of children and they laughed at him, murmuring in local dialect and then reforming the circle, some raising their arms in the air, squeezing closer towards him. He started to become paralyzed with fear.

Off in the distance, on the edges of the marketplace, the buzzing sound of a motorcycle caused a pause in the chant. The children seemed to know to whom the sound belonged and started to look around. *Rescue,* Oly thought to himself as the yovo chant hesitated. A spiral of dust crossed the horizon like the Tasmanian Devil in a Road Runner cartoon. The closer it got, the more the children looked toward it and away from Oly. When the encroaching storm became louder, approaching their location between the stalls, the chanting slowed and some ran away. A large Togolese *gendarme* with gigantic thighs and dressed in a tight olive drab uniform drove directly through the middle of the school children. He skidded to a stop, set the kickstand, and removed his belt, an action that caused the entire crowd of children to flee in a wave of brown khaki.

"*Vas-y!*" he yelled, taking a swipe at the legs of one of the taller boys.

"*Américain! Welllcome!*" he yelled when the last of the children ran off, several of them wailing from the beating they received. Removing a pair of dark sunglasses, he introduced himself in a combination of French and halted English. "My name Chalim! Welcome!" His hands were large and calloused, typical of people who worked in fields more hours than they slept. Pointing to Oly's bag and mattress, Chalim barked at several frightened children who had regrouped nearby and they grabbed his belongings with haste. "No problem, *mon ami*. They take to house," he said, and he pointed off into the distance. "*Montez!*" Chalim yelled, slapping the Vespa's dented rear wheel cover like a horse's hindquarter. As his duffel and mattress bounced away on the shoulders of children like a breadcrumb hoisted by ants, what would become the familiar pang of losing control settled into Oly's gut. He swung a leg over the rear seat of the Vespa, unsure whether or not to wrap his arms around Chalim's waist. The stench of sweat and body odor was overpowering. But for the first time since he had left home, he felt at ease.

Chalim careened through narrow alleys and dirt paths as he leaned into blind corners, making a game of surprising women and children who dove out of the way, often falling to the ground, wide-eyed with panic at the sight of a crazy *gendarme* with a white man on the back of his Vespa. One woman dropped an entire bag of charcoal balanced on her head, to the delight of Chalim, who guffawed as he waved and sped by.

Seconds later, they arrived at their destination, a ramshackle cinder block building with a rusty tin roof and faded Coca-Cola signs. The Karibi featured the only cold beer in town, compliments of a kerosene *frigo* commandeered from a local merchant by Chalim's colleagues. When they drove up, Oly's attention turned immediately to a cache of black AK-47s leaning conspicuously against a post on the front porch. As the cloud created by Chalim's Vespa settled around them, several men sitting on a bench in olive uniforms and black boots turned to see who had arrived. Their comrade had a trophy and wanted to share it. "*Mes amis! L'Américain est ici!*"

"*Bonne arrivée, Américain!*" they chanted in unison, raising glasses filled to the rim. A rifle slid from the post against which it was leaning and clanged to the floor. Oly's eyes darted to the corner, waiting for a bullet to discharge into his thigh. No one noticed. He guzzled the of-fered glass of Bière Benin, the legacy of Germany's pre-World War I col-onization of Togoland. Though the nation was ceded to the French after 1917, the German-run breweries had maintained a stubborn presence.

Six *grande* lagers later, Oly could hardly see. The omnipresent chil-dren staring at him from outside the Karibi became blurred figures in front of a dusty landscape. He had no concept of time, other than the fact that the sun was now a blood red blob finally sinking into the dis-tant horizon.

The next morning, Oly awoke, his head heavy like a brick and pressed into the mattress that the driver left him with. Several dark balloons floated over his head, giggling as they gradually came into focus. He tried to lift himself off the cement slab he had been sleeping on and they scattered, giggling and leaving dust in their wake. Oly found him-self sprawled in front of a mud house, his duffel bag nearby. He had no idea how he or his bags had gotten there. A short cement wall separated him from the rest of a compound. Chickens ran about, plucking insects off the dirt. The stench of boiling palm oil stirred his empty stomach. A woman walked by with a large bowl balanced on her head. "*Anasara, bonzoo,*" she said.

Oly stared in disbelief, blurting out a '*bonzoo*' in response. The wom-an laughed and kept walking. The buzz of the Vespa Oly recalled from the day before became louder as it approached. Chalim. He bellowed a greeting to someone passing as he approached and entered the com-pound with a loud roar of the engine. Oly heard two claps, the Togolese equivalent of knocking in a land where few dwellings had doors. Chalim was wearing the same military-issue khaki as the day before. His face was so dark it was difficult to read his expression. "*Américain!*" he cried, peering through the front screen. "Welcome! You're home! You like?"

Sitting up, Oly squinted into the blinding sun and considered the brown mud walls and the rusty tin roof of what was apparently his new home. It had been built for a family of at least five, maybe six, and he had it to himself. It had screen windows installed and a cement floor, all requirements of Peace Corps housing. There was an outside latrine and a space with a drain inside for bucket showers. There was no running water.

"*Oui, c'est bon,*" Oly replied, his *stagiare* French starting to come back to him.

"You have chief house," Chalim said, coming into focus for the first time. Looking over Oly's head, Chalim frowned and barked something in Kotokoli. A tall boy with a sinewy frame put down a pile of sticks and approached the soldier. Chalim rattled off several sentences and the boy glanced at Oly, then ran off in the opposite direction. Chalim looked down at Oly and smiled. "His name Taha. He help you."

CHAPTER 7

LA VIE TOGOLAIS

NOVEMBER, 1990

OLY THOUGHT ABOUT JEFF AND the fate of the other volunteers. He pictured Michelle lounging at a bayside retreat in Aneho, wrapped in a sarong as a German businessman with slicked back hair and Ray-Bans brought her a cold drink. After all the traveling and training, it had come down to Oly sitting with an armed soldier in the middle of nowhere, the life sweating out of him. His tin roof crinkled in pain from sun-induced expansion. Even the Africans described the heat like the sting of a scorpion. "*Ça pique*," they'd say. And yet, there was no way to cool down. No watering hole. And if there were, it'd be full of botflies and giardia bacteria, making it unswimmable.

At first, it made Oly uncomfortable to have a house boy, but when he attempted to do things like fetch water from the well, so many hands tried to take over that he dropped the bucket into the well and a small boy had to climb down and retrieve it. It didn't take long for him to compromise the idealism he'd shared in air-conditioned conference rooms before leaving for Africa. It was simply too difficult to do everything alone. From then on, Taha fetched water, cleaned the kerosene lamps, did small repairs, and retrieved chickens for dinner, facing them East toward Mecca before wringing their necks in proper Islamic tradition. He helped Oly wash clothes by hand and iron them so that botflies wouldn't lay their eggs in the wet fabric. When Taha wasn't doing some random task, he was sweeping, always sweeping the brown dust that covered everything.

With Taha's assistance, Oly found a *menusier* to build him a couple of tables and chairs, was introduced to the family who lived next door to him, and found a reliable rice and bean lady for meals. After a couple of weeks of being followed by a small crowd wherever he went, a flatbed truck with a shiny Yamaha DT-100 motorcycle and a propane stove arrived from Peace Corps headquarters in Lomé. As the vehicle approached his house, a horde of children followed, singing and chanting like giddy Parisians running down the Champs-Élysées after American jeeps in 1944. Oly wanted to kiss the driver. Instead, he signed the paper on a clipboard and read the fine print that said: Failure to wear helmet will result in immediate termination from Peace Corps.

He was so excited he gave the children rides on the back (another Peace Corps violation) and revved the engine as he drove in little circles, churning the cheering crowd into a fever pitch each time he did so. He drove to the *marché* at full speed, arriving like a superhero as he removed his helmet and raised his arms to the delight of onlookers. *I can do this*, he thought to himself for the first time.

It was easier to connect with his neighbors than he expected. They were curious but kept a respectful distance. The father, a teacher, admonished his kids when they started chanting the 'yovoyovobonsoir' song, and had a sense of humor. He listened to the BBC on a short wave radio each night to improve his English and invited Oly to discuss current events on the cement slab in front of his house. "*George Bush est fort,*" he'd say. "No one mess with George Bush. He show Saddam who's boss." Oly enjoyed the African perspective on the American president. There seemed to be a lot of respect for showing others who was *boss*, and it amused him that the Togolese thought of the country club president in such a way.

As the rainy season in late fall yielded to the oncoming *harmattan*, Oly established routines and adapted to the slow pace of Tchamba life. Taha began taking his Yamaha into town to purchase staples like soap, fruit, or bush meat. It seemed an economical idea, since prices doubled when Oly appeared in the market. Taha knew how to bargain and he'd keep whatever extra francs he earned in the transactions.

Oly's mission, as a construction volunteer, was to conduct a needs assessment of the area with the *Bureau des Travaux Publiques* that he had been assigned to in Sokodé, nearly 30 kilometers away. Then, it was his duty to find funding and labor for said project. He wasn't even sure if the 'TP' (as it was known), knew he was at post. The bureau had allegedly received a letter from Rollings indicating that he was to sponsor construction projects with them in the region. But with the mail such as it was and, of course, no phones or other communication, he figured it wouldn't be until he made the trek to headquarters in Sokodé that they'd even know he was in the country. "*L'heure Africain,*" he said to himself one day, smiling as he swung in his hammock, enjoying the peaceful calm of the shade during another sweltering day.

It had felt like an eternity since Oly said goodbye to his family. He recalled that Akundé had told the trainees that mail could take several weeks to reach post, and even then it was a crapshoot. Oly imagined care packages from his mother languishing in a Lomé warehouse or piling up in the house of a corrupt government official. Stopping at Tchamba's PTT (*Poste de Telegraphique du Togo*) became a frequent part of his routine. The imposing cement building sat at the entrance road to town and amused Oly with its size. No one ever received mail, and there were hardly any customers, yet it was bigger than the post office back home, and there were always two or three government workers behind the counter, somehow looking busy. The bureaucracy of Africa, a legacy installed by French colonization, added comic relief to Oly's day. It didn't matter that there was only one white person in town named Richard Olymeyer. All correspondence had to be properly logged, registered, verified by identification and sorted by some arcane method designed to look important. Oly learned not to act impatient as he waited behind the large counter, staring at packages that arrived with his mother's handwriting as the clerk painstakingly recorded names, dates, and destinations. He'd make the *fonctionnaires* laugh each time with his commentary on being the only white man in town. "*Je suis le seul blanc,*" he'd say, handing back his Peace Corps ID. But they never relented, asking for it every time.

Nothing made him feel farther from home than things that contained glimpses of America. Books. Tapes. M&Ms. He'd stare at the list of ingredients with awe at the wonders of modern industrialism. So organized. So efficient and satisfying. Letters were nearly impossible to read because they documented everything he desperately missed. Family cookouts, days at the beach, new baby cousins. His mother would often include *Time* magazine articles about the African AIDS epidemic or a drought in Niger - anything to make him want to get on a plane. His brother Andy often included his own surprises: a neatly folded page of *Boston Globe* box scores, maybe, and a random selection of swimsuit models. Oly pinned them up in his room like a G.I.

On lonely nights, as baboons barked in the distance behind his house and the scent of smoky fires filled the air, Taha would often join Oly for dinner. They divided the fare. Oly got the thighs and breast meat, while Taha devoured the delicacies of head, feet, and wings. Taha loved to talk about America, especially the leaders. "*Oh, Colin Powell, il est fort! Noir Américain. Oh, George Bush! Il est fort. La Maison Blanche.*"

On occasion, they'd go together to watch the tiny black-and-white television of the El-Hajji next door, powered via car battery. After lengthy productions of the Togolese president greeting random dignitaries, the 'news' would abruptly end, replaced by hours of local culture that mainly consisted of local villagers dancing in some scripted celebration for the president. Later in the evening, re-runs of *The Cosby Show* and *Dynasty* would broadcast, dubbed in French. The scene reminded Oly of his father's stories about gathering at a neighbor's house in the 1950s to watch *The Ed Sullivan Show* on the only television on the street.

In the first few months at post, Oly had become surprisingly comfortable in the village of the old man. Without the distractions of super malls, automobiles, and technology, his existence had boiled down to simple routines.

Jolt from bed and sprint to latrine.
Rice-and-bean lady for breakfast.
Laze around hammock in midday heat.
Visit area villages in late afternoon.
Hammock nap.
Street food at sunset.
Drink.
Sleep.

The thought of trying to develop a place that hadn't changed its farming practices in 3,000 years, let alone built schools for its children, allowed Oly to rationalize his procrastination, and focus on immediate concerns, like hooking up his kerosene-powered *frigo* and visiting the local *menusier* to have custom furniture built for him.

He thought about his family and wondered if they missed him. Holidays went by, unnoticed except for packages from home that arrived weeks later. Thanksgiving, Christmas. Just another day in hot, sub-Saharan Africa.

He had become a street-food addict since it was too hot to attempt cooking anything. His favorites were Anya, the rice-and-bean lady, and the 'omelet man' who for some reason never seemed to have any eggs, despite the fact that he always sat at his stall and appeared open. Oly got a delicious omelet on his first day at post and nothing since. It got to the point where he wouldn't dismount from his motorcycle. He'd pull up, ask if there were any omelets, and the main would patiently say, "No ekks," every single day.

"À *demain*," Oly would reply, before heading to Anya. She had become Oly's surrogate mother after a short time, always ready with a stick to shoo the children so he could eat in peace. She grew up in a village outside Tchamba, and was always draped in colorful wax hollandaise, the most expensive imported cloth in the market. The bright purple and pink tones contrasted so brightly with her skin that Oly often caught himself staring at her. She smelled of soap and always had huge mounds of warm rice in gigantic cuvettes covered with fresh white cotton cloth, awaiting him with pregnant anticipation. She had spent some time working in Ghana as well and could speak to him in English, a welcome break for Oly.

"Come my son," she'd say, arms spread wide. "*Viens manger! Viens manger!*" Two things were absolutely forbidden in Togo: talking about the president and killing wild game. Both were considered punishable offenses. But, on a particularly warm morning, after several farmers walked by, hoes over their shoulders, Anya lifted a pot to show Oly and gently scooped a large chunk onto his rice with a spoonful of gravy. He closed his eyes as he bit into the square piece of meat that had been tied together with thin grass reeds so it would stay together while it cooked. It was the most tender piece of flesh he had eaten since being in country and tasted like the corned beef he'd eat at Sunday dinners back home. He smiled, and Anya laughed, saying something in Kotokoli to her sister, who was helping out that day.

"What did you say?" Oly asked, gravy dripping from the corner of his mouth.

"*Tu es Togolais maintenant,*" she said, pointing at him, nodding. "You are now Togolese."

"Yes," he said. "And I can go to Togolese jail now for eating this, *non?*" he responded to the delight of Anya and her sister, who covered their mouths and jiggled with laughter.

"*Ta femme,*" she asked, no longer laughing, but wiping a tear from the laughter. "Where is your wife? What are you doing here?"

"No wife," he answered, surprised by the transition from wild game to marriage.

"Why you come here, so far? My seesta want to know why you leave America come here," she asked him, gently stirring a pot of red sauce next to her. He paused, caught by surprise. It was the first time a Togolese confronted him with the obvious question of what a white man was doing in the village. While he stalled for time, feeling a pang of guilt at his lack of production at post, Anya's spoon scooped the head of a young antelope that was simmering in the sauce. She held it in the air for a moment to test if it was cooked. The head was tilted on the spoon and its mouth grimaced, with an eyeball staring at Oly. *Well?* it seemed to implore, waiting along with Anya for an answer.

He felt a pang of guilt at his lack of production at post and looked down at the steaming bowl of rice and beans in front of him. Anya's sister giggled. "She think you don't know," Anya said. Anya made a sweeping gesture with the back of her hand. "You take her with you. Go to America."

He felt the sweat rolling down his back and tried to think of something funny to say. At a loss, he decided to thank both of them for the meal, getting up and leaving an extra thirty CFA for the meat. The next day he decided he'd adjusted long enough to post. It was time to go to work.

CHAPTER 8

AU SERVICE

ON A COOL, DUST-FREE OCTOBER morning in the village of the old man, Oly kick started his moto, swung by the omelette man to confirm that, once again, there were 'no ekks,' chowed down his rice and beans at Anya's with a sudden urgency, and headed off with new determination to ride the thirty kilometers to Sokodé to pay homage to his appointed Togolese supervisor.

The crumbling Travaux Publiques building, one of many overbuilt designs done by the Germans and French in the 1960s to get newly independent Togo on its feet, was constructed to withstand all that a complete lack of maintenance and African weather could dish out. Even though most of the paint had peeled off, giving the building an Alamo look, its walls were two feet thick and everything, even the inlaid benches along the walls, was made of concrete.

Oly smiled as he parked his bike and placed his helmet on one of the handlebars. A large plank connecting the main entrance to the road traversed a gigantic storm drain filled with fetid garbage and human waste. The agency's mission statement, printed on the front of the building, was faded and barely readable, an apt tribute to its symbolic effectiveness: '*Sanitation, Santé, Progrés.*' An aspiration.

The receptionist, Madam Kloure, was splayed out on a rickety wooden table, like a murder victim in a high school play. She was snoring when Oly walked in, instinctively waving one of her fat hands at an imaginary fly. Unsure what to do, Oly stood in front of the table, hoping to be noticed. After several minutes, two Togolese *fonctionnaires* walked by the desk, laughing with the words yovo mixed into their banter. "*Elle est morte,*" she's dead, one of them said, and laughed, slapping his colleague on the shoulder. Red-faced, Oly glared at the sleeping woman and followed the fonctionnaires up the stairs.

When he walked in, several official-looking men, all in the requisite polyester powder blue or grey fonctionnaire suits, were glued to a tiny black-and-white television plopped on a large dusty desk. One of the men kept adjusting an old car antenna stuck in the top for reception. With the exception of one man wearing thick-rimmed black glasses, they didn't look up so Oly figured whatever was happening was important. The man waved Oly over to see. Nelson Mandela was being freed from a twenty-seven-year imprisonment. "*Yovo, regard,*" one of them said to Oly, pointing to the television. Mandela was waving to hordes of well-wishers in a gigantic parade in Pretoria.

One of the fonctionnaires who was wearing a powder blue suit and had giant beads of sweat on his forehead said in English, "The white man takes, but sometimes gives."

The others grunted. Oly sat quietly, suddenly conscious of his presence as the only white person in the room. "*Je ne suis pas le chef des blancs,*" Oly said after a few seconds.

The man in the thick glasses laughed and looked up from the television. "*Excusez-moi, mon frère,*" he said, standing up. "I am distracted in this historic moment for Africa. Please…," he said, holding his arm out for Oly to enter his office next door.

Monsieur Bawendi, a plump fonctionnaire of Ewe descent, was a jovial, well-dressed man with a sense of décor and appreciation for all things American. He was very excited to see Oly, and all he wanted to do was talk about New York, where he had once visited a cousin who drove a taxi in Queens. "Beeg Apple, Beeg Apple," was all he kept saying, laughing aloud. His large wooden desk was completely empty with the exception of a dusty black phone that didn't look like it worked. A gigantic black-and-white portrait of President Eyadema hung directly over Bawendi's desk, so large that it caught Oly's attention and wouldn't let go. His expression was not menacing, but more self-satisfied.

"He is watching," Oly said to Bawendi, pointing with his eyes.

"Ha!" Bawendi laughed. "That is just a picture. The president is too busy to watch me." Oly decided not to ask a follow up, knowing that there was no love between the Ewe of the South and Eyadema's people of the Kabye. He had learned from Chalim that there was no love between the Ewe, who were blamed for acting like neo-colonialists in cahoots with the French, and the northern minority Kabye, who toppled the Ewe president in the 1960s and had ruled with an iron fist ever since.

They spent over an hour chatting in Bawendi's office in both French and English. Bawendi made a suggestion that he join him on *tournée*. It was a huge honor to be asked on tournée. It was a practice passed down by the president that consisted mainly of one thing: demonstrating power by showing up unannounced. To have a white passenger was the ultimate tournée. It garnered even more respect, and more importantly, *pouvoir*. Even though Peace Corps Volunteers were not supposed to get involved in politics, going on tournée gave volunteers access to villages they may not ordinarily come into contact with and sent a message to potentially uncooperative chiefs that they had the backing of the government. It was something they didn't cover during cross-cultural training in San Antonio, but Oly knew that an occasional show of pouvoir was a necessary evil.

CHAPTER 9

LA TOURNÉE

March, 1991

"Come," Bawendi said to Oly in English, reaching out his hand to hold Oly's. Oly flashed back to his cross-cultural training and remembered that Togolese men would often hold hands as a sign of trust and respect, nothing sexual implied. Oly wanted to giggle out loud as he and Bawendi walked, hand in hand, down the stairs past the men still watching Mandela's release and the receptionist, still snoring. "*Au revoir, Madame Kloure,*" he said, without even looking at her. "*President Eyadema viens demain,*" he said, smiling at Oly. She raised one arm and waved at a fly that had landed on her shoulder, then placed it back down and didn't move. Oly followed Bawendi down the back stairs that led to his vehicle. He never asked if Oly had the time or even wanted to go. It wasn't even a question of whether or not he'd give up the next six hours without notice.

Bawendi thrived on the reaction of villagers as they scrambled out of the way of his speeding car. The chauffeur didn't slow down at all, but rather leaned on the horn. Even a large herd of cattle crossing the road didn't call for braking. He just leaned on the horn about a kilometer in advance and watched the farmers hit the animals with sticks to get them across the road in time. Bawendi paid no attention to the chaos. "Oh, ho, ho," he laughed, his belly shaking with the vibration of the car. "*Papa est arrivée. Papa est arrivée.*" Bawendi described villages they passed not only by the projects underway (a German storehouse, a French latrine, a

Chinese bridge) but also by the delicacies that his chauffeur would find and pack into the vehicle, gratis. "*Mon ami, village de la mango,*" he'd say, pointing while he smacked his lips.

After nearly half an hour of bottoming out over potholes and swerving around fleeing children, Oly felt carsick and ready to roll down the window to vomit when they came to a skidding halt at the 'village of manioc,' home of a tasteless tuber that was shredded and boiled into one of Bawendi's favorite dishes. A screaming child came running through the woods, pleading for help, as Oly puked near the car. Bawendi grabbed the hysterical boy by the shirt. "*Qu'est-ce qu'il y a!?*" he demanded.

Jumping and pointing, the child yelled that everyone was sinking in the river. Bawendi gave quick orders to the child to alert the village and pointed at Oly and the chauffeur to get back in the car. When they arrived at the river's edge, it was such a surprise to see another vehicle, let alone one with a white person in it, that everyone trying to help took their eyes momentarily off the scene to look up. A Toyota bush taxi, top-heavy with cargo, was half sunken and listing in the muddy water. The crude log bridge that the taxi was attempting to cross had collapsed, dropping the vehicle and its contents below. The driver and his apprentices crawled up the riverbanks as dozens of passengers stood by, screaming and pointing at their lost packages. Three men held long sticks out toward the taxi, attempting to prod cargo still attached to the roof.

Screaming and waving his arms at Bawendi, the driver explained that before he tried to make the treacherous crossing, he had the passengers walk to keep the weight down, but that didn't help. Bubbles rose from the sinking truck and broke the surface as a baby goat tied to the roof wailed like a frightened child. The noise made Oly wince and he grabbed a long stick and scrambled down the riverbank, trying to reach the animal in the sluggish, brown water. The villagers chattered in the local language, pointing at his efforts. After several minutes of filling with water, the truck reached its tipping point and slowly rolled over, exposing its undercarriage. The murky water silenced the helpless beast and Oly dropped the stick, wiping a tear from his face. The crowd began to disperse as the taxi driver and his apprentice poked and prodded at the loose packages that floated near the banks. Bawendi smiled at the scene and pointed at the tumbled logs. "*Mon ami, votre projet,*" he announced in a booming Idi Amin voice.

He drove Oly back to the village and made introductions to the chief, making lengthy proclamations in local language. While Bawendi spoke, the village elders sitting around the chief looked back and forth between him and Oly, watching Bawendi's dramatic arcing motion with his arms, presumably a forecast of things to come. The toothless chief glanced at Oly, smiling and nodding his head up and down. The deal was done whether Oly liked it or not. Two women were loading bushels of manioc onto the top of Bawendi's car when Oly opened the back door. A bag of charcoal spilled out and a giant yam fell on his foot. The women stopped loading and stared at the white stranger, a look Oly had grown accustomed to in the smaller villages. "You sit up front, *avec moi*," Bawendi smiled, as the chauffeur started up the car and paid the women. Riding on the uncomfortable middle section of the bench seat, squeezing his legs against the stick shift, Oly couldn't help but feel like one of the bags of charcoal: a commodity. Bawendi peeled an orange and threw the rind out the window, smiling to himself as Oly looked over and reflected on what had just transpired. "*Le pont, c'est bon. Bon projet,*" Bawendi said, making an arcing motion with his hand. "You know, *mon ami*. We build together. Togo and America. *Le pont du chèvre.*" The Goat Bridge.

Bawendi held out half of an orange for Oly and laughed, throwing his head back and making a poking motion with his arm, imitating Oly's attempts to save the goat with the stick. The chauffeur joined in, surrounding Oly in a chorus of cackles that made him feel like he was tied to a table in a mad scientist's castle. "The chauffeur thinks you liked the goat," Bawendi laughed. "Not a lost meal, but a lost friend."

After a slow, teetering ride back to Sokodé with the car bottoming out several times due to the extra weight, Bawendi directed the chauffeur to drop the cargo off at his house on the outskirts of town. Oly's legs had completely fallen asleep from leaning against the stick shift.

Bawendi's home, a neat, two-story cement structure painted bright orange, had a large metal gate to separate it from the street. A crowd of children ran out from the house to greet the vehicle. They stopped in their tracks when they spotted Oly. Bawendi rattled off something in the local language and they let off a rousing cheer, jumping in the air and surrounding the car.

"What did you say?" Oly asked.

"*Mon ami,* I just buy you at the market. They think you are mine."

On the bumpy ride home, with several gift manioc from Bawendi attached to the back of his motorcycle, Oly felt happy, like he had made a big step toward answering Anya's question. *Why you come here so far?* Instead of ignoring the screaming children who ran out to the roadside to wave and yell when they heard the yovo on moto approaching from miles away, Oly stood up on his foot pegs and rode one-handed, pumping the other like Evel Knievel after completing a jump. He looked in his rearview mirror and the entire road had filled in with children waving their arms in his dust cloud. When he passed the post office, Oly noticed Chalim's Vespa parked out front. When he heard Oly approaching, Chalim came out and waved, the barrel of his rifle pointing over his left shoulder. "*Mon ami,* you like *manioc?*" he smiled, pointing at the moto. "*La nourriture africain.*"

"*C'est vrai,*" Oly replied, holding out five of the tubers for his armed friend.

CHAPTER 10

DANSE DES YOVOS

———

NOVEMBER, 1991

SEVERAL MONTHS INTO HIS STAY, in which the days passed quickly absent the transitions of changing seasons, Oly hunched over the hole in his latrine groaning in pain. The lunch with Bawendi was having its revenge. He should have known when the woman at the market 'washed' his calabash in dirty water before serving him tchouk that he was going to pay a price.

Why you come here so far? Oly had started to think of his experience like a combat soldier. He had just finished reading *All Quiet on the Western Front* (an old paperback edition he had packed away) and could relate. You arrive, equipped and trained for a mission, filled with idealism and purpose, but not sure exactly what you were getting into. And, after a short time in the trenches, when the idealism slips away into reality, the only thing that mattered was survival and your friends. He was managing to survive, and the friends were coming slowly. He wondered if Jeff was, in fact, surviving. It had been a while since he'd even thought of his friend as he had found himself becoming less attached to his past life and more conditioned to the present.

After a half hour on the latrine, after both legs had completely fallen asleep from compression on the cement blocks on both sides of the hole, Oly started to feel sorry for himself. No one knew his birthday was coming up. Packages from home would probably be several weeks late, and his mind was starting to drift towards Anya's question about why the hell he came there so far. Sweat poured down his face as he stood up, wiping himself with the remains of a toilet paper roll that was almost finished.

He decided that he needed a tournée of his own.

On his daily tour to the P.T.T., the only mail waiting for Oly was his copy of *The Griot*, the unofficial Peace Corps newsletter. It was just what he needed to reconnect. On the cover was a caricature of Rollings in local clothing, riding on top of a bush taxi holding a goat. No editors were listed and Oly wondered where it came from. Probably from the posh posts near Lomé, where volunteers had things like electricity and access to typewriters and copy machines. He imagined Jeff being somehow involved in the publication and Michelle typing copy as she sat on a balcony in a bathrobe overlooking the Bay of Benin. The stapled pages featured several disheartening stories of volunteer motorcycle accidents and a near drowning. The drama was balanced with several salacious poems about sexual encounters with Togolese and one story of a party at the German Embassy. On the last page, in a corner of an inconspicuous spoof ad for Milo, a chocolate sports drink, Oly found an announcement for the annual *Danse des Yovos,* a legendary party that had run uninterrupted in various discreet locations since the 1980s. He loved the fact that other yovos existed, who had not only used the term but could understand everything that went along with it. The dance would be cathartic for them all. An unleashing of their *yovoness* amongst their own kind. Oly had first heard about the celebration from a scrawny, wild-eyed volunteer visiting the Hotel Californie to give the new recruits a primer on motorcycle repair in the bush. He had grabbed Oly too hard from behind and breathed a whiskey question on him, asking where he was from. Oly made something up and bought him a *café au lait.* "Danse des Yovos, Kara" was all the volunteer could muster before stumbling off his stool and into the night.

Danse des Yovos was not sanctioned by Peace Corps Lomé. It was forbidden on many levels. First and foremost, PCVs were forbidden from leaving their regions with their Yamahas. Second, although the location was always a secret, the date was Christmas Day. Christmas was one of the most depressing days of the year for Peace Corps Volunteers. The combination of isolation, heat and sand instead of cold and snow, and the inability to be with family made it difficult on even the most hardened volunteers. Enter *la danse*. Lance Buck, a volunteer in the 1980s, was accredited not only with founding the party but also for personally slaying a wild boar for the feast. For several years, the fete featured 'Buck's boar' until it became too risky to obtain the contraband meat. He was even rumored to have driven through the local villages on his motorcycle in a complete Santa outfit, terrorizing small children as he ho-ho-ho'd his way through town. The Santa costume got passed down for several years, as the tradition lasted until approximately the mid '80s when it somehow disappeared after an ugly incident involving some American missionaries.

When Oly started to leave the P.T.T., reading *The Griot* as he walked, one of the postmen called out to him. "*Monsieur, attend,*" he said, asking Oly to wait. "*Quelque chose viens d'arriver.*"

It was a package. He hadn't received anything in weeks. The man held it out like a crown, filled with pride at delivering likely the only package the office had received all month. Oly loved examining the packages before opening them. They always looked like they worked hard to get to him. The corners of the brown cardboard box were all pushed in, and it was ripped on one side and re-taped where it had been checked by Togolese customs. The top was nearly covered with colored stamps from the U.S. The various P.T.T. officials from Lomé to Sokodé and even Tchamba had covered those stamps and the rest of the front with their own verification stamps, making the entire box a masterpiece of bureaucracy and administrative handling. It was from home. They remembered his birthday and Christmas, a full month in advance when it was sent. Oly couldn't wait to get home to open it. In addition to a card signed by everyone in his family, there were peanut M&Ms, several *Sports Illustrated* magazines, two books about travel in West Africa, and a cassette tape of music made by Andy and Brett. It featured hits like 'I Touch Myself,' 'Burnin' Down The House,' and 'You Can't Always Get What

You Want.' Oly smiled, as he knew exactly what not-so-subtle messages were being delivered in the selections. The card had been opened (most likely by customs people in Lomé looking for cash). It had a palm tree on the front and inside said, 'Wishing you were here.' Oly felt a catch in his throat as he looked at the 'I love yous' and signatures of his family. It was time to reconnect, even if the *yovos* weren't family.

On Christmas Eve, 1991, Oly packed up his moto and made the four-hour ride to the Kara region where Craig Fulton, an animal husbandry volunteer from Oregon, was posted. The mosquito buzz of two-cycle-powered Yamahas could be heard for miles, as volunteers descended upon Kara. The risk of getting thrown out of Togo was worth the potential reward: a chance to speak English and talk professional sports, drink tchouk, and hook up with another yovo. Volunteers from the northern desert region rumbled in like characters in a post-apocalyptic film, unshaven and dust-covered. They drove the final mile to the party in triangle formation like a biker gang, looking the part. One of them even wore a stars and stripes helmet like Peter Fonda in *Easy Rider*.

Rows of Yamaha DTs were already lined up when Oly pulled in, the distinctive yellow helmets dangling from the handlebars. He could hear pulsating music from within the compound and the distinct smell of bush meat. In less than a year, everyone from training had been transformed into shipwreck survivors. The men had all grown beards and lost half their body weight. Female volunteers had fared somewhat better and had actually gained weight in some cases. Everyone had abandoned their American t-shirts for the colorful cloth found in local markets. Many volunteers, veterans from earlier cohorts, Oly did not know, roamed about, sloshing overfilled calabashes of tchouk as they flirted with the new recruits. In one far corner, an emaciated man leaned over a Togolese woman ladling tchouk into the empty calabashes of eager volunteers. Jeff. Oly hardly recognized him. He appeared as though he hadn't shaved or cut his hair since training. He wore a soiled Togolese boubou and was in bare feet. After his calabash was filled, he raised the bowl and gulped the drink too fast, causing it to rush out the sides of his mouth and down his chest. When it was empty, he belched and threw the calabash over his shoulder onto the ground, screaming "GERONIMOOOOOO" at the top of his lungs.

Oly filled a bowl with homemade chili that the host volunteer had made from local beans and bush meat. The combination was more of a stew than chili, but Oly gorged on the food, hardly chewing. A group of volunteers, sitting under a grass *paillotte*, were laughing out loud as Oly approached, sharing tales of the two most popular PCV topics: bowels and food. Just hearing a language that Oly could understand—white people speaking his language—invited him to sit down and reconvene with his culture.

Two men Oly did not recognize, one wearing a tattered 'Reagan/ Bush' t-shirt, had captured the attention of the audience with the tale of a baboon they had roasted. "Once the hair was burned off, it looked like a human," the Reagan/Bush guy added. "It nearly made me puke, but the meat was pretty tasty."

A guy from Mango, one of the most northern posts, made all of the women sitting in the circle cry, "Ewwww" with his vivid description of cow anus soup. "Dude," he cried, spilling tchouk on the ground as he laughed. "It was pure anus delight."

The familiar beat of American rock music pulsated from within the host's house as Oly looked around for Jeff. He finally spotted him, stumbling toward a path on the edge of the bush, leading two attractive female volunteers. As the tchouk flowed and the dancing began, the real reason everyone made the journey became clear. It was risky on many levels, both physical and cultural, to have sex with a 'host-country national.' Everyone had saved their pent-up desires for Danse des Yovos. There was an unspoken rule that Peace Corps sex was exempt from all the trappings of Western romance. You hooked up. You used protection. That was it. No dating. No courting. The landscape began to swim before his eyes, as Oly refilled his calabash with tchouk and stumbled toward the path that Jeff had taken. A Police song, blaring to distortion from the house, accompanied a small group of sweaty and enthusiastic volunteers that Oly could see, singing along to 'Roxanne' through the porch.

Oly came upon a clearing with a large empty barrel elevated off the ground with a small fire burning beneath it. Several plastic tubes were inserted in holes on the sides. The still was in the middle of a palm grove, and several of the trees had been cut down to provide sap for the mixture. *Sotoubee*, or as Peace Corps Volunteers liked to call it, crazy water, was banned by the Togolese government, and for good reason. Distilled in empty petroleum barrels and insecticide containers, the brew was extremely potent—some would say poisonous—and caused a variety of ills not the least of which was extreme drunkenness. However, depending on the market, and the farther one went north, the coveted liquid could be found just about anywhere if one knew whom to ask.

Oly was taken aback at the scene of several volunteers lying around on the ground in various states of semi-consciousness, like visitors to an opium den. Jeff lay between the two female volunteers he led through the clearing. "Dude," he slurred. "*À la santé. À la santé.*" He stood up, spilling his tchouk and putting his arms out to hug Oly. Jeff looked and stank like something rotten when they hugged.

"How's post treating you, roomie?"

"Better than you, Jeff. What the hell are you living on, insects?"

Jeff smiled and poked at his ribs. "Merry Christmas to you, too. *Mon ami*, I spend more time on the can than I do in my bed. I used to begin my days with a jog in the park. Now it starts with a sprint to the latrine. That sonofabitch Rollings really hooked me up. There's no clean water for five miles, and the street food sucks. Some guy was trying to sell me a porcupine on a stick the other day. After my first month, I hitched a bus to Lomé and blew a month's allowance on a room at the Sarakawa. I had to sleep in a clean bed with air-conditioning. That and I paid a young lady for some company."

"Jesus, Jeff."

"No problemo. I used protection. You should try it, man. She was Nigerian. Spoke English and everything. It was awesome."

Oly looked around at the handful of volunteers who could hardly keep their heads up. The Togolese man who was tending the still handed him a glass of clear liquid and smiled, a toothless, inviting smile. Oly threw the sotoubee to the back of his throat, surprised by its smooth, smoky flavor.

"Is it the petroleum barrel, the pesticide storage container, or the plastic tubes causing the buzz?" he asked the man in English. Not understanding a word, the brew master smiled again. "I gotta get out of here," Oly signaled to Jeff.

"You look like you've got your hands full."

As the stew, tchouk, and sotoubee sloshed about his stomach, mixing a buzz with an unsettling nausea, Oly headed down the path toward the music, falling twice. Sweaty volunteers groped one another as Oly grabbed a full calabash of tchouk and pushed his way to the middle of the dance floor during Madonna's 'Lucky Star.' He caught the eye of Michelle, the hot bohemian from training, who intimidated most of the men and danced by herself. Her hair was cornrowed and she had wrapped a brightly colored sarong around her figure, leaving a split up the leg that would have caused a riot in any of Togo's Muslim villages. The infamous Peace Corps grapevine had buzzed with rumors of powerful expats like the German ambassador frequenting her residence.

The local liquid courage replenished Oly's dehydrated hormones with a desire fueled by desperation. It wasn't something he intended to do, but spilling tchouk on Michelle's back when he burst onto the floor got her attention. The stud in her left nostril flickered the moonlight as she turned in reaction. "Oooooo, I like my tchouk like that" she purred. Before he knew it, they were off in the neighbor's paillotte, getting reacquainted. A goat sniffing around for a midnight snack didn't inhibit her desire to disrobe him as they made do with her sarong as a mat. "Never thought the government would protect me like this," she giggled, as she threw four square blue packages of condoms on the ground. Oly was out of his league but the sotoubee compensated, just as Meister Bräu had in college. He fumbled to rip open one of the packages.

Michelle brought a new level to the sensibility of physical touch. It wasn't until she stroked him lightly with a fingernail that Oly realized he hadn't experienced human contact of any kind for months. She did a funky thing with her tongue, flicking his earlobe and the side of his neck. Her torso twisted in ways he thought not possible. As her auburn hair spilled over his shoulders and chest, the uninvited goat sneezed. She didn't flinch. Michelle focused on the moment, something Oly truly appreciated. She was in complete control and told him what to do and when to do it, a step-by-step guide for drunken males. She even told him when to put the condom on and how long to last, looking him directly in the eye when it was time to come. He'd never been with someone so experienced and it was intoxicating. When they finished, she placed her head on his chest and smiled. "So what brought you to the dark continent, white boy?"

"You."

She squeezed his side with a light tickle. "You put that on the application?"

"Maybe."

"Oh, look at you getting all mysterious and all. I bet this is the first time you've been out of America."

"Not true. I drove through New Mexico in college."

She hesitated, but laughed when she realized he wasn't being serious. Michelle toyed with a leather necklace Oly bought in the Lomé marché, touching the cowry shells that were attached. The quiet made him awkward. It'd been so long since he slept with a girl that he forgot his exit strategy. He was glad she didn't follow up on a real answer for why he came to Togo. "Where are you from, Michelle?"

"Around. My parents moved a lot and I spent time in several milieus. My standard line is born in Cincinnati, raised on the world." She stopped playing with his necklace and raised her head off his chest. "I'm so sleepy. You think there's a 7-Eleven somewhere we can grab a chili dog? Where's your moto? You buy, I'll drive."

"That hurts," Oly said, rubbing his stomach. "I can't take the food here."

"It's okay, yovo," she smiled. "I'll feed you." She gently moved her hand inside his pants.

The temperature started climbing quickly as night gave way to a sultry African dawn. While some of the party faithfuls began to stir, Michelle and Oly had noiseless sex, something that they both found difficult to do. Just after he finished, she tried to push Oly off. "No, just one more minute," he said, not wanting to move.

"No, I don't think so, yovo. I think our landlord is waking up." Her eyes followed the movement of a man coming out of the mud hut connected to the paillote. "Don't move, he hasn't seen us yet. I think he's going to his latrine."

The familiar scent of cooking fires burned in the distance. Nearby, women grunted salutations to one another in traditional language as they headed to market. Michelle sat up, her tanned arms pulled across bent legs. She frowned. "Women run this place, you know," she said, fixing her sarong.

The early morning sun pierced a grove of nearby palm trees and shot into Oly's eye like a laser. They both stood up, leaving the paillote and crossing the opening that led to the remnants of the party. "Yeah, it's crazy how much work they do." Oly tried to sit up, aware that the nightly magic had worn off.

She raised her head and looked toward the house. "No one's awake yet. Come on, let's get some rice and beans." As they quietly stepped over scores of bodies passed out on the porch, Oly kicked an empty calabash and watched it skid across the cement floor. Jeff, who was sprawled under a gigantic mango tree in the front yard, woke up and watched the two of them trying to sneak back.

"*Bonjour, yovos,*" he said, rubbing his head and smiling at Michelle and Oly. "So, you guys have fun last night? You disappeared during all the action. We started a big conga line through the village. It was awesome. That freaky physics guy was behind me and started rubbing my neck. I almost punched him out."

Michelle fixed her sarong and put her hands on her hips. "Oh, not too much fun," she said. "Monsieur Oly here got lost, so I helped him find his way," she purred, swiping her hand across Jeff's cheek as she walked past him like a Hollywood starlet. Oly shrugged his shoulders and followed, heading toward his motorcycle to retrieve some rice and beans.

When they returned to the house, most of the volunteers had woken up, some already packed and ready to head out. Michelle dismounted the back of Oly's motorcycle and walked away. Without even saying goodbye, she simply turned and blew him a kiss. He figured he would probably not see her again during his time in Togo. Just another notch in the belt for the mystery girl. Oly watched her drive away in a plume of dust and held a fist to his ear, pinky and thumb extended in the phone position. "Call me," he mouthed. Jeff caught it all.

"What the hell are you doing?" he said, slapping Oly on the shoulder. "I gotta hand it to you, man, you're about the last one I thought would bed her. Holy shit, she's hot. You're lucky I'm the only one that just saw you do that. Very uncool. You think I got a chance?"

"I don't think the castaway look is what chicks like that are looking for," Oly said. "You know she hooked up with the German Ambassador?"

"No shit?"

"Yeah, and look at you, Jeff. What the hell's the matter with you? Are you gonna make it?"

"Dude, I told you what it's like. I'm dyin' here. There's nothing in that shithole I'm living in. And speaking of which, I've been peeing out of my you-know-what since I got there."

Though it bordered on pathetic, Jeff's vulnerability allowed Oly to like him a lot more than the braggards from the north, whose false bravado caused them to keep a distance with other suffering volunteers. He appreciated Jeff's honesty, but after bailing him out on the French exam, had started to wonder if the cool and self-confident person that he had been attracted to in training was ever going to re-emerge.

As volunteers loaded up their bikes and said final goodbyes, Oly found it difficult to say farewell to Jeff. He imagined *The Griot* featuring a story of Jeff's 'early termination' for undetermined reasons and thought he may never see him again.

CHAPTER 11

LE CHANTIER

JANUARY, 1992

IN THE BEGINNING OF JANUARY, 1992, as the dry season depleted river beds and dust covered everything, a check for fifteen-thousand dollars arrived in Oly's name from the American Embassy 'self-help' fund. Volunteers referred to it as the 'help-yourself fund' known as it was for bad over-sight and a tendency for its funds to disappear into pockets rather than projects. It was a primary reason why it was so easy to get the funding as a Peace Corps Volunteer, as the Embassy knew that the money would be put to good use. As soon as he deposited it into his account at the Banque du Peoples Togolaises in Togo, Oly and Bawendi went on a spending spree, ordering everything from tools and reinforcement barto wooden planks and cement.

Several days later, Bawendi and Oly returned to Affem Boussou, the site of the taxi bush accident where Bawendi declared he would return with a *projet*.

Bawendi and Oly gathered the chiefs of Affem and the chief of the village on the other side of the prospective bridge to talk. During their conversation, translated from French to local language and back again, a gigantic cloud of dust rose in the distance like an Oklahoma twister. As it came closer, Bawendi turned to the chiefs. "*Allons-y!*" he yelled. "*Convoquez le village!*" Within minutes, two drummers appeared and be-gan pounding away. By the time the dust clouds were accompanied by the grind of diesel engines, over a hundred villagers had gathered, singing and clapping in expectation.

When the Mercedes flatbed finally came into sight, loaded with all of the project's supplies, the cheering had reached a fever pitch. Scores of children danced in front of the slow-moving truck, leading it to the middle of the village square. With a protesting hiss from its hydraulic brakes, the flatbed stopped, a cloud of dust settling on top of the crowd. The driver waved through a filthy window as the mammoth vehicle rested, overshadowing the primitive mud huts surrounding it. Bawendi ran to the passenger-side door, grabbed a stick from a boy and scrambled up the cab steps. Clinging to the door frame, he extended the stick-wielding arm, sending the crowd into a frenzy. Oly was mesmerized by the power of Bawendi's impulse: Togo's Fidel Castro. "*Mes amis,*" he began, silencing the mob. "*Nous sommes arrivées!*" he yelled, pumping the stick again, to deafening cheers. The driver pulled the air horn, causing a nearby flock of sheep to panic, which sent the crowd into hysterics. Bawendi ranted in Kotokoli, waving the stick like a scepter, pointing into the distance toward the bridge site. The word yovo was sprinkled in amongst the local dialect. The villagers looked at Oly when it was mentioned. Before he climbed down, Bawendi directed the throng to unload and smiled as they descended upon the truck like ants, grabbing everything within reach. Within an hour, an entire mud granary had been filled with planks and bags of cement.

When Oly tried to help, a villager would grab whatever he was carrying from his hands. Bawendi frowned at Oly when he saw him breaking the hierarchical code and waved him over. "*Monsieur Oly*, you are chief. *Ce n'est pas votre place.*"

Oly didn't like being chief. *What the hell,* he thought to himself, standing by as everyone did the work around him and Bawendi told him to relax. He knew that Bawendi was right, and that he couldn't disrespect the social norms of privilege and power, especially when it came to *yovo* status. Bawendi was protecting him. *Know your place.* It still made Oly resentful. One of the reasons he loved the Peace Corps was that it was supposed to break those conventions.

Despite the limitations on his involvement in the work, it felt good for Oly to be on site *au chantier.* At Danse des Yovos, his conscious weighed heavy with stories from other volunteers, who'd created health clinics, trained farmers in animal husbandry, and eliminated giardia in local water supplies. The bridge project not only gave him a sense of purpose but also distracted him from his loneliness and kept him from drinking the days away with Chalim and the local gendarmes.

The distinctive wail of loose fan belts in Bawendi's Peugeot could be heard through the jungle as Oly made his way to the work site each day. When the Peugeot pulled into Affem Boussou's village square, Bawendi always emerged in a colorful boubou and looked every part the well-fed corrupt government official. It was a role in which Bawendi thrived and was teaching Oly to accept, whether he liked it or not. The mantle of leadership. The only things missing were a pith helmet and a long bore rifle. Ever since the day the supply truck was unloaded, Oly felt a divide between him and the workers. In Tchamba, he accepted his role as the token white-man stranger. But when he went to work, he hoped things would be different: a chance to be one of the people. Every time he tried to pick up a shovel or a bucket, people would stop their work and watch. He was a source of entertainment. Bawendi would have to yell at them to get back at it and he'd have to give Oly a glare that hopefully the villagers didn't notice.

The Peace Corps Volunteers that Oly recalled seeing in black-and-white photos from the 1960s in the recruiting brochures in Boston looked so healthy, clean, and robust. The men wore gleaming white t-shirts and they seemed always to be standing next to some heavy-duty piece of farm equipment. Now that he thought about it, the not-pictured Africans were probably digging up the fields next to the posing Americans.

"*Patron,*" Bawendi smiled, pointing at the villagers heading toward the bridge site. "You bring happiness *au Togo, non?*"

"*Je suis le patron*," said Oly. Bawendi picked up on the disappointment in his voice and frowned.

"*Les Français, les Allemands n'aiment pas les Africains*," he barked, scolding Oly with a pointed finger. "They drive Mercedes and stay always at Hotel Deux Fevrier à Lomé. You are Togolais patron, like me. Look at you! African-American."

Oly gave Bawendi a deliberate look from head to toe and laughed. "*Et votre boubou? Le Peugeot? C'est quoi?*"

Bawendi's eyes widened at Oly and he threw his head back, laughing. "*C'est quoi? C'est quoi? C'est le patron! Nous deux! Les patrons!*"

Oly grew to accept that he was the patron, even going so far as to hand out CFA notes, on Bawendi's direction, to the hardest workers. "*C'est bien, ça*," he'd say, insisting that the cash helped keep the men on the bridge and away from tending their fields. Oly thought about Bawendi's patron comment. It was Bawendi's way of admitting that he and Oly had a lot in common. Yovo/patron. Foreigner/Ewe in Kotokoli country. He had to negotiate his relationships with the local population just like Oly, with the exception that being African allowed him to get a bit closer. But not that much. Oly could tell that it wasn't easy for Bawendi to be an outsider, despite his joking. Maybe it was easier being patron than trying to fit in.

"Who are those guys?" Oly asked Bawendi on an especially warm morning, gesturing toward a group of sweating, sinewy farmers mixing cement and hauling sand without stop.

"They're from Affem-Kabye, the village on the other side of our bridge. You should visit their chief," Bawendi said. "I hear rumors that they think you're the favorite of Affem-Boussou chief."

"Say what?"

"No worries. African politic. I speak to them with language that everyone understand," he smiled, making the international sign for money by rubbing an index finger and thumb together. No sooner had Bawendi stopped rubbing his fingers together then the yelling began. A group of men had dropped their hoes and were screaming and gesturing at one another. One man pushed another down to the sand. Bawendi marched toward the conflict, his robes flowing behind him.

Both groups of men turned their attention to him and started pleading their cases, gesturing, pointing at one another and yelling. One was even pointing at Oly, yelling a string of phrases sprinkled with yovo, yovo!

No one was able to make his point. Bawendi finally chose two of the leaders and headed off toward the shade of a nearby palm tree. The others refused to continue working until the problem had been resolved. Oly was left wondering what was going on.

After over half an hour, Bawendi emerged with a frown on his face. When Oly saw him approaching, he felt the hairs on his neck rise. *Here it comes*, he thought to himself, wondering how Bawendi was going to play him to work out the problem.

"This is not good," Bawendi said to Oly, gesturing for him to move over to a quiet, shaded area where they could talk. "The men accuse each other of stealing supplies last night. Cement. Wood planks. Iron bar. Everything. Accusation of *voleur* is the worst crime in Africa. You can be killed for being *voleur*. This is not good."

"So, we just tell both sides to stop. Can't we do that?" Oly pleaded.

"It's not that simple. They are refusing to work. And the men from Kabye say that it is the Boussou chief himself who is telling people to steal. They were ready to attack one another. We have only one choice," said Bawendi. "Council." Bawendi barked several clipped phrases to the chief's advisors and dismissed the group with a backhand sweep of his left arm. Two men ran toward Kabye, while a couple of others jogged into the chief's compound in Boussou.

"*Broussards*," Bawendi said under his breath, as he walked away. "These country people very stupid," he continued, pointing to his head as he spoke. Oly looked around to make sure no one could hear, glad that Bawendi was speaking English.

"That is why they will always live like this," he continued. "They don't see outside of their stupid little problems."

Oly stopped himself from asking how the rest of Togo was different.

Minutes after Bawendi's proclamation, the two men from the Boussou chief's compound reappeared, holding traditional cylinder drums under their armpits. Both began pounding the worn leather tops in unison with short, curved sticks as they marched throughout the village. The beat was angry and staccatic, both men sweating profusely while their sinewy arms moved at great speed to augment the urgency of sound. It was a calling as it had been for centuries, to summon the villages. The same thing was happening in Kabye. Gradually, people began to appear. First from the interior of Boussou's maze of mud huts, then from the perimeter forest, then in small groups from the Kabye road that led from the worksite. Oly was amazed at the effectiveness of the drums. People simply dropped what they were doing and came. It was the most effective communication strategy Oly had seen since his arrival in Togo. It made him think about the sense of community he'd missed. Maybe things weren't always better in America, where only tragedy, it seemed, brought people together. He wondered why they hadn't volunteered to use it in the mornings for the worksite. *Overplay*, he thought to himself.

Bawendi waited with his arms folded, unimpressed with the scene he triggered. Oly wondered how the chiefs felt, being upstaged by this boubou-wearing Ewe from the South. Bawendi was many miles from his people in a place that decided nearly everything on race and ethnicity.

It took less than fifteen minutes to assemble what appeared to be the majority population of both villages. Men rested hoes on their shoulders and women heading to market carried cuvettes on their heads, babies tightly wrapped on their backs. Small groups of children, many dressed in their khaki school outfits, danced as they followed the adults, some singing the *yovo* song when they recognized Oly.

The crowd gathered outside the Boussou chief's compound, while the drummers continued to play. Some of the women began to clap and move their hips to the beat. The drummers from Kabye walked from the bridge road with a small group of followers, including the Kabye chief, their distant sound matching the intensity of the Boussou players. Minutes later, the drummers from both villages joined together in front of the gathering crowd. The sound of all four men playing in unison drowned out everything else. The Kabye chief stood next to Bawendi, surveying the crowd. He summoned three of his advisors and they walked into the Boussou compound, followed by Bawendi who signaled for Oly to follow. They entered the largest mud hut in Boussou, the council chamber. It was dark and cool inside, and the acrid body odor mixed with the aroma from a large cauldron of tchouk in the middle. There were small wooden stools around the outside, half of them occupied by the Boussou chief and his elders, the other half vacant for Bawendi, Oly and the Kabye council. Everyone but Oly was dressed in his best boubou. "You didn't tell me this was a party," Oly whispered to Bawendi.

Both chiefs were expressionless as they greeted one another. Then the councils of both sides acknowledged one another with traditional bows, hands over hearts, and the requisite grunting sounds that accompanied the salutations. Oly sat awkwardly during the unfolding scene. No one acknowledged him.

The Boussou chief, dressed in a 'wax hollandaise' purple and white boubou, sat in marked contrast to the Kabye chief, who wore a slightly soiled, traditional pullover, similar to many of those on his council. A man of the people.

When the salutations were finished and everyone took their seats, the Boussou chief reached out for one of the calabashes next to the cauldron and dipped, handing it to the Kabye chief. They acknowledged one another, said a few phrases in each of their respective dialects, and poured the drink on the dirt floor, an offering to the spirits. One of the Boussou elders then took over, filling each of the calabashes and handing them out. When everyone had theirs, Bawendi looked over at Oly and signaled for him to follow the group. Oly accidently poured more than he had hoped, splashing the feet of the elder beside him and setting off a chain reaction of murmurs and snickering by the elders.

"I'm glad I could provide some comic relief," he said to Bawendi.

"Eeets okay, Monsieur Oly. They say your ancestors must be thirsty. They have never seen a white man do this before. They appreciate your efforts," Bawendi said, giving a perfect pour and acknowledging the group.

After several minutes of sipping tchouk in silence, it began. The Boussou chief spoke to the elder beside him who in turn translated in French to Bawendi who then in turn spoke to the Kabye elders. (His Kabye, he admitted, while not perfect, was manageable.) The rapid dialogue continued for several minutes, punctuated by serious-sounding groans, head nods, and rubbing of chins. It felt like the satirical comedy of a chief's meeting, with each chief becoming more animated as the time went on. Oly had a hard time following the rapid French translations to Bawendi and couldn't tell by the tone if they were making progress. He tried to read the faces of the elders. Occasionally, a comment would set off a murmuring and Bawendi would have to put his hands up to calm everyone. At one point, an elder stood up and started waving his hands about, making his case about something. Bawendi was sweating profusely and had to wipe his brow, looking over at Oly as the man swept his arm from left to right. Oly listened carefully for the magic y-word to see if the man was talking about him. It started to get very warm in the hut.

Whether or not it was a coincidence that the conversation ended when the last calabash was filled, Oly was relieved when Bawendi stood up, nearly an hour after the conversation began. "We have reached conclusion," he said to Oly in English. "Now comes the hard part. I have to tell the village what happened."

Oly could barely open his eyes due to the glaring sun that greeted him when he emerged from the darkness of the council hut. The huge gathering of villagers was still waiting outside and the drummers jumped to their feet, playing in celebration while calling the crowd to attention. Bawendi waited to emerge last, just after the two chiefs. When he exited the small entrance of the hut, he held his arms straight up in the air. Touchdown. The crowd went wild. Oly wondered what the chiefs must have thought of his grandstanding.

The crowd gathered around him and the two chiefs. The drumming stopped, as did the dancing. "*Mes amis,*" he said, pausing for effect, as all good politicians did. "*Nous avons decidé.*" (He waited for one of the elders from each village to translate.) And then what seemed like an over-explanation that confused the crowd more than anything else, went on to say that something about *gri gri* (curse) from somewhere, which was standing in the way of the villages getting the project done. Oly heard yovo at least three times, which concerned him, but Bawendi seemed to be having his way with the crowd. He waved to the sky, made sweeping hand gestures similar to the elder in the hut, and clenched his fists. The chiefs and the elders kept their poker faces and nodded as Bawendi spoke. Once in a while, they'd murmur to one another, but Bawendi seemed to be having his way with them. Oly concluded that what Bawendi was telling the villagers had more to do with a story they could relate to, rather than the politicking that took place inside. Oly could tell that he was keeping the message simple, direct, and repetitive. *Do this work and the Gods will be happy. Do this work and the yovo will bring you gifts. Do this work and live in prosperity. Do this work.*

Bawendi, sweating profusely and making a final gesture to the drummers to start playing again, turned to Oly and smiled. "*C'est fini.* They will continue work. After both villages sacrifice a couple of chickens that you will provide," he laughed, patting Oly on the back.

That evening, after several more calabashes of thouk, a delicious bowl of rice and beans with wild antelope meat, and a couple of shots of soutoubee, Oly was invited to crash at Bawendi's country house for one of the biggest holidays of the year: the 13th of January, affectionately referred to as *la treize*. It was officially Togo's 'independence day', when President Eyadema shot and killed his predecessor as he attempted to escape into the American Embassy compound next door. To celebrate Eyadema's 'liberation' of the country, no one was allowed to work.

"It is best that we stay at my country home," Bawendi told Oly. "You can never predict how the military is going to 'celebrate' this questionable occasion. You know, like sacrificing a white man to the gods," he smiled.

Bawendi's chauffeur had taken his car for repairs, so they took a bush taxi from a nearby village. Oly give up what he referred to as the 'death seat' (he refrained from sharing the name with Bawendi) to Bawendi while he sat in the back, pinned between two women holding small children. The slow-moving bush taxi barely had enough horsepower as it climbed a treacherous portion of the *Route Nationale*, aptly named the Cliffs of Aledjo. A large tanker truck had overturned and was lying in the road like a wounded beast, gasoline flowing down the middle of the road in broad, rippling sheets. Women and children from nearby villages ran to the site with buckets and *cuvettes* to gather the spilling fuel. Just beyond the accident site was a one-way tunnel dug into the side of a steep cliff by German engineers in the early 1900s. Normally, traffic ascending the mountain took the outside pass, skirting the cliff, while descending vehicles squeezed through the narrow underpass. Due to the rollover, all vehicles were using the tunnel, which was only built for one car or truck at a time.

As the taxi crept toward the accident, the driver didn't slow down to see if cars were coming from the other direction. A complete feeling of horror gripped Oly, as passengers began to yell. *"Attention! Attention!"* screamed a man clutching a leather briefcase. Bawendi let out a laugh, but gripped the dashboard with his fingertips. Oly joined the chorus and the helplessness as the taxi entered the darkness. The woman next to him clutched her infant and mouthed something to the window. Her resignation made him want to holler. The Arabic lettering across the windshield praising Allah was the last thing Oly saw before the light went out in the dark tunnel. The black, wet, stone interior of the cliff felt like a one-way trip to hell. Staccato bursts of the van's horn echoed off the rocky chamber like the death cry of a wounded animal. Oly knew it would be too late if a tanker truck descended in the other direction.

Instinctively, he crouched over and put his head between his knees, like an obedient passenger in an airline safety video. Halfway through the darkness, he noticed that the screaming had ceased. The only sound left was the wailing horn. They had resigned themselves to their fate, a sensibility that clashed violently with Oly's American can-do-ness. It was a tension that caused Oly to feel everything from resentment to a spiritual acceptance over his time in Togo. He could hear the child's heavy breathing next to him, as the mother fell still. They were preparing to die.

He pictured women gathering fuel spilled from the van next to his lifeless body. Then it was over. Sunlight splashed across the windows and the Arabic lettering came back on the windshield. 'God is Great,' it said. *But for the grace of God go thee,* Oly thought to himself, sweat dripping down his back. They had made it. People around him started laughing. He heard 'yovo' interspersed throughout conversations. Bawendi was pointing to the windshield, instructing the driver on something, possibly to do a better job of looking out next time. It was the first time Oly had cheated death. They were veterans. *"Chauffeur, tu est fou!"* Oly yelled. The passengers guffawed in unison with Bawendi. He was horrified and exhilarated, like at the end of a roller coaster ride.

The driver's face appeared in the rearview mirror. "You African!" he cried, smiling to reveal a toothless mouth. Oly turned to the woman clutching her infant. The child's mouth was attached to one of the mother's exposed breasts, as though nothing had happened. Back to normal, whatever that meant. He had tasted what they lived every day. A freefall into the will of God. He had decided they should live today. They laughed. Oly thought of the people collecting the spilled gas and wondered if they felt the same way. He recalled a BBC report about hundreds of Nigerians dying in a huge explosion while they collected fuel from a ruptured pipeline. Part resentment, part spiritual acceptance, he sat with the post-traumatic euphoria shared by all and wiped the sweat from his forehead. He was beginning to understand why it was so difficult to access the culture. The brush with death was a shared experience that brought Togolese together, sheltering the community after near tragedy. This life-and-death bonding, a fact of daily life, was something that yovos had delegated to nursing homes, churches, hospitals, and categories that separated death, categorized it away from daily life. On that day, Oly was able to cross over the experience that kept him apart as a yovo and drew him closer to the other African survivors in the van.

As a fonctionnaire collecting a government salary (not to mention the graft from various projects), Bawendi was able to afford a compound larger than most. Five rounded mud houses with turrets, like miniature medieval castles, were connected by a four-foot mud wall to keep out snakes and other undesirable predators. It was a practice in African construction that went back thousands of years. Each of his three wives had their own separate house, which they shared with their children. Bawendi's mud castle, on the north corner of the compound, was twice the size of the others and shared with no one, unless he requested female company. Oly couldn't help noticing the smooth cement floors and quickly repressed the thought that popped into his head regarding the missing bags of cement from the bridge project. The thatched roofs were fresh and everything had its place. The common space where children played and meals were prepared was neatly swept and free of debris. A large wooden mortar and pestle for mashing corn stood against one of the walls.

After a spicy meal of foufou and chicken, Oly sat under the moonlight on a stool with the women and listened to Bawendi's children laughing as they bantered in Kotokoli. He picked up a stick and started to clean his teeth as he had witnessed many times. The children took notice and started giggling and pointing, their dialogue sprinkled with the requisite 'yovos'. The women stared at Oly, their faces flickering by the firelight. He smiled a mouth full of wood splinters and spat them on the ground. They were chit-chatting in Kotokoli when Bawendi walked in. "They say you are a white African."

"After my brush with death in the taxi with you, am I not?" Bawendi laughed and told the women the reason Oly believed he was a white African. He even re-enacted the expressions on Oly's face as they headed into the tunnel. The women's faces lit up with laughter and they bent over, slapping one another in hysterics as they recounted the yovo's horror. *Laughing at death, literally,* Oly thought to himself, trying to nod as though he appreciated their laughter at his near demise.

One of the women started bantering with Bawendi and gesturing and he started answering back, as if the translation turned into another conversation. She was making a swirling motion with her right hand and pointing down at the ground. Bawendi raised his voice a bit and then gave a lengthy response, accentuating it with various 'yovos' and glances at Oly. It was a moment where Oly felt as close to acceptance as he could get, with the understanding that there was a limit.

Oly's head hurt when he emerged from Bawendi's hut the next day. It took him a minute to remember where he was. The scent of a smoldering fire made him cough. It was already getting hot. The sun rose hard and dropped like a rock in Togo. It could be eighty degrees by eight in the morning. Bawendi sat in the middle of his compound on a stool, brushing his teeth with a short stick.

"Ah, my friend. You sleep well?" he said when he noticed Oly. "Well done yesterday. The project will be a success."

"I didn't do anything."

"Oh yes you did," Bawendi smiled, spitting pieces of the stick onto the dirt.

"I tell them that white God angry. Strong *gri-gri*. Will dry up wells and destroy crops."

Oly stared at Bawendi to see if he was joking. "You didn't do that."

"Ah yes. It worked very well. I am glad I thought of that."

"Are you crazy?" Oly said, surprising Bawendi with his protest. Bawendi lost his patience for the first time since Oly had known him.

"Look around you. You are white man in Africa. White man. Not black man. You come here," he said, pointing angrily at the soil. "And you come as many before. For what? To show the African what? To build bridge because he say so? You think you first white man to come? The last? No, no, no my friend. No. I know many stories. I know how white man come in ships to Dixcove in Ghana and take many people away. I know these things. I know it!"

Oly was shocked at the bluntness of Bawendi's comments. He had never heard anything remotely addressing racial tension in the time he had been in Togo. His pounding heart compounded by the smoke and the warming morning made it difficult for him to think, let alone react. "So you told them that I have special powers that could ruin them?" Oly said.

"I had no choice. They were ready to fight one another. I cannot have that. They will be here long after you go. It is more important."

"The scapegoat," Oly murmured under his breath. He felt himself getting angry at the divide between them. So much for patron/yovo. He felt used by Bawendi and now understood the tension when Bawendi caught him trying to work with the villagers. This was the price. He didn't understand his place, so Bawendi framed it for him. It was a lot easier to use the yovo than to try to delve into the politics between the two sides. Especially since Bawendi was an outsider himself. It was a clever political move.

"What?" Bawendi asked.

"Nothing. I have to go," he said, looking toward his motorcycle. A stomach ache joined his head in a symphony of pain.

CHAPTER 12

LES BANDITS

LATE JANUARY, 1992

OLY DROVE TOO FAST WHEN he left Bawendi's village, speeding through villages, oblivious to the darting chickens that crossed his path. He could feel a tightening in his throat as he twisted the throttle, his wrist starting to hurt from squeezing it too hard. The salty taste of tears reached his mouth. He felt like a fool. "YOVOOOOOO!" he screamed in anger as he flew through the village of Kpano, standing up on his foot pegs and terrifying the children that dived for cover from the speeding motorcycle. "*Yovoyovobonsoirçavabienmerci! Yovoyovobonsoirçavabienmerci!*" he chanted over and over until he reached the outskirts of Tchamba, feeling crazier and crazier each time he yelled it.

It didn't matter what the hell he did. He was yovo. He knew there was another conversation that took place with Bawendi and his wives that fed his defensiveness. It must have been about the cement. And now his bridge was going to be finished out of threats of white gri-gri. "Stupid fucking shit," he said out loud, skidding to a stop outside the P.T.T. When Oly entered the foyer, helmet under his armpit, he was still angry. The clerk waved at him with enthusiasm, disarming some of the emotion. "*Un colis est arrivée. Un colis! Pour vous! D'amérique!*" The man smiled with pride as he held out a brown paper package. Oly felt his anger melting away.

"*Attends*," Oly said, surprising the clerk and holding his hand up. He reached for his back pocket and pulled out his Peace Corps identity card. The clerk laughed out loud and covered his mouth.

"*Tu as raison*," he said, and played along by checking Oly's I.D.

When he tore open the package, several ground nuts poured out along with a letter that was written on crumpled graph paper, the kind that the students had in their notebooks at school. On the paper was scribbled a note in crayon.

> *Patron, Tu vis?*
> Enjoy the gift. There is more where that
> came from. Visit soon and you will see.
> *À la prochaine fois.*
> Kjadouge Jeff

Danse des Yovos felt like a lifetime away. Oly wiped the sweat from his face as he looked at the clerk who handed him a pen to sign the ledger. Jeff's scribbled note was an obvious ploy that smelled of loneliness and desperation disguised with adventure. It was just what Oly needed to forget Bawendi and the doldrums of the bridge project. Jeff would help Oly get over his feeling of being the outsider. He was always involved in some scam that he called his *petits projets*. A popular story on the Peace Corps grapevine that Oly had heard from a volunteer passing through Sokodé was nicknamed 'speakeasy.' It had become embellished in its many tellings in dusty bars across the Togo land, but the one message that stayed consistent was Jeff's knack for trouble. According to the volunteer, Jeff had shown an interest in the sotoubee market and talked constantly about where he could find barrels, copper tubing, and funnels, all of which he was able to obtain thanks to a diverted small-projects grant from the United Nations Fund for Development. Sales of the liquor were so profitable in Jeff's village that an ostentatious purchase of two hundred sheep from a Tuareg trader tipped off the local gendarmes who in turn demanded a piece of the action (in exchange for his safety).

Even after the arrangement with the gendarmes, the village was able to build schools, fix roads, and even purchase a tractor. The diverted seed money never made it into the UN report on small-project grants, but the chief made Jeff an honorary member of his counsel and offered him one of his most beautiful daughters, Assana. Guessing that the girl looked no older than thirteen, Jeff declined and accepted several goats and platters of *wagashi* (local cheese) instead. The gendarmes invited Jeff to a number of their bashes, complete with village girls, banned bush meat, and unauthorized discharging of military rifles.

When Oly pulled up to Jeff's hut on a sweltering afternoon in the mid-winter of 1992, Jeff had just arrived and was dismounting from his Yamaha, which was laden down with two large sacks of what looked like nuts. Without even greeting Oly, Jeff threw the sack down and yelled as if Oly had been there the whole time. "Dude, getta load of this! You like cashews? Here, all you can eat." He poured them onto the ground, grabbing a fistful and letting them spill through his fingers like a diamond merchant.

"I know I'm supposed to ask you where they came from, but I don't want to know the answer," Oly said, knowing that his mere presence made him an accomplice.

"*Très drole, mon ami,* there's a huge grove about five miles that way," he said, pointing toward the south. "It's kinda hidden, but once you get there, the place is unbelievable."

"Speakeasy."

"What did you say?" Jeff asked.

"I said speakeasy. I heard the story from a Kara volunteer passing through Sokodé a few weeks ago.

"No shit. Is that what they're calling it? Man, that was fun. You hear about the chief's daughter, too?" (Oly nodded). "Good thing I didn't get messed up in that. She looked twelve!"

"And this is the part where I say, 'That grove probably belongs to someone who might have a reason to hurt us.' And then you say, 'It's no big deal'."

Jeff dropped the rest of the cashews and squinted at Oly. "Then why did you come, yovo?"

Oly felt his anger rising, but realized Jeff was right. "You want to know why, yovo? Because I was bored, that's why. Because I was angry at a friend of mine who treated me like a yovo after I thought we were friends. And because you sent me the first package I've received in months. You happy, yovo?"

Jeff threw a cashew at Oly that just missed his head. "I knew it, you bastard. I knew you'd come when I sent that."

"I'm going to get my *petits commerçantes* to sell them in the market. Maybe we can even export some of them," he added, cracking one open and popping it in his mouth. "Damn, they're good. C'mon, let's go back and get some more," he said, throwing a nut at Oly's chest and grabbing his motorcycle helmet.

Two miles into the ride, Oly began to get an unsettled feeling and downshifted into third gear. Cashew groves didn't just appear in the wild. He had heard stories of the president's plantations throughout the country and didn't think it a coincidence that one of the most expensive nuts in the world popped up in the middle of Togo. As they approached the grove, Oly noticed a series of two-track roads that Jeff had failed to mention. They appeared to be well travelled with what appeared to be the recent treads of a four-wheel vehicle. Military. The part that scared Oly the most was that there were no warning signs or fences at all. Oly saw that as an extra reason to stay away. Jeff saw it as an invitation.

They parked below a tree in full bloom. Jeff unloaded an empty sack and started filling it as if he were at Goodale Orchards in Ipswich on an October afternoon. He even whistled.

"I don't think we should do this, Jeff."

"I'm not forcing you to stay."

Oly watched for several minutes as Jeff filled the sack, whistling while he worked, completely ignoring Oly. It started off as a low, rumbling noise far off to the east. The unmistakable noise of a diesel engine. Oly forced himself not to say anything until Jeff spoke first. When he couldn't wait any longer, Oly asked if he had any idea where the noise came from.

"Probably some farmer," he said without breaking stride. He had almost filled one sack. The rumbling grew louder and closer. This time it came from the opposite direction.

"Jeff, I think there's two of them, and they don't sound like tractors. I think it's time to go."

A large shadow followed by a gigantic dust cloud broke through a clearing in the grove, packed with men wearing helmets. "They're not here for the nuts," Oly yelled, running to his bike. Jeff fumbled with a bungee cord, as he tried to strap one of the sacks onto his bike when the several branches broke off just above their heads followed by a whizzing sound.

"For Christ's sake, Jeff, drop it. They're fucking shooting!"

Oly jammed his foot hard on the kick-start, slipping off and banging his shin on the footrest, drawing blood. The shots went full automatic, showering the two with leaves just before the gigantic vehicle came into full view. Men starting jumping over the sides before it came to a stop, about a hundred yards away. Jeff gave up on the sack and jump-started his bike.

"We're fucking dead, Jeff. Drop the goddamn nuts! They'll kill us!" Jeff spilled the sack onto the ground and dropped his helmet. He jumped on his bike and jump-started it immediately, actually smiling when a large branch fell just beside him. By now they could clearly hear the men yelling. Jeff leaned forward over the handlebars and spun out, coaxing as much torque as he could from the tiny 100cc engine.

While he tried to follow Jeff, nearly losing control in the soft sand, Oly glanced in his rearview mirror and saw the men crouching to get better aim at them. One of the soldiers picked up Jeff's helmet and waved it at them. When they could no longer hear the crack of rifles, Jeff slowed down and stood up on his foot pegs, waving his fist in the air. "You take one in the leg?" he said, pointing at Jeff's bloody shin. Oly had forgotten about his shin during the escape and looked down at the red stain on his shoe.

"No, I'll be alright."

It was pitch dark by the time that they finally got back to Jeff's house. Neither said a word when they dismounted their bikes, as the reality that they could have died finally sunk in. Jeff's face was caked with dust and his hair stayed in a permanent windblown position. For once, Jeff didn't have a comment to make. Jeff went into his house and came out seconds later, swigging from a bottle of clear liquid. He held it out to Oly, who took a deep swig. "Easy buddy," Jeff said. "They don't call it crazy juice for nothing."

"Here's to putting my life in your hands. Again. I'm going to bed."

After what felt like five minutes of sleep, Oly was jarred awake early the next morning by someone yelling. When he popped up, the sun streamed across his face, igniting a headache that felt like a knitting needle piercing his skull. It was Jeff's houseboy, Mikalo, pounding on the front door.

"*Monsieur Jeff, viens. C'est serieux, Ils vous cherchent. Ils demandent après vous. La militaire. Ils vous demandent!*"

Jeff and Oly looked at one another.

"Your helmet, Jeff. It has a Peace Corps sticker on it."

Seconds later, a white Peugeot 504 pulled up to Jeff's, accompanied by an armed soldier on a Vespa. Chalim. Unlike the impeccably dressed man who emerged from the backseat, he wasn't smiling. The man wore a Western-style suit, white shirt and blue tie. He had the classic black-frame fonctionnaire glasses and nodded to Chalim, who helped him with the door. His chauffeur handed the man the helmet that he grasped with several golden-ringed fingers. The chauffeur pushed Mikalo aside and knocked on the door. Chalim stood behind the man, grimacing and holding a rifle at the ready. He had a faraway, terrifying look on his face. Jeff answered, wearing a Chicago Bulls t-shirt and a towel wrapped around his midsection. "I am sorry," he said through the screen in

English. "I don't want any raffle tickets." The chauffeur looked puzzled and pulled hard on the locked screen door. The man stepped forward calmly and nodded to the chauffeur. He spoke quietly in perfect, university English.

"My friends, allow me. My name is Francis Owangube. Welcome to Togo. Peace Corps, correct? Ahh, yes. President Kennedy. Tragedy, his death. Like the untimely deaths of so many, *non*? Was it Billy Joel who said that only the good die young? In any case, I believe I have something that belongs to you."

The click of Jeff opening the screen door was the only thing that broke the silence. One hour and two bottles of sotoubee later, they'd learned that Mr. Owangube was a businessman who owned several apartments on New York's Central Park West, considered the Togolese president a personal friend, and would kill them if they ever visited the cashew plantation again. After they'd agreed to the terms, Owangube wished them well and said something in local dialect to Chalim, who nodded without smiling. As he got back in the backseat of the Peugeot, Owangube smiled, exposing a gold tooth, and said, "Enjoy the nuts. Very good with tchouk."

In his sotoubee-induced haze, Jeff smiled back and waved. *"Merci, mon frère!"*

Oly tried to catch Chalim's eye, but the gendarme acted as if he didn't know him, a feeling that sent a chill through Oly, making him wonder what would happen when he returned to Tchamba.

CHAPTER 13

LE RELAIS

———◆———

HUNG-OVER, SUNBURNED, UNSHAVEN, AND STARVING, Oly felt like a rescued shipwreck survivor turning his back on a life at sea. The misadventures had left him with a desire for *la vie simple* and a return to the predictable chaos in Tchamba. *Brushes with Jeff,* he thought to himself.

The dry season in mid-winter would soon turn to rain in the early spring, making it impossible to complete the bridge project unless he moved up the timeline. Political upheaval surrounding recent elections in Togo had caused rioting in Lomé, and the Peace Corps had urged all volunteers to remain at post until things quieted down. 'Unbeknownst' to the president, scores of bodies not of his ethnic group had turned up in a city lagoon, forcing the declaration of a shoot-to-kill curfew to restore order. Though it had been over a week since the cashew incident, Oly now understood why the soldiers had been so unusually aggressive and fired actual bullets at yovos. Volunteers were instructed in an official memo wired to each region to create an escape plan should things get really ugly, the subtext being that no one was coming to the rescue. Tchamba was only fifteen kilometers from Benin's border, so Oly had a plan. He laughed to himself as he wrote the directions down on paper.

Left at large yam field, continue five kilometres past baobab tree. Pass old mosque over bridge and continue past three mud huts on the left. Ask for yovo.

The slow process of waiting for more cement to be delivered held up the next phase of the bridge project, and all reports were that the storage hut in Affem Boussou had become a free-for-all. Bawendi was in Benin's capital, Cotonou, on extended family business and Chalim had become scarce after the cashew incident. Weighing his options, Oly headed to Sokodé to figure things out.

The Relais, an expat bar tucked away on one of Sokodé's side streets, was the oasis of choice for yovos seeking to escape the heat, monotony, and cultural isolation of third-world life. Run by the eccentric Rouan and Patrice (two nomadic restaurateurs from France, recently chased out of Bamako for unexplained reasons), the Relais offered cold beer, country and western music, and sharp conversation.

Amongst the regulars was Stefan, a white South African military contractor, who always wore a white button-down shirt and perched himself at the corner bar stool. He drove a black 1100cc BMW motorcycle, on which he had crossed the Sahara Desert. He liked to smoke Fine brand cigarettes and blow rings whenever he held court with local girls, which was often.

German entrepreneur, Otto Brundhauer, only needed a helmet with a spike on top and he could have led the effort to restore Togo back to its pre-WWI Prussian glory. Instead, he ran a public latrine project for Doctors Without Borders and quoted excerpts from *The Economist* to whoever would listen. He had a bushy mustache, mutton chop sideburns and loved to slam his glass on the bar when it was empty, which was often. When he tired of that, he would rip the locals. One time, he complained loudly that the Togolese would steal the pull chains from his newly built stalls, rendering them useless so that people simply crapped on the floor. Otto hired young boys to keep the latrines clean and had them charge people two francs for toilet paper.

When Oly told him that it was free to shit in the woods, he sneered. "Fokking American yankee, why don't you just fokking bomb the place." A white ball of spit clung to his mustache, while he stared at Oly with bulging eyes.

Jean-Paul, a skinny Frenchman from Lyon, was sent to Africa in lieu of compulsory military service. He hated everything about Togo: the heat, the dirt, the food, the people, the lack of electricity, the bad cigarettes. Everything. He was supposed to be teaching Togolese women how to start

According to Rouan; the only thing Jean-Paul did was smoke, sit on the toilet, and ehsleep with the local girls. One time, he apparently ordered a shipment of nuts from Lomé for a cooperative. The truck tipped over going too fast around a curve, killing the driver and leaving the local villagers with two hundred bags of unshelled peanuts. He didn't even go to the accident scene to offer assistance. Patrice banned him from the bar for a month when she'd heard of his callousness, and, when he was finally allowed to return, hardly anyone looked him in the eye.

Oly was chatting with Patrice about the recent troubles in Lomé, when a white Peace Corps van pulled up front. Oly resisted the urge to look, trying to play it cool. Otto swore out loud, slamming his empty glass on the bar and muttering something in German. Seconds later, ten trainees piled into the Relais like third graders on a museum field trip. Their chit-chatter distracted everyone at the bar.

The cool, clean, white skin of new trainees from places like San Diego, California, and Madison, Wisconsin stood in marked contrast to that of the battle-weary expats. Rollings was wearing a tomato-red Hawaiian shirt covered with tiny toucans, and flipped his detachable sun visors up when he entered. He pretended not to recognize Oly. After the recruits were seated, he walked over to Oly at the bar. "Well, look who it is. Wise guy number two. I thought you and your buddy there would have been behind bars by now. How's the dysentery treating you these days?"

"It's great!" Oly said, noticing Patrice's smile from behind the bar. "I have a guinea worm poking out of my belly button; you want me to show it to the new stagiaires?"

Rollings squinted his eyes at Oly and laughed it off. "No, I don't think we need to do that. Look how scared they are. Well, it's good to see you've toughened up. How 'bout a beer, compliments of Uncle Sam?"

"If Jeff could see me now," Oly said, as they clinked glasses.

"How is that sonofabitch anyway? You see him much?"

"Yeah, I actually saw him recently."

"Yeah? Was it during visiting hours at the gendarmerie?"

Oly spewed his beer on the bar and pretended to cough. Otto swore in German and stood up. Rollings laughed, "I don't want to even hear it." After a few minutes of small talk, in which Rollings didn't seem so bad once he had a few beers in him, Oly's gaze fixed on one recruit wearing a tight Izod shirt. Rollings noticed. "Samantha's out of your league. Maybe you should shower next time."

"*Tais-toi,*" Oly said, gulping down his second beer and slamming it down on the counter. He smiled at Otto and wiped his mouth on his sleeve.

Beneath a large stuffed gazelle's head hovering over the bar, Otto was spewing his drunken anti-Americanism onto Samantha and two other wide-eyed recruits. "You fokking imperialists call anything you support freedom. Fokking democracy. You want to control the fokking world so you can keep driving those fokking Cadillacs. They called Germans imperialist pigs. You make us look like fokking Canada."

When she finally excused herself to visit the bathroom, Oly hopped off his stool and caught Samantha near the entrance, nearly tripping over a banana plant.

"Hi, welcome to Togo," he said, righting the plant before it fell over. Her laugh broke the ice and he caught her giving him a once over. Samantha's curly chestnut hair was so clean that Oly wanted to sniff it and rub her all over himself. He hadn't shaved in two weeks and was wearing a denim jacket that hadn't been washed since it left America. A tingling sensation in his groin added to the awkwardness. It had been a really long time, and he hoped she didn't pick that up. He tried to keep eye contact.

"Oh, hi, aren't you Oly?" she asked, confirming what she already knew.

"How do you know my name?"

She giggled. "Oh, you know, the Peace Corps grapevine. People talk."

"They do? What do they say?" *I walk around with erections?*

Ten minutes later, he'd found out she knew more about him than he did about her. She heard about his hookup with Michelle and even about his fall from a baobab tree when he got attacked by army ants at the training center. As she spoke, a second conversation was talking place, the subliminal kind that happens when two people find one another and it clicks. The kind that made Oly want to say stupid things like *I feel like I've known you for a long time,* or even worse, *Have we met?* He gulped the rest of his beer before it got too warm and felt more alive than he had in months. He was hoping that he wasn't giving off too much of the 'man scent' that haunted him all throughout college when he tried to pick women up.

Rollings caught Oly's eye as he ordered two *grande lagers.* Oly raised his glass and winked at him. "Don't look now," he whispered to Samantha. "But did you know that Rollings is CIA?"

"Really?" she asked with flirtatious curiosity.

"Yeah, and you know what his code name is?"

"Can't even guess. What is it?"

"Pencildick."

Samantha spewed a stream of beer at Oly and he laughed out loud, leaning back from the mist. He spilled his beer down his shirt and slammed the empty mug on the bar. "Rouan, my glass is empty!" he screamed. Rollings cast them a dirty look and two tables of trainees looked up at them.

"You're dangerous, aren't you?" she laughed. "I've never met a dangerous man like you."

"You ain't seen nothin' yet, baby. Want a ride on my DT-100?" Oly blushed.

"Did you just call me baby?" she laughed. "I'd love to," she said, leaning forward, tilting her head toward Rollings. "But I'm with them. Besides, I hardly know you." She caught him staring at her breasts pushing against her shirt. A faint scent of laundry detergent and fruity shampoo drifted in his direction as she flipped her hair. "What are you looking at, yovo?" She looked at him with a daring curiosity that rattled Oly. She wasn't accosting him, but looking to see how he'd respond. She liked the game.

"Something I haven't seen in a long time," he blurted out before he could think.

She reached out with a finger and touched his chin, looking him directly in the eye. "You poor thing, you must really be suffering way up there all by your lonesome in Tch-Tch-Tchamba," she said for effect. "I'd give you my number, but turns out I don't have a phone," she laughed, just as Rollings yelled from the doorway that it was time to get on the bus.

CHAPTER 14
EN BROUSSE, II

———◆———

WHEN OLY FOUND OUT FROM a volunteer passing through the marché in Sokodé that Samantha's post was only forty minutes from Tchamba, he went directly to the tailor and picked out a fresh new boubou with purple and yellow designs. The next day, he skipped a visit to the bridge project and plotted a surprise visit during her second week at post. He drove so fast that he flew over the washboard ripples in the road that normally slowed him down, and ran over several chickens without stopping to pay for them or apologize. When he passed by her house (it wasn't hard to find out from the locals where the yovo lived), he didn't stop but rather revved his engine just enough so it would guarantee that she'd hear the distinctive Peace Corps' Yamaha DT-100 sound. As he made his way to the marché in the center of town, he looked in the rearview and saw her come out of her gate, towel wrapped around her, fresh from the shower as she ran out to see who it was. *Perfect*, he smiled to himself. After an appropriate time at the marché and a few calabashes of tchouk to loosen things up, he headed back down to her house and glided to a stop next to the open gate.

"I know that's you, Oly," she yelled from inside. "That was smooth. Did you actually buy anything at the market or did you just circle around for a while, rehearsing your excuse for visiting?" she said, this time in person as she walked outside, hands on her hips. "A couple of yams maybe?" she joked, cupping both of her breasts and laughing. Oly took his helmet off and bowed, the gallant knight dismounting his steed. "Well?" she asked, smiling, hands still on hips.

"You got me," he answered, completely at a loss for words. Her wit was faster and better than his, stripping him of any ability to give a clever response. "I didn't even bring any money," he said, shrugging his shoulders.

"Hmm. Yovo away from his post? Not sure what he's doing in unfamiliar territory? Sounds like a psycho-vac situation if you ask me. Well, c'mon inside, cowboy, and I'll give you a moment to think of a better answer," she gestured, looking past him at a gathering crowd of curious children.

When Oly stepped into the coolness of her cement house interior, he was reminded how difficult it was to first arrive at post. She had no furniture, hadn't set up her petrol powered *frigo*, and her food was still sitting on the floor.

"You need to get some cupboards built, sister," Oly said. "The mice are gonna have a field day in here."

"Is that what that noise is at night?" she said. "It freaks me out." Despite her confident exterior, Oly saw a glimpse of her vulnerability and fear. He could tell she was really glad he surprised her. The same Peace Corps calendar Oly was given during training hung on her wall. It was open to January, with a picture of a lily-white volunteer juxtaposed with hordes of dark-skinned Nepalese children, the Himalayas rising in the background.

"If you turn to June, you'll see a picture of me perched over my latrine," Oly joked, flipping the pages. She looked serious for a moment as she looked at Oly, but caught herself and smiled. A strand of hair flopped over her nose and she blew it aside.

"When do you start turning cynical over here? Could you let me be the idealistic newbie at least until I unpack?"

There were several pictures of Samantha spread out on a bag, some with family members and one with a guy with his arm around her. Oly hoped it was a brother. He filed the image away to ask about later. Her Peace Corps mattress lay on the floor with the government-issued mosquito net dangling above it.

"You wanna come with me to Crate and Barrel?"

"Pretty pathetic, huh?" she said, looking at her half-unpacked bags. "It's alright; hop on my bike and we'll go shopping."

Though Oly was only vaguely familiar with Koussountou, he knew enough about the standard marché items that he could take her around town and look the part of the veteran volunteer. Which soap to buy. The blue net-like scrubby cloth that he couldn't live without. The extra wicks for lanterns. The magic mosquito coils that were probably filled with formaldehyde. They even stopped for a plate of warm rice and beans with wagashi, a local favorite.

Oly thanked the woman serving them in Kotokoli, surprising her and impressing Samantha. His confidence was coming back as he could sense she was smitten. "She wants me," he joked to Samantha, while he smiled at the woman. Oly scooped a steaming morsel of wagashi into his mouth. "Damn, I love this stuff. You can't get it in Tchamba."

Samantha picked up a piece with her fingers and looked at it. "Careful, yovo," Oly said. "That's not culturally sensitive. Just eat it."

"Easy for you to say. My stomach has been turning like a butter churn since I got here."

"Ah yes, the virgin stomach. That's okay. You'll get used to it. Sort of. Wait until your first G and L on your motorcycle. That's when you've arrived."

"What the hell is that?" she said, in between mouthfuls of rice.

"You really want to know?"

"No, but okay."

"It's when you can't control your bowel as you bounce along the road. You gamble with just farting to relieve it, because you think you can. But you can't, so you lose. G and L."

"That's disgusting. Why did you tell me that?"

"Because I want you to be prepared for anything," he said, smiling and popping another piece of wagashi in his mouth. They sat quietly for a few moments, eating in silence, their minds racing about what to say next, but enjoying the fact that they didn't have to say anything. "So why did you…" they both said at the same time. "Jinx, buy me a coke!" they both blurted out, causing the wagashi lady to laugh and cover her mouth at the bizarre exchange in a language she didn't follow.

"Join the Peace Corps?" Samantha finished. "It's not that interesting, really. I'm just an innocent girl from South Carolina who wanted to see the world."

"Bullshit."

"Okay, know it all," she said, pointing her spoon at Oly. "Tell me about myself."

"First of all, don't take this the wrong way, but you're not that innocent. Second, you're not from South Carolina. Your parents moved there. And probably not too long ago, because you don't really have an accent. And third, you're doing this to prove something. Just like the rest of us. Except, for the first time in your life, you're not sure you're going to succeed, unlike all of your previous efforts that probably resulted in various accolades and scholarships."

Samantha stared at him, the rims of her eyes turning slightly red with emotion, caught off guard at how closely he read her. She popped a piece of wagashi in her mouth and smiled, regrouping. "Not bad, yovo. Not bad. Where did I go to school?"

"Hell, I don't know," Oly said. "I'm not a charlatan. Okay, somewhere out west. I'm playing the something-to-prove card."

"Score again. UCLA. What about you, white boy? What's your story?"

"I'll let you know on the second date. I have to get to know you first."

"You bastard," she said, causing the woman serving the wagashi to look over at them. "I think she understood me," Samantha laughed.

Before leaving, Oly invited her to join him the next weekend for the big *Deux Fevrier* celebration. "Let me check my busy calendar," she smiled, agreeing to the date.

The *Deux Fevrier*, affectionately known as *le retour triomphale* was the day in 1969 that Togo's President Eyadema had allegedly survived a plane crash/assassination attempt on his life.

Since that glorious day in Togo's history, everyone had been forced to commemorate the president's triumphal return by wearing white and participating in some sort of march. Peace Corps Volunteers had been strictly warned against any sort of political activity, so they merely became bystanders to the whole charade. Bawendi had invited Oly to join him at the Karabie, and he'd agreed, adding he was bringing a *jolie fille*.

Samantha drove to Oly's house on her new motorcycle that had just arrived. He smiled when he heard her over-revving the throttle, having just recently learned how to drive. The indigo *complet* that she was wearing fluttered in the breeze as she made the final, shaky turn to his house. The deep blue contrasted nicely with her newly tanned complexion and chestnut hair. Oly found he couldn't help but get himself aroused when she shook her hair loose after removing her motorcycle helmet, even if it was like a scene from a cheesy Bond movie.

She looked nervous, an emotion that seemed to dissipate once she took notice of Oly's wardrobe. He'd been unable to resist wearing one of the prints that he'd picked up in Kara. One featured a man shimmying up a palm tree, stuck between a snake coiled at the top and a lion attempting to climb the trunk. The caption read, *dieu sauve moi*. The other, two birds fleeing a cage on a pink background with a caption that read *si tu sors, je sors*. Even though it seemed pleading, he put on the cage-bird shirt.

"Even though I barely graduated from Peace Corps Academy, my third-grade French is pretty good," she smiled. "Can't say I've ever read a pickup line on a guy's shirt."

"Don't flatter yourself. What it means is that if we're not having a good time, we can go someplace else. It's Togolese hospitality."

"Okay, *Monsieur Oly*, you just keep telling yourself that."

"Hey, Evel Knievel, I think I should drive. Your dress might get caught in your chain." He hopped on his motorcycle and patted the back of the seat like the saddle on a horse. "Jump on," he teased. During the quick two-minute drive to the Karabie, she pulled him a bit tighter with her arms around him.

"Here we are," he said, pulling in front of the only bar in town. When they dismounted, she boldly hooked her arm around his and they entered the bar like a couple at a brightly colored debutante ball.

The rickety tables spread along the edges of the outside courtyard were surrounded by Togolese men in the mandatory white boubous. The scene had an eerie, religious feel to it, and it felt as if the god in this case would make anyone not wearing one disappear. The uncomfortable irony to the forced celebration was that everyone was on notice. If you were on the government payroll and didn't show, it was a bad career move, not to mention a potentially life-threatening decision. Every gendarme in town was present, including Chalim, and the Prefet wore enough white cloth to cover a king-sized bed. Oly wondered if that was on everyone's mind as they emptied scores of Bière Benins.

None of the women in the courtyard were recognizable, but they were beautiful. With the exception of the *Prefet*, the men didn't bring their wives to political celebrations. These were city girls imported by the Prefet, who knew what it was like to sleep with a man in an air-conditioned room with sheets. Oly spotted Bawendi holding court with an exceptionally attractive girl wearing long, braided hair attachments. His bleach-white boubou cut a regal figure on his six-foot frame. Oly couldn't imagine where or how such an item was kept so clean in a country where dust from the *harmattan* winds penetrated the deepest recesses of everyone's existence.

"I hope they didn't rent a girl for me!" he yelled into Samantha's ear over the blaring music. Several minutes later, Bawendi approached with a toothy smile and three grande lagers. "*Monsieur President!*" Oly announced, with arms held out. Bawendi held his fingers loosely in a large, soft, fonctionnaire grip and a wave of cheap Nigerian perfume wafted over him. Oly pictured two large jugs of 'One Man Show' and 'Rambo Style' like he'd seen in the markets on his bureau. An Alpha Blondy tune blasted beyond distortion off the cement walls surrounding the outside dance floor of the Karabie, while Bawendi stuck his hand out, inviting Samantha to the dance floor.

Bawendi led her with his West African dance moves, enveloping her in abundant white cloth as their flip-flops shuffled on the sandy cement. On a good night at the Karabie, the only sound you could hear was the pulsating rhythm of steel guitars and the shhh-shhh of three hundred legs moving together as one.

Thousands of miles from home, sipping a beer with strangers not of his race and with a woman he hardly knew, Oly was starting to feel at home. After three grande lagers and two interminable Pepé Kale hits, Oly hopped up to join the dance. The crowded floor smelled of cologne, beer, and sweat as Oly pushed through dancing couples and across the floor toward the large man in the white boubou. Samantha looked glad to see him.

"*Mon père*," he said to Bawendi. "*C'est ma femme!*" Two couples next to them laughed and chattered in local dialect sprinkled with 'yovos.'

Bawendi raised his arms in the air, welcoming his friend, and obliged. "*Si tu sors, je sors!*"

"Can you believe we're here?" Oly yelled in her ear, causing Samantha to wince.

"Do I want another beer?" she yelled back, confused.

"Here! Here!" Oly yelled again.

"No, I can't hear!" she laughed. Oly gave up, putting his arms around her. She held him tight in return in the midst of the sweaty mob. Unable to talk above the noise, Oly pointed at the sky. Samantha smiled and looked up at a universe, uninterrupted by the light pollution of America. The music paused, offering silence for the first time in two hours, then a familiar chord emerged from the loudspeaker. Oly's gaze whipped over to the table where he caught Bawendi standing next to the DJ, with a gigantic smile on his face, waving and signaling with a thumbs up. It was Billy Joel's 'Just the Way You Are.' Oly pulled Samantha in tighter and they danced quietly for several minutes, two white strangers in a crowd of Africans, dressed in ridiculous clothes, holding onto one another.

"Oh, I love this song. Was this your idea, Oly?"

"Look over at the table in the corner."

As she turned, her hair brushed against his cheek and he rubbed against her. It was almost too much to take. She spotted Bawendi laughing - dancing with an invisible partner.

"He so American. Where did you meet him?"

"He's my Togolese boss."

"I need a Togolese boss," she teased, looking into his eyes. "You want to be my Togolese boss?"

"Stop."

"Why?"

"I can't explain right now."

She laughed, pushing away from him. "You men are all the same."

After the dance, as the stars began to fade and the guests jumped on their Vespas with female companions on the back, they left Bawendi and returned to Oly's place on his motorcycle. Her arms clung tightly around his waist as they sped past several yam fields toward the edge of town. The heat of the day that had been absorbed by his tin roof radiated into the house at night, making it too hot to sit inside, so they sat under a mango tree on his front porch.

"The closest thing I have to a late-night stop at Denny's," Oly said, holding up a precious can of ravioli he'd bought in Sokodé.

As he heated up the food inside, he spoke through a window screen. "So, I have to ask you the inmate question. What are you in for?"

"What do you mean?"

"You know. Why'd you sign up?"

She didn't answer until he reappeared from the house, holding two aluminum bowls of steaming ravioli.

"Do you want my interview answer or the real answer?"

"Start with interview."

"I want to give back and, in return, learn about other cultures."

"Now the real answer."

"I was scared to death of getting a real job after college and being on the treadmill for the next thirty years."

"Nice! Welcome to the toughest job you'll ever love!"

"But now that I'm here, I'm excited to do my project. They assigned me to work with a local women's cooperative. Women in small business or something like that. I think it's going to be fun. We have already set up a bunch of meetings and the women have started contacting suppliers to negotiate price together. It's really amazing."

"Yeah, fun," he answered, trying to refrain from being jealous. She seemed to be so much more organized than him, like the girl who sat next to him in math, always turning her homework in on time. They sat silently, savoring the small taste of the West.

"*Allahhhhhhhhhhh, akbar. Alllllllllllahhhhhhhhhhhh, akbar.*" The local mosque was doing its first call to prayer, just before sunrise. "When you hear that, it's an official all-nighter," he said, reaching into Samantha's bowl for an extra bite of ravioli. "This stuff is like gold. Sorry, I'm starving."

They talked about everything from their favorite villages to other Peace Corps Volunteers to the things they missed most. Samantha's restlessness formed as an 'air force brat' came out when she described having life in several states, Guam, and Manila. When her dad chose his Filipino girlfriend over the family, the family divided, and Samantha had checked out after college.

"Can't say I've been any farther than Canada," Oly said. He told her about his brothers, the day he knocked a bully down on the playground at Cutler Elementary, and the day he got accepted into Peace Corps. "I lied about most of my construction experience. I mostly made trips to the lumber yard and fetched lunch."

Samantha scraped her bowl one last time, licking the spoon in a way that caused him to stare at her mouth. She then tapped the spoon on her nose and had a serious expression on her face.

"Do you feel like it matters that we're here?" she asked.

"Matters? That's a loaded word. I can tell you that your opinion of that word will change dramatically from now until the time you leave. When I first got here, I thought about matters like an American. Rally the people. Get stuff done. Move on. About a year ago, I had a dump truck in Affem Boussou loaded with two hundred bags of cement break down just before a rainstorm hit. There was no place to go. While I stood under a tree with the villagers and Bawendi, he looked up to the sky and laughed. As the rain poured off his face, he smiled and said that Allah was teaching us a lesson. I yelled at him asking what kind of lesson that could possibly be. *We should have waited until the dry season*, he said. While we waited for help, two of the workers climbed a tree and captured a flying squirrel. They cooked it on an open fire under the tree, while we helplessly watched the cement get soaked. I lost five-hundred dollars-worth of cement that we had to dump on the road. Thinking back, though, Bawendi was right. I totally ignored nature's timeline. He warned me about that, but I didn't listen. What *mattered* was that I paid attention to how those men handled it. They didn't despair or say everything was ruined or go home. They cooked a squirrel and took it in stride while we waited for the rain to stop. I created a mantra from it. *Cook the squirrel*, I say to myself when I think I'm losing it."

Samantha sat in silence, inches from Oly, as they stared into an ink-black sky. The blinking red light of a satellite pulsed thousands of miles overhead. "Really?" she laughed. "That's your mantra? Cook the squirrel?" She flipped her hair back and pointed the spoon at him. "You're a funny yovo."

Things went quiet for a moment and she looked down, thinking. "Do you miss it?" she asked.

"Miss what?"

"The whole thing. The rat race. Television. Burger King."

"No. I miss mint chocolate-chip ice cream. I miss the fact that things work in America. But I like being in a place where no one cares what you do. There's so much pressure to do something back home."

Samantha put her empty bowl down and reached behind her head to put her hair in a ponytail. "Are you getting sentimental on me, Oly? Have you been to the *dispensaire* lately? People suffer here. They eat the same thing every day if they can get it. Medieval Europe had a better sewage system. And when they're not growing something to eat, there's absolutely nothing to do."

"True, but for a couple of years it's nice."

A group of women, audible but not visible in the darkness, greeted one another in Kotokoli as they passed Oly's house. In spite of fatigue and fifteen-hour days, they always took time for the elaborate greeting. It was like a dance that started with various grunts and phrases and ended with both women echoing the other in a crouching position. Oly moved his hand over Samantha's mouth before she could ask about the noise. She didn't move. "You want to kiss me, don't you?" Oly whispered. As she nodded her head, he removed the hand that covered her mouth and moved toward her to close the deal. "Can you believe how dark it is here?" Oly said, breaking the silence after the kiss. "I mean there's no electricity for miles. It's like the sky is just swallowing up the world. Have you ever seen so many stars?"

"It's kind of a reminder, don't you think?"

"Of what?"

"You know, about what your friend told you about who was in charge."

Just as the orange sun peeked over the horizon, Oly invited Samantha into his mosquito net-covered bed, feeling a way he hadn't felt a long time since his last heartache in college. She climbed in and giggled. "Are we going to cook some squirrels?" she laughed, throwing herself down on the kapok mattress and grabbing him to join her.

CHAPTER 15

BON TRAVAIL

THE THROATY, DISTINCTIVE RUMBLE OF a large diesel engine rolled toward Oly's gate, sounding as if it would ride directly through the wall. The hydraulics squealed and hissed in protest as the driver set the brakes. Oly jumped up in a daze, traumatized by the same noise as the military transport in the cashew field. It couldn't be. He reached under his bed for the machete that he kept for protection and then let go of it when he saw Samantha stir. She awoke, startled, and covered herself. Her hair was mussed up, which aroused him, a good morning smile making its way to her lips. Outside, as the sun peeked above the half-finished cement mosque in the distance, Bawendi waved frantically from the front seat of a brand-new white GMC 9000 super-duty dump truck with the distinctive baby-blue logo of the United Nations embossed on the driver's-side door. In the bed of the vehicle, on top of a load of cement, stood a white man surrounded by Togolese laborers. Jeff.

"*Patron, leve-toi! Le travail nous attend!*" he cried, pumping a fist. In the background, the call to prayer floated across a neighboring manioc field. The laborers jumped from the truck bed and fell to the ground with their mats. "See?" Jeff insisted. "God's calling you! Wake uuuup, white man."

Samantha emerged from the house, a purple Holland Wax panya wrapped around her. She rubbed her eyes as the men went silent.

"Oh," Jeff said. "*Bonjour.* Is Oly there?"

"I don't know. Let me check," she said, calmly throwing her hair back. The only sound that could be heard as she re-entered the house was the sound of the idling diesel. Several seconds later she re-emerged. "No, he is not here, you must have the wrong house. Please check on the other side of town, I think there's another white man who lives there."

Bawendi leaned on the air horn, literally frightening the shit out of a nearby goat, causing the men on the truck to laugh and point. Oly emerged from the house and the men cheered. Bawendi let up on the horn.

Oly could barely see through his sleep-deprived eyes and squinted into the image of Jeff pumping his fist and Bawendi waving. "How the hell did you two meet?" he said. "Now my life is officially hell."

"Ease up, yovo," Jeff replied, "I saw this gleaming white truck full of cement passing through town and knew you must have something to do with it. What the hell were you doing last night anyway, besides meeting lovely…"

"Samantha," she cut in, appearing behind Oly.

"Nevermind. You don't need to explain. It's nice to meet you," he said. Ten minutes later, Samantha was riding on the back of Oly's Yamaha as he led the convoy toward Affem. Jeff rode on top of the cement with the laborers, leading chants like a Liberian warlord on CNN riding into Monrovia on a ramshackle Toyota 4Runner. Minus the AK-47. Watching Jeff through the round circle of his vibrating rearview mirror, Oly felt the nausea of losing control that haunted him every time Jeff was around. Samantha clutched his waist and giggled as they rattled over the washboard ripples on the road to Affem. The bridge project had dragged on for twice as long as he had planned and his two years was coming to an end. Stalled shipments of cement and inadequate numbers of village volunteers had set the timeline back. On top of the delays, the rainy season had arrived early, halting all progress on pouring cement.

When they arrived at the construction site, the Affem Kabye chief jogged from the *grande paillotte* followed by four of his children, arms raised in exaltation. The water from the previous rains had subsided and the UN truck was able to drive to the bridge site without getting stuck in the mud. The sight of three white people and a gigantic vehicle full of cement was enough to bring nearly the entire village out to greet the convoy.

"*Bon arrivée*," the chief cried, displaying a yellow-toothed grin.

Bawendi quickly explained that their lengthy absence had been due to the rains and that today would be the day to complete the bridge, so that both villages could prosper. He was exceptional at delivering flowery rhetoric that brought nods and laughter whenever he spoke. As the men jumped down from the UN truck and villagers descended upon the load of cement, Samantha and Jeff paid respects to the chief with Bawendi translating. The chief then became very animated, complaining that the neighboring village, Boussou, hardly ever sent people to work on the project. Bawendi sent a young boy sprinting off into the distance. Minutes later, he appeared with a drum. "*Allons-y*," Bawendi said, pointing at Oly's motorcycle.

Leaving Samantha and Jeff to supervise the unloading of cement, Bawendi and Oly left on the motorcycle, Bawendi's large frame pushing Oly against the gas tank as he struggled to control the handlebars. When they arrived at Boussou, it was totally quiet, save for two pigs that snorted their way across the village center.

"*Regardez!*" Bawendi snarled, grabbing the drum and dismounting his bike. Bawendi's eyes bugged out as he thrashed the drum and howled in angry bursts of Kotokoli. The veins in his neck swelled and pulsated in rhythm with his hot-blooded cries. Suddenly, one, then several villagers came running. Within minutes, dozens of people had appeared from all directions, heeding Bawendi's wailing cry. No explanation necessary, waves of men sprinted to the river and chattered with excited panic.

Oly stared in disbelief, wondering what could have caused such a reaction. Bawendi peeled the shirt off his back as he ran toward the river at full speed. By the time Oly weaved his motorcycle through the sprinting villagers to the sandy banks of the river, Bawendi was standing waist deep and shirtless in a narrow section of the river, the villagers splashing about as they crowded around to see what had happened.

"*Au secours! Au secours!*" Bawendi yelled, tossing his head back with a laughter that washed over the confused villagers. Bawendi climbed out of the water, grabbing his shirt from the ground as the crowd parted. He pointed to the sky and then at the truck, chattering in rapid staccato phrases that mobilized half of the crowd. The rest yelled in return, pointing at their heads and headed back toward the village.

"What did you tell them?" Samantha asked, stunned as a group of skinny teenagers peeled off around her, several headed to help unload the cement.

"I tell them that a little girl fell into the water. But I am not sure. It is possible that she is okay," Bawendi smiled, clutching the drum under his arm.

"That's wrong," she said, turning to Oly. "How could you do that?"

"I had nothing to do with it," Oly replied, annoyed at the accusatory tone in her voice. He looked over at the villagers heading to the site. "You have to admit, it got their attention."

Samantha abandoned her protests when the men bent over with laughter at Bawendi, mimicking his cries for help and pointing to the river. Bawendi's dramatics amused them and they began to help.

The most difficult phase of the bridge project had begun. With two chiefs and a full complement of labor on hand (the Boussou chief finally showed up on a bicycle), the opportunity had arrived to finish the work. The main deck of the bridge, tangled with a network of heavy rebar and wood forms, had to be poured in a day. Without machines to mix the cement, large numbers of people needed to coordinate both mixing and pouring without wasting any time. Bawendi directed all of the activity and hardly slowed down to eat once the operation began.

By late afternoon, nearly a hundred villagers were busy mixing, pouring, and transporting the cement to the deck. For all his theatrics, Bawendi was meticulous when it came to construction. He screamed when someone grabbed a shovel full of dirt instead of sand to mix with cement, and made sure that the water was as clean as possible.

Oly sat under the shade of an ancient baobab tree with Jeff and Samantha. They didn't want to be there, but every time they tried to help, the villagers would grab the buckets or shovels from their hands. They weren't accustomed to white laborers and it caused too much disruption, so they played reluctant overseers.

"All I need right now is a pith helmet and a bull whip," cracked Jeff. He jogged down to the riverbank and inserted himself into the brigade of villagers passing buckets of water from the muddy river to mix cement. After a flurry of protests and karate chopping hands from the bucket he grabbed, the villagers finally accepted Jeff into the line.

Nine hours later, with the sun starting to dip towards the horizon, the entire deck of the bridge was nearly finished. Three men poked at the poured cement to make sure it filled in all the holes between the rebar, while a young boy draped large palm fronds over it to make sure it didn't dry too fast. Several women were arguing on the side over the empty cement bags that were used in the market to wrap peanuts.

When the final bucket was ready to be poured, Bawendi stopped the work and called the two chiefs over. Scores of villagers clung to the riverbanks, jostling for a view. Bawendi held a bucket between them and announced something to the observing crowds. He took each of their hands like a referee ready to announce the winner of a heavyweight fight and placed them either side of the handle. It reminded Oly of the old black-and-white photos he recalled from high school history classes, when the Union and Pacific railroads finally met and the last spike was driven into the ground. The chiefs, bitter rivals at best, raised the empty bucket in the air to the cheering crowds, aged politicians putting their differences aside to pander to their constituents. Bawendi motioned for Samantha to join him and Jeff, who was howling with several of the workers from Affem.

After years of rolling the dice with various log-and-mud structures, the citizens of two ancient villages could finally cross over the river that divided them, year round, without wondering if they could make it back. Oly felt good, in spite of the setbacks. After barking some final orders in Kotokoli, Bawendi turned and smiled, "It's time for the Guinness, my friends."

Samantha put her helmet on, but was distracted by an argument taking place near a pile of planks. The men were fighting over left-over supplies. "I guess that's to be expected," she said, reading Oly's disappointment. As they pulled away, following Bawendi in the truck with Jeff, the men continued arguing and didn't look up. Even though Samantha's clutch around his waist brought him comfort, the satisfaction of completing the project dissipated like the dust behind his rear tire. Oly should have known better, but he had envisioned the villagers lifting him over their heads like a place kicker after a game-winning field goal. Instead, his parting memory was watching the villagers squabble over leftover supplies.

Oly went over the events of the day, starting with the frustration he'd felt having to beg the villagers to finish work that they'd supposedly asked for. He felt himself going too fast over the jarring washboard road, trying to run over flailing chickens.

"*Doucement,* yovo," Samantha said, her voice muffled through her helmet.

The charade led by Bawendi to motivate the villagers had been funny at the time, but it was infuriating now that Oly thought about it. It had taken months of cajoling, pleading, and threatening to get workers to show up to help and for them to stop stealing the inventory stored on site. If the bridge was built, so be it. If it wasn't, so be it. How could they have stared at that river for so many decades without trying to find a better way to cross it? And why was it so anticlimactic when it was over?

When they pulled up to the edge of the last manioc field on the outskirts of Affem Kabye, Samantha tapped on Oly's helmet, gesturing for him to look to his right. Two men were sprinting out of the field, motioning to Oly, one wearing a filthy t-shirt with the logo 'Virginia is for lovers.' It was an elderly farmer with his son. The two were panting heavily when Oly stopped, a cloud of red motorcycle dust settling around them. The man looked at him, his face deeply lined with the cracks formed from decades of manual labor in the sun. He held an ancient hoe by his side and gestured to the boy to speak.

"*Monsieur*," the boy began. Oly waited several minutes, as the man rattled in Kotokoli, waving his sinewy arms about, making an arc like a bridge and, at one point, clasping his hands together and looking skyward. Oly felt a lump form in his throat as he watched, straddling his motorcycle with Samantha holding on. He took his helmet off to hear the translation from the boy. "He say God bring you. He say *merci* to God for you. He say happy to family and life." The boy smiled, proud of his elementary English.

Rather than trying to start a dialogue, Oly held the old man's calloused hands in his and repeated, "*Merci, merci, merci.*" He felt Samantha pull him tighter as he kick-started the motorcycle and the man gave a final goodbye in Kotokoli.

The white UN truck was already parked in front of the Karibi when Oly and Samantha arrived. The radio was blaring an Alpha Blondy song and Oly could hear Jeff's yelling. When Samantha and Oly walked in, there was already an empty bottle in front of Bawendi and Jeff. Several more grande lagers appeared at the table. Bawendi poured the drinks, spilling some on the table, and raised his glass in exultation. "*Dieu merci, le pont est fini!*" he cried.

"What took you guys so long?" Jeff said to Samantha, as he took a huge gulp and slammed the glass down.

"This old farmer stopped us to say thanks."

"No shit. The last thing I saw was everyone fighting over the leftover planks. I couldn't get out of there fast enough. I dumped so much dirty water in that cement, I'll be surprised if it lasts a couple years. Don't tell Oly that part." Samantha looked over at Oly who was backslapping with Bawendi and drinking what looked like a shot of sotoubee.

Several hours later, as Oly's head began to swim from the dust, drink, and fifteenth playing of an old AC/DC cassette, he staggered to his feet to get up. *"Patron,"* said Bawendi. *"Tu depart?"* Without responding, Oly kept walking and exited to an alley on the side. With one hand on the seat of his Yamaha, Oly puked his brains out next to a goat that was tethered next to a post. Several children appeared from a nearby hut as Oly continued with the guttural groans of a man purging his body.

"Yovo,yovobonsoirçavabienmerciiiiii!" they sang in the loud staccato bursts that annoyed Oly even when he was sober. While puking, it enraged him. Nothing that he had done over the last two years changed the fact that he was nothing more than a yovo. Not living in town. Not eating local food. Not wearing the clothing. Not building the bridge. Not speaking phrases in Kotokoli. It was like he'd just arrived. He felt like he had done his part to belong. He was shedding himself of the things from America that caused him to judge. But now that he was leaning more towards acceptance and opening himself up, he had hoped that Togo would do the same. He imagined himself the trapeze artist, waiting for a bar to swing close enough so that he could grab it and let go of the one he'd been holding onto. The only problem was that it was just out of reach.

He grabbed a nearby rock and lost his balance as he hurled the stone in their direction. A child screamed from a direct hit, and Oly collapsed to the ground, just as Jeff had appeared.

"Jesus, dude," he gasped, pulling Oly to his feet. "You're wasted, man," he said, grabbing Oly's shoulders and looking him in the eye. His face pasted with dirt, Oly mumbled something and lurched forward to puke again. As he did, a man came marching from one of the huts with one of the boys in tow.

"Yovo?" he cried. *"Yovo? Tu blesse mon enfant? C'est toi? Ça fait mal, non? Tu vois?"* he said, holding the crying child's bleeding arm up for him to see. Jeff stood in between them, putting up his arms like a referee, as Oly slouched against a nearby mud wall.

"Doucement, mon ami. Il est malade," Jeff explained, making the universal signal for crazy by circling his ear with a pointed index finger. The

man looked suspiciously past Jeff, squinting his eyes, not sure what to believe. As he did so, Jeff reached out with a thousand francs, telling the man to bring the boy to the *disponsaire* and that he was sorry.

The man walked away with his son, and Jeff hoisted Oly from the ground and helped him into the Karibi, just as Samantha was coming out to see what had happened. "Is he okay?" she asked Jeff, as Oly's head began bobbing up and down.

"Not sure. He beaned a kid with a rock and was yelling some crazy shit."

"Man, he looks bad," she said, trying to lift Oly's chin up.

"*Encore une bière,*" Oly slurred, putting his hand up. Jeff and Samantha looked at one another, laughing.

"Dude, no more for you," Jeff said. Turning to Samantha, he smiled. "Hey Sam, did they teach us this part during cultural sensitivity training?"

Laughing out loud, Samantha shook her head and put her arm around Oly. "C'mon, let's throw him in the truck. I'll take his bike home."

It wasn't the way Oly wanted to end things in Tchamba. With only days left on his contract, he awoke the next day with a pounding headache and no idea how he got there. He heard some clinking outside his window. Samantha was sitting at a stool, washing dishes under his mango tree. There was a note from Jeff on his kitchen table.

You were wasted and hit a kid with a rock. You owe me a thousand francs. Nice bridge, though. I'll catch up with you again someday. Maybe. Good luck with the return.

"Hey," Oly whispered through a screened window. She looked up and stopped scrubbing.

"Hey. You okay?" she asked.

"I'm not sure. I am really sorry if I did anything crazy yesterday. That goddamn sotoubee…"

"I don't think it was just that," she said. "You were really upset how the bridge ended. I know you've been here longer than me, but you can't leave like this. You gotta let go of that stuff. You're going to be disappointed no matter what, even when you return to America. They didn't ask you to build that bridge, you know. Their life goes on, whether or not you help."

He rubbed his head and walked out onto the porch under the mango tree. "I think I'm falling in love with you."

She reached in the washing bowl and threw a handful of soap at him. "Tell me that when you're not hung-over, you crazy yovo."

"No, I mean it. I am." Oly looked down at her and she put her hand up to block the sun.

"So, what are we going to do about it?" she asked. "You're leaving and I'm staying."

"I know, but it's not forever. I'm going to see you again, right?" He put his hand out and pulled her up to him. When she stood, there were tears in her eyes. He brushed them away and kissed her on the cheek.

"Okay, maybe I'm falling a bit in love with you, too," she said, as tears started rolling down her cheeks. They hugged for a long time, swaying for a few seconds, and then staying still. Neither wanted to let go.

CHAPTER 16

LES TOURISTES

SUMMER, 1992

"MONSIEUR OLY!" THE BOY FROM next door cried. *"Monsieur Oly! Yovos! Yovos! À Tchamba!"*

Samantha and Oly broke off their hug as the boy ran onto his porch, his eyes wild with excitement as he pointed off in the distance. "I need to get back to my village," she said, wiping her tears. "I've got some projects to tend to, but I'll be thinking of you every day. Have a good trip back and I'll see you before you know it." She walked past Oly to grab her helmet. The boy watched quietly as he noticed that she had been crying. "Let me know how things turn out with the yovos," she said, as she got on her motorcycle. Oly absorbed every detail he could of Samantha as she started her motorcycle and drove off, not knowing when he'd see her again. As she drove away, she waved. He watched her until she became a speck and he could no longer hear the sound of the motorcycle.

Curiosity and the boy's persistence got the better of Oly, and he put on a traditional boubou given to him by a local chief and invited the boy to jump on the back of his Yamaha. He drove in first gear as he struggled to keep the handlebars straight due to the weight on the back and his pounding hangover. When they pulled up to the *Affaires Sociales* building in the center of town, Oly noticed a white Toyota van parked in front, but it resembled any of the local taxis. Loud music and singing emanated from within the building as a crowd of khaki-clothed students crowded around the entrance to see what was going on. When Oly squeezed through the students and entered the main courtyard, he saw scores of children wearing blue panyas performing *animation* - a line dance reserved for political demonstrations and holidays. Something was up.

What didn't add up was that he saw no white faces or important looking government types. They were usually easy to spot because they wore crisp fonctionnaire suits and looked very unimpressed most of the time. The blaring music reverberated through his aching body. He grabbed the boy who brought him by the back of the shirt. "Yovo?"

The boy pointed to a crowd of well-dressed black people seated with an older gentleman wearing glasses. Two of the strangers wore t-shirts with Howard University on the front. Several sipped orange sodas. One held a camcorder pointed at the *animation*. Americans. Like a mutual *What the hell are you doing here?* the college students looked up at Oly with contempt before diverting their attention back to the animation.

Ignoring them, Oly smiled to himself and took a seat next to an attractive female student wearing a white t-shirt and a leather tourist bracelet common to the Lomé markets. "Welcome to Tchamba," he announced over the music, hoping the noise was the reason she ignored him.

The older gentleman stood up and moved over to Oly, hand extended. "Hello, you must be the local Peace Corps Volunteer. Professor Gunning, Howard University, Washington D.C."

"No shit," Oly responded, half yelling. "Excuse my French, I just didn't expect..."

"Blacks?" Gunning retorted without hesitation. Gunning had been to Africa so many times and dealt with so much misunderstanding about being black and in Africa that he no longer meandered around the point. He laughed. "That's one ironic twist in Kennedy's vision. It tapped into the white man's vision of a 'new frontier' but didn't touch the imagination of African-Americans wishing to help the homeland. I surmise it might be a bit more complicated for us in the context of what was happening to our people in America, you know, with the fire hoses and all."

Oly's head started to pound. He didn't how to respond. A black yovo challenging a white one in his own backyard. Oly started to feel angry at Gunning for making *him* feel like the stranger, an imposter. He wanted to rip off the boubou and throw it on the ground. He tried to upstage Gunning with a smug comment about the *animation*. "I don't mean to rain on your parade," Oly yelled over the noise. "But you know these kids get pulled out of school for this stuff?"

"Ah yes, I know. It is unfortunate, but as you know, it is the culture that we are not apt to change, yes? We're on a semester here at the University of Benin. We learned about the traditional market of Tchamba and wanted to see it. Your mayor has treated us to this lovely dance performance. I'm sure you understand the implications of telling him we are not interested."

Oly felt angry again, this time at Gunning's access to the mayor. He was going to offer to introduce Gunning to the mayor, to show him *his town*. The students continued to ignore Oly and watch the midday spectacle put on by the gyrating *animateurs*. Oly and Gunning stepped out to the street, where they could talk without having to yell over the noise.

"I'm sorry for the behavior of my students," Gunning said. "They are my pre-doctorals in the African-studies program. This is their first trip to Africa and they're very sensitive. Some of the girls cry every night when we return to the hotel. The culture shock is worse when they're your own people. And, unfortunately, you crashed the party. Please don't take it personally."

"Not at all, professor. I was just glad to see some Americans." Oly looked down at himself, starting to feel less angry and more self-conscious. "A white guy pulling up in a boubou isn't exactly Nelson Mandela. Good thing I didn't show up riding my elephant."

Gunning burst out laughing and removed his glasses to wipe a tear with his hand. "Yes, your elephant. That would have been perfectly colonial," he said, still laughing. Gunning reached for his wallet when the music from the *animation* stopped and the audience clapped and whistled their approval. "Here's my card," he said, reaching out to Oly. "Please, keep in touch. I would like to hear how you do upon returning to America."

Oly nodded, flattered that the professor had shown an interest in him but wondered if he actually meant it. "No problem, Professor. Enjoy the market. Oh, and look for Anya when you go. She has the best vegetables and good yovo prices."

Oly signaled for the boy to jump back on his bike and revved the engine deliberately so that the students looked. "*Au revoir, yovos!*" he yelled, waving to the glares from the students.

CHAPTER 17
LE DÉPART

———◆———

LATE SUMMER, 1992

OLY COULDN'T STOP THINKING ABOUT his interaction with the Howard students, as the reality of returning home became imminent. The visiting Americans were like an albatross floating about a ship that he had sailed for two years. It was time for the voyage to end. He held out Gunning's card and looked at it. It had an email address, phone number and fax: symbols of a busy world that wasn't slowing down or waiting for him. He pictured the disappointed faces of the Howard students when they saw him. *But they're yovos, too,* he thought to himself, annoyed. Being American didn't connect him with the students. And living in a village wearing a boubou didn't connect him to Tchamba. *What the hell,* he thought.

Oly had a duffel bag filled with African textiles and carvings rather than toothpaste and cassette tapes. He had let go of the tethers of home, but was barely hanging onto his new surroundings. Two dry and two wet seasons had gone by in such a blur - Oly felt like he'd just arrived. In America, the changing of seasons at least made him feel the passage of time. But in equatorial Africa, every day was as hot as the next, and the months passed like minutes. The Howard students made him feel like he was fooling himself. *What the hell are YOU doing here?* was all he could think about. He felt ashamed at himself for thinking he had integrated into his new home. Now it was time to leave.

He wandered around his cement house, barefoot on the cool cement floor as images of the past couple of years flipped through his memory. Samantha. Jeff. Chalim. Bawendi. He felt sick about how long it may be until he saw Samantha again.

The slideshow of memories kept replaying itself as he made small piles of things he planned to give away or sell. Sweat dripped from his forehead, making dark circles on the cement floor as he imagined the man climbing the mosque next door to give the call to prayer, the toothless chief laughing over Saddam's letter, and flirting with the women in the marketplace.

As the images washed together, Oly felt foolish for starting to believe that he had mistaken the rituals of adjustment with being accepted. *Who the hell did you think you were, driving up on them like that?* he thought to himself, playing the scene with Gunning over and over. *You think they were going to run around and embrace you?*

As he folded Kente blankets and wrapped bronze carvings in his socks, the familiar rumbling of Bawendi's Peugeot pulled up to the gate. The squeaky door opened and closed, followed by Bawendi's clap to announce his arrival.

Oly responded. "*Non, je ne suis pas la. Laisse-moi.* Leave me alone."

"*Tu n'est pas la?*" answered Bawendi. "Eets a thief? I bring police, non?"

Oly opened the door to Bawendi, who had a big smile on his face and had his arms out wide. He picked up on Oly's expression.

"Give me the ticket," he said. "I will take your place. You stay here."

Oly considered the gesture. He at least had a choice. Bawendi would, in fact, have traded places with him in a second.

"Are you ready, yovo?" Bawendi asked.

"No, I am not," Oly answered in English. "*Je suis devenu Africain.*"

Bawendi laughed. "Then I will find you some wives. And you must go to the fields and I will take plane."

The door to the Peugeot was open, a portal to Western civilization waiting for him to enter. A small group of children had gathered, witnesses to Oly's hesitation outside of the idling vehicle. None of them were chanting or singing. They knew who he was after watching him for two years, and gave him the space and respect as they may have done with one of their own elders. They waited to see what he was going to do, unaware that once he stepped into the 'portal' that it was likely he'd never return. He reached his hand out to one of the children, who returned the gesture by touching Oly's fingertips. Oly felt himself getting emotional and wondered why, after all this time, he allowed resentment at being called 'yovo' to cloud the simple act of making a connection. The children giggled when their fingers touched, and Oly smiled. Bawendi came around the car to see what was delaying them and tried to shoo the children away. Oly put his hand up to stop him. "*Ça va*," Oly said, a tear rolling down his cheek. "They're just saying goodbye."

CHAPTER 18

AU PAYS AMÉRICAIN

END OF SUMMER, 1992

TWO MONTHS HAD PASSED BY quickly after Oly's return to Boston in the summer of 1992. The usual readjustment to stimulation overload and fifty brands of peanut butter overwhelmed him, along with the overt pressure of having to *do something* with himself. After the visits to relatives and catching up with old friends had run its course, it was back to the Olymeyer house - a return to familiarity that made Tchamba seem like a dream rather than something real.

His original acceptance letter was still posted on the fridge, a third-world subpoena to remind his mother that she had lost her son. Oly's absence had heightened his sensitivity to everything about being home, from the height of the trees to the material fortune of average people.

"If you took our house and plopped it in Lomé, it'd be the nicest place in the city," he announced one night over a chicken casserole. Oly was confused, wondering why he wasn't as happy as he thought he should be exchanging the struggles of life in Tchamba for the conveniences of takeout pizza.

He felt himself thinking a lot about his early childhood, trying to reprogram himself to the feelings of being home. He spent hours in the attic, pouring over old photographs, college essays, and report cards from the third grade.

"Mom, where's my Boston album?" he'd yell from the fold up ladder that led to the crawl space.

"I think Andy took it a few years ago, sweetie. Sorry!" she'd yell from the kitchen.

"What about my crew jacket? Did he take that, too?"

"I don't know. We can't keep everything, you know! I think it got thrown out."

The cardboard boxes and scattered remnants of his past made Oly feel interrupted rather than connected. It didn't help. Except for the yearbook quote, the scraps of his former life didn't connect to his current reality. He climbed down from the attic, sweating from the stifling heat, clutching several photos and wearing his old letter jacket. His arms extended several inches beyond the ends of the sleeves and he couldn't button the front. It still had his varsity pins attached. "Mom, I'm going out for while," he said, walking through the kitchen. "Oh, honey, you found that old thing. My God, it barely fits you!"

"Mom, c'mon, I wasn't serious. I can't believe I saved this stuff."

She laughed and went back to pouring herself a cup of tea. "You want some? Do you remember we used to do this when you were little? We had the nicest conversations."

"Sure, I'll have some. You still have my 'Richard with a capital R' mug?"

"Yes, I do, sweetie. It's in here somewhere."

After fixing their tea, they sat in the living room. Oly looked around at the framed family pictures on the wall and thought about the attic. "Mom, what happened when I was gone?"

"You mean after I was done crying?"

"Did that leave any time?"

"Very funny," she said, smiling and taking a sip of tea. "There were times when it felt like an eternity and, others, when life just went on. It was very hard around the holidays. I hated the holidays without you," she said, red circles forming around her eyes. "Your dad and I used to talk about how proud we were of you and then I'd find myself standing in your room—which, by the way, I had to constantly chase your brothers out of."

"Thanks. My baseball card collection is still missing, and I know I'll never see my Larry Bird posters again."

"It was so hard just not being able to talk to you, Oly. If I could have just picked up the phone and said hello, I think it would have made it easier. It was just so hard not knowing if you were safe."

"It was really hard to make phone calls. You know that. But I thought about you guys all the time."

She caught him staring at the pictures on the wall and the World Book Encyclopedias that had been on the shelf since the late 1970s. "You seem distant, Richard. You've had that look on your face a lot: like you're not sure about something."

He wasn't sure about a lot of things, most of all why he wasn't entirely happy to be home. He knew that he couldn't express that without hurting his mother's feelings, so he modified his response. "I'm just tired, I guess. It's taking me a while to adjust to everything. I'll be alright. It's great to be home, don't get me wrong," he said, feeling insincere and hoping his mother didn't pick up on it.

"I know, sweetie. When you left, you were just out of college. Now look at you, all grown up. It might take a while to readjust but we love you, you know," she said, touching his cheek with an extended hand. He wasn't sure it was just a question of time. Maybe if Samantha and Jeff were around it would have been a little easier, but he couldn't rationalize why it wasn't better being home. Old friends and family were around, a change in seasons, Mexican food, and all the things he dreamt about as he lay sweating away the lonely hours in his hammock, as children stared at him. He felt like he needed a halfway house, a decompression chamber between the first and third worlds, like the astronauts had when they returned from space.

He loved having tea with his mother, but he felt like he couldn't tell her half the things that were on his mind because they'd upset her and she wouldn't understand what he was talking about. He had pushed a pause button when he left and now it was time to hit play again as though nothing had changed. What was he going to say? How he almost died picking cashews? Killing wild monkeys at *La Chasse*? Chasing the children with a stick?

After floating in and out of the conversation with his mother around relatives, news of his high school classmates, the town, his brothers, he realized that the neighborhood was completely quiet except for the sound of leaf blowers. No one was outside, heading to the fields or the market. They were either inside or at work. *How do you connect with people here?* he thought, taking the last sip of his tea and standing up as his mother excused herself to run some errands.

When he'd try to walk into town, people who recognized him would stop and ask if he needed a ride. He'd decline the offers, feeling depressed that everyone assumed something was wrong when he just wanted to take his time. He'd make calls to temp agencies and then walk several times into downtown Essex, as he often did in Tchamba, where he'd greet passersby and chat with the old men at the rice-and-bean lady. Except in Essex, there wasn't a rice-and-bean lady, and the old men were all inside. No one was on the streets. Everyone had somewhere to go, and they stayed in their cars.

One afternoon, some high school friends called, wanting to go out for lunch. Oly met them at the Mug 'n' Muffin, a diner that had been in town since the Eisenhower administration. Chris Falkner and Jimmy Thompson ran track with Oly at Essex High in the 1980s. Oly had sent them postcards from Tchamba on occasion and they'd kept in touch. Once, when Oly went to the Tchamba post office for his daily run Mr. Unumbe, the clerk, gave him a disapproving look as he handed over a package that had been mysteriously opened in transit. Loosely wrapped in the remaining brown paper were two Hustler magazines from Jimmy.

The three old friends sat over coffee in heavy, white diner mugs, and Jimmy and Chris peppered Oly with questions.

"So, did you sleep with any?" Jimmy asked, as he surveyed the menu.

"Jesus, Jimmy, give it up, will you?" Chris interjected. "The guy just got back and you're making him feel like an idiot. Order some goddamn eggs and get over it."

Then Chris turned to Oly. "So did ya?" They all laughed hysterically, causing an electrician in blue Dickies to turn on his seat at the counter to eyeball the commotion.

Oly reached down and itched his crotch under the table for effect. "Yeah man. Don't get too close, Jimmy, or I'll rub it on you."

After a round of pancakes, eggs, and sausage, and details about living with no toilet or electricity for two years, Oly sat back and wiped his mouth with a napkin. "Damn, that was good. I've been dreaming of that breakfast for a long time."

"No shit," Jimmy replied. "You're all skin and bones."

"Funny you should use that expression," Oly replied. "Because I haven't taken a real crap in two years either. But I'll leave that one alone."

As they left the diner, Oly felt a lot better about being back. The connection with old friends was a step toward feeling normal again, and they seemed to accept him back.

"You need a ride?" Jimmy asked as they got in their cars and Oly stood alone in front of the diner.

"No, all set," he replied, looking down the street toward home. And just for an instant, Oly caught the two friends glancing at one another. Everything wasn't alright. No one rejected a ride home in America. *What the hell,* he thought. *I'm a yovo in my own country?*

On the way home, he passed a video store. They were a novelty that was just beginning to appear when he left for Africa. The man at the counter smiled when he walked in. "Welcome to Video Barn, can I help you find anything?"

Oly stalled in front of the counter, pausing as a thought flashed across his mind. *Yeah, I've been living in a hut on the other side of the world for the past two years, eating goat intestines and crapping over a hole. Can you tell me what a video is?* "No thanks, I'm just looking," he said.

From the 'top picks' list, Oly picked up a copy of 'Born on the Fourth of July' starring Tom Cruise and brought it to the counter. He remembered seeing Top Gun before he left and liking it.

"Account number?" the man asked.

"Um, I don't have one."

"Oh, okay, the clerk replied, reaching under the counter. "All you have to do is fill this out."

Staring at the lime-green sheet, Oly saw how disconnected he had become. Address, credit card information, phone number, etc. All of it someone else's. And he didn't have a credit card. After filling out the top part, Oly hesitated. "I'm kind of in transition right now and don't have my new credit card. Is there any way I can…"

"What you can do is give us someone else's you may know, or maybe they have an account with us and you can do it that way. We just have to contact them and put you on their account."

"Okay," Oly replied. "Let's try that."

"Sure, who are we looking up?"

Oly threw his mother's name out.

"Yup, here she is. Rebecca Olymeyer, 14 Seaside. Is that correct?"

Oly nodded.

"Okay, now all I have to do is call to verify that you can be on the account and we're all set." As the clerk picked up the phone, Oly's pulse quickened and shame washed over him. The man was calling his mother to see if he could rent a video.

"Yes," the man said into the receiver. "I'm calling from Video Plus. I have a Richard Olymeyer here and want to see if I can add him to your account … Oh, sure, here he is."

He handed the receiver to Oly.

"Richard?" his mother said. "What are you doing? I was wondering where you were. Are you in town?"

"Yes," Oly replied, checking to make sure the store clerk wasn't smirking.

"How did you get there? I noticed that both cars were here when you left."

"I walked."

"You need a ride?"

"No, I don't need a ride." Oly said deliberately, trying not to sound impatient with his mother.

"Okay, sweetie. We'll see you later." Oly handed the phone back to the man, who smiled.

"Okay then," the clerk said, taking the green sheet back. "Two dollars and you're all set. It'll be due on Thursday."

As Oly left the store, the shame of the last ten minutes washed over him. He had built a bridge in Africa, but couldn't rent a video without his mother's permission. When he got home, a message written in Rebecca Olymeyer's parochial-school cursive was waiting for him:

Jeff called. He said you know him and that he wants you to call him. Also, a lady from 'Pro-Temp' called and wants you to work this week at Vintage Software in Cambridge, 1100 Mass. Ave. She said something about calling if you can't make it but that they need your help all week.

Love, Mom

CHAPTER 19

JEFF, DEUXIÈME FOIS

FALL, 1992

OLY LOOKED AT THE NUMBER for Jeff and noticed it was a local area code. He shoved the note in his pocket, threw the video on the couch, and skipped steps to use the upstairs phone. Jeff answered.

"*Bonjour, chez Jeff. C'est qui?*"

Oly laughed. "*Ta mère, le chèvre.*"

"*Oh, le chèvre. Ma mère. Merci.*" They both laughed again.

"*Ça fait longtemps.*"

"*Oui, mon frère. Longtemps.*"

Oly thought about how strange it was to be speaking French in America. "Where the hell are you?" Oly asked.

"Central Square somewhere."

"What? Boston?"

"Yeah, dude, Cambridge. It's a free country, right?"

"I thought you were from Wisconsin or something."

"I was."

The unease of being back in America quickly succumbed to the uncertainty of dealing with Jeff. The resistance that Oly would have given to Jeff's offer under normal circumstances could not withstand the reverse homesickness that Oly felt. He was game for just about anything, even if it involved cashews.

"*Demain soir. La ville de Cambridge. Bistro Cantab. J'arrive avec une personne mysterieuse.*"

"*À tout à l'heure,*" Jeff finished, hanging up the phone.

Oly's mother was cutting a green pepper for dinner when he came back downstairs and looked up. "Your French sounds so nice, honey," she smiled.

"Mom, why are you listening to my conversations?" Oly protested.

"I wasn't, sweetie. I picked up the phone for one second to make a call. I didn't know you were on it. It's so nice that you feel comfortable speaking like that with your friends."

After a quiet dinner of meatloaf and rice and small talk with his parents, *The Presidential election is tomorrow, did you know that? Do you need anything at Marshall's? Your father is going to need help moving something from the basement…* Oly left his parents to their nightly reading routine and went to the living room to watch the video. He hadn't expected the return of soldiers from combat to resonate with his emotions. During the scene where the two war buddies got drunk and fought with one another, tipping over their wheelchairs as they argued about readjusting to American life, Oly started sobbing uncontrollably, resting his head in his hands, not caring if his mother was listening in or not.

CHAPTER 20

LE CANTAB ET LE PRÉSIDENT

———————

NOVEMBER, 1992

THE CANTAB LOUNGE STOOD ON the front line of a gentrification war. Its shabby, faux-brick front withstood its glitzy neighbors and didn't care, like a man on the beach wearing dark socks and shoes. It looked like an old insurance office or a place where you would rent a car. If not for the sign, you'd never know what happened inside. Through a foggy window yellowed over time, the shadowy movements of a warm-up band mixed with the pulsating sounds of amps distorted by maximum output. A biting November wind caused the small line near the entrance to huddle close to the wall. As people exited, a burst of music, warmth, loud conversation, and cigarette smoke floated past the line.

"This better be worth it," Oly said to Jeff, who stood next to him and blew into his bare hands. "I haven't bought a pair of gloves yet."

"Tell me about it," Jeff said. "I'm thinking of moving to LA for the same reason. Don't worry, *mon ami*, it will be worth it. Hey, did you vote today?"

"For what?" Oly asked.

"President, you idiot. Today's election day."

"No, shit. I totally forgot. Who's running?"

Jeff laughed and patted Oly on the shoulder. "Maybe you should go back to Togo. You don't have to worry about elections there."

When they finally made it through the narrow entrance, a myriad of blacks and whites, young and old, stood and sat shoulder to shoulder as they took in the rhythms of the warm-up band and awaited the main act. College kids in worn baseball caps slugged cheap Buds next to local forty-somethings in Members Only jackets and plain-pocket jeans. Older black men leaned over the rail separating the bands from the bar crowd, and several nondescript groups awkwardly hung out at tables because it seemed like a funky place to be. Jeff yelled over the cacophony for a passing waitress to bring two pitchers of beer.

The warm-up band looked like a displaced jazz ensemble from New Orleans in the 1950s. Ancient sound equipment rested on plastic milk crates. The speakers had a cheap, second-hand look with big dials and buttons on them like a 1970s hi-fi system. The sax player sported a rental tux, while the tall bass player wore a 'seen-it-all' grin and quietly plucked his chords on the tiny stage. The amps rattled horribly through it all. It was the type of place that got better the more one drank. The drummer sat squeezed under a window covered with a plastic holiday tablecloth that had Santa Claus faces on it. There was hardly enough room for the man to sit, wedged between speakers and the front-door alcove, but he had a raging face and was impossible to ignore. With an oversized Hawaiian shirt and a voice like a game-show host, he was the main event until Little Joe made his appearance.

Little Joe Cook and the Thrillers (featured nightly, Tuesday through Saturday) were a time-warp novelty out of place in the cold American northeast. The all-black, all-New Orleans members were still together since their first hit 'Peanut' hit the billboard charts in the 1950s. Wearing a variety of rumpled tweeds and polyester shirts, the band entertained a mostly all-white audience, a mixture of college kids and Cambridge hipsters looking to rub elbows with diversity.

While the Thrillers played a warm-up number and Jeff ordered beers, a bowlegged man of about seventy stood off to the side, leaning on a rail as though he were waiting for a friend. His face wore a distant expression, as though he wondered whether he had left the stove on. He wore a cheap sports coat about two sizes too small and thick glasses. Minus the glasses, he reminded Oly of Chalim. Oly figured he had to be Little Joe. Oly looked around him at all the young, white faces and wondered if they were amused by Little Joe as in a novelty act or whether they actually came to listen to some music, or maybe a little of both. He looked at Jeff, swigging a beer and felt divided on whether he related more to the band or his countrymen. Little Joe was obviously not African, but Oly felt a desire to sit near him, to talk to him, to hang out. He didn't feel like that about the college students. He wondered if that was the reason Jeff brought him, to confuse him and see if he could handle the experience of being with Americans out of Africa.

The drummer yelled into a mic near his head, while pounding on the cheap drum set and encouraged the crowd to begin clapping their hands. He worked the group into a frenzy, chanting "JOE COOK, JOE COOK" as the bowlegged man looked at his fingernails, pretending to act uninterested. "JOE COOK, JOE COOK," a table of Fidelity interns screamed, pounding on their table and knocking empty Coronas to the floor. When the hysteria reached a level that seemed satisfactory to him, Little Joe grabbed a microphone, took center stage and acknowledged the crowd with a dismissive wave.

Jeff had a huge smile on his face and yelled to Oly over the noise. "Not what you expected?"

"There's always a method to your madness, isn't there?" Oly yelled back, catching the eye of a brunette college student swigging a beer.

"I don't know if I'd call it a method, but it's definitely madness! Messes with your head, doesn't it? I want to run up there and start talking bad French to Little Joe, but I know he won't understand a word! It's nuts, isn't it?"

Oly said nothing, taking a big swig from his beer.

Little Joe broke into a bluesy tune filled with sexual connotations called 'Hot Nuts.' He approached people at the tables and got them to participate by singing embarrassing lines. During the tune, a member of Little Joe's entourage began dancing about with CDs of his latest release called 'Lady from the Beauty Shop.' Jeff waved the man over and bought one. It had a large peanut on the cover and looked hand-drawn. When 'Hot Nuts' ended, the band took a short breather and Little Joe announced that his band was available for Bar Mitzvahs, birthdays, and weddings. Oly looked at Jeff and laughed at the thought of Little Joe belting out 'Hot Nuts' at a Bar Mitzvah in the downtown Sheraton.

After the announcements, Little Joe welcomed the crowd and yelled, "You know why there's a ring around the tub? Cause it means I left you clean!" As the crowd roared and tried to figure out what that meant, he burst into another tune, called 'Jelly Roll.' Jeff ordered more beers. Little Joe walked the floor near Oly and Jeff, testing the long black extension cord tying him to the amps.

After the first set, the band dispersed and Little Joe simply sat on a high chair on the stage, clipping his nails. No groupies, no media, no fans; just Little Joe clipping his nails like a disinterested chief on his throne. He looked up through the crowd and signaled with a pointed finger. One of the men from the band came over and whispered something in Little Joe's ear. Little Joe nodded, put his clippers down and grabbed the microphone, "Ladies and germs, you have a new president; the only man with more female fans than yours truly, Mr. Bill Clinton." The Boston crowd cheered at once, a number of them holding up their beer bottles and clinking them together.

Jeff hollered and slapped Oly on the back. "No new taxes!" he yelled, clinking his bottle with people at the next table. Little Joe put the microphone back down and picked up his nail clippers to finish the job, as though nothing had happened. Oly felt numb and buzzed from the now-warm beer he had been nursing. Even though the election of a new president filled the college crowd with new life to energize the evening even more, Oly felt distant: a witness to his own culture, as opposed to a participant. He glanced over at Jeff and noticed the same vibe, even though he seemed to be getting over it, as he chatted up a co-ed seated next to him.

Oly got up to go to the men's room, walking through groups of people high fiving and talking about the new president. He had missed out on all the hype from Tchamba and was not as interested as he thought he'd be, though he was satisfied that the Gulf War would probably be finished. When he walked down a narrow corridor to the men's room, he noticed several framed pictures and newspaper articles of Little Joe. Couched in fine print and browned paper, he saw glimpses of young, dapper African-American males holding shiny brass instruments and smiling for the cameras. One of the captions read, 'Joe Cook, Sonny Flair, Jonny Billings, and company play Thursday at the Cantab.' The place looked open and clean, with sharply dressed young men and women smiling and hanging onto one another.

Little Joe's resemblance to Bawendi made Oly think of the last time they were together and how misplaced he felt being in the middle of a city so far away from his friend. It made him feel connected to Little Joe in a way that didn't seem right. Just because he was the first black guy he'd seen since he got back? Oly wanted to ask him about Sonny and Jonny and what happened to the Cantab in Louisiana. He wanted to ask him why he left New Orleans and what he was doing in Boston all these years. He wanted to tell him about Bawendi and drink a Guinness.

When Bawendi and Oly went on their *tournées*, Oly was always focused on budgets, cement deliveries, and whether or not he'd survive the chauffeur's driving. Bawendi would ignore the situation around him, comfortably peeling an orange, as they flew down dirt roads, sending chickens and small children running in all directions. They were going to blow a tire and die. Bawendi ate. Oly worried. Now back home, safe again, with Jeff next to him, Oly felt the familiar resignation that clutched him during the helpless moments in Togo. And it brought him peace.

Five songs into the second set, the drummer grabbed the mic as he sweated profusely beneath the stage lights. "Ladies and gentlemen," he yelled. "May I have your attention as we now bring to you the song made famous around the world by our one and only, legendary JOE COOK!" Little Joe untangled the long, black cord attached to the microphone and stepped forward. In a startling voice, that most people would need helium to produce, he belted out the old favorite, famous throughout the world and eulogized forever on the door of his yellow Lincoln.

When the waitress brought their third round of beers, Jeff asked her if Little Joe sang 'Peanut' every night. "Are you kidding?" she answered. "Sometimes three or four times!" "Hey!" Oly screamed into Jeff's ear, as the waitress walked away. "Where the hell is this mystery guest you were talking about?"

In a drunken slur, Jeff replied, "*C'est lui,*" he said, smiling and pointing the neck of his Bud Light toward Little Joe.

A slideshow of nostalgic images flittered through Oly's mind as they stumbled out of the Cantab and into a cheap Indian food dive on Mass Avenue: Riding through tropical rainstorms on the way back from the bridge project. Laughing with Anya over rice and beans. Playing with the local kids, even when they sang the yovo song. Hanging out with Bawendi beneath a full African moon.

Jeff lit a cigarette over his stained menu and let out a raucous laugh that turned heads. "Dude, let's get some fuckin' vindaloo," he announced. "Vindalooooo!" he screamed, as a nervous waiter approached their table.

"Please sir," the man implored with his arms out. "No smoking in this establishment. We will lose our license." Jeff slow blinked and blew a stream of smoke in the air.

"Party pooper. They're all asleep, man," he said, his eyes blinking even slower as the cigarette dipped down in his fingers. "No one will know."

Oly took the cigarette out of Jeff's hand and stubbed it out on a plate. "Sorry," Oly said, to the waiter's relief. "Just bring us some vindaloo and a bunch of rice."

After a spicy meal that Oly knew he'd regret, he woke up several hours later, face down on an old moldy couch. The sun beamed on his face through a crack in the curtains. His stomach turned over from the vindaloo when a familiar 'latrine sprint panic' started to make him sweat. He fumbled with two door handles until he found the right one, just in time. He barely got his pants down, now sweating profusely as he bent over, putting his head down on his knees. *This can't be happening,* he said to himself, a bead of sweat falling from his forehead onto his crumpled pants that were wrapped around his shoes.

"Oh, shit," he said out loud, remembering the temp job message from his mother. He fumbled at the pants pocket for the address. His head was throbbing with a hangover and his stomach growled out loud as he fumbled again with the door handles seeking Jeff. "Jeff," he said in a panicked whisper, not sure of other people who were in the apartment. "Jeff!" At the third door, he found Jeff, sprawled out on a bed without covers, in his underwear.

"Hey," he said, this time louder.

Jeff groaned, hardly moving. "C'mon man, what's your problem."

"I gotta get out of here. I have a job."

Jeff barely lifted his head off the bed. "That's what your readjustment allowance is for."

"Shut up. I need to go," Oly insisted. "By the way, you wreak. That vindaloo was a bad idea." Oly closed the door and Jeff emerged, several minutes later, his hair disheveled and his face displaying several days' growth.

"What the hell are you going to wear?" he asked, looking Oly up and down, wiping his eyes. "The same smelly shit from last night?"

"It's a software company," Oly said. "Mickey Mouse t-shirts and flip-flops."

Jeff shuffled past Oly towards the kitchen without responding. "My fucking head is killing me," he said, clambering in the kitchen. "You want some breakfast? You're already late."

Oly looked around as Jeff scrambled eggs and made instant coffee from packets that looked like they were taken from a hotel. He was wearing a *panya* shirt that had faces of President Eyadema printed on it with the phrase, *Merci Papa Eyadema* below each image.

"Nice shirt. You're a fan now?"

"Gotta support the Republic," he said, smiling. "Low crime. A chicken in every cuvette. What's not to love?"

"Oh, I don't know. Why don't we start with soldiers who shoot at cashew pickers?"

"Private property. I would have done the same thing," Jeff said, shoving a spoonful of eggs in his mouth. Oly started to feel unsettled, like Jeff was about to tell him something that was going to pull him away from any attempt to integrate back into American life.

"How did you end up here?" Oly asked.

Jeff paused to remove something from his teeth before he answered. "I ran into a Ghana volunteer right before I left home and he needed someone to look into this place for a few weeks while he travelled. Being jobless and homeless it seemed like a no brainer."

"Nice coincidence that it also happens to be a couple of miles from where I grew up," Oly said, wondering what Jeff was up to, as he helped himself to more eggs. "So, you haven't been home yet?"

"Not exactly. I needed some time to adjust. They think I'm travelling around and coming back in a few months. Oly looked up from his food to see Jeff's facial expression when he talked about not seeing his family.

"Who's *they*?" Oly asked, realizing for the first time since he'd known Jeff that little had ever been revealed about his family.

"Not really that important," he said, looking down at his plate. "Moved around a lot. Dad came and went. Mom struggled with prescription meds. Sister ran off with boyfriend. American tragedy shit. I was out when I finished high school. That enough bio for you?"

Jeff got up and quietly rinsed his dishes off and threw them in the sink, his back to Oly. Oly took the hint not to pursue any more questions. He took the deflection as one of the reasons Jeff always seemed to be on the run.

"Did Clinton really win president last night?" Jeff asked, changing the topic to fill the awkward silence. "I'm totally out of touch with America. I didn't even remember to vote."

"We were at the Cantab, remember?" Oly said.

"How could I forget Little Joe and vindaloo," Jeff said, smacking his lips with disgust.

"Shit, I was smoking too wasn't I? I think I'm going to puke." Jeff leaned over Oly as he finished his eggs and grabbed the plate from him, close enough so that Oly could smell his cigarette vindaloo breath. "Don't want you to be late for your big job."

Oly looked up and backed away from Jeff, waving the air. "What the hell is that supposed to mean?"

"What do you think it means?" Jeff answered, his bloodshot eyes staring at Oly.

"Oh, I don't know … that I have a job?"

"Fuck that, let's go to D.C." Jeff said. "You're running late, let's go," he said before Oly could respond.

Oly got up, looking at the clock, calculating that even if he hurried he'd be at least an hour late for work. Jeff kept talking as they headed out of the apartment, becoming more animated as he spoke. "It's hopping with RPCVs and the new president always hires tons of stupid idealistic idiots like us, willing to work fourteen-hour days for hardly any pay. And don't we get that government-preferential-hiring-status thing for a year? It's perfect for us."

"Us?"

"Oh, sorry. I didn't know that the job you are hours late for was a promising new career. I thought we'd check it out."

"We?" Oly asked. His stomach gurgled so both of them could hear.

"*Oui* yovo. WE. Get it? You like that?"

"I think I'll stick to my boring temp job for now. Wearing a stained Mickey Mouse shirt sounds promising compared to getting shot at in another cashew field."

"You went with me to see Little Joe for a reason, you bastard," Jeff said, pointing at Oly, knowing that he was tempted to say yes.

"I'll get the taxi and take you to your future. You can have a think while you're bringing pizza to your new boss."

"Taxi?"

"Stay here, I'll be right back," Jeff said, as he ran off behind the apartment building.

CHAPTER 21

LE TUNNEL

———◆———

OLY WAITED SEVERAL MINUTES OUTSIDE the dingy brick entrance of the apartment building, contemplating the derailment of his flirtation with a normal life. A rattling mechanical sound followed by a rusty surplus U.S. Postal Service truck pulled up from behind the apartment complex. A cloud of choking blue exhaust emerged from the back followed by a loud backfire noise that sounded like a shotgun blast.

The truck's blue-eagle emblem was still visible through a thin coat of white paint. It had one seat on the right-hand side. Oly stared at Jeff through the driver's side glass for several seconds.

"Special delivery!" Jeff yelled through the sliding side door. Oly looked down at the sidewalk and shook his head. "Government surplus!" Jeff yelled. "Five hundred bucks in Southie!"

"Yeah, and look at that, no seats," Oly said, poking his head in the open window.

"Relax, you get to drive later."

Oly sat in the back where the mail bags were once stored and clutched a strap as Jeff grinded the gears and headed into Cambridge.

"So, what do you think of the plan, buddy?" Jeff said, turning through Central Square toward Massachusetts Avenue. Oly stared out the dirty back window at the billowing exhaust blinding drivers behind them.

"Well, I'm going to temp for a few weeks, try to keep my readjustment allowance from disappearing, and then we'll re-evaluate."

"No, you idiot," Jeff snapped, swerving the wheel on purpose so that Oly slammed his shoulder against the wall of the truck. "I mean the plan! Moving to the capitol! Getting on with it!" Jeff said, with a diabolical look through the rearview mirror.

"You're fucking crazy," Oly said, feeling as though he couldn't remember how many times he'd said or thought that about Jeff.

"Well, I'll keep it simple for you," he said. "You can hang out with your parents watching late-night TV, logging temp jobs, and hoping your girlfriend comes back and remembers you. OR you could get on with your life and see the future."

"Why do I feel like I'm about to get on a motorcycle and head into a cashew field?" Oly asked, feeling like he was going to vomit vindaloo all over the back of the seatless truck.

"Because you are," Jeff laughed, swerving onto Mass Avenue.

"Why is the gas needle on 'E'?" Oly asked, trying to hold himself on his knees to see through the front window.

"Don't worry about it. It's broken."

"Then how do you know when you need gas?" Oly asked, watching helplessly as they passed a Sunoco station.

"Would you shut up?" Jeff snapped, impatiently. "Did you learn nothing in Togo? *Homme propose, dieu dispose!* If we make it, it's Allah's wish. If not, it wasn't to be."

"I think I'm going to throw up," Oly said, staring at an old mail bag that was bunched up next to him. Seconds later, Jeff yelled for Oly to hold on as he turned abruptly down a one-way street and nearly hitting an unsuspecting pedestrian.

"What the hell are you doing?" Oly cried.

"Chill out, man," Jeff barked impatiently. "We're never going to make it through this traffic. I'm cutting around."

"Against a one way? You'll get thrown in jail!"

"Only if I get caught," he said, leaning on the horn.

Oly felt a coolness on his scalp where he hit his head on the side during one of Jeff's quick turns. "Oww, my head. I think I'm bleeding," he said.

Jeff ignored him, accelerating and causing another backfire.

"Jesus, Jeff," Oly sputtered, the blood from his head now running down his temple. "I really don't need to get there that bad." He could only see the back of Jeff's head now, as he felt woozy and crouched down on the floor of the vehicle. Just when Jeff swerved back to enter a tunnel that went below an overpass adjacent to Mass Ave., the truck lurched forward and gasped, then rolled to a complete stop in the tunnel.

"Shit!" Jeff yelled, banging his hand on the steering wheel.

"You're kidding!" Oly said. "You're fucking kidding! What the hell just happened?"

"Shut up for a second, I gotta think," Jeff said, resting his head on the steering wheel.

"Think about what? How you're an idiot and we're going to die!"

Jeff turned on the hazard signal and jumped out, yelling through an open sliding window above the deafening roar of rush-hour traffic, "Dude, stay here. I'll be right back," as though he had done this before.

"What? You're just going to leave me here?" Oly replied, as oncoming traffic passed inches from the truck and beeped as it went by. A bearded man in a green *Boston Globe* delivery truck gave Jeff and Oly the one-fingered salute and yelled profanities out his window. Jeff yelled back and threatened bodily harm.

"Jeff!" Oly yelled, terrified as Jeff jumped out between cars that screeched to avoid him. Jeff didn't hear and was already crossing the tunnel against traffic, his hair flapping from the wind of passing cars. A gigantic yellow MBTA bus hurtled by, barely avoiding the stranded truck. No one stopped. Fearing the worst, Oly climbed out after Jeff, holding his head and feeling a vomit coming on.

Oly started to forget his anger at the helplessness of his situation. He started to laugh at the honking cars and waved at them as he watched Jeff make his way all the way across the tunnel and disappear up a maintenance ladder. Oly held his arms in the air in victory as he pinned himself against the dirty wall of the tunnel. The beeping cars, glaring faces, curses and gestures, the danger, all became a surreal comic backdrop of the civilized world as he started to howl with pain, laughter, and nausea.

The cliffs of Aledjo flashed in front of him. He thought of the woman with the baby. The crazy driver. The acceptance so common in Togo associated with handing your life over to someone else. After twenty minutes, when he started hearing a siren approaching, he looked over at Jeff sprinting back across the tunnel with a jug and knew he was, for some reason, going to end up in D.C.

Jeff barely avoided a truck that decided not to slow down and jumped up on the narrow curb, holding a jerry jug. He was drenched in sweat, but smiling. "Shit, there was a gas station right around the corner. They totally hooked me up even though I'm out of cash." He opened the cap to a full jerry jug and began pouring it into the truck.

"Oh shit, sounds like we're going to have company," he said, tipping the jug forward.

"Well, at least they won't be shooting at us! You proud of yourself?"

"I am, actually," Jeff smiled. "I'll get you to work before lunchtime and you'll be back in your high-school bedroom by nightfall. By the way, you look like shit. You better clean up that blood. *Homme propose, dieu dispose!*" he yelled, as he finished the jug and threw it in the back. "Now jump in before the cops get here." The truck started after a brief whirr and Jeff accelerated back into traffic.

"How about *homme* get gas and God do something better with his time?"

"That's too much for the side of a bus," Jeff laughed, finishing up the gas fill. Jeff looked in the rearview. "I see you smiling, you bastard," he said. "You love this shit. D.C. or bust baby!"

Several minutes later they finally arrived at Oly's first job in America post Peace Corps. And he had arrived on Africa time, two hours late. Oly walked into the reception area of Vintage Software, an obscure high-tech company in a half-renovated Cambridge warehouse, looking like he lost a fight with a dumpster, his shirt stained with perspiration, some blood and mail-truck dirt. A man wearing a Tasmanian devil sweatshirt and flip-flops gave Oly a second look as he passed by. "You must be the temp. You get in an accident or something?" Oly took the out.

"Yes, actually. But I'm okay. Sorry." He paused for a minute.

"Well, go get yourself cleaned up. You're the third temp in a week; at least you showed up. There's a bathroom out back. There's the phone. Use the call sheet to transfer calls. Oh, and whatever you do, do not under any circumstance forward calls directly to Tom, or today will be your last. Good luck."

Even though he was sweating profusely, with a soiled shirt and a bit of blood drying on his forehead, no one bothered him at the quirky company. He even got invited to a game of ultimate frisbee during lunch, leaving the phone unattended. All he could think about was Jeff and the potential of moving to D.C. Then all he could think about was Samantha's disapproval when she returned in a couple of months.

Oly was in the middle of trying to call his brother Andy to ask his opinion on the D.C. move, when the man to whom he was not supposed to transfer calls stood over his desk. Tom Heward wore camouflage cargo shorts, flip-flops, and a Jetsons t-shirt. He had graduated second in his class at MIT. He knew Bill Gates, the CEO of a new company that was making personal computers. His BMW 522i had a Starfleet Academy sticker on the rear windshield. Heward's office was laden with coffee cups, empty pizza boxes, and piles of hard drives that he had dismantled for some reason. Oly's brain raced to remember if he accidentally forwarded any calls and was expecting to be fired. Instead, he asked Oly how his day was going and requested that he make a reservation for him at the MGM Grand in Las Vegas (executive suite, if Mr. Gates didn't already book it) for an upcoming exposition.

Oly kept looking out the window, half hoping that the mail truck would glide by. He laughed to himself at the breakdown and the night at the Cantab. He never imagined that Jeff could put his life in danger in the first world as well as the third, though it seemed to make sense. And now he was considering a move with him that was even less logical.

Oly looked across at the techies clacking away in their cubicles, munching on cold pizza. It was all so safe, so comfortable. He could get a sales job, then move up the ranks. Maybe even take in a trip or two. Samantha would be proud of him. Maybe. He wondered if she had moved on, hooking up with another volunteer. Or maybe a high-ranking Dutch aid worker, with an air-conditioned Land Rover. She'd move back to Europe, settle into a walkup apartment in Amsterdam, and ride a bike to market with two little kids in tow. He couldn't bear to think about it. It had been a long time since he'd heard from her. The last letter was somewhat general, talking more about work and loneliness than anything related to being with him again. He tried to read between the lines, but it was no use. Oly found himself gravitating towards Jeff's idea, but knew that a steady job and resistance to Jeff's sophomoric plots were a better formula for earning Samantha's approval.

At quarter to five, it began to get dark and Oly wondered how he was going to get home. The Tasmanian devil shirt guy walked over to Oly's desk. "Well, you made it. Nice job. Now if you can be on time tomorrow and not look like you committed a crime, you might even get a free t-shirt." He laughed. "Oh, and there's a strange-looking dude who just pulled up in a mail truck. He said something about 'yovo' or yogurt or something and mentioned you."

Oly jumped up and peered out a large picture window overlooking the parking lot. Jeff was leaning against the hood of the mail truck, holding two bottles and greeting the Vantage employees as they passed him on the way home for the night. Oly considered leaving out the back door and never seeing Jeff again. He knew that if he went down to see him he was going to D.C. and throwing his fate into a cashew field. He wished he had gotten through to his brother to talk to him about it. Oly left through the front, feeling light headed as he went down the stairs.

"*Salut, mon ami,*" Jeff said, handing a beer to Oly. "Bière Benin. I found them in an African grocery in Cambridge. Cost five bucks apiece, but worth it. You believe it?" He waved over Oly's shoulder at Tom

Heward getting into his car. "Nice dude, that guy," Jeff said, taking a swig. "Who is he?"

"He's a man who made more before he turned thirty than either of us will make in a lifetime."

"Good for him," Jeff said, pointing his bottle in his direction. "Hey, I'm sorry 'bout this morning. But I got you here and it looks like you made it through the day. Tell you what, I'll let you drive this time." Jeff tossed the keys to Oly and jumped in the back.

CHAPTER 22

L'ETRANGER

THANKSGIVING MORNING, 1992

A LASER BEAM OF SUNLIGHT poked through the curtains of Oly's bedroom and reflected off his face, waking him up. For a moment he thought he was back at Jeff's, but looked down at his aching feet that extended over the end of his short childhood bedframe, and remembered. The grumbling in his stomach reminded him of the Jeff vindaloo adventure and he sprinted to the toilet, groaning in pain as he sat for several minutes. There was no clock in the room, but he could smell scrambled eggs and coffee wafting up the stairs. There was a box full of photos in the corner of the room that his parents had developed for him. He grabbed a stack, flipping through images of thatched huts and muddy roads, his arms around Bawendi with Samantha standing nearby. He didn't know why he missed it so much. He remembered counting the days in Tchamba while he lay swaying alone in his hammock in the heat of the day, his stomach grumbling, children screaming 'yovo' all day. Maybe it was because in spite of the angst and loneliness he had somewhat of a defined purpose and people around him who weren't judging everything he did. Yes, there was the usual yovo judgement. Yovo, why do you burn your trash? Yovo, why do you live by yourself in a big house? Yovo, why won't you give me money? But after a while, he became accepted. He had his place, and life went on. At home, there was never a sense of acceptance. Nothing was good enough, even in the place he was raised. Things weren't geared around community and survival. It was all postering and comparing. The Joneses. The ambition. Maybe as a yovo he didn't pick up on that in Togo, but back in his own culture it was obvious.

He pulled out a picture of himself standing in the pouring rain next to an old dump truck, full of cement, with a flat tire. He had been too angry at the time to notice the expression painted on the windshield. *Homme propose, dieu dispose.* How did he miss the signals? And now that he was back where things actually worked, why did he miss what he left behind? All he dreamed about was being back where he had some semblance of control. Now he was on the verge of reuniting with Jeff, the catalyst of chaos. Oly's portal back to the third world.

He held up a photo of him and Jeff, standing next to their motorcycles, wearing panya shirts. A group of villagers were around them. It was near the end of Oly's stay. He had a big smile on his face. It was starting to make sense now. He tossed the pictures back in the box and ran downstairs for breakfast.

Oly's mother quietly scooped the eggs onto a plate and had the counter covered with various root vegetables for the dinner. He hadn't had a real Thanksgiving dinner in years. The last one he tried to pull together was with Chalim: a guinea fowl, and some yams from the market. It wasn't the same. Oly smiled at his explanation in bad French at how the yovos came from another country and took over, but celebrated with the local people to thank them. "Thank them for what?" Chalim kept asking.

Oly knew something was wrong when he entered the kitchen and his mother quietly chopped vegetables. The turkey was already in the oven. He knew that her behavior was probably related to his disappearance of the night before. He didn't want to talk about it, but knew he had to. He felt like he was in high school again.

"Are you upset, Mom?" She didn't respond. He was starving but knew it wasn't the time to stuff his face, so he let the eggs get cold. She just kept chopping.

"What is it?"

She finally put the knife down, but didn't turn to face him. He could tell from her voice that she had been crying.

"I can't take this, Richard. You ... you come home for the first time in two years and then disappear to who knows where? I had no idea what happened to you. I thought once you came home I wouldn't have to worry anymore. I really can't take this. I really can't." She was sobbing. Oly stood up and tried to console her. He was surprised that his mother was so upset. What would have happened to him? Kidnapping? Struck by lightning? His mind raced to come up with a story since the truth would have made it worse.

"I ... I had to stay in the city with my friend because his truck broke down and I would have been really late coming back home. I am sorry. I should have tried to call."

She put both hands on the counter, her back still to him, and started sobbing. He moved away from her and sat down again, her head in her hands. "I don't know, Richard. I just don't know."

"Don't know what?"

"I don't know what is going on with you. We've hardly spoken since you've been home and we miss you so much. I thought when you returned it would be over, but it's not. I still miss you, even though you're here."

Oly felt bad, but not overly empathetic. He wanted to say *What the hell do you want from me? I've been shitting over a hole for two years!* but he did not. He felt detached, like a part of him hadn't come home yet. It was the opposite of homesickness.

His mother continued chopping, wiping a tear from her face. "Your father and I were talking and we think you might get back on your feet easier if you strike out on your own." She turned around, her face streaked with tears. "Of course, you're welcome to stay here as long as you want, but we think it's for the best until you get settled."

Oly started to feel angry and abandoned. Go out on your own until you get settled. *Isn't that a contradiction?* he thought to himself. Life was too complicated in America. He had forgotten the social norms around communication and felt like a foreigner in his own home. He wanted his old routine back. He paused before speaking to soften his reaction, but it only increased the tension.

"Mom, I know it's been weird since I've been home. I'm temping and trying to get back in the swing. I haven't really been home that long and it's been hard for me, too. It's just going to take some time."

He could see the worry lines in his mother's face. The same ones he used to see when he'd talk to her about old girlfriend troubles or painful adolescent episodes he didn't understand.

"I know it's hard, sweetie. Maybe your brother will let you stay with him a while. You can talk about things and he can help you get back on your feet. We just think it's for the best. It's just too difficult to have you here but somewhere else." For the best. He pondered the phrase. For whose best? He knew it would be a mistake to react and felt a tightening in his throat.

Oly hadn't seen much of Andy and Brett since his return. They had gotten together once or twice, but the sense that he wasn't the same became exaggerated around them, and they'd call him out. "Dude, what the hell is wrong with you?" they'd say. "You drinking too much jungle juice?" They were observations that only siblings could make, and he wasn't ready to face them. The brothers pulled into the driveway together in a new BMW that Andy bought from the profits of a new Internet business he was starting. The car made the familiar sound of tires on crushed stone as they pulled in, a nostalgic reminder of Oly's pre-Peace Corps days.

Oly's mother looked up, relieved that they'd break up the awkward tension. He knew from his mother's reaction that she wasn't going to back down on his moving out.

Oly had a complicated relationship with his brothers. He was several years older and entered university before either of them made it to high school. The other two grew together, while he grew apart. In Togo, he had only heard from them a couple of times and wasn't even sure what they had been doing over the past couple of years. Oly had sensed some jealousy over his travels and the attention he had received, but didn't know how to make light of it without getting annoyed at them. Andy had graduated from Boston College while he was away and Brett was finishing at UMass. More milestones that Oly had missed out on. Brett slammed the door when they entered.

"Give me that back," Brett barked at Andy, pushing him to get the bottle of wine back that Andy grabbed from him on the way in.

"Look what I got you, Ma," Andy mocked. "It was on sale." Oly was treated like the third 'grownup' in the eyes of Brett and Andy and was never in on their antics. They burst into the kitchen.

"What's up, Tarzan!" Brett blurted out.

"Not much, Jane," Oly responded, impressed with the speed of his own response. Andy plopped down in a chair and grabbed a piece of fruit from a basket on the table.

"Nice," he said, pointing the apple at Oly. "Man, I hadn't noticed how skinny you got. Ma! Extra pie for Tarzan!"

Oly noticed that his mother spoke to the boys in a more casual voice than she did with him. Like a mother. The conversation was less measured than her conversations with Oly since he'd been home. "Andy, I got some turnips that need squashing. Brett, go upstairs and get your father to carve the turkey; it's almost ready to come out of the oven."

"I can carve the turkey," Oly said. The three looked at him.

"What? Are you nuts?" Brett said. "Dad's the turkey carver. You forget that in the jungle?"

"I wasn't in the jungle," Oly said, feeling angry.

While Brett ran upstairs, Andy crabbed a handful of cashews from a bowl that was sitting on the counter. There was an awkward silence while their mother chopped and Andy chewed. He looked at the floor while they listened to the muffled voices upstairs and the footsteps on the floorboards above. "So, how's it been since you've been home?" Andy started. "You know you're not getting your Police cassettes back."

"It's been great. I can't believe how much I missed the food."

"And us?" he added.

"Of course. You and buffalo wings. Almost on the same par."

"Did I hear buffalo wings?" Brett said, entering the kitchen with his father. "Hail to the turkey carver, everyone," he said, bowing in submission as his dad walked by and gave him a playful slap to the midsection.

"Oly, great to have you home again for Thanksgiving, son," he said, reminding Oly that he hadn't had the meal at his parents' house in over two years.

Peter Olymeyer was aging well. His full head of hair and slightly greying sideburns complimented a tan face that displayed confidence at all times. He wore a comfortable grey t-shirt that said the name of Oly's college on the front (Williams) and faded jeans. After forty years spent managing a firm that exported sporting goods around the world, he was finally pursuing his passion: fly fishing. "Just got back from an incredible trip to Canada," he said to the three boys.

"Catch anything?" Andy asked.

"Three large and a bunch of smallmouth. And it only rained once. It was great. Rob Jeffries caught a monster pike that almost pulled him in."

Rebecca wiped her hands on a white apron that she was wearing and untied it, turning around as she did so. She was not following the conversation and looked distracted. "Pete, would you please carve the bird? And boys, get the table set."

Andy and Brett shoved one another as they made their way to the cabinet where the plates were stored. They left Oly to set the silverware himself. "You sure you can trust me with these knives?" he said, holding a large steak knife in the air.

"Watch out, Tarzan on the loose!" Brett cried, using a plate as a shield. Oly pretended to lunge at him.

"Boys, knock it off. Someone's going to get hurt," Rebecca warned, holding a pot of steaming turnips. The Olymeyer boys all laughed, slapping one another on the back. It was the same warning they'd been hearing since they were little.

"Ma, I'm a college graduate, remember?" Andy said, putting his arms out to help with the turnips.

"Wait," Brett said. "Let me get the electric knife and we'll have a duel." He went into the kitchen, laughing, mimicking *someone's going to get hurt* as he plugged in the knife. Rebecca stood with her hands on her hips.

"Peter, are you going to just sit there?"

Pete shrugged. "Honey, c'mon, they're just having fun. Brett, give me that electric knife before you hurt someone. Or the turkey."

"See, Richard, what you missed?" his father said, taking the knife from Brett and turning in towards the turkey rather than his eldest son. Oly watched his father carve the turkey as his brothers finished setting the table. He felt a sudden sadness at his father's comment because he wasn't sure what he had really missed. He didn't miss rough housing in the kitchen or jokes at his mother's expense. He thought he did on the countless lonely nights he had rocked in his hammock, drenched with sweat, swigging from a bottle of warm beer. But he didn't. He felt like he was watching the scene around him rather than participating in it.

Peter brought a platter of freshly carved turkey to the table and they sat down. Rebecca put her hands out on both sides, a traditional gesture that had been in the family for as long as they could remember, to hold hands with the person next to you and to give thanks, a tradition that excluded Oly in recent memory. Oly wondered if they left a space for him or if they just slid down at the table. He sat in between his father and Brett, his father surprising Oly with a tighter squeeze as if to compensate for the lack of words expressing how much he had missed him.

They ate quietly. Oly's mind wandered to the pre-dinner conversation about whether or not he should move out in order to get settled. "So," Oly started, after he swallowed a large bite of mashed turnip. "What do I need to know about America that I missed?"

Brett and Andy looked at one another. "I'll take that one," Brett said. "Bird retired. This crazy thing called the Internet was invented. You probably know all about the Gulf War, so that's not news. And the Cold War basically ended. Other than that, nothing."

Oly pointed his fork at Brett. "The Bird thing is tragic. The rest of it sounds boring."

"What about Africa?" Andy asked. "What do we need to know that *we* missed?"

Oly had a mouth filled with turkey and looked around the table, trying to chew his food before answering. "First of all, Africa is four times the size of the U.S., so I can't tell you everything." Although it was barely susceptible, he could feel that his comment put a space between him and his family. He was calling out their ignorance, but it flopped. Andy and Brett looked at one another.

"Uhh, thanks," Andy said. "Anything else?"

"Yes, there is something else," Oly said, picking up on the awkwardness around the table. "I need you to know that I spent more hours than I'd like to admit lying in my hammock, missing you but unable to call because I didn't have a telephone. It was really difficult to be away from you guys," he said, looking over at his mother who had tears welling up in her eyes.

"And Andy and Brett," he said, looking back over at his brothers and picking up his glass of wine. "I thought of both of you when I was spreading my cheeks over the latrine in my backyard."

"Whoooahhhhh, that's what I'm talking about!" Brett yelled, slapping his hand on the table.

"That's enough," Rebecca said, turning a scorned eye towards Oly and Brett.

"Now you're back," Andy said, clinking glasses with Oly. "We thought we'd lost you."

When the meal was over, signaled by Andy and Brett fighting over who was going to load the dishwasher, Andy tapped Oly on the shoulder and asked him if he wanted to take a walk. He threw his jacket on while Brett and their parents sat down to watch a football game on the television. "We'll be back in a few," Andy yelled. "Just going to get some fresh air."

"Why do I feel like Fredo in The Godfather?" Oly said to Andy. "Where's the fishing boat and the lake?"

"Don't be so friggin' dramatic," Andy replied, lighting a cigarette.

"Since when do you smoke?" Oly asked.

"Since I had to start my own company and I didn't know how I was going to put food on the table." He offered Oly one and blew out a stream of smoke. Oly shook his head and looked at his brother, realizing how much he'd actually missed.

It was starting to get dark when Andy and Oly left the house. A breeze blew crispy oak leaves that scraped across the street and the scent of Andy's cigarette smoke blended in with the cool fall air.

"Man, I miss this," Oly said, putting his arms out.

"Miss what?"

"This cool air. The changing of seasons. The leaves. The moon. I miss it all."

Oly noticed that the trees and shrubs around the house had gotten a lot bigger in his absence. Andy pointed out all of the people who had moved during his absence and how the neighborhood was changing. Their old basketball hoop that was on the street attached to a telephone pole was starting to rust and the rim had broken off. They made small talk, and Oly sensed right away that his brother was leading up to something by the way he dragged deep on his cigarette and seemed to be lost in thought.

"Dude, what the fuck, are you okay?" Oly finally asked.

"Yeah, I guess. Mom told me what she talked to you about."

"Great."

"Listen, I know it's rough, but she cried a lot when you were gone. She's having a rough time adjusting to you being back."

"What does that mean?"

"I don't know," he said, taking another drag. "I think she somehow thought nothing would change with you or that you'd be like you were when you left, which obviously you are not. I even noticed it."

"So what's your point? I already know she doesn't want me around, which makes no sense to me at all."

"I know it's weird. Maybe she needs some space of her own to get used to your making it home in one piece or something and being all weird. I don't know."

"Fine, you don't have to explain. So, what is this walk about besides telling me something I already know?"

"I am offering you to crash with me for a while. Until you get back on your feet."

Oly felt a flash of anger. *Really? Is it that bad?* He made up an excuse. "I know I'm supposed to seem grateful, but I can't do that. You got your new company and shit. I can't be in your way."

"You're my brother. You're not in my way." Andy finished his cigarette and flicked it into a drain where it fizzed out in the murky water below.

"Let me think about it," Oly said.

"No hurry," Andy said, as they turned and headed back down their street.

Before they got back to the house, Oly made up his mind to move to D.C.

CHAPTER 23

ALLEZ REVENIR, II

———

OLY'S DEPARTURE FROM ESSEX LACKED the fanfare of the last time he'd packed his hockey bag to leave home. This time, his mother's face had a look of concern, rather than sorrow. She seemed more comfortable sending him off to Africa than with an unshaven man in a used postal truck. He gave her a hug that lasted longer than the usual *good to see you, ma* hug, reminding him of the one he gave her at Logan Airport a couple years earlier. *What the hell am I doing?* he thought, as she pulled away from him and touched his cheek.

"You be safe now"

"I'm not going back to Togo, Mom. It's just Washington."

She glanced over at Jeff, who was laughing along with his brothers next to the truck. "I know, but you're my baby and I don't know when I'll see you again. I'm proud of you, Richard, you know that. We want what's best for you." Her lip started quivering.

"Hey, Tarzan!" Brett yelled from behind them. "Your buddy is giving us the real story. Getting shot at? Really?"

Jeff shrugged and watched Rebecca's jaw drop. "I think I'll make sure the bags are ready to go," he said, patting Brett and Andy on the shoulder.

Jeff grinded the gears and lurched forward out of the Olymeyer's driveway. Sitting on the floor in the back of the truck, Oly felt like a dog going to the kennel and looked one last time at his parents through the scratched rear window, while they stood and held one another with trepidation.

Jeff didn't talk until they reached the entrance to 95 South, the interstate that ran directly to the nation's capitol. "*C'est la route nationale, mon ami!*" he cried. The postal truck lurched and wheezed through Rhode Island and Connecticut, drinking gas like it was going out of style, overheating in Connecticut, and in need of a new fan belt in New Jersey. When they passed through New York, Jeff pointed at the Statue of Liberty. "Hey, look, she's calling us! We're tired, restless, shiftless, poor, or whatever it says..."

Oly was sleeping uncomfortably on his hockey bag in the back, pretending not to hear. Jeff jerked the steering wheel, causing Oly to fall off onto the floor of the truck and wake up.

"What the..."

"Sorry man, I just needed you to look out the window. Show some respect to the Lady."

Oly looked out the dirty window of the truck, rubbing his head. "Yeah, I know, land of opportunity, blah blah blah. Too bad we're not going to New York. We could be tour guides."

"Man, your attitude is holding you back. You gotta work on your positivity."

"Positivity?" Oly said, starting to feel angry.

"I basically just got kicked out of my parent's house. I have no job, a piddly readjustment allowance rattling around my wallet, who knows how many amoebas ratting around my gut, friends who treat me like strangers, strange friends like you, and my life is in the back of an old mail truck. Positivity?"

"I knew you'd come around, man. Look, Lady Liberty don't care. She loves you. She wants you to succeed. See that smile on her face? That look of determination? She's in your corner. She's got your back."

"Fuck off," Oly said, feeling better. "And don't roll the truck again while I'm trying to sleep or I'll puke on you."

"Land of opportunity, man." Jeff said, keeping the wheel straight. "Land of opportunity."

Several hours later, after one flat tire and a near miss with a folding chair that was lying in the passing lane, they pulled onto the Washington beltway. The hum of traffic filling all four lanes and the inability of Oly (who was driving at the time) to get enough acceleration out of the truck to keep pace was a fitting metaphor that did not pass him by. "Look," Oly said, lurching the wheel so that Jeff rolled around and hit his head in the back, "Life is passing us by."

Oly felt nauseous now that they had reached their destination. He thought about his family the whole way down and could not calculate why he decided to throw his fate in with Jeff rather than give it a go.

It was now late afternoon, just enough time to pop into the Peace Corps headquarters on K Street to find housing (another piece of Jeff's master plan). "I heard there's some sort of halfway house we can crash at," he said at the time.

The career center for RPCVs was housed in a tiny office off the main floor of the Peace Corps headquarters, a building that had the attraction of a shopping mall complete with escalators and fast food outlets. The office was teeming with returned volunteers wearing colorful clothes from their former host countries. Although Oly had a bag full of similar clothing, he couldn't bring himself to wear the stuff in America. The matching *complets* just didn't look right on white people and he was tired of standing out in a crowd and just wanted to blend in again. The men in the office were unshaven and several of the women still had their hair in corn rows. It was like a transit station for volunteers not ready to join America. An attractive African-American woman, who happened to look good in a complet, sat on the couch looking very relaxed, reading a dog-eared copy of Harper's. Her colorful cotton top was splattered with oversized begonias and palm trees.

"Excuse me," Jeff said, interrupting her reading. "Do you know if there's a house or place nearby where RPCVs can crash?" She looked up briefly, gave Jeff a disapproving onceover and pointed at the bulletin board. There was a yellow index card stapled to the right hand corner.

Maison du Paysage
110 U Street
Ten bucks a night. Cash only.

He smiled and thanked her. She looked back at her magazine and said, "*Pas de quoi*" causing Jeff to wonder if she knew him from somewhere. Just as it was getting dark, Jeff and Oly turned onto U Street, the truck engine now making a chugging noise that sounded like it was about to give up. They pulled in front of a decrepit brick townhouse built in the early industrial age and not updated since. A shaggy-haired RPCV wearing a red shirt with a black print of Che Guevara's face on the front was putting out the trash. He looked up, bleary-eyed, at the postal truck, confused by the civilian-dressed passengers. Jeff let out a hearty Kotokoli greeting, turning the man's confusion into a knowing smile.

"*Mes amis,* welcome," he said, as he put the lid on the last barrel. And, as with all Peace Corps greetings, it was quickly followed by name of post and years of service.

"We're both Togo, 89–91," Jeff answered.

"No shit," the shaggy volunteer replied. "I was in Benin. Man, Lomé's like Disney. What a town. The beer alone was worth the trip. Damn commies. Cotonou was messed up with that shit. Even the Chinese cars sucked."

Oly glanced at shaggy's shirt, confused, but decided not to ask. They followed him into the hostel, a waft of pot smoke assaulting their nostrils as they entered. A beaded curtain separated a dark living room from the kitchen as they walked down the hall. An attractive female with stringy brown hair and a tie-dyed top looked up from a day-old *Washington Post* and smiled. Jeff waved. Shaggy led them up a set of rickety stairs, stopping at the top in front of a closed door with a small Grateful Dead sticker on it.

"I think they're sleeping," he said, putting his ear close to the door. "Grady and Paige, they're a married couple from West Virginia. Your friendly house parents. They screw like rabbits when they're not high," he chuckled. Oly and Jeff looked at one another. "But, hey, we're family, right?"

Oly looked down the hall at the sun filtering through a dirty window, dust particles dancing in the dim hallway light. He dropped his hockey bag on the floor as he had the day Rollings left him in Tchamba, wondering if he had made the right decision.

"That's cool," said Jeff, breaking the silence. "We'll just leave our stuff here and come back later."

"*Ça marche*," said Shaggy. "I gotta go, but make yourself at home. There's a signup sheet on the fridge for vacuuming and bathroom duty. Other than that, we're pretty self-sufficient. Just put ten bucks a day in the cookie jar and chill."

CHAPTER 24

LA MAISON BLANCHE

———◆———

THE PRESIDENT-ELECT'S TRANSITION-TEAM OFFICE ON M Street was a beehive of activity. When Jeff and Oly drove past the entrance, the mail truck's exhaust backfired, causing three Secret Service agents standing in front to reach for their vest pockets, staring in their direction, one touching a finger to his ear piece to listen, just like in the movies.

Oly laughed. "Maybe he's being told to take the shot." Once the agents realized the source of the noise, they regained their composure.

"You heard of going out with a bang?" Jeff said. "Well, we're going in with one."

"Nice," Oly said. "I just don't want the bang to be accompanied by a hail of bullets."

Their entrance into the nerve center of the new leader of the free world was not what they expected. Rather than Marine guards and advisors holding briefcases, they were greeted by a large carpeted space divided by portable cubicle dividers. Computer wires were taped all over the carpeted floor of a gigantic rented office divided into hastily assembled cubicles. It was very unpresidential-like and had the appearance of a shady insurance company. Phones rang, rows of fax machines spewed out copy, several televisions played the major networks, four coffee machines sputtered to keep up with demand, and people both young and old scurried about like waiters in a busy restaurant, instinctively passing one another without a word.

Jeff stared at an eight-by-eight-foot whiteboard covered with blue numbers and hastily written information on scheduling and priorities. A list on the right-hand side in bright red magic marker had two exclamation points under the heading 'hot potatoes.' There were four items: Gennifer Flowers, the draft, drugs, health care. They both stared at everything around them, paralyzed by the action. Several minutes passed until they were approached by a young bespectacled man in a coffee-stained, white, button-down shirt and a blue tie decorated with a white democrat donkey pattern. He exited from one of the temporary offices separated from the mayhem in the middle by a glass door, so Oly figured he must have been someone important. He didn't introduce himself.

"You must be new since you're the only ones standing still," he said, holding a cell phone to his ear. "Yeah, I'll be right there," he said, interrupting the conversation. Without hesitation, he snapped the phone shut and looked at Jeff. "You two sign in? You can't start unless you sign in. They need some help over in correspondence. I see you've already previewed the white board. Don't bother me unless there's a fire, and, whatever you do, do not answer the phones." His phone rang again and he walked away from Jeff and Oly without acknowledging whether they were on board with the campaign, Republican spies, or just passing through to find a toilet.

They walked over to a corner of the room under a large sign on cardboard that had the word 'correspondence' written on it with an arrow pointing down. Half a dozen people were already in place, tearing through envelopes with letter openers and tossing them in a recycling bin as they scanned each letter in seconds. Jeff removed several boxes that were piled on a couple of stools nearby and handed one to Oly. They sat next to a young woman who wore black-rimmed glasses and had girl-next-door looks. She didn't look up when they sat down, but held an arm out with a fistful of unopened letters. Then she reached over and handed them another stack of loosely collated typewritten pages on official looking masthead. Oly flipped through them and noticed that they were policy statements and generic responses for most of the correspondence they received. She looked over the top of her glasses at Oly. "You gonna help out or do you need an instructional manual?" she said, not smiling.

"Are you from the same place as the prick in the office over there?"

She stopped sorting and smiled. "If you are referring to Bill Denson who chaired the Little Rock campaign headquarters then, yes, I guess I am."

Oly was impressed, but didn't act it.

"Sorry," she continued. I'm working on caffeine and three hours' sleep. Got here at five and haven't stopped much since."

"Five in the morning?" Jeff asked.

"Yeah. We're under a bit of pressure. The letters keep piling in and they want us to get through most of them by next week at the latest." She put her hand out to Oly and then Jeff. "Susan," she said, with a handshake that was firm and corporate.

"I'm Oly and this is Jeff," Oly replied.

"We're returned Peace Corps Volunteers," Jeff chimed in, causing Oly to look at him like he was bragging about selling the most Girl Scout cookies.

"Cool," Susan said, turning her attention back to the pile of envelopes and response letters. "You guys stick around long enough you should make sure to get to know some of those pricks. It's the only way you might land a job down the road. Don't expect the West Wing, but they're looking for a lot of people. Just keep your head down and work until you drop."

"Thanks, I'll remember that as I work for free," Oly replied, looking around one more time before reading his first letter and trying to match it up with a response.

Jeff eyeballed the people coming in and out of the various offices surrounding the work area. *So self-important*, he thought to himself. *Pricks. Probably have never left the country.* Whether Jeff or Oly liked it or not, the *pricks* were the ones standing between them and the type of opportunity they thought they had left Massachusetts for. Though it became clear in a matter of minutes where they stood on the president-elect's food chain, Oly and Jeff felt energized for the first time since their return to America. After several hours of correspondence work, they sat out in the mail truck, sharing a tuna pocket and chips they picked up at a nearby deli.

"I have an idea," Jeff said when he was finished.

"Let me guess," Oly replied, his mouth full of sandwich. "We walk up to the White House and tell the guards that we're two unemployed Peace Corps Volunteers looking for a break."

"Shit," Jeff said, honestly taken aback. "That was pretty close."

"I was joking, you fuck. I don't want to hear your idea if that was close."

He ignored Oly and continued. "I overheard a conversation when I went to the bathroom. Clinton's going to be downtown at some rally to thank the transition team tomorrow. I say we work our way in and get some face time."

"With who, jackass?" Oly asked, wiping the remaining tuna off his mouth and throwing the napkin in the back of the truck.

"With whoever will listen. If it's Bill, Al, Stephanopoulos. Hilary. I don't care. Someone."

"Does it involve cashews?" Oly asked.

"You know what I'm starting to learn about you?" Jeff said in an accusing tone, continuing without waiting for a response. "You make sarcastic remarks about my ideas. You say they are crazy. You make me feel like a chump. And yet you don't have any better ideas and on top of it, you go along with my shit. So, unless you finally come up with something, why don't you go your own way or shut the hell up 'cause I'm not holding you back."

Oly glared at Jeff. He wanted to hit him. He knew that Jeff was right and was surprised that he had that kind of insight into their relationship. Oly looked at the door to the truck and Jeff caught him. "Go ahead, big boy. Go for it. It's a big wide world out there. Go make something of yourself. Build a bridge."

Oly felt a tightening in his throat like he did when he was bullied on the playground as a child. Without thinking, he lunged at Jeff and knocked him against one of the sidewalls of the truck, making a loud bang. Jeff hit his head and immediately put his hands to the pain. "FUCK!" he yelled out loud. "FUCK that hurt! What the fuck is your problem?"

Oly said nothing and didn't feel bad. He felt relieved, like he took some power back from Jeff, even though it was an infantile. "Sorry, but I feel much better," Oly said. "Let's go to the rally. Give me the keys, I'll drive."

The next day, they skipped out of work and parked two blocks from the Washington Hilton, three hours before the rally was scheduled to start. Dozens of people had already lined up by the front entrance. "So much for your insider information," Oly said.

"Don't hit me," Jeff said, holding his arms up in a mock defensive position.

"I tried."

They squeezed into a spot near the entrance in front of the same flagstone wall where John Hinckley had fired his shots at Reagan over a decade earlier. Two hours passed and the crowd began to fill in, the air seemed to fill with anticipation. Minutes later in the distance they heard the wailing sirens of a police motorcade as it wound through the surrounding neighborhoods. "Here they come," said a woman standing next to them pushing a baby stroller. "Bill and Al are on their way."

The crowd watched several large, shiny Crown Victoria limousines followed by two black Chevy Suburbans with tinted windows pull behind a dozen state police motorcycles with flashing blue lights. Out of the vehicles jumped several large, Secret Service agents in tightly fitting cheap suits and dark shades, all wearing funny noodle-shaped wires attached to their ears, just like in the movies. A number of aides and other officials exited the cars, causing a distraction for which car to focus on. Finally, a roar went up from the crowd when a Secret Service agent opened one of the doors of the third limousine. All Jeff and Oly could see was Clinton's silvery mane above the waving arms and crushing crowd of people, barely held back by police barriers. "Shit, there he is!" yelled Jeff, knocking a coffee out of the hand of a lady in a Redskins t-shirt standing next to him.

Clinton absorbed the energy of the crowd, looking completely relaxed and happy, as though he had been doing this all his life. He walked with purpose toward the screaming mob, a flock of aides scrambling behind him along with numerous agents, and proceeded to grab and shake hands. Oly and Jeff leaned forward, craning their necks to get a better view. Jeff started jumping up and down, making Oly nervous, as it seemed to draw the attention of one of the officers.

The woman with the baby carriage fell behind Oly and Jeff and rammed Oly's calves with the front wheels, trying to get a better look. When Oly looked back after swinging his head around to the lady in reaction to the pain, Jeff had disappeared into the crowd, following the President-elect and his entourage. *Shit*, Oly thought to himself. *Shit.*

As Oly made his way along the infamous flagstone wall, the crowd seemed to envelop the president-elect like an amoeba, despite the efforts of the Secret Service. One agent was holding Clinton's belt from behind to keep his movements controlled and give him a chance to pull the president-elect back, just in case. Clinton kept moving along the crowd, smiling non-stop, grabbing hands, shaking, touching, and soaking up the attention.

Seconds later, with Oly watching from a distance, a wave of people fell back as though a wind had pushed them. Several women screamed and the crowd parted near where Oly last spotted Jeff. Oly's stomach lurched and everything started moving in slow motion as he caught a glimpse of Jeff's head and the movement of several large men in suits.

Oly could see the silvery mane moving quickly backwards and towards the hotel lobby, a reaction by the agents to whatever was happening in front of them. Through the crowd that was now parting, Oly could see two of the agents open their coats to reveal shiny black Tec-9mm semiautomatics. There were screams and chaos as people panicked and starting moving away, rather than towards, where Clinton was last.

"You're fucking hurting me!" Jeff screamed. "What the fuck!" he cried again. As the crowd quickly dispersed, Oly was able to get closer and see what was happening. The woman with the baby stroller had picked up the baby and was holding it close, starting to run from the scene, leaving the stroller behind for Oly to nearly trip over.

A blur of muscular arms in synthetic fiber jackets fluttered around him as he edged closer to the commotion. The lady in the Redskins shirt pulled back in the midst of the violence, and suddenly Jeff was nowhere to be seen. Oly began to panic as the bodies around him pushed to get away and onlookers tried to see what was going on. The president's entourage had already made its way to the hotel, as had most of the crowd.

An agent, whose shades were broken from the scuffle, put a strong arm on Oly and told him to back up. Jeff was being picked up off the ground by two agents like a rag doll. His hands were attached behind his back by handcuffs and his nose was bleeding. Profanities streamed from his twisted mouth. "You're killing me, man! Let go! Jesus, what the fuck?"

The agents holding Jeff, one whose jacket had ripped neatly along the center seam in his back, handed him over to two waiting D.C. cops. "Book this asshole, 51-2," the one with the ripped jacket said, and the cop nodded. Unable to summon the strength to speak, Oly stood alone and stared at the sequence of events unfolding before him. The agent holding Oly back turned to him as the rest of the Secret Service agents walked away toward the hotel and the cops dragged Jeff to a waiting cruiser.

"You with him?" he asked, squinting his eyes at Oly, the only person who hadn't run from the scene.

"Me?" Oly responded.

"Yeah, you. He with you?" he said, pointing over his shoulder with his thumb. Oly could see Jeff spit some blood onto the pavement, as two officers shoved him in the back of a cruiser.

"What's a 51-2?" Oly asked, not answering the agent's question.

"It means your buddy is fucked. I suggest you find your way to central booking before he makes too many friends down there, if you know what I mean." Oly didn't answer but simply nodded, slowly stepping backwards and feeling as though he was going to vomit on the wall where President Reagan was nearly killed.

Oly drove the mail truck back to the hostel like a zombie, completely blocking out the world around him. He had no recollection of the drive back as he pulled up in front of the hostel, relieved by the quiet of the street. He noticed that his shirt was completely drenched in sweat. When he went inside, the familiar stench of pot was reassuring to Oly, like homemade bread in the oven, as he collapsed on the couch and considered joining the party, in need of something to take the edge off. Grady was sitting in an old barco lounger in shorts with no shirt, taking drags from a four-foot-high bong. He nodded at Oly as he exhaled from a long drag. Oly sat, stone-faced, his mind racing through the day's events in disbelief, replaying them in slow motion, from twenty different angles. He cursed himself for being seduced yet again by Jeff's foolish promises of adventure and a new beginning. And, like the times before when he'd gotten caught up in the whirlpool of Jeff's misadventures, he thought of Samantha and started to get depressed. He walked over to Grady and the bong and took a long hit, hoping tomorrow would never come.

He knew that when Samantha arrived back in the United States she'd have a plan. She always did. Probably grad school or something reasonable. Her women's cooperative in Koussountou had taken off, empowering hundreds of women like a well-organized machine. He recalled the late-night conversations they'd had together about his bridge project and the simple answers she gave to his dilemmas, while he ruminated about distractions like personality conflicts and disloyalties. Self-pity tinged with doubt sank into Oly's stomach as he took repeated drags from the pipe, feeling the wooziness of getting high wash over him.

CHAPTER 25

HOMME PROPOSE

———

CENTRAL BOOKING WAS AN UGLY brick building on the corner of a busy intersection. Inside, it was packed with hookers, crack addicts, and people with whom one should avoid eye contact. Oly walked up the front stairs and held the door for two officers who were escorting a man in dreadlocks with his hands cuffed behind his back. "Thanks," one of them said, giving Oly no mention. Oly saw a sign that directed him to the intake area and approached a large officer who sat high above him at a counter behind a dirty Plexiglas screen. The officer took no notice of Oly and was writing on a pad.

"Excuse me," Oly said, in a quiet voice. The officer didn't move but instead picked up the phone. When he was done with the conversation, the officer hung up and looked down at Oly, not saying a word.

"Let me guess," the officer said after a few seconds. "You must be Jeff Hinckley's boyfriend," he said.

"He's not my..." Oly started, but then realized it was futile to respond. "Yes, he's my friend. Do I get to see him?"

"Four-thousand dollars, cash, money order or check, and you can see your boyfriend until his court date which will be..." he paused to look at a ledger in front of him. "Next Tuesday at nine. We make special arrangements for threats on the president."

"He wasn't threatening..." again, Oly stopped himself short when the officer glared at him.

Oly found an ATM that was conveniently located in the central booking lobby and drained almost all of his readjustment allowance to get Jeff out of jail. When he handed the officer the cash, it was quickly counted, put in a drawer below him, and Oly was handed a receipt. "You get this back after the court date," he said, and then pushed a button below his desk.

Several minutes later, Jeff was accompanied by two guards who looked like they had experience hurting people. Jeff looked half dead as he dropped onto a wooden bench near the waiting area. His clothes were filthy and there were what looked like blood stains around his mouth and on his collar. Several bandages covered a wound on his head. Oly wanted to feel bad, but he did not. The bail money had decimated his bank account, and he wondered if he was ever going to see it again.

One of the guards handed Oly some paperwork to sign and glared at Jeff like the pathetic piece of shit that he was. "Looks like buddy boy here won't be delivering my mail in a couple of lifetimes. He's in federal, state, and local computers now. Shit, he's even posted on Interpol. Better build in some extra travel time next time you fly. He's gonna set off flags everywhere he goes. If you're his friend, good luck," he said to Oly before walking away.

After a long silence driving back in the truck, with Jeff moaning in the back, Oly looked in the rearview, glaring down at Jeff who was holding his head. "Don't say a friggin' word, Jeff. I've had enough of this shit. You are a friggin' idiot. You were so right. I keep telling you how fucked up everything is but keep following along. This is it. This is fucking it."

When they got back to the hostel someone had written on a piece of paper that the transition team had called and they were not to bother showing up to work anymore. "Great," Oly said, throwing the paper in the trash. "We're blacklisted in the goddamn nation's capital, all my money is gone and you're registered on Interpol."

Jeff started to move his lips, leaning on the kitchen counter as he did so. Oly felt a choking sensation in the back of his throat and didn't wait for Jeff to speak. "I'm out. I'm going back to Boston." The silence passed between them for two minutes before Jeff spoke, looking at Oly in the eye.

"*C'est fini. Entre nous. Fini!* Go ahead. *Vas-y.* Go home, yovo. Go and do what? *Quoi? Pourquoi?* Be a farmer? Work for your dad?" Through the blood-stained gauze covering his forehead, Oly could see Jeff's face flush with anger. His eyes were bloodshot and had welled up with tears. "You remember all those conversations we had in Togo about how all this shit meant nothing in Africa? The fast food, the corporate ladder. It's all bullshit. *Homme propose, dieu dispose,* right? You forgot all that? You think I wanted it to be like this? Those pukes on M Street weren't going to hook us up. The whole thing was a sham. I didn't mean to lunge at Clinton. I was just trying to shake his hand and they freaked out on me."

"Oh, so you're a martyr now?" Oly said. "That's the problem, Jeff. In your so-called spontaneity, you forgot we're not in Togo anymore. You can't do this shit here. What about that day in the tunnel? What was that? God's will? Those rules don't apply here, man. Shit doesn't work in Togo because they don't have a choice, not because they want it that way. It's just a big game so they can face the next day. You think they'd survive if they blamed themselves every time one of their kids died before its first birthday? Get real, man. Get fucking real." He continued without letting Jeff respond. "You don't think I have goals? You don't think I want to do things? I want to do things, Jeff. I joined the Peace Corps just like you did—to get away from this nine-to-five crap and see the world, to make a difference. I can take chances, too. I just don't need to die on the highway or at the end of a Secret Service gun to prove it." Oly could feel his legs getting weak. He felt exhausted as a teardrop fell onto his pant leg. Jeff didn't say a word as Oly walked away to lie down. For the rest of the night, they didn't speak, and Oly went to bed without saying goodnight. He stared at the ceiling and couldn't sleep. At 2am, he threw his pillow and headed to the couch in the common room, the smell of fried plantains wafting from the kitchen. Ladysmith Black Mambazo was playing on a radio accompanied by the whistles of Ron, a new arrival who slept all day and stayed awake all night.

Oly felt angry at Ron for wearing African clothes that looked bad on him, making foods from places he'd never see again, trying to fight off the inevitable transition to reality. He wanted to scream that it was over and wondered whether the hostel was an oasis or halfway house. The pathetic band of returned volunteers had sequestered itself, together, resisting their return to reality with exotic foods, bizarre shirts, and illicit drugs. He stared out the bay window onto the moon lit street. The thwack, thwack, thwack sound of helicopter blades broke the silence of his thoughts and brought him back to Bawendi and thoughts of Samantha. As sirens approached, a straining engine roared down the street, wheels screeching. A police helicopter's searchlight flooded the street, turning the inky blackness midday-bright. A dark green car flew by the house, and the searchlight washed over Oly's face. He felt the desperation of the people inside the car and wondered if they were running from the same things as he, when he plopped down on the couch and fell into a deep sleep.

CHAPTER 26

AFRICAIN, AMÉRICAIN

———

A LOUD FAN BELT AND a blaring radio from an early commuter starting her car just outside the hostel's living room window woke Oly up from a bad sleep. A dim light in the kitchen cast shadows from someone making an early breakfast. It was Grady. Oly's subconscious planted an image of Samantha in his head.

"Yeah, I know. I get it," he said aloud.

"What?" Grady's voice said from the kitchen.

"Nothing. Good morning."

"Morning. Want some organic bean dip and toast?"

"Sure," Oly replied, making a face.

Samantha symbolized everything he was running from to everything he wanted to be and be with. Her stability and common sense gravitated him toward Jeff in Togo. Her warnings were parent-like even though he always ended up with her at the end of the day. He desperately wanted to be with her and felt panicky that she was coming home soon. He had nothing to show for himself since his return and it made him depressed. He was mad at himself for getting caught up with Jeff again, but couldn't figure out a better alternative. *Hang out with the folks? High school chums? Brothers? I should have stayed with the friggin' temp job. How could I be so stupid to think this was going to work?* He felt the urge to go into Jeff's room and smother him with a pillow.

"You coming?" Grady yelled from the kitchen.

Oly got up from the couch. "Yeah, sorry," he said. "Just getting my pants on."

"What the hell are you doing crashing on the couch? Late night?"

"You might say that," Oly said, getting up from the couch. Grady handed him a toasted organic bean dip sandwich and had a cup of black coffee waiting for him. The coffee cup was a heavy diner mug with a thick handle. It had a fading blue label on the side: Eat Maggie's Muffins, Madison, Wisconsin.

"There's sugar there and milk in the fridge if you want. I don't know how you take it," Grady said. An unexpected wave of emotion welled up in Oly, as he experienced the most normal routine, however small, since he had left home. He imagined Samantha in place of Grady. Maybe that's all he wanted. A routine. A good morning. A cup of coffee and an organic bean sandwich.

Pictures of yesterday's trauma flashed in his head, as Grady asked him how things were going. Oly couldn't tell him what happened and gave vague answers about temping, like everyone else in the hostel. "You know, 9 to 5. Back to the American reintegration program."

Grady took a bite of his sandwich and paused, taking a leather necklace that was hanging outside of his t-shirt and tucking it inside. "Yeah, man. I get it. Look, I got something if you're interested" he said, reaching in his pocket and pulling out a card that looked like it was for a dentist appointment. "I don't think Paige and I are going to stick around much longer. We're gonna hit the road soon and do some hiking out west with a buddy." He handed the crumpled yellow card to Oly. "Someone at Peace Corps set me up with these people for a chat. It's some kind of development agency. You can go in my stead if you want. See what happens."

Oly thanked him and took the card, looking at it like a Willy Wonka golden ticket. "This is for today," Oly said, looking at the card.

"Yeah, no shit. And you better clean yourself up a bit. You look like crap."

Delirious from lack of rest, Oly pulled on his only clean button-down and rifled through his pants pockets, examining the tattered remains of phone numbers he had written down weeks ago at home, prior to Jeff's transition-team plot. One of the most promising openings was at a well-established NGO called the African Development Agency.

Oly shoved ten dollars in the cookie jar on the kitchen counter before heading out to walk the four blocks to the Metro stop. No one else was awake yet as the sun poured through the curtains, illuminating the dust that floated in the air. He glanced at Jeff's Postal Service truck parked on the street, covered with leaves, one of its tires now flat, and smiled at the irony of his friend driving a vehicle from the government that had blacklisted him for life.

The African Development Agency was one of the better-known and well-respected NGOs in town. When he arrived at the reception area, a pleasant African-American woman welcomed him with a buttery accent. She was wearing a blouse with a kente pattern. Oly looked up at several large poster-sized photos hanging in the reception area. Victoria Falls. A herd of antelope. A group of children waving. A mud hut. The pictures were beautiful, but he wondered why a development agency perpetuated the myth of Africa as it had been for thousands of years rather than what it hoped to be. There were cities and highways too, after all.

"Hello," he said, deciding not to use West African French in case she was neither African nor French speaking.

"It's nice to meet you, Richard. My name is Frieda Kwonde. I am the associate director for recruitment. I see on your application you spent a couple of years in Peace Corps," she said, annunciating the 'P' at the end of Corps, so it sounded like 'corpse.' "We have many Peace 'Corpse' Volunteers here. Very dedicated. So nice. Tell me, what is it that brings you here today?"

"Well," Oly said, stifling a laugh from the image of a peace corpse. "I saw your posting and thought I'd be a good match for your small-business-development initiatives overseas."

"Yes, tell me more."

"I really want to help those places like Africa that are trying to … develop." He felt himself getting warm inside his shirt, becoming uncomfortable with his lack of preparation. *When did I last have an interview?* he wondered, trying to sit up straighter.

"Hmm," she said, pausing. Oly could sense Frieda's initial friendliness melting into skepticism. "And which initiatives looked interesting to you?"

He had no idea, so he guessed. "Umm, well, women in development, for example. Women in villages nccd support to start their own businesses." Frieda showed a hint of an encouraging smile, but could tell he was improvising. "My experience in Togo gave me a greater understanding of the needs of women in Africa, and I feel I could really assist the development of that." Pictures of the rice-and-bean ladies and the ones carrying water on their heads or selling things at the market drifted in and out of his head. They never seemed to need his help. The warmth under his shirt was condensing to sweat as he felt the conversation slipping away.

Frieda threw Oly a lifeline, switching the topic from exposing his lack of preparation to what he actually did in Peace 'Corpse.' He wanted to correct her to at least get something right, but stopped short, knowing it would probably make it worse.

The last part of the interview was a role play in which he had to create a budget for a $5,000 project to establish a small textile cooperative in Ghana. Since Oly felt he had no chance at the position, he relaxed in his chair and decided to give up on trying to impress her.

"Well, Frieda, half of that money is not going to be in the budget. If you want to transport the goods from one place to another, you must invest, shall we say, in the right people. Once you buy the cloth, say for two thousand, I'd put aside one thousand to make sure the merchant doesn't sell it elsewhere before you pick it up. Then, I'd add another thousand to the transportation cost to see that the driver and his apprentice guard the cloth, then another couple hundred or so for the soldiers at various checkpoints to make sure they don't decide to partake in the shipment. It doesn't hurt to get to know the local gendarmerie, if you know what I mean. Then, when the cloth arrived, I'd make sure that two bolts of it made its way to the local chief, so he doesn't interfere in our affairs. Then, finally, with whatever is left, I'd get the project started and hope we can climb out of debt."

She raised her eyebrows at the end of Oly's explanation and she smiled, somewhat out of pity, for the first time since the interview began. She stood, extending a hand. "Mr. Olymeyer, it is evident that you have experience in the third world. I thank you for your candor. We shall be in touch should we be interested in further discussions. Thank you for coming in." She didn't ask how best to reach him, and he knew that he'd never hear from her again. I guess I am a *peace corpse*, he wanted to say on his way out.

Oly walked the ten blocks to the hostel, eliciting stares from umbrella-wielding pedestrians as a steady rain matted his interview clothes against his skin. He was feeling depressed and starting to go to a dark place. Thoughts of Samantha were not even helping, and seemed to make it worse. He was reaching the proverbial rock bottom. When he arrived back at the hostel, soaking wet, the mail truck was gone. Oly was relieved and wondered how Jeff managed to drive it with a flat. A new 'tenant' whom Oly didn't recognize was piling bean sprouts on a large sandwich and didn't appear to see him. Oly walked past not wanting to chat and dove into his hockey bag, digging in a panic until he found Gunning's card. He went back to the living room and dialed the number on it.

"Hello?" the familiar voice answered, surprising Oly that it worked. "This is Professor Gunning."

"Professor, it's Richard Olymeyer. We met about a year ago in Togo."

After a brief pause, during which Oly could hear Gunning saying something muffled to someone in his office, he returned. "Sorry, I was with a student. How are you? I was actually wondering if you'd made it back to America safely."

"Yes, I did. Thanks."

"Well, this is a wonderful coincidence. I called the Peace Corps headquarters a week ago, actually, to see if they knew where you were. Of course, they give no information."

"You did?"

"Yes. Listen, I have a very busy afternoon, but I want to treat you to lunch. What do you say? Tomorrow at around 2? There's a place in Dupont Circle with a Senegalese chef who makes peanut sauce from the old country. I forget the name, but it begins with an 'A.' We'll share memories of your village, and I'll fill you in on the rest of our trip."

CHAPTER 27

Bon Appétit

AKOLO'S, A TRENDY BISTRO IN D.C.'s leafy Dupont Circle district, was nestled between a tobacco shop and a secondhand bookstore. Oly walked in at a little after two and stood near the corner of the bar. A handful of scraggly PCV types were sprinkled at various tables mixed in with African-Americans and several African diplomats. Two dusty antelope heads hung over the bar, one missing an eye. An attractive hostess with braided hair extensions and a flowery smell approached Oly. She seemed to walk in synch with the techno world music beat that played in the background. Oly was transfixed. She stood in front of him and smiled.

"Welcome to Akolo's," she purred, in a throaty West-African accent. "Ken I geet you a beverage?"

"Yes, my sista, do you have tchouk?"

"No, sah," she smiled with an expression that said *Congratulations, you are the 26th returned Peace Corps Volunteer who has asked me that.*

"Okay, how about Pepsi?"

"Yes, Pepsi. We have Pepsi."

Oly looked around them and understood immediately why she was not impressed by his question. The place was littered with RPCVs. The men were thin, angry-looking, and had unkempt beards. They wore colorful *panya* shirts that looked odd on yovos in West Africa and horrible on them in America. The African Hawaiian shirt. *What was with the homeless look?* he thought to himself. *Africans were so clean and orderly. Who did they think they were, dressing like that?* They had worked so hard not to look like Westerners that they looked like crazy people.

From a table in the corner, beneath a large wooden mask, Professor Gunning waved in Oly's direction. Oly had forgotten what he looked like but remembered his thick, black, retro eyeglass frames. He sat across from a man wearing a white button-down shirt with a pen in the front pocket: the uniform of the educated African elite. Oly didn't recognize him. The men stood, smiling, and shook Oly's hand. Several papers were spread on the table, as though they had been meeting long before Oly arrived.

"Sit down, my friend, thank you for coming," Gunning said. "I brought a friend of mine visiting from Atlanta. I hope you don't mind the extra company." Without waiting to see if Oly objected, he continued. "Mr. Soyere, this is my Peace Corps friend Oly. He surprised my Howard University students when they went to see the real Africa. You should have seen their faces when my white friend drove up on his motorcycle."

Soyere grinned politely and tapped his left index finger on the papers, somewhat impatiently. "It's so nice to see you, Monsieur Oly. I take it your return to America has gone okay? What have you been up to?"

Oly decided not to tell the truth. The waitress' arrival with drinks bought him some time. "I have mostly been visiting with family and eating lots of hamburgers." Soyere grinned again, but didn't tap his finger.

Gunning sensed the awkwardness in the room and ordered for the table in French. As the waitress walked away, he followed her with his eyes in an attempt to distract from the moment.

"She's Beninoise. Françoise. Beautiful girl. Daughter of the former Ambassador."

One of the scraggly white men looked over at Oly, giving the yovo with the black friends a once over. Oly felt self-conscious and proud at the same time. He was a yovo, but in his own land. He winked at the man for some reason, causing him to look away.

"You know him?" Gunning asked, noticing the exchange.

"No, but I feel like I do. He's probably a returned volunteer drowning his sorrows."

Gunning took a sip of water and smacked his lips. "You Americans are a strange lot. You go off to save the world, then come back and don't know what to do with yourselves. And when you're away, you still seem lost. It cannot be easy."

"It's not," Oly said, disarmed by Gunning's sharp insight.

"Why did you join the Peace Corpse?" Soyere asked.

"I'm sorry," Oly said before answering. "Corpse is a dead person. You say it *core*, like apple core."

"Ah, yes." Soyere smiled, somewhat embarrassed by Oly's correction. He inadvertently started tapping the papers again, waiting for Oly to answer.

"You know, Mr. Soyere, I give a different answer every time someone asks me. To be honest, I just didn't want to get a job after college."

Before Soyere could respond, a heaping platter of chicken smothered in peanut sauce arrived at the table. "*Dieu merci*," Gunning responded, smiling at Françoise. The three ate in silence for several minutes while Oly caught Soyere looking at him and wondered what the hell was going on. He had started to feel like he was being vetted.

"A funny thing happened to me on the way to the mud hut," Oly said, wiping his face with a napkin and taking a sip of water.

Soyere nodded his head. "What do you mean?"

"You know, when you go into the *Core*, you have all these ideas about saving the world. It takes about six months for that to wear off, and then your eyes open."

"Would you say things fall apart?" Soyere joked.

"Maybe," Oly answered. "Yes, I would agree. But it's more than that. Things don't just fall apart. They do everything. Right in front of you. People die. Animals give birth. Disease. Starvation. In the U.S., you have to look a little harder to find all those things. It's not all right out in the open like it is in Africa. I even saw my first dead person there. He was lying right in the middle of the road, and the traffic was just going around him."

Soyere and Gunning looked down as they ate, making Oly unsure as to whether or not they were listening. Gunning finally put down his piece of chicken after chewing all the meat off and wiped his mouth. "Africa has it all, doesn't it?" he smiled.

"Speaking of having it all, Professor, I could not help notice that you seemed to be having some sort of meeting before I got here," he said, looking down at papers that Soyere had stacked into a neat pile. "What were you talking about, if I could be so forward?"

Gunning looked over at Soyere who tried to give a quick shake of his head like a pitcher waving off a catcher, but it was too obvious as Oly looked directly at him. Soyere smiled and Gunning spoke. "A small nonprofit organization called the Friends of Sapelo is having some land issues in Georgia and they contacted me, I mean us. Mr. Soyere is an associate with the NAACP with whom I have been working since the Sixties. We were doing some strategizing. It's a difficult and somewhat unpleasant issue, the details of which may or may not interest you."

Oly paused before answering. He took a sip of his Pepsi and glanced over at one of the antelope heads. He imagined it talking back to him. *Well? Do the details interest you?* Soyere filled the silence. "You built a bridge in Africa, yes?"

"How did you...?" Oly jumped in, looking at Gunning.

"Right, your little meeting before I got here. So you've been talking a bit. What's the yovo angle?"

"Excuse me?" Soyere answered, squinting, with a displeased look on his face.

"The *yovo.* Why do you need a white guy? Why me? It's the only reason you need me, let's face it. I'm really no other use to you. I have no job; no real prospects as of late. My readjustment allowance is about to run out and my college loans kick in at the end of the month. I'd say being a yovo is about the only thing I have in my corner. *Qu'est ce que vous voulez?*"

Soyere sat back in his chair and considered Oly. He folded his arms. "The Peace *Corps*," he said, with exaggerated emphasis, "is a very well-respected organization. Yes, we could have secured the services of a great number of people, that is true."

"But you handled yourself quite well during my visit," Gunning cut in. "And we believe that once you begin something like this you will see it through." Before he had a chance to respond to the flattery, Soyere started spreading the papers out on the table. They were a mixed pile of documents, copies of land deeds, depositions with writing in the margins, and copies of hand-written notes that looked very old.

Soyere and Gunning looked at one another, wondering how Oly was going to react. He was the fifth yovo they had approached - the others, a variety of liberal activists and recent law grads, all turned them down for one reason or another. "The people of the Sea Islands are direct descendants of freed African slaves," Gunning began, gauging Oly's reaction. "The Freedmen. You probably remember that from high school history class." He paused and took a sip of water. "The Friends are having a hearing that they wanted me to attend about some casino or something that they're trying to block because it will take over a significant plot of land that you see here," he said, unfolding one of the papers to show a topographical map filled with lines and coordinates. "It's not complicated, but they want outside help because there has been some, how shall we put it...," he paused, looking over at Soyere, who finished his sentence.

"Intimidation."

"You're joking," Oly said, laughing. "Who the hell do you think I am? Why don't they call the police?" Neither smiled, but gave Oly a look that exposed the great divide between whites, blacks, and the law.

"You said you wanted the yovo angle," Gunning finished. "There you have it. We considered the media, the NAACP, all the usual routes. And those are certainly options for us. But we know that long after things quiet down, that whoever is behind this will cause great suffering. That's why we thought that, potentially, an advocate of your profile may just be able to work out a reasonable settlement."

A reasonable settlement, Oly thought to himself. *What the hell did that mean?* The conversation reminded Oly of a time during cotton harvest season when he came upon a small village near Affem Boussou that was weighing its crop for the government buyers from SOTOCO (Société Togolaise de Coton). When he drove up on his motorcycle to innocently see what was happening with the gigantic fluffy bales of crop, the entire operation stopped and one of the men from SOTOCO (who happened to be white), started gesturing to the men from the village asking in angry French what he (Oly) was doing there. It didn't take long for Oly to figure out that the man had been hired by SOTOCO to add some *yovo power* to the government operation to swindle villagers out of millions of francs in cotton payments. An unannounced yovo visit by a stranger was not part of the plan. "*C'est qui?*" the man insisted, pointing at Oly. "*C'est qui?*" he kept yelling. The villagers looked around, some laughing and pointing at the angry yovo, while others looked confused, looking to the chief for direction. Oly had decided to hang around, waiting to see what impact his simple presence would have on the operation.

Eventually, a teacher from the village approached Oly, smiling with an outreached hand while everyone watched. "My friend," he said in a pleading voice in English. This man has come to do business with the village and will not continue until you leave. We are sorry for this, but I hope you understand this situation."

"I'll do it," Oly said, breaking out of his daydream.

"Do what?" Gunning said, looking to make sure he understood what Oly was agreeing to.

"You know, go to the meeting, be a yovo, whatever."

"*Whatever?*" Soyere did not like his casual tone. "You refer to a generation of my people, the descendants of slaves as *whatever*? Maybe this is not for you. This is serious."

"Serious?" Oly shot back. "So serious that you proposed it to an unemployed returned Peace Corps Volunteer who is living off a dwindling allowance in a halfway house?"

Gunning laughed to break the tension. "He got you there, Samuel," he said, using Soyere's name for the first time. "Let's be reasonable about this," Gunning said, while Soyere started to gather the papers back into a neat pile.

"How do I get there?" Oly asked.

"I will get your ticket, but I have to agree with Mr. Soyere about this situation," Gunning answered. Oly considered the antelope head, the beautiful waitress walking across the restaurant floor, the scrawny volunteer getting up to leave, and took a deep breath. He closed his eyes for a moment and thought about Jeff, whether he'd see Samantha again, and Bawendi. When he opened his eyes a few seconds later, Soyere and Gunning were staring at him.

"Give me a day or two and I'll let you know," Oly said, as Soyere put the papers away.

Gunning reached into his jacket and gave Oly a card. "You reach me at Howard and let me know."

It wasn't until his walk back to the hostel that Oly realized the entire lunch date was a ruse. *You idiot,* he said to himself, wondering what he had done. *Of course the papers were out on the table. They knew I'd be interested in what they were doing and they needed a yovo to do their dirty work.* "Sonofabitch!" he said out loud, wishing that he hadn't allowed himself to walk into the false hope that Gunning might have simply wanted to connect with him. He wondered if Gunning hatched the plot when they first met in Tchamba.

CHAPTER 28

HOMME PROPOSE, II

———◆———

DECEMBER, 1992

JEFF AND OLY HADN'T SPOKEN since the bailout and Jeff's disappearance from the hostel. The next morning, Oly called for a cab and put twenty dollars in the cookie jar next to a moldy cassava root. A new arrival, whose name he did not know, was making a sandwich in the kitchen. He was barefoot, wore a Mickey Mouse t-shirt and had terrible body odor. Oly avoided eye contact and looked around the living room, getting one last imprint and wondering if he'd ever see the place again. He took a cab to the airport and bought a one-way plane ticket to Boston. Washington had always been known as a city of transition, a place where the world crossed paths on a temporary basis. Oly clutched his bag as the driver turned onto Rock Creek Parkway, thinking about his family and the unsettled feeling of his own transition that he wished would disappear.

"It's all your fault," he said, looking at the bag. The driver looked in the rearview, a puzzled look on his face. "I'd have a job and probably a life if it wasn't for you," he said, angry that he had allowed himself to get caught up in Gunning's scheme.

"Hey buddy, I don't have a problem with you. I'm just taking you to the airport," the driver said, sounding as though he'd had practice dealing with crazy people. Oly laughed, feeling relieved that he was with someone who had no pretenses about who he was or what he wanted. As the cab drove along the final stretch of road to the airport, Oly became more anxious. He had been gone less than two months. He couldn't go back to his parents. Andy had just started up his own company and might have some room at his apartment, but had his own life. Samantha would not be impressed, he thought to himself.

Oly never felt comfortable landing at Logan. Each time he did so, it felt as if the plane was landing in the ocean until the very last minute when a runway appeared. He always looked for the landmarks that reassured him that it was going to be all right: first the outer harbor islands and an occasional tanker, then Deer Island, followed by Nahant and Winthrop. This time he didn't look. The familiarity of landmarks didn't comfort him, and he waited until the plane abruptly bumped the tarmac before looking around.

The world moved in slow motion around Oly, as he remained seated, staring at swirling snowflakes out the window while passengers unclicked seatbelts and wrestled with the overhead compartments. Announcements blared over the speakers and passengers grabbed their belongings. Oly waited. He had no one to call and couldn't bring himself to stand up until everyone had disembarked.

"Sir?" enquired a voice next to him. It was one of the flight attendants. "Sir? Do you need assistance?"

Oly snapped out of his trance and looked around. He was the last person on the plane. The attendant's name-tag read 'Terri' and she had an attractive smile with a concerned look around her eyes. Oly figured she was somewhere from the Midwest. Too friendly to be from the Northeast. Her hair was pulled back in a ponytail. Oly imagined her as a runner type, who lived the dream in a condo with floor-to-ceiling windows and a successful boyfriend in sales.

"Oh, sorry," Oly said, trying to pull himself together. "I was just thinking."

"I know how that can be," she said, reaching across a neighboring seat to pick up several empty cups and papers. "I'm supposed to clear every-one out, you know, with the new security rules and all, but if you need…"

"That's okay," he interrupted, grabbing his bag and wondering if she thought he was a terrorist.

"You have a Merry Christmas now, okay?" she said in a sympathetic way that made him feel as if she knew he had no plans.

Which he didn't.

Unlike the excited travellers and families around him, he had nowhere to go. He spotted a man checking a cell phone and wondered what his parents' reaction would have been if he called. He had come full circle from just a few years earlier, when his entire family had come to wish him well on a future that seemed so focused and certain. *My son is going to Africa.*

He stood for a few minutes, watching a young mother apply Chapstick to her toddler son. A young couple clutched one another, possibly whispering about meeting the in-laws for the first time. *How did everything get so fucking complicated?* he thought to himself, wishing things could just be normal again. *Samantha would just get on with it,* he thought. *Would probably already be enrolled in a couple of grad programs and interning somewhere.*

He jumped on a random hotel shuttle just to get out of the airport and the memories it triggered. When the van stopped at the Radisson, a short distance from Logan in nearby East Boston, he asked the driver where he could get a bite for cheap. Fucilli's, a neighborhood restaurant nestled into a brick townhouse since 1957 apparently had the best eggplant parm in town.

"You can't beat it with a stick, buddy," the van driver said before he sped off.

Christmas ... and no one knows where I am, he thought to himself, as he walked towards the cursive neon lights of Fucilli's. From the second and third-floor porches, Christmas lights glowed on plastic snowman faces and likenesses of Jesus that looked down on him. He smiled to himself, wondering how he would have explained the mixed icons Bawendi.

Fucilli's was exactly what Oly needed: a homey, comfortable place without pretension that didn't judge and just let him be. He needed that right now. Glass windows looked out onto the street, as several customers sat eating at the counter. *Manicotti or eggplant parm special* was written in grease pencil on paper plates tacked above the grill. Oly ordered the eggplant special, which arrived just a couple of minutes later on a heavy, warm, porcelain plate. The waitress, Linda, wore her hair in a bun, had an apron like a waitress from a '50s diner, and had hands that looked as though they had been familiar with hard work.

"Home for the holidays, hon?" she asked, sizing him up.

"Sort of," he said, shoving a piece of bread in his mouth.

"Oh, so you used to live here and then moved away."

"Yeah, I kinda lived in D.C. but it didn't work out."

"Oh yeah? Bush fire you?" she said, nodding to a regular who walked in behind them. "It's a long story."

"They always are, sweetheart," she said, as the customer, a man wearing a Bruins sweatshirt, took a seat at a booth across from them.

Oly stared at the steam rising from the food in front of him and she took the hint.

"Okay, hon, I'll leave you to it. Enjoy," she said, looking up at the clock and snapping her gum. "Give a holler if you need anything."

A gentle sleet began spitting against the front window and Oly shoveled the food in his mouth, not remembering the last time he had such a good home-cooked meal. Linda had her back to him as she made small talk with the man in the Bruins sweatshirt. Oly watched a fuzzy television screen covering the traffic to the airport and mulled over the prospect of showing unannounced at his parents' house, wondering how he was going to explain himself.

"Shit," he said out loud, causing Linda to turn.

"Something wrong, sweetheart?"

"No, I'm good," he said, catching the eye of the Bruins sweatshirt guy. "Just thinking."

He blew on a piece of cheese-covered eggplant and started thinking about Samantha and what she would do if she were with him. *Probably call her parents with a reasonable explanation about why she came back.*

It wouldn't be too long before she'd be back home and he knew that if he didn't have his shit together she'd probably end up moving on while he 'sorted things out.' She had never liked Jeff and what he did to Oly's head. She would have had no patience for what happened in D.C. and would likely have told him to make a choice between her and that, whatever that was.

Oly watched Linda wipe down a table, while he nursed a lukewarm coffee. It saddened him to think that there was so much love in his life and here he was, sitting alone, less than twenty miles from where he grew up, feeling like a complete stranger. He couldn't bring himself to pick up the phone and call his family. The thought of sitting in his parents' house for Christmas made him wish he had never come home.

He thought of Phil Thompson, the pasty volunteer from Nebraska, who had taken to the animal husbandry project in Atakpame and decided to make a life of it. *Could I have stayed?* Oly asked himself. Settled down with a wife or two in the plateau region, maybe an apartment in Lomé. Bought a farm, a few goats, lived off the land. He never found out exactly what had happened to Phil, but he did heard through the grapevine that he spent a lot of time grubbing for food from local expats.

It was unthinkable to call upon Andy and Brett for help, having gone from overseas adventurer to domestic beggar. *From saving the world to saving up for my next meal,* he thought to himself, finishing the last bite of green beans and eggplant parm.

A stained apron came into view as Linda stood over Oly, balancing a tray full of dishes on her hip.

"Hon, you've been staring at the rain over that cup for a half-hour. You waiting for someone? Want a refill?"

"I'm not waiting for anyone," he answered without looking at her. She shifted the tray and looked down at his bag. He imagined she could relate to his desperation, a feeling that a lot of customers may have brought with them to the eatery in its working-class surroundings. She carried the tray over to the opening to the kitchen and set it down on a stainless-steel counter for the tattooed arms of the dishwasher to take away. She grabbed a wet cleaning rag and started working on a table next to Oly, who didn't look over.

"She'll come back," she said, putting the rag down to straighten out several laminated menus. The hairy arm of the cook rose over the stainless steel warming shelf and broke the silence with a ring of the bell that had been on top. The man in the Bruins sweatshirt, who was still sipping a coffee and thumbing through an old copy of *The Herald*, looked up to watch Linda bring him his order - the same plate as Oly's. When she came back toward Oly, she wiped her hands on her apron and glanced down at his bag.

"You got plans for Christmas, sweetie?"

"No," he said, realizing it was tomorrow.

"Where is she, if you don't mind my asking?"

"Africa."

She laughed, surprised by the answer. "Well, you got on the wrong plane, hon!" making a joke that caused him to break a smile. She put her hands on his table and looked him in the eye. "You look like a smart guy, you'll figure it out, don't be so hard on yourself. And when you find a good one, don't let her go! Ain't that right, George?" she yelled in the direction of the kitchen. The cook rang the bell again, this time calling out her name. "Don't let the good one go, George!" she yelled again, laughing as she headed to retrieve another plate on the warming counter. "Can't let the meatloaf get cold," she said, as she passed by Oly to put the plate in front of a couple that had just arrived. "Hey, nice talkin' to you. Take care, okay? Don't let the good ones get away."

The blood rushed from Oly's face, as her words echoed through his head. Linda had turned her attention to other customers, but she gave him a sympathetic look as paid his check and headed toward the door, leaving a few dollars on her table as he walked out. She looked at him one last time, winking as he walked out into a light snow. He put his face up towards the gray sky and let some of the flakes fall on his face. He couldn't remember the last time he experienced snow.

The duffel bag straps dug into Oly's shoulder as he scanned the street, looking for a pay phone. His fingers floated above the numbers for information while he considered what his brother's reaction would be. After two hang-ups to the number he was provided, the third call went through. Andy's enthusiasm was a lifeline.

"Was that you hanging up on me? Where the hell are you calling from, a tunnel?"

"I'm close to a tunnel, but it has an Irish name."

"What? You're in Boston, you crazy bastard? Mom and Dad have been asking a lot about you. They know you're here? You just took off with that mail-truck freak and that was it."

"Things didn't quite work out down there. Listen, I don't know how to..."

"Of course you can, Oly," Andy broke in, saving him from having to actually ask. "For as long as you want. Sort of. You sound pathetic, man. On Christmas and everything. What the fuck? You need me to pick you up?"

"I can manage. Don't tell Mom and Dad, okay?" Oly asked, before hanging up. "I'm not ready for that drama right now."

"Whatever you say, big brother. That's kinda whacked, but I get where you're coming from."

Andy had recently purchased a fixer upper two-family in Saugus, a working-class town of aluminum-sided townhouses a few miles north of Boston. It was considered where immigrants from East Boston moved when they had finally 'made it.' Andy was in the process of converting the unfinished half to the latest startup business rage called 'internet cafés.' He couldn't bear the cubicle life after college and decided to build his dream with the easy loans flowing around anything related to a 'dot-com.' He named it The Connection.

Oly's cab pulled up in front of the house. Andy had gone out, but left the light on. Oly quietly let himself in and was happy that his brother wasn't home. He had left a cot in the unfinished section with a note: *My house is yours. Catch you in the AM. Andy.* He dropped the duffel bag, put his head in his hands, and sobbed.

DIEU DISPOSE

CHRISTMAS, 1992

ON CHRISTMAS DAY, 1992, OLY heard the sounds of Andy turning on the shower and headed over. He waited outside the bathroom door, sitting on a giant queen-sized bed that was in the dining room. Andy had made it his bedroom as it had three large floor-to-ceiling bay and space for several computer stations. As Andy hummed in the shower, Oly looked around the room at the photos of girls he hadn't met, of camping trips, of holiday gatherings - all without him in the picture. How much of life he had missed.

Andy stepped out a few minutes later, his waist wrapped in a Boston Celtics beach towel, his hair dripping-wet. "Shit," he said, startled at Oly being in the room on his bed. "You freaked me out." "Merry Christmas to you, too," Oly said, examining a photo of an attractive redhead mounted on a horse that was by the bedside table.

"Yeah, I guess," he said, dropping the towel to get dressed.

"What the fuck are you doing? Why did you just show up? Are you losing it?"

Despite the fact that the thought had circulated in his brain for a while since D.C., it was the first time that someone else had verbalized the question.

Oly had always been the one keeping his younger brothers in line, and out of harm's way with their parents. He watched as Andy slipped on a pair of plaid boxers and pulled a clean black t-shirt out of his bureau. "Well?" he said, spraying his armpits with deodorant. "You're like a fugitive. I'm supposed to go over Mom's and do what? Pretend you're not here? Show up with you? Merry Christmas! Look who I found!"

Andy's anger confused Oly. "Why are you so mad, Andy? What did I do to you?"

"Oh, I don't know. You're gone for a couple of years and you're all Mom talks about. Then you come back, disappear to D.C., and we don't hear from you and then you pop up on Christmas Day like you're wanted by the police." Andy tugged on a pair of jeans and started combing his hair. "Do whatever the fuck you want, big brother. Just remember that it's not just about you. What you do affects other people, in case you hadn't figured it out."

Oly was taken aback by his younger brother's perception. He really hadn't thought about the effect of his departure - or return - on his brothers. They seemed to take it in stride. He watched while Andy slipped his shoes on, a pair of worn docksiders.

"I'll call Mom, okay?" Oly said, as Andy put a belt on.

"That's not the point, Oly, and you know it," he said, looking up at the ceiling with exasperation.

"I'm sorry, Andy. I was being selfish when I got back. You think I'm acting like a freak? Well, I feel like one. I don't feel like this is my home anymore. I feel like a foreigner. I didn't think you guys noticed, but I could tell by the way Mom acted that something was wrong. I'm sorry." He looked at his brother and felt a tear roll down his cheek.

"Oh shit, you're not crying," Andy laughed. "You're a mess, dude. Put on some friggin' clothes and let's go surprise Mom and Dad. I'll tell them you were panhandling at North Station."

The brothers man-hugged, Oly holding on even when Andy tried to pull away. He had never exposed himself to being vulnerable and scared in front of his brothers before. The family dynamic had shifted, leaving Andy as the heir while Oly searched for himself.

"C'mon, let's go," Andy said. "This place is yours if you can deal with the remodeling. Stay as long as you need and we'll figure things out. Throw on a better shirt so you look like a normal person."

Oly thought about his last Christmas, which he spent at Bawendi's, chowing on porcupine stew and tchouk, trying to numb the pain of being three thousand miles from home in hundred-degree heat.

While they drove across town in Andy's new black BMW, Oly stared out the window at the dusting of snow on the vinyl-clad triple-deckers and realized that he and his brother had reversed positions in the family. Andy wasn't supposed to be driving the nice car on the way to his parents with his long-lost brother next to him. That was supposed to be Oly in the driver's seat. Literally. He looked over at Andy, who irradiated confidence behind a pair of aviator Rayban sunglasses. "Look at you, asshole," Oly said.

"What?" Andy smiled. "You like the ride? Bet they don't have these in Togo."

"Well, actually they do. It's just that you can count the number on one hand."

They drove silently for a bit, only stopping once to get a couple of bottles of wine, which Andy paid for. "So, little shit, how'd you grow up so fast?" Oly asked when they pulled out of the parking lot.

"Oh, I don't know. I guess after college I probably felt like you, not knowing what the hell I wanted. Working at a regular job sucked. Maybe starting my own thing was like running off to Africa, except I didn't get all crazy like you did."

"Crazy? What do you mean?" Oly laughed, feeling relieved that his brother seemed to relate.

"Crazy like how Mom is going to be when she sees you," Andy smiled, as they pulled into the Olymeyer driveway.

CHAPTER 30

ELEPHANT FOU FURIEUX

———◆———

DURING THE DRY SEASON OF 1991, while the Affem bridge project waited
for supplies, Oly would relax in a hammock attached to the mango tree
in front of his house with his latest copy of *La Nouvelle Marche*, Togo's
one and only newspaper. The title loosely translated as 'the new direction.' Though not strong in content, *La Marche* gave Oly a chance to
practice his French. Each edition carried one, and only one, cover story
every day: President Eyadema's daily activities. *La Marche* comforted its
readership, consisting mostly of government fonctionnaires doing bureaucratic things. It was the patriarchal African society in print form.
Eyadema greeting the French ambassador. Eyadema holding audience
with a group of businessmen. Smiling with the head of the ruling party,
the *Rassemblement du Peuple Togolais*. The photo ops usually took place
in the same room, on bright white leather couches that somehow made
the guests look small and the president gigantic. Except for practicing
his French grammar, Oly had no use for the rag; it never reported on
anything actually happening in the country, good or bad. But that all
changed on January 15, 1991, two days after the annual celebration of
the president's rise to power. The headline read, *Elephant Fou-Furieux:
Menace du Pays*. A renegade elephant, separated from its herd, had apparently gone insane, inflicting terror upon villages in the South. It was
illegal in Togo to kill wild game. But rumors of trampled pregnant wom-
en called for action—and provided an opportunity for the president to
add to the folklore that kept him in power. It had been a while since

Eyadema had fed his propaganda machine with new feats of his courage, and news had begun to spread of budding opposition parties, inspired by a wave of *la democracie* in faraway places like Tiananmen Square and the collapsing Soviet Union.

The last time Eyadema was challenged, in the early seventies, a plane carrying him from Lomé allegedly crashed outside Sarakawa in the North, killing the French pilots and everyone else on board. The president walked away, miraculously unscathed, claimed sabotage from the opposition party, and declared the day a national holiday. Parades were organized, children were released from school, and the annual *Fête du Retour Triomphale* was born. The Chinese government, in its never-ending ambition to win favor with African governments in exchange for generous trade agreements, built a museum around the charred wreckage of the plane, where visitors could gawk at a fifty-foot statue of a Mao-like Eyadema waving to the adjacent yam fields. The plane wreck didn't even look real. It was a heap of metal that looked like it was taken from a scrap yard.

Oly read in fascination as the newspaper reported that the elephant, separated from its herd, was terrorizing the president's home region of Kara; villagers stood by helplessly as yam fields were destroyed and houses toppled by the beast. *La Marche* featured photos of everything except dead pregnant women, a conspicuously absent detail that amused Oly as he sensed the manipulation. It was *Retour Triomphale, Part Deux*.

Below the fold, in a photo from the archives, a younger President Eyadema was shown next to his helicopter in a triumphant pose, brandishing a gigantic rifle that dated from the Colonial era. He was a collector of sorts. What captured Oly's attention was what the president stood on top of: the carcass of a humpback whale. Oly had heard stories about the president shooting into the ocean from his helicopter in the Bay of Benin, but now there were apparently photos to back it up. Oly remembered Bawendi telling him once that Europeans tried so hard to make everyone forget their colonial past. "*En Afrique*," he explained, "*le gouvernement et le peuple ne sont pas la meme.*" He was right. There were two different worlds. Unlike in America, where everyone wanted to touch their leaders, see their frailties, see pictures of them in blue jeans on the weekends - in places like Togo, the leaders were mysterious, inaccessible, and dangerous. The story explained that Eyadema interrupted a reception with the French foreign minister to board his private helicopter and level the elephant *fou-furieux* with a submachine gun, just as it was readying to eviscerate another defenseless expecting mother.

The twisted carcass of the dead beast was hoisted onto a flatbed truck and toured about the country for all to see. Brilliant. *The Republican Party would love this guy*, Oly thought to himself. Eyadema intimidated his people and saved them, all in one shot. Impressive. He didn't have to say a word. The photos of the bloody carcass spoke for themselves. *Everything's alright now everyone. You can even see for yourself. By the way, this is just a friendly reminder that I'm the guy with the helicopters and the guns.* Oly put the paper down and fell into a slumber, dreaming of hoisting a rifle to throngs of cheering well-wishers. He was awakened by the distinctive buzz of a Peace Corps–issued DT-100, which grew louder, then muffled as it passed behind the grand mosque, then louder again as it turned onto his road. A few moments later, Samantha appeared, holding her yellow helmet in her hands as she took off her jean jacket in the heat.

"Hey neighbor, I was visiting your marché and thought I'd drop by. I didn't interrupt your siesta, did I?"

Oly peered over the top of his paper, leaning back in the hammock pretending to be asleep. He groaned. "I'm sick. Doesn't anyone ever call first anymore?" She laughed and pushed the hammock.

"Sick, my ass. Hey, I heard there was some dead elephant coming through Sokodé. Everyone's lining the streets to see it. Something about the president involved that I didn't catch."

Oly threw the paper off his chest. "You're joking, right?"

"No, your friend Chalim told me about it. I bumped into him at the marché. It'll be here this afternoon. What is it, anyway?"

He pointed to the paper resting under the hammock. "It's the biggest news in this place since the big crash at Sarakawa. This guy is a piece of work."

"You wanna check it out? Not like you're rushing off to work or anything," she said, sliding her helmet back on. "*On y va*, yovo?" Oly groaned again and slid off the hammock, deciding that an afternoon with Samantha was better than anything he could come up with in the sweltering heat.

The road from Tchamba to Sokode, a dusty thirty kilometers full of potholes and domestic fowl, wound through ten villages that huddled along its banks like street beggars. Riding on the back of Oly's Yamaha, Samantha grabbed his waist, her slender arms pulling tighter each time they went over a bump. At one point she tickled his ribs and giggled, a sensation that caused an erection that was painful as he jammed himself against the gas tank.

When they arrived in Sokode, choked with dust from the long ride, the streets were packed in anticipation of the caravan. Drums pounded in the distance as ramshackle bush taxis made their way past the grande marché, packed with howling revelers. It was an occasion to celebrate and a break from the routine (that and the fact that most of them had never seen an elephant before, dead or alive). A low guttural diesel sound rumbled in the distance, north of the city, causing a pause in the ruckus on the streets that was followed by a cry of anticipation.

The caravan, including twenty large black motorcycles mounted by Eyadema's personal republican guard, had arrived. Oly got a chill as he eyed the escorts. Wearing dark goggles and looking straight ahead, these were the special forces of the president, the ones that made people disappear in the night. They were like the SS shock troops of Togo. The procession was so loud that it drowned out the crowd as it passed. Then, on the heels of the slow-moving escort detail was the prize, a gigantic Mercedes diesel semi towing a flatbed, a mound of grey fleshy carcass chained on top. The moment was almost anticlimactic compared to the melodrama that surrounded it, particularly when the 'ferocious' mother-killer came into view. Shriveled from having spent days in the sun, the chained animal looked pathetic, its bloodstained body contorted into an unnatural position, flies swarming at will. Samantha looked away. "I can't stand this, it's so sad," she cried, as the stench from the carcass caught up with the procession. The crowd roared its approval as the caravan inched by, a cavalcade of armed soldiers standing on top of the truck and the elephant's torso, brandishing rifles in victory. One was flapping the elephant's ear up and down to the approval of the crowd. They loved it. Bringing up the rear were scores of joyous Togolese, many pounding drums alongside the caravan.

"Let's go," Samantha said, tugging on Oly's arm. "I don't know why I thought this would be a good idea. It's making me sick."

They ducked into a bar called Jackson Five, which featured a faded, chipping mural of the famous singers on the outside wall. Oly ordered two grande lagers and watched as Samantha took a gigantic swig.

"I can't believe that," she lamented. "I thought I had seen it all. But that was so barbaric."

Oly halfheartedly agreed; in spite of the barbarity, he was fascinated by the spectacle and wanted to stay. "Yeah, but think of the street cred he got out of it."

"The what?"

"You know, street cred, respect, attitude. It's part of the culture."

"Culture?" she cried, causing the bartender and a fonctionnaire drinking a half-finished Guinness to look over at them.

"That was disgusting. That wasn't culture."

"Don't be so judgmental," he said, taking a swig from the lukewarm beer, starting to feel the euphoria of the moment slipping.

On the ride back to Oly's house, Samantha held on but didn't tickle or talk at all. Oly felt a soreness below directly related to a feeling that the opportunity to fulfill some natural urges was slipping away after the elephant disagreement. When they got back to his house, he quickly conceded so that he could get back into favorability. "Don't get me wrong, I think it's horrible what they did," he said, walking closer to her, trying unsuccessfully to not sound patronizing. "Absolutely horrible. So mean to that poor Dumbo."

She looked at him with a skeptical expression and put her arm out. "Wait just a minute there, soldier. All that killing get your primal juices flowing?" she looked up at him, close enough so that he could see the sweat droplets on her neck.

"If I were the dictator and you lived in one of those villages, would you want me to protect you?" Oly asked, pushing against her arm so that it started to bend.

"That depends," she said, no longer resisting his advancement. "On what you did after you protected me."

"I'd use protection, of course," Oly said, proud of his segue.

"Oh, you're so clever, aren't you?" she smiled, as he rubbed against her. "Which reminds me," she said, while looking past Oly. "I'm a bit low on supplies."

"Hmm," Oly said, unbuttoning the front of her shirt. "Maybe I can have some delivered with the next shipment of cement."

The memory was vivid to Oly and made him feel disconnected from the present. Samantha was the only person who could ground him, to act as that catalyst between the first world and the third. He thought about the look on her face when he left Togo for the last time, a mixture of uncertainty and sadness as she touched his cheek at the airport. He needed her in his life.

CHAPTER 31

QUELLE SURPRISE

———

OLY'S MOTHER DIDN'T HAVE A chance to scream when he walked in the door with Andy. Before she could react, Andy put his arm around his older brother and announced, "Look what I found by the mailbox!" and they all hugged. "But, but…" was all she could say as Oly held her and Andy with a combination of awkwardness and affection.

"You don't need to say anything, Mom," Oly said, holding onto her. "It's okay, things just didn't work out. And don't worry, I didn't bring my bag with me."

She looked up from the hug, her eyes glassy with tears. "I would never turn you away, Richard. I only want what is best for you."

Before they could continue the conversation, Brett burst in while his father yelled from the kitchen, "Who is it Rebecca? Another of those panhandlers?"

"What?" Brett yelled, feigning disappointment. "Now there's less turkey for us?"

After the initial joy of Oly's surprise return passed, an awkwardness took over. The Olymeyer dynamic had seemed to work around his absence and now had to re-calibrate. Hushed conversations took place in the kitchen while he sat in the living room with his father explaining at least five times how things went bad in Washington and how he ended up at Andy's. The subtext in Oly's mind was that they were moving on without him and his sudden reappearance caught them off guard. In some ways, he wished he had never come. Not long after they finished eating and retired to the living room, he feigned illness and asked Andy to take him back to his place. Rebecca started crying when she hugged him at the door. "I am glad you are alright, Richard. I hope that we see you again soon."

Brett, never one for the sentimental moments, reached over and grabbed Oly's earlobe. "And let us know so there's enough turkey you knucklehead," he jabbed.

Oly's father came from doing dishes in the kitchen and stood behind Rebecca. Ever the dutiful husband, he rested his hands on her shoulders. "You know you're always welcome, Richard," he said, looking concerned while his mother broke off the hug. "We're always here for you."

CHAPTER 32
BRUSHING UP

———

A FEW DAYS AFTER CHRISTMAS, a misty rain sputtered over Andy's neighborhood. Togo never had a misty rain. It either poured buckets or not at all for months. Most of the snow in the neighborhood had melted, making the Christmas lawn decorations look out of place against the brown grass. Andy had left the house early and Oly hadn't spoken with him much since Christmas dinner. Oly reached into his still unpacked duffel bag and pulled out a purple and yellow *panya* shirt that he had made on one of his last days in Tchamba. He realized that he didn't have any winter clothes and grabbed an old sweatshirt of Andy's that was lying in a dirty laundry pile on the floor. When he looked in his wallet at a lonely twenty dollar bill, he realized that his readjustment allowance from Peace Corps was only going to last another month or two. It had been a couple of weeks and he was starting to lose hope in Gunning contacting him. He remembered that he had not told his parents that he was going to be in the area or that Gunning was possibly going to call.

He walked two blocks out of Andy's to The Daily Grind, a local breakfast stop. A gigantic black Ford F250 diesel with four aluminum ladders neatly strapped to the top was parked out front. The body was perfectly clean in spite of the dirty, slushy winter streets. Printed on the door in white cursive was:

Brushing Up:
Covering the North Shore since 1980
Free estimates (978-468-4538)

A comforting aroma of coffee laced with frying grease greeted Oly as he entered. All except one of the counter stools were taken by various tradesmen wearing the requisite Carhartt gear. They hadn't noticed him until he sat down next to a gigantic man with black, spiked hair. The man glanced over at Oly as he took the stool. "Sorry, is this taken?" Oly asked.

The man took a sip from his coffee and looked straight ahead. "If my buddy shows up it will be." He lifted the cup again with two sausage fingers, its thick, porcelain rim disappearing beneath a bushy salt-and-pepper mustache. A detectable scent of Old Spice mixed with the greasy aroma made Oly feel queasy. Without asking, a middle-aged waitress who reminded Oly of Louise placed a mug of hot coffee in front of Oly. She giving him a menu when the man spoke to her.

"You just can't find any good help these days, Barb. Every friggin' day it's the same crap. And Mondays and Fridays? Ain't happenin'."

Barbara responded in a rehearsed manner that indicated she had similar statements hundreds of times over the years. She was the breakfast equivalent of the bartender. "Whatchya gonna do?" she asked. "Be a great place to work if it wasn't for the help."

"Exactly," the man said. "Exactly."

Barbara set down a paper placemat and silverware and then proceeded to ask Oly if he was eating. He wondered how she would have reacted if he had said no.

"Yes, the belly buster, please." Oly took a swig of the coffee, which was so strong it made him cough.

"Easy killer," the man said. "That stuff'll get you through the day."

Several of the men got up to leave, but the man stayed, accepting another refill from Barbara. "Looks like inside work today," he said, indirectly to Oly.

"Is that your truck outside?" Oly asked.

"Yeah, why, lights on again?"

"No, I just like the name."

"You like that? My wife thought of it."

The awkward pause that followed was interrupted by Barbara bringing a steaming belly buster plate of ham, eggs, toast, hash browns, and beans. "You're gonna need a nap after that," the man said, sipping again from his coffee. "Name's Bobby by the way. Montero. Bobby Montero. You're not from here I take it."

"Not exactly," Oly said. "I'm Richard. Olymeyer. Go by the name of Oly. I'm crashing at my brother's place a couple blocks away.

"You looking for work?"

"The last time I painted something was in high school art class."

"Did you miss the part I was telling Barbara about not being able to find help? You have two arms and legs and you don't look like a drunk. Works for me."

Oly smiled. "Four years of college and this is the qualification for my first real job. I wish I knew that several years ago."

Bobby waved over to Barbara for the check. "Let me share something with you, kid. I have a house on the Cape and more money in the bank than most of the college boys I know. Who said that 80% of life was showing up? He got that shit right." Bobby paid the bill, including Oly's breakfast, without saying a word.

"Thanks," Oly said.

"No worries. And if you show up on time tomorrow, I won't take it out of your paycheck. Gotta go chase down some drunks and finish a living room. See you tomorrow, 6:30 at the Dunkies off exit 7 in Manchester. Thanks again, Barbara," he said, getting up.

Oly watched Bobby Montero leave the restaurant and felt normal for the first time since he had returned home.

The mist had stopped when Oly left the warmth of the diner, but it was just enough to leave a chill in the air and add extra slush to the already-melting brown snow. When he got back to Andy's, several construction pickups were parked on the curb. The front door was open and two burly workers lugged twelve-foot sheet rock through the front door. Andy was bent over, fiddling with some wire connections to a new computer in the dining room when Oly walked in.

"Some serious work going on here."

Andy spoke without looking. "There you are. I thought you ran away. Where the hell you been?"

"Getting a life. Hey, I got a job at The Daily Grind."

"No shit. Dish boy?"

"No, not *at* the Grind. I met a guy from a painting company. He was complaining about not being able to find good help, so I spoke up."

"And how do you fulfill the good help requirement?" Andy asked, smiling as he finished the wiring and stood up.

"I survived two years in Africa and built a bridge."

"Great, did you tell him that?"

"Not exactly. I told him I wasn't a drunk and would show up. Those were his requirements."

"Hmm. Well, I think you're good on one of those."

"Funny. Funny man. One small problem." Oly muttered.

"Let me guess. You're supposed to show up to work tomorrow but your Big Wheel is still in mom and dad's garage."

Oly was glad he didn't have to ask Andy for the help. "I've got some things to do tomorrow but I can drop you off at the train, that okay?"

"And if I say no, where does that leave me?"

"Good point. What time you need to be there?"

"6:30am"

"Bastard."

CHAPTER 33

AU CHANTIER

———

JANUARY, 1993

ON A CHILLY JANUARY MORNING at 6:25am, two full-sized Dodge Ram pickups stacked with ladders and scaffolding frames idled next to Montero's black Ford F-250 in the Dunkin' Donuts parking lot. The dull thump of a stereo bass and the scent of cigarette smoke greeted Oly when he walked up to the trucks. Montero rolled his window down. "Didn't think you'd show up. Right on time." He looked past Oly for his point of origin. "You walk? Where's your ride?"

"I got dropped off. Crashing at my brother's place."

One of the men returned from Dunkies, holding a tray full of extra large styrofoam coffee cups. Montero grabbed two and handed one to Oly without asking whether he even wanted one. "This is Mo, Paul and Buddy," Montero said, taking a sip. They nodded at Oly, appearing somewhat surprised that Montero had brought on new help. "Well don't just stand there, assholes, say hello or something."

One by one, the three men reached out a hand and shook Oly's, saying their names as they did so. Buddy, muscle bound with tattoos and a crisp white t-shirt, nearly crushed Oly's hand. Paul, lanky and somewhere in his late twenties, wore a soiled Bruins baseball cap and a black t-shirt with the phrase *Chicks Dig Me* printed in white letters. Mo was stocky and overweight, and had a sarcastic look on his face as he shook Oly's hand. His hands were chubby and calloused and he reeked of cigarettes. He wore a fluorescent pink t-shirt with various paint stains on it. "Watch out for him," Montero said, when Oly and Mo greeted one another. "Mo can be cranky in the morning. Drink your coffee, big guy."

They all sipped their coffees for a few minutes, while the fumes from Montero's rumbling diesel wafted over them.

"Where you from?" Mo asked.

"Essex."

"A clammer, huh?" Mo said with a smirk, looking Oly up and down.

"I've actually never clammed."

"Then what the hell are you doing in Essex?"

Oly felt like a new prisoner in the ward, having to either prove himself or forever submit. "I'm suckin' cock," Oly said, not smiling "You wanna see?" He puckered his lips while maintaining his gaze on Mo. Buddy and Paul burst out laughing, giving Oly permission to break off his gaze and smile, slapping Mo on the shoulder.

"Okay, ladies, let's hit it," Montero broke in, looking at the crew with curiosity at what they were laughing at.

Oly climbed into Montero's truck, a move that instantly offered him both protection but also resentment from the crew. The inside of the vehicle was a working man's temple. Nothing was out of place and there wasn't a splatter of paint anywhere. The carpet had the recent markings of having been vacuumed. It smelled like pine, and a small box of maps sat on the floor. The storage container between the driver and passenger was filled with new pencils and a calculator. It felt good for Oly to be back in something so American and so real. "Okay, Oly, here's the deal," Bobby started. "You'll figure this out on your own, but Paul is going to fuck with you. He's somewhat of a disaster and has a lot of shit going on. Wife left him; daughter won't talk to him. You know the drill. He works hard and I've known him for a while, but just don't let him get to you. He's an angry chap. Anyways," he said driving through downtown Manchester. "We're working on a big-ass inside job in West Gloucester. Monster son of a bitch with twelve-foot ceilings and shit loads of molding that they want a different color of course. You like painting ceilings?"

Oly lied and nodded his head.

"Good, then you and Mo can start up high and work from there. You bring your lunch? The little lady make you something?"

"No, I didn't. And I don't have a little lady."

"Lucky bastard. Keep it that way. Know what I'm sayin'?" Montero laughed and pounded the steering wheel with one hand. Oly gave a polite chuckle and lowered his eyes. He felt a CD cover under his foot and looked down at it. Montero caught him staring at the picture of Enya on the front. "Yeah, I know what you're thinking. The guys give me shit about that all the time."

"No, really, I wasn't thinking anything."

Montero explained anyway. "I got high blood pressure. During the day I get all worked up, you know, and it helps me relax. Brenda got it for me. It's pretty good shit once you get used to it. I like that song Save the Whales. It's real peaceful. And I love whales and all."

"Sail Away."

"What?"

"It's called Sail Away."

"Oh, it is? You listen to it too, huh? You're a college kid, right? Smart guy. And here you are working for me, a drop out. Hey, at least you college kids show up on time, right Oly?" he said as he turned onto the gravel driveway of the West Gloucester house.

Montero hadn't held a paintbrush since 1987, when he discovered that the money was in getting the paint to the wall rather than putting it on the wall. He hired friends who couldn't hold steady jobs and spent most of his day buying materials and making sure everyone showed up on time. Mo Brancone, a local high-school-football-hall-of-famer-turned-Michelin-tire-associate-turned-security-guard, managed the crew with Paul Amarillo, his security pal and best friend since grade school. Paul's career trajectory paralleled Mo's. He quit the Michelin shop on the same day that Mo was fired for threatening a customer with bodily harm. They cheated their way through North Shore Community College together.

Neither could hold steady work, and grudgingly accepted Bobby being the boss. He was also the only one in the crew who didn't lose his temper with customers. Unrealized dreams made the men keenly focused on the drama of present life and all its trivial drama.

"We're on it, kid," Mo said, grabbing his styrofoam Dunkies from the cup holder and getting out of the truck. "Not one to give much advice, but keeping it shut goes a long way with these ham and eggers. Especially Paul." He took a sip and stared at Oly over the top of the cup, wondering how long he was going to last. Oly hadn't taken a step towards the house when he felt a tuck on the shirt around his neck. Bobby stuffed a handful of drop cloths under his arm and handed him a box of tools. "Last time I bail you out, college boy. Boys see me doing that, you're doomed. Start thinking ahead and go get 'em."

Paul gave Oly a *wassup* look as he walked by with the armful of supplies. Thanks to Bobby, he had passed the first test. The house was set back from the road and surrounded by old New England growth. The weathered shingles were peeling and Bobby took notice. Possible job in the spring. Rhododendron bushes and hostia clutched the front porch. A faint light flicked on in the living room when the men walked up on the porch, their boots creaking on the loose boards. An elderly woman opened the front door and smiled. A dog gave a half-hearted bark in the background. "Brushing Up ready to serve, Mrs. Henderson," Bobby Montero said in a soft, patronizing voice. Mrs. Henderson opened the door, releasing a waft of grandmother house scent: the attic smell with the faint remains of last night's dinner. Pot roast, most likely. "Wipe your feet, gentlemen," Montero said without looking. He looked around the cluttered living room when he walked in. The grandfather clock. Threadbare sofa with old afghans draped over it. Classic Yankee décor. Although, you could never tell how much money these people had, he thought to himself. The shabby ones were usually the most loaded. The men left their boots by the door as they walked in, one of the first impression 'graces' that Bobby insisted on.

"I tried to get my grandson to move the beds like you requested, Mr. Montero. I hope it was good enough for you to get in there."

"No worries, Ma'am. That's why I brought the muscle."

"Coffee? I think I got some cake here, too, if you like."

"Sure," Bobby said. "Now it's the two upstairs on the right, yeah?"

"Yes, that's it."

When they got upstairs, the beds had hardly been moved. "What the fuck?" Mo said, audibly enough that Bobby snapped his head around.

"Shut it, Mo. You and the kid pull 'em out in the hall. You can always go home and jerk off if you want." Oly was amazed at how quickly Montero transitioned between his customer-relations voice with Mrs. Henderson and his voice with the boys.

After the beds were moved, they spread out the drop cloths. Oly, being low man, had to make various trips back to the truck for step ladders, work lamps, the radio, several cans of paint, brushes, and buckets, putting his boots on and taking them off each time. Mrs. Henderson left a tray with several ceramic mugs, a platter of cake and a pot of coffee at the bottom of the stairs.

Oly tried to heed Bobby's advice to think ahead but found himself getting in the way, bumping into Paul when he tried to set up a ladder and stepping on Mo's foot when he set up a drop cloth. Everyone had a routine and a space. Oly decided to wait until everyone was settled. Paul was setting up a roller brush when he noticed Oly standing off to the side. He tossed a caulking gun to Oly. "College boy, grab your caulk and put it in those cracks," he said to the pleasure of Mo.

Montero poked his head in the door, holding a cell phone to his ear. "You boys behave now, I'm going to Magnolia to pick up a few things. No paint on the floor you giamokes. And keep the language down." Oly could feel a tightness in his breath as he realized that nothing could protect him now.

He got to work, caulking cracks and doing his best to smear the silicone without making a mess. He could feel the eyes of Paul and Mo on his back.

"Hey, Oly," Paul said. "You get laid last night?"

"No, why?"

"Cause you're caulking that wall like you got a hard on."

Oly didn't turn around but kept working. Thankfully, Mo turned on the radio to break the silence. The men finally settled into their space, each taking a wall in a large bedroom, and worked quietly for almost an hour, only interrupted by occasional laughter at the crude commentary of *Dennis and Callahan* on WEEI, a local sports talk station. One of the topics in between call-ins about the Celtics and Patriots was the new president's *don't ask, don't tell* policy regarding gays in the military.

"Who cares if you're a fag?" Paul said, dipping his roller in a paint tray. "You're shooting terrorists, who gives a shit."

"What about the shower?" Mo said, as he opened a new can of paint.

"Fuck you talking about?"

"You know … I don't want some dude staring at my cock," Mo answered, clutching the pants between his legs for effect.

"You wish some guy would stare at your cock." Paul laughed. "Speaking of cock, had another DJ gig last week. You should have seen the talent there. Holy shit."

Paul turned almost every conversation to sex. He was the most frustrated man Oly had ever met since Peace Corps. He prided himself on being the ugly friend with a brave heart. He could get girls to do things that better-looking guys could not. Getting girls to display tattoos in revealing locations and signing body parts were his go-to stories.

Oly knew better than to question their validity and he instead focused on the reactions of the crew. They were mesmerized in their own fantasy worlds, as Paul stopped working to detail his story. He put his roller down and talked, pretending to pull his pants down at the hip. "So she turns to me and says, *You wanna see my clovers?* I could barely get out a nod and she pulls her jeans halfway down her leg, like this." (He demonstrated). Paul let the fantasy sink and then started painting again with a big smile on his face, murmuring *Yeah I wanna see your clovers, baby* to the delight of the crew. Oly noticed that whenever Paul told a story, he stopped working while everyone else continued on. No one ever called him out on it.

The work banter made Oly think about the *chantier* in Togo and a similar feeling of being left out of the discussion. Even though it was rare that the villagers would let him work alongside them on the bridge, when he insisted on helping fetch water or dig sand, he was able to observe a level of communication that he completely missed when he observed from the riverbanks. Each day, one of the workers, a sinewy man from Affem with a torn straw hat and yellow teeth, would cease working and tell long stories to the delight of the men who continued to haul sand, water and cement. Oly never knew what the stories were about and felt like an outsider, but could tell that the man was very popular and offered much detail, whether or not the stories were true. It was similar to the experience of working with the Brushing Up crew. It didn't matter what the content was about, it was a distraction from work, a fantasy that allowed the time to pass. Oly considered telling them that Paul reminded him of the guy from Affem, but knew it would be awkward and fall flat. He feared that Paul would then have to one-up him with some racist epithet that would piss him off and turn confrontational, so he kept quiet.

After a commercial break from the radio rant about homosexuals in the military, Paul asked Mo if he wanted to join him on a DJ gig he was setting up for the weekend. Oly didn't mind not being asked, as the arrangements involved complicated excuses to get away from their wives, which Oly could never keep straight anyway. "You remember Ronnie Thompson's cousin? He's getting married on the Cape. We go down a day early to price a job and hit the party. You wanna do it?"

"Is there going to be any talent?" Mo needed to know.

"The bride invited her entire sorority and I think they're all going," Paul said, gauging whether the trip would be worth it.

"None of that crazy shit like last time, Paul," Mo said, pointing his brush at him. "My wife was not happy about that."

"Quit your worrying and loosen your skirt," Paul said, finally picking up his roller again after another long pause. Oly figured that he had done exactly twice the amount of work as Paul by that point.

The talk and the plotting swirled around Oly as if he didn't exist. An occasional comment would float his way but he was left alone to work, and think. It didn't get past the crew that he more than covered his share, which built up an acceptable level of respect. Keeping his head down, lost in his thoughts and the routine, centered him, but got him thinking about whether or not he was making himself more (or less) desirable to Samantha when she returned. *Look honey, I'm a painter!* he imagined himself saying to her, sarcastically.

On the third day of work at the house, Oly decided to break his silence with one of his old college memories. "Hey guys, I have one for you, but watch me as I talk *and* work." This made everyone except Paul laugh. He recalled in detail how two sisters convinced him to join them naked in a dormitory sauna. "They were drunk and dared me to. I had both of them going at the same time, if you know what I mean. We got caught by the security guard when one of them couldn't stop making noise, but it was awesome."

"Are you sure the noise wasn't calls for help?" Paul interrupted.

Without thinking, Oly flicked his paintbrush at Paul, splattering him in the face. Paul dropped his brush and glared at Oly, giving him a thousand-yard stare that terrified Oly. He hadn't been in a fight since grade school and figured that Paul got in them on a regular basis. He looked down at Paul's fists, which were tightly clenched and started to feel panic. Mo sensed that things weren't going to end well and put his roller down, stepping between the two.

"Take it easy, ladies. We don't need any paint spillage, if you know what I mean."

"I'll fuck you up," Paul said, picking up his brush and pointing it at Oly's head. "I'll fuck you up so you'll be eating out of a fucking straw." Paul's voice had changed in a way that made Oly think he was never going to challenge anyone like him again.

"Actually, he's right about that," Mo said, closing ranks on Oly. "That is something he will definitely do. Don't piss your pants. That was a good story, though."

They painted quietly after lunch, the tension hanging in the air as the mind-numbing debates continued on the sports radio. *What was going to happen with the Celtics after Larry Bird? Are the Bruins ever going to make any good trades? What do the Sox pitching staff look like?*

Late in the afternoon, punctuated by the fourth edition of sports radio hosts (same mind-numbing topics, different callers), Mrs. Henderson came up with stairs holding a tray of snacks followed by the heavy footsteps of Bobby. Oly was almost excited to see him. "Oh, it looks wonderful up here," she exclaimed, putting the tray down on a plastic covered side table.

Bobby said nothing and gave a skeptical look around. "Glad you like it, Mrs. H. These boys are good for something every now and then." Nobody spoke or turned to the two visitors. Oly noticed the change in the room. He didn't dare speak but kept moving his roller in the hallway, taking extra care not to splatter. Bobby came out in the hall to inspect.

"Well, you survived," he said, smiling. "I thought for sure Paul would have killed you by now. Probably why you're in the hallway. He turned his attention back to Mrs. H. "Well Mrs. H," he said, putting his hands on his hips. "Thanks for the treats and we should wrap it up today. Mo and Paul will make sure those corners are covered and we'll be out of your hair. Sound good?" She nodded and smiled. Mo quickly moved to apply some extra paint to the corners Bobby referred to.

Oly learned that quitting time was a loosely arranged moment when Bobby would come back from pricing jobs or running errands to schmooze and wrap up with the homeowner. Paul started the breakdown by cleaning his rollers and brushes and doing a final look around. When he walked by Oly, he poked him in the ribs, causing Oly to flinch. "Good story today, college boy. But stick to painting," he said, looking around the hall. "You're better at it."

When they were done cleaning up and filling their trucks with the equipment, the winter sun started setting even though it was only 4:30 in the afternoon. Oly noticed the men gravitating towards Bobby who was standing by his truck, handing out blank puffy envelopes as the men blew into their hands in the chilly air. Oly walked over, unsure, and waited. Bobby looked up after handing Mo and Paul theirs, which happened to look thicker than the one he was about to receive. "Not bad today, kid. You didn't kick over any paint and nobody gave you a black eye. Yet."

"Thanks, I think."

Oly noticed Paul and Mo peeling off their work clothes next to their trucks, changing in the cold to clean shirts. "What the hell?" Oly said, looking down at his paint-covered sweatshirt. We going out?"

"Rookie," Mo said, as he pulled on a tight black sweater.

"Hey," Bobby said, pointing his finger at Mo and Paul. "I need the kid tomorrow. That means I'm holding both of you responsible."

"Whatever," Paul said. "I think college boy can handle it."

"That's what I'm worried about. I'm not shitting. Either of you," he finished, hopping in his truck and revving the diesel before pulling out of the driveway, making Oly wonder if he was going to make it back to Andy's at any point.

Mo put his arm around Oly, who was still holding his thin envelope. "C'mon college boy, let's go make that envelope a little thinner."

They ended up at The Rhumb Line, a place Oly hadn't been to since he was first legal to drink. It hadn't changed much - even the dirty wooden floors badly in need of refinishing. Before they sat at the bar, three Coors Lights appeared. The bartender, an attractive brunette with shoulder-length hair and a black low-cut t-shirt, gave them a smile. "Hey, Justine," Paul said, putting his arm around Oly. "I want you to meet someone. He just escaped from a village in Africa and hasn't been with a white girl in years." She looked Oly up and down and had a concerned look on her face, throwing a bar towel over her shoulder.

"Too skinny."

"Whoaaa!" Mo and Paul said in unison. Oly took a deep swig from his beer.

"Yeah, but that's only the part you can see," Oly responded, putting his beer on the bar and looking Justine directly in the eye. She flipped her hair back and leaned over the bar, exposing cleavage that caused Paul's eyes to bulge. Putting her hand out, she invited Oly to lean forward, which he did. She cupped his chin in her hand and spoke softly.

"You want me to find out?" she said, having practiced her flirty moves behind the bar so many times they were now automatic. Oly felt himself getting aroused and had trouble keeping his composure. He was no match for the seasoned bartender and the female attention made him think instantly of Samantha and how much he ached for her. She grabbed his empty beer bottle with French-tipped fingernails and turned away from them, displaying hips in perfectly contoured jeans with embroidered pockets. She turned her head back before walking away.

"She just ruined you," Paul said, laughing at Oly. "Hey Mo, look at the kid. It's like he just saw a ghost!" he said, laughing and slapping Oly on the back so he almost choked. "A fucking ghost!" he shouted, laughing as he took a giant swig from his beer.

They stayed until Oly's envelope went from thin to empty. He didn't notice and didn't care that a hundred-and-fifty bucks in twenties was gone. What he did notice was that he was starving, still wore his painting clothes, and it was nearly eight o'clock. Justine's act put Samantha in his head and made her stick. He found himself staring at her several times and she caught him twice, giving a smile but then a quick look-away. She was definitely not interested, he thought to himself.

Mo's cell phone went off just as they sat down to a tray of greasy hamburgers that Oly tore into, fueled by drunken hunger. Mo's expression changed as he spoke into the phone, placing one hand over his free ear so that he could listen over the bar noise. "Yeah, I know, I'm just out for a few drinks with Paul. What? Yeah, I know what time it is. Alright, I'm coming. Jesus." He hung up and shoved the phone into his jeans without looking at Paul and Oly. "Fucking buzzkill," he said to the burger in front of him.

"I thought you already told her what you were doing?" Paul said, through a mouthful of food.

"I did. It wasn't really permission. I should have known."

"Wife rope. Damn." Paul said. "Just enough to hang yourself. Yeah, you should have known. Sorry."

Mo chowed his burger in silence and stood up, throwing his napkin down on the chair. "Think twice before you tie the knot, college boy." He gave Paul a man hug and stumbled off, waving to Justine as he headed out the door.

Paul laughed as he put his arm around Oly, breathing the stench of stale beer and pretzels on him. "Looks like it's just you and me, honey," he laughed, making Oly feel sick. "Don't worry, sweetheart, I'll get you home safe."

A half-hour later, he drove Oly home to his brother's place. Paul was a different person when he wasn't in front of the crew. He drove a red Chevy Malibu with a car seat in the back and old Cheerios on the floor. He asked about Peace Corps, where his family lived, and what he was planning to do next, as if painting were not the end all.

Paul let out a huge belch as he made the turn onto Andy's street. Oly was impressed with himself for remembering where Andy lived and with Paul for managing to drive drunk without crashing. "So, college boy, what's the plan? You gonna use that degree to hold up your paintbrushes or what?"

"Maybe."

The conversation was interrupted when they pulled up in front of Andy's. Oly jumped out and thanked Paul for the ride. His head was pounding. Paul reached his hand out. "Hey, college boy. Sorry about the empty envelope, but good work today. Don't forget tomorrow at Dunkies. You want a pick up?" he said, looking around as if to memorize the location.

"Sure," Oly said, feeling accepted. "That would be great."

For two months, well into the early spring of 1993, Oly fell into a routine that cleared his mind and made him feel for the first time since his return that living in the present wasn't so bad after all. Hard work, swearing, farting in the open, Italian cold-cut subs, and beer did the body and soul good—life was simple.

He had lost contact with Jeff but was counting the days when Samantha would return. He never mentioned her to the crew, fearing that it would reveal a side to him that could serve as ammunition. Every day after work he'd call his parents to see if she'd sent any letters. When they arrived, he ripped them open, usually tearing the Togolese stamps he liked to preserve that were glued onto the tissue paper-like envelopes. Her letters were almost always reassuring, catching him up on her projects, how much she missed him, the villagers, and whether the bridge was still standing. He wrote back to her twice a week, filling her in on details about everything in his life except for his employment situation. He mentioned the painting as an 'odd job' and would emphasize his mythological career ambitions before returning to small talk about pizza, family, his longing for her, and the weather.

The crew, meanwhile, had accepted Oly as a full-time member and even stopped making him pay for drinks. His envelope stayed full in his pocket. He worked hard, learned the rhythms of when to joke or stay quiet, and impressed Montero with his staying power, which raised his suspicions. One late afternoon, when they ran low on paint and quit early, Montero drove Oly to his brother's. Oly could sense something was coming by the quiet that led up to Bobby speaking.

"You're settling in pretty well, kid. Didn't think it would work out, but looks like you're on the crew. That how you planned it? Graduating to ham n' egger?" he said, peering over to Oly after saying *egger* with an edge to his voice.

"I have a dad, thanks," he responded, regretting the words as soon as they left his mouth.

Bobby took his eyes off the road as he turned the wheel onto Andy's street while he hit the windshield fluid button. It responded with an empty whirring noise. "Hear that sound? That's you," he said, ignoring Oly's dad reference. "You're spending all your money with these jamokes and going nowhere."

Oly reached for the door handle, wanting to escape Montero's intervention. "What's your point, *dad*?" Oly yelled, raising his voice at Montero for the first time.

Bobby hit the brakes hard in front of Andy's house. "Okay, fuck the advice," he said, as he jerked the truck's gear into park and surprised Oly with an uncharacteristic flare of his temper. He went silent and looked straight ahead through the dirty windshield.

"I'm sorry," Oly said, placing his hand on the inside door handle. "That wasn't right. I know you were just trying to help."

Bobby kept looking straight ahead and gripped the steering wheel, his knuckles turning white. "I gave up drinking ten years ago. I have a business and a wife. You have a lot going for you. Don't fuck it up. Don't be one of these idiots. They're like family, but I can't save them. I just watch the train wreck lives they have and it pains me to watch it. That's enough. Get the hell out of my truck so I can listen to Save the Whales."

Oly stepped out into a pile of brown slush that soaked his shoes and the bottom of his pant leg. When he was in the middle of swearing about the misfortune, the passenger-side window slid down. "I don't mean to add insult to injury, slush puppy, but things are going to slow down quite a bit, so we're just doing inside work until the spring."

"When were you going to tell me this?"

"Sorry, Mo was supposed to tell you today but I guess he forgot to. If anyone gets sick or we get a big job in the meantime, I'll give a holler, okay? Sorry, but sometimes it does suck to be low man."

Oly lifted a numb foot out of the slush. "Right, low man. Nice term."

"Hey, keep your chin up. Things will work out. We'll be in touch."

As the window went up, Oly could hear the first verse of Sail Away, the irony of which was not lost on him. He watched Bobby drive away, spraying slush in his wake onto the cars parked on the side of the road and thought about what a cold, heartless place America could be.

CHAPTER 34
SI TU SORS, JE SORS

———◆———

SPRING, 1993

GIVE UP DRINKING AND GET a wife, Oly said out loud to himself as he entered Andy's. Thankfully, there was no one home to overhear his phone call to Samantha's parents' house. It was a call he had been putting off for weeks, but knew that she would be coming home soon and he couldn't delay it any longer. He called three wrong Cummingses before he got the right one from information; it was Samantha's mother who answered. Her voice jumped an octave when she realized it was Oly, the man she'd mentioned so many times in letters home. "Oh, Oly, it's so good to finally hear your voice! Samantha has written about you so many times! What have you been up to? Are you in Boston? Did you know that Samantha's coming home tomorrow?"

"Yeah, that's kinda why I called."

"I think her flight might actually be stopping over in Boston if you want to see her."

Oly filled her in on the past month, letting her know of his successful transition and pending work with vague references to interviewing. She listened politely and acted impressed with how well he'd landed on his feet. After several more minutes of awkward small talk, she gave him the flight information. He hung up the phone with promises to possibly make a trip to meet the family and ended up staring at the paper, paralyzed.

Oly stood in the half-constructed room, the plastic covering on windows not yet installed billowing with the breeze outside. Cans of plaster and cut drywall covered the floor. Several screws and nails were strewn about the floor. The air smelled of fresh sawdust and paint. A work in progress. His brother had goals, ambitions, and was working towards them. He had a shrinking readjustment allowance, a menial job that paid for a drinking habit, and the dwindling hopes of a real relationship on a piece of paper. It made him think of the simple possibilities in America. Determination, good ideas, a bit of cash flow, a little bit of luck, and you could get stuff done. If only some of that could have translated to Togo, he thought, wondering if the bridge was still standing. A carton of drywall screws made a convenient seat as Oly sat down, clutching the paper with Samantha's flight info. Andy's car passed in front of the house, the tires making a loud slurping noise as it passed through the slush. Oly stood up and looked out as Andy backed into one of the spaces on the street. He put the paper in his pocket, wishing he had more time to think about what he was going to do before Andy came home. Oly watched him unload the trunk of several Home Depot bags and a heavy bucket of paint.

"I got it, I'm good," Andy yelled, sarcastically.

"I got the door, girlfriend. And I don't want to get my socks wet."

"Shit, this crap is heavy," he said, squeezing past Oly and dropping the paint on the floor. They must still be putting lead in it." Andy looked his brother over, inspecting him. "How you been, bro? Seems like I haven't seen you in a while. I got some paint for ya now that you're an expert," he slapped Oly on the shoulder.

"How's, what's it called, Brushing Out?"

"Up."

"Right."

Andy looked past Oly at the room and put his hands on his hips. "Things are starting to shape up. Drywall guy comes tomorrow, electrical almost done. Still waiting on the terminals and some furniture. Getting there, bro, living the dream," he said, in a way that got under Oly's skin.

"Oh yeah, the dream. Gotta have those," Oly said in a pathetic way that revealed more than he had hoped.

"C'mon, big brother, chin up. You'll figure it out. You're brushing your way to the top, right?"

"Asshole."

Oly pretended he had errands to run and asked to borrow the car. He didn't feel like being around his brother's dream and drove around the neighborhood, finding himself taking solace in an extra large roast beef sandwich at Nick's just a few blocks away. As the construction workers came in and out, most grabbing takeout bags with greasy bottoms, Oly wallowed in self pity as he debated whether or not to meet Samantha. He pulled the paper from his pocket and stared at it again. What would she think of him? Did she have a new boyfriend? Would she approve of his new line of work? He had hardly saved any money since the cash went mostly toward drinking, takeout food, and helping Andy with some of the house bills. He was treading water, something that would not go over well with her.

On the return to the house, he opened the car window and enjoyed an unseasonably warm breeze that accompanied the sounds of slush running under the wheels. Repressed memories of Jeff came to mind: imaginary voices telling him to get out of Dodge and stop wasting his time with the painting. He pictured Montero and Samantha standing side by side, arms crossed, shaking their heads side to side, disapprovingly. And what about Gunning? Was he ever going to call? He had his parents' number. Did he lose it? Oly forgot to ask his parents if they had heard anything the last time he dropped by to get letters from Samantha.

When he pulled up to Andy's, it was already getting dark at 5:30 in the afternoon. It was the time of year he hated most in New England. He missed the long days in Togo and his morning routine, accompanied by the sounds of the waking village. What he really missed was that everything was outside and accessible. Food, markets, neighbors. In America, everything seemed hidden. You had to drive everywhere and make plans ahead of time.

Nothing was spontaneous and no one walked to places. You never saw your neighbors, especially in the winter. Oly wouldn't know if a family or a serial killer lived next to Andy. When he got back, he managed to squeeze the car into a spot in front of the house, bumping a large SUV at the back of him, hoping no one noticed. The roast beef had started to gurgle in his stomach when he stepped out of the car into a deep slush puddle near the sidewalk that soaked half of his leg.

"You *love* messing with me, don't you!" he yelled, looking up. "What is it? You don't want me to get too comfortable? You can't stand that, can you?" He saw his reflection in one of the windows of the SUV, his face scraggly and bearded, his hair in bad need of a cut. He had put on some of the weight he lost in Togo, but still looked haggard.

A stack of mail was sitting next to a phone in Andy's entrance that was propped up on a box of tiles against the wall. Even though he never got any mail at Andy's he flipped through the letters until he saw one in a light blue envelope with the distinctive red and white candy-cane airmail striping along the sides. Half of it was covered with Togo stamps featuring likenesses of President Eyadema and various government buildings and historic sites. It was addressed to his parents' home but had been forwarded to Andy's. He tore it open.

> *Dear Oly,*
>
> *It's been so long I hope that you are doing well. It feels like an eternity since you left and I'm glad that you're getting my letters. I love yours as well. Things here have been pretty much the same, except for Anya's (the rice-and-bean lady) baby dying of something. Everyone asks about you and, yes, the bridge is still standing. Have you seen much of Jeff? What are you up to? Anyway, probably no use in responding since I'll be heading back by the time you get this. It's really hard to say goodbye to everyone but I can't wait to get back and have a hamburger! I will be passing through Logan Airport March 27 if you get this in time and have a brief layover. It would be great to see you.*
> *Sam*

Andy came in from the kitchen. "Holy shit, I thought I heard someone come in. What the hell happened? You get hit by a snowplow?"

Oly dropped the letter on the table, ignoring his brother's question. "What's today's date?"

"Shit, I don't know. The 26th or something. Seriously, what the hell happened?"

Oly's mind was racing and he walked past Andy, dripping across the unfinished floor. "I don't know, I gotta go. Talk to you later." Even though Oly was still living out of a bag and had not done any shopping for new clothes, he knew exactly what he would wear to the airport. He also made sure to shave.

The next day came fast and Oly had hardly slept, his mind racing with what he'd say when he first saw Samantha and wondering what her reaction to him would be. At the international terminal doors, he took notice of the people who appeared to be arriving from Africa, many wearing the wax hollandaise panyas, badly underdressed for the Boston winter, their luggage piled extra high on the pushcarts. He imagined the bags stuffed with yams.

Oly thought of how long ago it had seemed that he came through the same doors, similarly underdressed and bleary-eyed from the long trip. He took out the paper with Samantha's flight information to check it for the umpteenth time. His stomach fluttered with anticipation. It had felt like decades since his family dropped him off at the same terminal less than three years earlier. He remembered how awkward it was with his brothers who didn't really understand why he was going away, and his parents who seemed stunned. He still had the old jean jacket he was wearing on that day, now with kente cloth attached at the collar. It was torn and dirty and somewhere in a box at his parents' house. His life had changed so much, but being back in the airport where it all started seemed so surreal, as if nothing at all had happened.

Oly's eyes locked onto Samantha as soon as she passed through the door, partially obstructed by a family pushing several baggage carts. She hadn't noticed him yet and was wearing the exact same shirt as he, a bright pink button down with open birdcages printed on it. Below birds escaping the cages was printed the words, *Si tu sors, je sors,* an expression that inferred both freedom and commitment. She finally noticed him, waving, and smiled in spite of the travel fatigue. Her hair was pulled back in a ponytail, allowing Oly to see how thin she had become since he last saw her. She was dragging a large bag behind her and wore a backpack caked with dirt from two long years of West African life. Oly's heart started beating fast as she got closer, their pink shirts gravitating like magnets. The man from the African family pushing the carts took notice of the two yovos in the similar dress and pointed, laughing and saying, "*Si tu sors, je sors,*" out loud.

Samantha stopped dragging the heavy bag and pulled the backpack off when she reached Oly. They hugged hard for several seconds. He stroked the back of her head and breathed in her smell. Neither wanted to be the first to peel away. "Nice shirt," Oly said, finally, causing her to release and step back.

"You too, yovo," she said, grabbing his lapel between two fingers and then stroking his face. "I missed you terribly. Look at you, American boy. You're all fattened up again."

He patted his stomach. "Nick's Roast Beef, right there. I had to make up for years of neglect. Speaking of which, can I treat you to your first American meal?"

They wandered through the Logan food court, Samantha completely overwhelmed and unable to decide on anything. "It's hard, isn't it?" Oly said, resisting the impulse to take her hand. "I went through the same thing. You think this is bad, wait until you go to the grocery store."

Legal Seafoods had comfortable seating at the bar and several screens above showing a Celtics game, which caught Oly's attention. The bartender, a young woman with curly brown hair and a crisp white shirt, smiled at the couple in matching pink shirts while she wiped down the bar. "Hmm," she smiled, as they sat down. "I think you two know one another from somewhere. Is that French? What does it say?"

Oly blushed when he looked at Samantha and translated for the bartender. "It means if you go out, so do I."

"Aww, that's sweet. Well, you both got that part right. What can I get you?"

Samantha was so tired; Oly ordered a drink for her and a combo plate of shrimp and broiled scallops. When the steaming plate of food arrived, she gasped. "God, this is amazing. I didn't realize how much I missed this food. Aren't you getting anything?"

"No, I'll just have a beer."

He watched her while the Celtics game filled the background with the comforting noise of an American sports program. "You look great."

"So do you."

"No, I mean it. I really missed you. You look great."

"Oly, you're embarrassing me. Has it been that long?"

"Are you kidding me? I've been counting the minutes. It's a lot harder to wait for someone, you know, than to be the one arriving."

"I guess.

"How's Togo? How's Bawendi and Chalim?"

"They're good. I didn't see Chalim much after you left. He seemed to really miss you, though, the one time I saw him at the Karibi. Of course, he wants to know why you haven't written. Bawendi had a baby that died. It was very sad. Then his mother died and he spent some time in her village. I didn't see much of him the last few months either. But it was really hard to say goodbye to them. I hated it." She picked up a scallop with her hand and popped it in her mouth, smiling afterwards. "Old habits die hard. God, I miss this food." She closed her eyes, savoring the food before opening them again to ask about Jeff.

"Shit, do we have to start on him during our precious minutes? Long story short, I ditched him after a nightmare in DC that I'll have to tell you about over much stronger drinks. He's been like a cold that won't go away."

"Touchy, touchy."

"It's not that. I keep thinking things are going to be different, that it can be normal to be around him. Then I get caught in some scheme and regret the whole thing. And then when I'm at the end of my rope, he pops up again. That's the extent of our relationship."

Samantha laughed, popping another scallop in her mouth. "I thought you'd never gain clarity on him. That's pretty good. But he brings out a side of you that keeps you going back. I don't think you're through with him yet."

"Whatever," Oly responded, feeling uncomfortable that she had so accurately assessed his friendship and turned the conversation on him. He drank his beer too fast, starting to feel angry, and ordered another. Her connecting flight was less than three hours away and things weren't going the way he'd hoped. The Celtics game entered the fourth quarter and they watched in awkward silence for a few seconds.

"So, I applied to law school at the embassy," Samantha offered, testing his reaction. "I don't know if I'll get in, but we'll see."

Oly tried not to think how that excluded him. "Where did you apply?"

"The usual. Chicago, Michigan, and a couple in Boston, of course."

"Where do you want to go?"

"Oh, I don't know, which one do you think would be good?"

"Chicago has terrible winters."

"So does Boston."

He felt pathetic and pleading, the exact opposite of what he had hoped to present. He reached for a french fry from her plate.

"Oly, this is scary for both of us," she held his hand. Oly started to feel embarrassed that she was the one consoling him. "I don't know where I'm going to end up, but it's going to take a while to figure things out. You must know how that feels."

A couple of overweight young men wearing Bruins t-shirts plopped down hard in the barstools next to them, bumping Oly's seat. Oly looked over, annoyed. "Nice shirt," one of them said, not bothering to apologize. "You two know each other?" the other added with a wise-guy smirk. Oly looked down at his shirt and feigned surprise.

"Holy shit, lady, who are you? Where did you get that?" The response pulled Sam and Oly out of their awkward moment, while the Bruins boys looked sheepish and went back to their beers. Oly took a large gulp from his beer and then wiped his mouth on his sleeve.

"So, do we know each other?" Oly said so only Samantha could hear. She played with her fork for a minute, looking down at her plate.

"Africa messed with my head. I just want to go home and settle in for a bit before I make any big decisions." She put the fork down and reached out for Oly's hand. "I have really strong feelings, Oly, but I'm scared. I really don't know what I want other than I just need to go home and sleep in my bed for a while. Alone." Samantha smiled, squeezing his hand.

After another awkward pause, Samantha glanced at the Budweiser clock. "So, what have you been doing?"

Oly didn't want to reinforce her uncertainty, but couldn't come up with a suitable lie for the moment. "Eating. Painting houses. Getting re-acquainted with life."

She let his hand go and turned to eat her last scallop, looking pensive, an expression that Oly interpreted as disappointment.

"Yeah, I know that look. You're unsure because you don't think I have my shit together. I knew you'd be like this."

"Like what?"

"All judgmental and shit."

She reached over, grabbed his beer, gulped it down and slammed it on the bar, catching the attention of the Bruins boys who nodded with approval. "Goddamn it, I just got off the plane wearing this ridiculous shirt to see you. I'm jet lagged, hungry, and have no frigging idea what's going to happen next. You've had time to get your feet on the ground." The bartender slid a fresh beer next to him without being asked, like a water boy at a prize-fight. They both looked at it and Samantha shook her head.

"I think I love you," Oly blurted out.

"You think?" she laughed, looking at the beer. "Was that you talking or your friend Bud?"

His head was swimming as he tried to pull his thoughts together on what to say next. "I meant I know, I think, I know I miss you and I think that…"

"Shut up," she smiled, reaching over and taking a sip of the beer. "I know exactly what you mean. I think, I know too."

"I've been invited to help out with some land dispute in Georgia."

Samantha reached for the beer and took another sip. "Talk about having no idea what's going to happen next."

"I'm not kidding. It's this group related to that guy who popped up with the Howard students in Tchamba. He kept in touch and they need me for something."

"What?" she said, sliding off the barstool, as she glanced at the clock again.

"I don't know exactly. It's something about descendants of slaves, some deal they're trying to make."

"Sounds dicey," she said, now standing and reaching for her carryon.

"What do you mean by that?"

"What do you think I mean? How do you know these people? What do they want?"

"They want me to go to some place off the coast to represent some non-profit group working on a land dispute."

"Really? And what in the world do you know about that?"

The Bruins boys looked up as Oly slid off the barstool. "Take it easy, pinkie," one of them joked, slapping him on the shoulder.

"I don't know anything about it," he said, surprised by the emotion in his own voice. "I don't know about a lot of things except that I…"

Samantha interrupted him by putting a finger on his lip. "I do, too. I just don't want you to get hurt so I can have you when I come back." She looked at the clock one last time and reached for her purse to pay.

"I got this," Oly said, realizing that his readjustment allowance was nearly wiped out.

Samantha threw her arms around Oly's neck, pulled him down to her and kissed him hard on the mouth, oblivious to the people around them. Off to the side, the Bruins boys started clapping. "That's what I'm talking about," one of them said.

After several seconds, disengaging, Samantha grabbed her bag. "I gotta go. You gotta go. We'll figure this out, but I need to go home and get my feet on the ground. Literally. I don't know what this thing is about that you're going to but watch your ass, I'm going to need it later."

Samantha turned to him when they reached the security line, her eyes filled with tears. She pulled on her shirt and held it against Oly's. "*Si tu sors, je sors.* I'll be in touch and let you know what happens with the college thing."

Oly started to feel anxious and sick, like she was saying goodbye for good. "Yeah, well I'll let you know what I'm up to. He handed her a coaster from the bar on which he'd written his brother's phone number. "Here. And say hi to your folks for me."

She wiped her tears with a sleeve and hugged him. They both shook as they started sobbing, his head nestled in her hair. Samantha pulled away first. Oly's face was red and tear streaked. Passengers were gawking at the oddly dressed, crying couple. "If I follow what our shirts say then I'm supposed to get on that plane with you."

She held his hand up to her lips and gave it a kiss. Oly watched with the same sadness he had when he looked at Bawendi and Chalim for the last time. He tried to slow every detail into slow motion, blocking everything else out and preserving the moment for what may become his last memory of her. They tried to keep eye contact almost the entire time she wound through the security line, as if they were the only two in the room. She blew him kisses, smiled, and wiped her face with the back of her hand as he waved.

Oly felt light-headed when she was gone. He walked in a daze back to 'The T' (the subway) and didn't remember how he got on the right train to the North Shore. When he asked the conductor, he got a funny look that reminded him of what he was wearing. An overwhelming fatigue fueled by emotion washed over him when the train pulled slowly from the station. He planted his head against the dirty window and stared at the grungy junk-filled backyards of Lynn pass by. The blur of trees and houses was exactly how he had felt since he'd been home. He pictured Samantha at ease, sitting back on a comfortable plane ride home, plan in hand. *She always had a fucking plan,* he thought to himself. She had seemed more well adjusted than him and she wasn't even home yet. He wondered if he had made a mistake in not getting on the plane with her or if the moonshot to Georgia was going to make him feel any more normal.

Andy was asleep when he got back and had left a light on. A yellow post-it was on the refrigerator: *Jeff called, wants you to give him a ring at this number.*

CHAPTER 35

BARPCV

SPRING, 1993

THE BOSTON AREA RETURNED PEACE Corps Volunteers (BARPCV) was the local organization of returned volunteers known for their cookouts, their work in the Boston public schools, and their softball team. Oly had resisted contacting them earlier because he wanted to see if he could move on without clinging to the past. He pictured them all sitting around in their bad yovo panya shirts, guzzling Bière du Benin from some boutique liquor store and lamenting their unemployment status. Along with the community projects, the BARPCV produced a friendly newsletter full of essays, goings on, career advice, and details on the latest get-togethers. It was an oasis of hope for the scores of bearded folks, living in their parents' basements, draining their readjustment allowances, and wondering what the hell happened to them.

Annie Cotter, a legendary RPCV who served in the Philippines in the 1960s, hosted an annual cookout at her house in Concord. It was tomorrow. She had become well known throughout the Peace Corps community as an activist, party-thrower, and overall maladjusted returned volunteer. Oly couldn't hold out any longer. He took the latest newsletter that had been forwarded to Andy's from his parents' and read the listing for Cotter's party. The cookout announcement said that "goat and other third-world delicacies" including local brews and potions, would be on hand. He wondered if there would be any other Togo RPCVs in the area that would attend.

Oly couldn't believe he was putting on a purple *complet* that he hadn't worn since he got home. "No, you aren't," Andy said, handing him the keys.

"Yes, afraid I am." Oly said.

"I don't know you anymore, older brother."

"That ain't the half of it," he said, jogging to the car with an enthusiasm he hadn't felt in months.

Annie's house was not visible from the street and he passed the over-grown dirt driveway three times before he spotted the rusty mailbox obstructed by vines. The word 'house' did not properly describe the dwelling, as it had an earthen roof and was built into the slope of a hill. The angle of the open side was constructed to face the sunrise, so that solar heat penetrated the living space and heated the black slate floor. Two cisterns designed to collect rainwater guarded both corners of the roof. A variety of wind chimes, accompanied by the tired bark of an aged golden retriever planted on the side porch, greeted Oly. Several vehicles and motorcycles were parked in various directions in a neighboring field. A beat-up Volvo station wagon with a rainbow sticker on the rear window. A vintage Triumph 400 road bike with a leather backpack attached to the rear. A modified green VW campervan with rust on the doors. It looked as much like a movie about returned volunteers as it did an actual event.

Oly gently pulled into the bumpy field, feeling self-conscious and hoping that he didn't bottom out. A bearded man wearing a tie-dye shirt peed out in the open with a cigarette hanging out of his mouth. His head turned to Oly. "Hey, man, no Republicans allowed," he yelled, the cigarette bouncing up and down on his lips as he zipped up.

Oly slammed the door as he got out. "Oh, this old thing? It's just to throw off the cops. The trunk is full of weed."

The volunteer laughed and gave Oly a hug, nodding at Oly's *complet.* "Nice threads, *chef. Afrique de l'Ouest?*"

"Yeah, how did you know?"

"Name's Ted. I was in Benin. Ninety to ninety-two. I think I recognize you from some party we had at the beach.

"Yeah, maybe. All you bearded types start to run together after a while.

"Cool. C'mon, man. Welcome to the party. Let's get you a beverage and introduce you." He put his arm around Oly and led him to towards the distinct, gamey scent of goat and burning hair.

"Ah," Oly said. "That takes me back. I can almost taste the baseball-glove meat now."

Alice Cottrell's appearance dispelled any notion that it was necessary to fully readjust to America after living overseas. A faint scent of incense lingering behind her, she hugged Oly a bit too hard, holding on a few seconds too long as she went on about how glad she was that he'd made it. Below her Carole King hair in shades of chestnut brown with streaks of grey, she wore a floor-length, tie-dyed summer dress with prints of giraffes on it. Thirty-five years after her departure from Manila, Alice looked like the maladjusted volunteer—a nebulous condition that isolated RPCVs both from America and from their countries of service.

"This here is Oly, from Togo," Ted announced. "Now, I'll got get you some liquid refreshment while you two get friendly."

"I'm so glad you are here," Alice crowed, arms raised in the welcome stance. "Now, where did you come from?"

"North of Boston."

"No," she smiled, "Where did you *come* from?"

"Oh, right, you mean posted. I was in Tchamba, Central Region."

"Oh, that's great. We have lots of Africa people here. Scott's over there with his wife, Comfort. Over there is Linda Watkins—she was in Gabon—and there's some other folks over there by the goat. The pond's great for swimming, so please make yourself at home. *Maligayang pagdating.*"

Oly's mind drifted towards Samantha, wondering how she would have reacted at the party. *Freaks,* he smiled to himself. Jeff would have been right at home. Scott Herrick and his wife, Comfort, met after his first year in the northern part of the Sahel of Niger. She was working at a local health clinic and he was weighing babies. He said he couldn't resist a woman named Comfort and 'had to have her.' Out of curiosity, Oly asked Comfort how she liked America. Like a child on the first day of school, she looked down at the ground and quietly whispered, "Ees okay."

Scott cut in. "Comfort's taking English lessons. Show them what you can say."

She didn't look up. "I like America fine."

"What do you like about it?" Oly asked.

"Teevee."

"What else?"

"People rushing all the time. Everybody run, run," she said, pumping her arms back and forth like a runner and laughing as she looked over at Scott in a seeming gesture for approval. "I know the feeling," Oly empathized, looking to Scott who finished the conversation.

"She's having a little difficulty adjusting to the pace. I brought her into Boston on The T and I thought she was going to pass out. We're trying to take it slow. She spends a lot of time in the apartment, but we're doing better. She has no way to communicate with family, so it's been a challenge." Comfort continued to look at the ground as they spoke and looked very sad.

Oly tried a Kotokoli greeting and her eyes lit up with excitement. "*Ca prends du temps,*" he reassured her.

In contrast to the RPCVs, a small group of nervous-looking young people in regular t-shirts and jeans stood sipping beers in plastic cups, trying not to look astonished at the strange behavior of the veterans. Oly watched as a haggard RPCV in a flowing yellow and purple panya shirt walked over to them, chewing on a charred goat hoof. One girl, wearing a Wesleyan t-shirt, recoiled as he approached her and belched.

Samantha and Jeff, Oly thought to himself, smiling as he walked over to intervene.

"Hey, buddy," Oly said to the man. "Annie just told me they're firing up the sotoubee shots. You better get over there!" Like a dog whose master had just thrown a tennis ball, the man dropped the hoof on the ground and stumbled in the direction of the house.

"Thanks," one of the recruits said, sipping his beer with relief.

"Hi," Oly said, eyeing their clean skin as he inhaled their intoxicating fresh smells, remembering the time he first met Samantha at The Relais. The group semi-circled around Oly, sensing him as a low threat while they introduced themselves.

A thin recruit, wearing a tucked-in blue polo, looked at Oly with nervous eyes. "The Peace Corps office put us in touch with Annie to give us an 'experience at speaking with returned volunteers.'" Oly laughed, looking behind them at a congo line that had started to a popular Brazilian tune blaring to distortion from the house.

"And how's that going?"

The girl in the Wesleyan shirt spoke up. "I don't think I want to join anymore." Oly paused, imagining Samantha having a similar reaction if she had witnessed the party for the first time. He thought of the glaring differences between the returnees and the recruits, wondering if they knew how difficult it would be for them to come back home once they 'crossed over.'

"It's okay," Oly replied. "They're just letting lose. A lot of people don't understand what it's like when you get back. They're just being themselves, slightly intoxicated." They nodded and stared as Oly explained, mesmerized like a group of med students watching their first surgery with the chief resident.

"Right," said a recruit wearing a Bush/Quayle 88 shirt.

After a few more minutes of small talk about where they were from and where they were going to be posted, Oly gave them assurances about how it was going to be alright and change their lives forever, so long as they didn't get sick or mede-vaced. "Toughest job you'll ever love," he finished, feeling stupidly trite as he walked away.

When Oly rejoined the group of RPCV revelers, he felt at ease, almost comfortable with the hoof eaters. His anxiety had lifted since he first stepped off the plane. He wasn't judged and no one asked him what he was going to do next. It was instant acceptance. It was hard not to imagine how Samantha and Jeff would have liked the party. He had considered asking Jeff but wasn't in the mood for the likelihood of dealing with his drunkenness and getting him home.

It turned out that Annie's was a nice halfway house. He sat on a stump, watching the badly dressed African RPCVs telling old stories, sharing laughs with Comfort. He imagined that Jeff would have embraced the scene, but Samantha would have lost her patience. He started feeling ill and didn't want to be asked why he needed to leave so he wandered off without saying goodbye. When Oly got to Andy's car, he heard muffled voices coming from a Volvo station wagon parked nearby in the field. The car was rocking back and forth and he saw two mounds of pale white ass flesh rocking back and forth, occasionally touching the side panel window. He couldn't get into Andy's car without looking. When he opened the driver's door, it bumped the Volvo and the fleshy mounds stopped, abruptly and just hung in the air. They then rolled off out of view and he could make out two blurry figures rolling around, reaching for crumpled clothing. Oly waved, not knowing what else to do. The couple ignored him, paralyzed like animals in the wild trying to blend in with the landscape.

A waft of burning goat-hair smoke washed over him, making him nauseous. A loud thumping noise started in the distance as a number of the partyers banged away on several of the drums that Annie had displayed in her living room. It reminded Oly of the late nights in Tchamba when he lay awake in his bed sweating, alone, unable to sleep from similar drumming in the background. At the time, he recalled that all of the feelings of loneliness and displacement would disappear if he could just hold out for the return to America. Now he wondered if the feelings would ever go away.

CHAPTER 36

PETIT COMMERÇANT

———◆———

LATE SPRING, 1993

ANDY WAS HALFWAY THROUGH A bowl of Captain Crunch, reading the newspaper, when Oly came down the next morning. Andy was wearing a Doors t-shirt, but his hair was always perfect. Corporate casual. He looked up and grinned. "Hey, Shaggy, how was Woodstock?"

Oly found it hard not to put Andy's comments in a condescending light. The tension of being the oldest and feeling less successful had created a constant tension. "Oh, you know, leave your clothes at the door, tofu, incense, reefers and the like. You're just jealous. When's the last time you made it to a party where everyone was naked?"

When Oly told him about Comfort's 'discomfort,' he looked up from his bowl. "That's crazy. Why do guys bring those women home? Is that allowed? It sounds creepy."

"What? Haven't you heard of the ex-pat boost? These guys do twice as well as they'd do with American girls. The women are ten times better looking than anyone who'd give them the time of day in the States. Second, not that I advocate for this, but the women are totally dependent on them and some guys get off on that. The sad part is that it's usually bad for the girls if they're not educated or in a city where they can get out and see other Africans. Comfort told me she stays in and watches the tube nine hours a day, waiting for her husband to come home."

There was an awkward pause while Andy looked back at his magazine, pretending to flip through, but seeming distracted. Oly knew he wanted to say something, but he didn't bail him out by asking. He poured himself some cereal and waited. Oly's sense told him that it probably had something to do with the downstairs almost being completed and him ready to open shop and throw his brother on the street. Then there was the girl Andy had been seeing and she probably wanted to move in and didn't want the brother around. "Yeah, I know what you're thinking, your car is all muddy from the summer of love festival. I'll wash it."

"Yeah, thanks," Andy said, without looking up.

"There's been something we need to talk about."

"Okay, the hair in the sink. No toilet paper. It wasn't me but I'll replace the old roll next time."

"Funny. You're enjoying this aren't you because you know what I'm going to say."

"Oh, let's see. You are almost finished dry walling downstairs. This girl you have been dating seems unable to be around when I am here. What am I missing? I'll pack today."

"C'mon, you are not moving out today. Don't be like that."

"Like what? You know what they say about relatives and dead fish."

"We're having the opening this weekend. I don't want it to be awkward for you."

"I think I got over awkward when I asked my younger brother if I could sleep on his couch. I'll get over it."

Andy's Internet café, to be named 'The Connection,' had gone from the downstairs living room in a dilapidated three-family walk-up to a completely refurbished, air-conditioned example of information-age entrepreneurship. The sky-blue painted walls had been complemented by a local artist Andy had commissioned with gigantic likenesses of Scooby Doo, Mickey Mouse, Darth Vader, and various Star Wars landscapes. It was a computer-nerd fantasy playroom. The ribbon-cutting ceremony was attended by friends, their parents, his brother Brett, a few clients he had designed websites for, and Rachel, the mystery girl.

Oly's parents gave him a sympathetic look when they first saw him, and his mother touched his cheek like she did when he was little. "Are you doing okay, sweetie? You getting enough sleep?"

Oly's father shook his hand and gave him a hug, but there was an insincerity that Oly felt, as if they were estranged. "How you doin', son?" he asked, patting Oly on the shoulders after the hug. "Hanging in there?" The expression on his dad's face revealed a pain that Oly had not noticed before. Oly knew that his dad struggled with an inability to solve problems, made worse by the inability to understand them. Oly's quirky readjustment to America ticked both boxes.

"Yeah, Dad. I'm fine. Andy's been good. I've been interviewing at a few jobs and I'll be out on my own before you know it."

His father seemed taken aback by Oly's calling him out and cut the conversation short by looking over his shoulder at Andy. "Okay, son. Well, you know we're here if you need anything," he finished before heading over to the group surrounding Andy.

Brett noticed their father walking away from Andy and went over to fill the void. He took a swig from a beer and belched at Andy. "From prodigal son to problem child."

"What makes you think that?" Oly responded.

"I went to college while you were away, big boy. I know Dad's disappointed face from miles away." He pointed the neck of the beer bottle towards Andy, surrounded by a group of people, including their parents. "Looks like you've been knocked off the pedestal. Good run though," he smiled, taking another swig. They both watched the group in silence. Oly was surprised at the insight of his little brother. "Don't worry about Mom and Dad," Brett continued. They're just freaking out worrying about you. Just don't be too honest with them. They can't handle it."

Oly had not remembered ever having a real conversation with Brett and felt emotion creeping into his voice. "Along with great power comes great responsibility," Oly said, grabbing Brett's bottle and taking a swig. "I hope he can handle it."

"Ladies and Gentlemen," Andy announced from the middle of the group that had been gathered around him. "If someone would please cut the lights." Several seconds after a guest flipped the switch, Andy turned on a neon sign that had been hung in the front window. *The Connection is Open* blinked as the group cheered. Andy proposed a toast, hoisting a champagne flute with a strawberry stuck to the rim, while the other arm wrapped around Rachel.

Brett poked Oly in the ribs. "Top of the pedestal, buddy. Top of the pedestal." In a strange way, Oly felt relieved as he watched his brother raise his glass.

"Excuse me," Andy continued. "I am sorry to interrupt the festivity, but would everyone please grab a glass and join in. He paused while everyone grabbed a glass and looked around the room for a few seconds. "To The Connection. May she always be true, reap dividends and friendships, and never, ever crash." The audience bellowed with a parliamentary *hear hear* as Andy held his glass aloft. "Okay, that's good for me, now let's get that music back on," he finished, before giving Rachel a kiss.

Brett clinked Oly's glass. "Where you gonna sleep now, big brother? I know you're not going back to Mom and Dad's."

"Who knows? Maybe I'll build a mud hut in the front yard and start raising cattle. You think that will get their attention?" Oly was feeling buzzed and lightheaded from the champagne, which blurred his thinking. He felt his little brother staring at him.

"What?" Oly said, annoyed.

"Nothing. I'm just proud of you, Oly. I know this must suck, but I never could have done what you did. It's pretty cool."

Oly felt a burning at the corners of his eyes. "Quit messing with me, asshole."

"No really. You set the bar for me. I know you're dying watching all this, but what you did can't compare. You'll get back on your feet." Before Oly could respond, Brett looked over his shoulder. "Here comes Dad and Mom. Sober up."

Oly felt his parents coming up beside him, one on either side. They were standoffish, as if sensing Oly's vulnerability. They had their coats on, ready to leave the party. "It's so nice to see you boys together again. We're so proud of you," their mother said, while Oly and Brett looked at one another. Oly's dad had his hand out to him. It was always the weird formalities that bothered Oly when his dad didn't know what else to do or say.

Oly ignored the hand and put his arms around his dad, patting him on the back. "Thanks for everything, Dad, I appreciate it," he said into his ear, while he held the hug. "I'm not moving back in, so don't worry."

His dad pushed off lightly and looked at him face to face. "I wasn't worried, son. You know you're always welcome. Your mom and I just don't think it's the best thing for you. Things will work out. You know we're always here for you."

Brett looked awkwardly towards the door, watching several guests putting on their coats and heading out. "Well, looks like this is our cue." Oly watched as his parents and youngest brother walked out of the house, imagining it could be a long time before he'd see them again.

Andy and Rachel were sitting on the couch watching Oly when he turned into the now-empty room. He wanted to laugh because they looked just like his parents did when he was in high school and they wanted to talk about something. "Hell of a party, bro'," Oly said before Andy had a chance to direct the conversation. Oly knew that Rachel had put him up to something.

"Yeah," Andy said, taking a sip from a Heineken.

"You turning the sign on tomorrow?"

"Nah, a few more days. I need to have the electrician check the power on the server before it's official."

"Listen, I already have a few leads on places and I'll be out in a few days. I'm really happy that you're…"

"I'm not kicking you out, Oly, so relax," he said, taking a confident swig from the Heineken while Rachel watched him, looking slightly disappointed. She focused on Andy's mouth while he sipped, in that annoying way new couples do when they think everything about their partner is amazing. Andy put the bottle down on the table. "I already have a plan for you to help me get started."

Top of the pedestal, Oly thought to himself.

CHAPTER 37

LA VERITÉ

―――――――――

LATE SPRING, 1993

EVEN THOUGH OLY HAD TO move into Andy's side of the duplex and crash near his bedroom door, the plan that Andy devised included Oly minding the store from midnight to five a.m. to capture the creepy all-night crowd during his initial opening. He wanted to say no and stick to painting during the day, but Andy needed him, and the guilt of living rent free was convincing enough.

The people who came to The Connection after midnight seemed as though they had been waiting for this moment their whole lives. A regular group quickly formed and Oly knew them all by name. Paul wore the same Def Leppard concert t-shirt every night. Terry was a weather scientist and came religiously to log onto the new online libraries that he could access around the world. Anita was a real-estate broker who was moonlighting to get in on the new online shopping business so she could follow her dream of selling doll collectibles. Then there was Frank who spoke to no one, wore a creepy brown suit jacket, thick glasses, and always sat at terminal six. Oly noticed that his hands were dirty, not from doing anything like gardening but an urban-grime kind of filth that most people would have washed off.

One evening, as he tried to look over Frank's shoulder, Oly decided to open up an email account with America On Line to see if, somehow, he could find Samantha. After a painstaking amount of searching every online directory he could find in the Chicago area (with a little help from Terry), he came upon several Samanthas with the same last name until he finally found the one that matched her last address. He opened up his first email account under togoyovo.com and sent a simple test message to Samantha, unable to mask his desperation. *Finally joined the digital age. It's hard to be in the same country but not with you. Let me know if you get this message. Oly.* He then did a search for Professor Gunning (who was much easier to find), and sent a message laced with a similar desperation. *Dear Professor; I hope all is well. I thought I'd use my new email account to reach out to you to see the status of your project. I am very interested in pursuing this initiative and look forward to your response. I do not check this email much but you can also call me at (617) 468-7865.*

Days after sending the emails, Oly found himself logging into his account several times an hour, wondering if Gunning or Samantha even checked their accounts.

One evening, as he sat at a terminal, constantly refreshing his 'inbox' to see if it had changed, he looked at the surfing histories of the customers to make sure that no one was running a gambling ring from the house (Andy had warned him about the number of ways the café could be shut down). Some of the links indicated that terminal six (Frank's) were from a number of illegal but somehow unblocked child porn sites. Oly printed out the history to show Andy, whom he rarely spoke to as they worked opposite hours. Andy seemed impatient with Oly, as though he knew of the problem but didn't want to be lectured by his older sibling.

"Oly, can you just speak to the guy and tell him to knock it off. Maybe it was a mistake." Oly considered the word. *Mistake.* He had made so many mistakes. Letting Samantha go at the airport. Moving to his parents'. Working for his brother.

"Andy, if he's soliciting kiddie porn on the Internet and it's traced back here, the FBI will crawl up your ass, so to speak."

Trying to look concerned, Andy glanced at the sheet. "You look like shit, Oly. Get some sleep. Why don't you take a couple of days off? I can close up during the night if you want. You've got bags under your eyes. Look, I know Frank is a sicko, but for every one of him, there are a hundred clients who don't abuse it. I'm trying to put up more firewalls. But the less access I give, the fewer clients I get. These cafés are springing up like weeds and word gets out fast on the censored ones. It's business, Oly. You wouldn't understand."

Oly felt the anger well up inside him at being patronized by his brother. "What the hell does that mean?"

"Nothing. Sorry I didn't mean it like that. Don't worry about it. I just mean that I'm running a business and there's some risk involved. You know about risk, right?"

"Yeah, I know about risk. I just want to know why you think you need to talk down to me like that."

"Relax, Oly. What's your problem?"

Oly paused, tempted to lay into his brother for his answer to the question. He took a breath and decided against answering, knowing that once he started he could not guarantee that he could pull himself back. "I don't think we need to get into that. Look, I want to thank you for letting me crash. I've obviously overstayed my welcome and I'll be out in a couple of days."

Andy could practically feel Rachel pushing him into the confrontation from behind. He knew it was his chance to cut Oly loose but couldn't do it. He could sense Oly's vulnerability and it wasn't worth it. "Okay, let's back up. You're right about Frank. Cut him loose. Or I can. It's not worth it. It would kill my business overnight. Imagine the headlines, "Client breaks The Connection." Andy felt relieved when Oly smiled, taking the lifeline.

"Alright, well, we're still friends, but I'm moving out soon so you and Rachel can start procreating."

CHAPTER 38
ÇA FAIT LONGTEMPS

——◆——

LATE SPRING, 1993

"*OUI, ALLO?*" JEFF ANSWERED THE phone in French, his voice sleepy, with a tinge of hangover.

Oly paused. "Yovo?"

"*C'est qui?*"

"*Ta mère.*"

"Oh, Tchambaaaaaahhhhh! *C'est toi?*"

"*Oui, c'est moi.* Please switch to English before you get arrested again for destroying a beautiful language."

Jeff ignored him. "*Patron, ça fait longtemps. C'est toi, yovo?*" Oly refused to answer and waited. Jeff relented. "Tchamba too tense. He in America too long," Jeff said, starting to wake up.

"Cut the shit," Oly said. "You left me hanging in D.C. I know you were pissed, but man, you cut bait. That was weak."

"What do you want, man? I got enough shit to deal with." It was the first time that Oly ever heard Jeff annoyed. The distant sound in his voice bothered Oly at a time when he thought he was reaching out to one of the only friends he had.

"Sorry, Jeff. *Tu m'as manqué.* And you're the one who called and left a number." Silence. "Right. Anyway, I noticed from the number you gave me that you're back in my area code. How'd you get back, anyway?"

"Goddamn mail truck. Pooped out on 95 somewhere in Connecticut. Some trucker picked me up. I've been crashing at various places."

"Jeff."

"What?"

"*C'est à moi.*"

"I thought we were cutting the French shit."

"Right. It's my turn."

"I know what it means, jackass. For what?"

"To do what *you* usually do. Propose something insane that has a high likelihood of jail or injury. I met this guy in Tchamba way back. A professor at Howard." He was waiting for Jeff to interrupt but it was silent. "He is on the board for some group that is helping a bunch of African descendants off the coast of Georgia fight for land rights against casino developers. They asked for my help and now I'm asking for yours if it works out."

Jeff finally spoke. "You?"

"Yeah, me," Oly answered, annoyed.

"What do they want?"

"Yovos, you idiot." Oly was beginning to think that including Jeff was a bad idea. "They don't have any whites on the board and they need a yovo to go down and testify for them. I had dinner with him and a friend of his in D.C. shortly before I left and asked the same question. For some reason, being a Peace Corps Volunteer qualified me to do it. What do you think?" To Oly's surprise, Jeff didn't answer. "Hello?"

"Yeah, I'm here. Sounds sketchy."

"Hmm. I guess it does, since tripping over one president and stealing cashews from another is normal."

"Bitch."

"Yovo."

"Isn't Samantha back by now?" Jeff asked, surprising Oly.

"Why? What does that matter?"

"I was just wondering," Jeff responded without a follow-up.

"Just wondering? About what?" Oly was starting to get angry again. "About whether or not I could handle it?"

"Hey, I didn't say anything, man. I was just wondering."

Oly felt angry at the distraction. Samantha said she needed time to get her feet on the ground and apply to law schools. The painting, Internet café and temp jobs were going nowhere. The project seemed the perfect distraction. Until Jeff messed with him.

"You don't have to be so touchy, man. I was just wondering. That's all. Seems like you're guilty or something." After a pause, Jeff said he'd think about the potential offer. It was the first time in their relationship that Oly had proposed something that made Jeff think.

"I'm living at my brother's and just threw myself out."

"What?" Jeff paused on the line for a moment. "I'll think about it," he finished. "I've got some shit to sort out."

"You do that, then call me." Oly gave him a new phone number. *Montero.*

The next day, before he walked out from Andy's with the hockey bag again packed with his earthly belongings, Oly sent an email to Frank, pretending to be from the FBI and attached a note to Andy's computer, thanking him for everything and wishing him all the best. The taxi he had called idled in front of Andy's house, a Buick Century with a missing hubcap and bad suspension that caused it to tilt to one side. Boston Cab was written in cursive on the banged up door and the toxic fumes from the exhaust wafted over Oly as he walked to the car. He gave Andy a hug and promised to keep in touch.

"Hey, man," Andy said, looking sad for his brother. "Stay in touch and do me a favor."

"What's that?"

"Quit starting over."

Oly was surprised by Andy's insight and tried not to be angry by the advice. "Toughest job you'll ever love," he replied, hugging him tight. "And thanks for letting me crash. I won't forget it. Tell Mom and Dad I love them, too."

The driver got out to help, interrupting the goodbye. "You two done?" he asked impatiently, giving the hockey bag the once over.

"Looks like a breakup move," he said, hoisting the bag with a groan, completely oblivious to Oly's annoyed expression. The cabbie's indifference to his reaction reminded Oly how refreshing it was to be around people who simply called things like they were and didn't give a rat what others thought. Montero.

"Where to?" he asked, slamming the trunk lid on the bag.

"How much gas you got?"

"Believe it or not, you're not the first person who has asked me that. You wanna go city or country, coast or inland?"

"I'd like to do all four, but I got a friend I need to drop in on, so to speak." When Oly reached for the front door handle it was his turn to ignore a disapproving glare. The cabbie grudgingly moved several notebooks, pads of paper, and a worn Bruins cap to make room for him.

"Sorry, I like to ride in front. Makes me feel part of the action."

James Weldon (according to the identification tag mounted on the dash), pushed the button on the meter and waited, saying nothing.

"Oh, right, sorry. Can I make a quick call on your phone?"

James picked up the handheld phone attached to a box between the seats and handed it to him. "You're pushing it, buddy."

CHAPTER 39

LE PATRON

———◆———

SUMMER, 1993

"MONTERO," THE VOICE ANSWERED, BUSINESSLIKE, waiting for instructions. Oly paused.

"Hello?"

"Yeah, I was wondering if you have any high ceilings that need painting." Oly heard some muffled sounds as if Montero were moving off a ladder or getting to a place he could talk.

"Hey, what's going on kid? Me and the boys were just talking about you the other day, wondering what you've been up to. You're not really looking for work already, are you? I told you I'd call."

"Work? No, not exactly. I'm in a cab outside my brother's house and the meter is running."

There was a pause and more ruffling. Montero was moving out of earshot of the crew. He got back on after a minute. "I'm not one to ask a lot of questions when people are in trouble but I am assuming you've already ruled out your family."

"It's complicated. I've played that card. It'll only be for a few days. I promise. I'm planning a trip."

"Right. We all are. And the girl?" Oly paused, not answering.

"Yeah, I thought so," Montero responded. "Forget it. We'll talk about that later. 98 Odell. Beverly. Key is under a brick on the walkway. Don't scare my wife, she'll be home in a bit. Maybe I can squeeze you into the next job. You do realize the boys are going to ruin you."

"Thanks."

Montero hung up without responding. Oly knew that it was a stupid desperation move and he hated himself for making the call. Montero probably had enough problems. Oly handed the phone to the cabbie and thanked him.

"Anything else, pal?" James answered, looking annoyed.

"Let's go for a swim on the backshore." Oly loved the ocean in the winter. It was the time of year when nature rested and prepared for the onslaught of tourists in the coming months. The breakers on the backshores of Beverly and Gloucester mesmerized him as the cab drove along the water's edge. The sun was especially brilliant without the hazy humidity of summer and its reflection sparkled on the tips of waves. A lobster boat chugged along, its occupants in orange rubber overalls reaching over one side as the winch pulled in a string of pots.

"That's the life," Oly said, cracking open a window.

"Yeah, that's what everyone says. You ever done that in February when it's raining out there and the rollers are making you puke? Eight years of that shit was enough for me. This is my boat now," he said, tapping the steering wheel.

"You lobstered?"

"Yeah, back when it paid. Don't pay shit now. Fuel, insurance, guys quitting all the time. It was the pits. No boss, though. I loved that part." Oly gave James the address after they completed a tour along the coast of Magnolia and Gloucester's backshore. They passed two houses that Oly and Montero's crew painted the summer before.

Montero's house, in contrast to the hard exterior that he presented, was a picture of Old World Italian-American comfort. As an ironic twist to the expression that the painter's house is always peeling, the colonial was wrapped in beige aluminum siding. It was as if the house were airlifted from East Boston where Montero grew up and onto a plot of land on the North Shore. Oly overpaid James with his dwindling cash reserves, forcing a smile and assistance with removing the hockey bag from the trunk. James gave the house a once over and looked at Oly. "Couldn't help overhearing your conversation in the car. All the best, kid," he patted Oly on the shoulder and drove off, leaving Oly standing on the side of the road with his bag, a memory of the Tchamba drop off that felt light years away.

Oly lifted several bricks before finding the key and hoped that the neighbors hadn't noticed and called the police. He let himself in and let out the obligatory *hello?* even though he knew no one was home. A worn fabric couch with a flowery pattern sat beneath a framed reprint of Fitz Henry Lane's Gloucester Harbor. The kitchen was the original, with worn wooden cabinets, a gas stove, cast-iron pots and pans that hung over a center island, and a casement window over the sink that looked onto a robust garden. The faint smell of a home-cooked meal from the night before still hung in the air. Framed pictures of Montero's family hung in a hallway that led to the staircase upstairs. He picked up the small painted model of a wooden fishing boat that was on a windowsill and stared at it for several minutes. It didn't seem right to feel more at home at Montero's than his parents'. But without the reminders of his childhood and the feeling that he was going backwards after Peace Corps, Montero's was perfect. A home without baggage.

Oly explored a bit more and walked down the basement stairs to a half-finished veneer-paneled space that smelled like the musty warmth of a wool sweater. He lay down on a bed that had several boxes piled on it and fell into a deep sleep. After what seemed like hours, the door at the top of the stairs opened, spilling light into the now dark basement in the late afternoon.

"You better be folding laundry down there!"

Oly was startled by Montero's voice and jumped up. It took him several seconds to remember where he was. "Oh shit," he said to himself, wiping drool from his mouth and heading up the stairs. Oly's hair had all the signs of sleep and he squinted his eyes when he reached the light that filled the first floor.

Montero's wife was stirring something on the stove and turned around. "Em, this is Oly, owner of said hockey bag that you nearly tripped over, causing you to almost call the police because I hadn't told you we were having company. Oly, Em, the love of my life." She smiled and reached out a hand that was soft, yet delivered a firm handshake. Her green eyes penetrated his with the confidence of a woman who had known hard work and lived a full life. "You don't look good. Go upstairs and take a shower. You don't have to sleep with the laundry you didn't fold. There's a guest room up here by the back room that's yours. We eat together every night at six sharp. You won't be late, and as long as you're here you're family. Got it? Oh, and I might have a big house in Gloucester coming up that you can work on. Depending on how much you eat, I may or may not pay you." Em gave Montero a look. "Just kidding. We'll worry about that later. And when you see the boys, do yourself a big favor and don't tell them this is your new home, but I guess you could figure that out yourself," Montero said, smiling as he slapped Oly on the back with a force that nearly separated his shoulder.

Oly had a sense that Montero's lack of judgment and questioning meant that Montero was no stranger to hard luck. It was hospitality without strings, a helping hand in desperate times without the politics of family. Though it was never openly discussed with the boys, they all knew that Montero had battled for years with a severe drinking problem, losing jobs and often being carried home by the guys. Though those days were long past, Montero knew what it was to reach out when someone was down.

Oly sat on a creaky bed in the guest room, his mind swirling with what he was about to enter with Gunning. He felt a desperation that seemed insatiable. Being in Montero's house made him want to go back to his parents and start over. *Call Samantha, get this over with. Start a life.* He looked at an old Radio Shack computer on a small desk cluttered with binders of customer billing records. When he clicked it on, the cooling fan made a loud noise that Oly hoped Montero couldn't hear. Minutes later, he managed to log onto his email. There were two messages waiting for him, one from Samantha and the other from Gunning. The subject line in Samantha's email read The Future while Gunning's simply stated fact: Plan A. He read 'The Future' first.

Hey Yovo; I wanted you to know that life is good in Chicago but that I miss you terribly. I feel like an alien in my own country. Everything moves so fast around me and I can't make sense of it all! My family is good and it's so nice to eat regular food again. I think I've put on a few pounds. I have some news for you! I was going to call your parents to find out where you were but thought email might be better. I got a fellowship from Harvard and will be coming east in a few weeks! Si tu sors, je sors I guess! Let me know what you are doing, I can't wait to hear. Although Oly was hoping for more, she signed it simply, *Samantha.*

Before he even read Gunning's email, Oly feared it would interfere with the good news from Samantha. *Good day my friend,* it began. *A series of events is beginning to unfold that may have created an optimal opportunity for you to join us on our march towards justice with the Friends of Sapelo. I am wondering if you are still interested in this venture, as we are preparing in the next few weeks to commit our resources and time to this project and its success. Please respond accordingly and we'll proceed. I hope this email finds you in good health and well-being. Sincerely, Professor Gunning.*

CHAPTER 40

LA LUTTE

THE SWEETNESS OF NEW ENGLAND summer had arrived and Oly was back in the routine with the old crew, perched on the scaffolding of an old Gloucester house with a view of the sparkling harbor, daydreaming whether he would ever see Samantha again if he decided to go to Sapelo when she came out. He decided to delay his response to Gunning but wrote back immediately to Samantha, expressing his enthusiasm for her decision without filling her in on his own dilemma.

The job was a gigantic colonial that was in bad need of repair. Many of the clapboards were rotten and needed replacing which slowed the work down and it had all kinds of peaks and gables that caused the boys to curse. The paint was peeling from everywhere, exacerbated by the salty sea air. It should have been painted five years earlier and, to top it off, the owner wanted a color change. Brown to white, the worst. The crew surprisingly welcomed Oly back with little questioning or the usual crap. Even though it had only been the winter months, he felt they had missed him and there was a sense that he was down and out, something they could all relate to and knew when to back off. Though Montero and Oly had arrived together, no one dared mention out loud the possibility that he was crashing at Montero's. Their quiet acceptance of Oly and healthy fear of Montero protected him. Oly volunteered to scrape the high dormers, the high areas, and the boys left him alone. He worked harder than ever, as the simplicity of physical labor focused his thoughts on one task at hand.

After several days on the job, on a day when the sun hung high and steady in the sky and the ocean breeze finally started to turn a bit warmer, Bobby showed up with the envelopes, which meant that they were just about done with the project. He had a smile on his face. "Gentlemen, even though it took you twice as long as a real crew, you done good and we're going to chill for a few days." Mo's mouth opened, but Montero raised his hand before he could speak. "From painting that is. You're still gonna work and you'll still get paid. I made a little wager with an old friend, shall we say, and I need your help. You too, college boy. You ever been in a boat before, other than your daddy's yacht?"

"Actually, I rowed crew for three years."

"What, one of those girlie boats that you can lift over your head with one hand? I'm talking real working boats with real working men. Seine boats. Ever heard of them?"

"Actually yes, they were called that because of the seiner nets that they used to surround the..."

"As I was saying," Montero interrupted, turning to the crew. "Time's a wasting and as much as we'd like a lesson from crew boy, we need to get our asses in shape. And fast. And speaking of fasting, you all need to lay off the sauce until we win this thing." He glared at the crew for a response. Mo winced but said nothing, although Montero was daring him to.

"What's that, Mo? You got something for daddy?"

"You paying us?"

"Damn straight. Bonus if we win."

"Where we going to get a boat?"

Montero glared at Mo. "Just show your sorry asses up at the State Fish Pier tomorrow afternoon."

The rest of the day was filled with conversation around who would sit where in the boat, on which side and, of course, who would steer. "I would think Bobby would steer, don't you?" Mo said, scraping a section of window.

"Who the hell knows, he's such a control freak he'll probably want to be in front," Oly answered.

They finished the final side of the house in less than two hours and had everything stacked up on the trucks by 5:30. Montero was quiet on the drive home, and Enya kept them both in their own thoughts. "You know something about Seine boats?" Montero broke the silence.

"A little bit."

"My father and his father worked these boats when men set sail, not diesel, to make a living off Georges. You know how the races started?" Without waiting for a response, he continued. "They set the boats stern to stern and raced away from one another in a giant circle to surround the fish coming into the harbor. Whoever completed their half of the circle first, won."

"And your father and his father before him, how did they do?"

"All I know is that Monteros don't lose."

Even though Oly felt intimidated by Bobby at work, when they got to his house he treated him like a son. A stew simmered on the stove that filled the house with warmth, a reward for the long day and a reminder of Oly's homelessness. Em was on the phone and waved at the two as they entered. She reminded Oly of what he hoped Samantha would be like if they settled down. Warm, relaxed, loving, at peace. That was all he wanted. He knew it was the reason he delayed his response to Gunning. The table was already set.

"Okay, I gotta go," she ended the conversation, hanging up a heavy black receiver on an old Ma Bell original with a circular dial. She smiled at Oly and then turned her attention to Bobby.

"Hey guys. You finish that house?"

"That we did," Bobby answered, leaning over give her a quick peck on the cheek. She held her head up to him when he did it, an intimate gesture that made Oly feel awkward but accepted.

"You got anything else lined up?"

Bobby darted a 'shut up' glance over at Oly in case he was about to spill the beans about the race. "Yeah. Big one coming up near the shore," Montero said, winking at Oly. "Big job. Let's eat."

"Hmm," Em answered, sensing something by Montero's reaction. "It's June, big job coming up but you won't tell. It's nearly Fiesta time. I think I know what's happening. I thought we agreed that you weren't going to do these races anymore after the last time. Remember?" She said, looking disappointed.

"Yes, I know Em, but this is the last one. And I have to show the kid what it's all about. It won't be like last time. You know I've been sober for months and that will never happen again." Oly was surprised at Montero's openness in front of him regarding sobriety and was curious to know what *that* was but figured it was not good. Em didn't object again, but bowed her head for grace, slowly shaking her head.

Montero bowed his head, signaling for Oly to do the same. Oly managed to peek at the two with his head bowed, taking in the humble moment of quiet contemplation and modesty. He looked at the top of Montero's head, the top starting to thin and bald, several flakes of dandruff (or was it sawdust?) resting on top.

"Lord, we thank you for this humble meal, for this bounty that you have placed before us, and for the time that we have together on this planet. May our vessels float like St. Peter's in the storm and may all of your blessings be received. Amen." he finished, giving Oly a quick look when he opened his eyes. He quietly put a slice of meat in his mouth and chewed, winking at Oly.

"Amen," Em finished with a silent prayer of her own. "That last part about St. Peter was nice, honey. Thank you for those words and I hope he looks after you. You're going to need it."

"Of course, honey. I need all the help I can get," he said, looking at Oly to ensure that he kept his mouth shut.

The next morning, when they drove up to the Gloucester State Fish Pier after making a detour through a Dunkies' drive-thru in West Gloucester for four Big Ones (extra cream, extra sugar), Oly felt the happiest he had been since he left Peace Corps. Even if he joined Gunning's project, he'd likely be back by the time Samantha showed up. Things seemed to be taking shape for the first time since he'd returned. He had even managed to call his parents a couple of times to let them know he was working and found a place to stay (though he left that part vague). Andy had left him a couple of emails as well, thanking him for chasing off the pedophile and how much more misery his actions had saved him.

While Oly jumped out with the tray of coffees, Montero turned to his Tuff Box attached to the bed of his truck and pulled out a variety of tools. Cordless drill, duct tape, box of screws, and a bait bucket full of thole pins.

"We building an ark?" Oly said to Montero, as he carried the equipment towards the dock.

"This ain't no college banana boat. This is the real deal."

"So real you didn't want to tell your wife?"

"So real you say that again you'll be pulling these pins out of your arse."

Oly distributed the coffees and put his hands on his hips, peering over the harbor with his hand shielding his eyes. "Ayy mateees," he said in a pirate accent. "She's a blowin' a bit from the east but a fine day for a row, me laddies!"

"Beats painting, Captain Hook," Mo said, taking a sip. Montero led them down to the dock where the Pinta rocked gently alongside the Santa Maria and the Nina.

"Looks like a real speed demon," Oly said, giving the wooden vessel a once over.

"Less talk, more action," Montero jumped in, ignoring him and putting the equipment down. He started drilling at one of the footboards immediately, making adjustments. The rest of the crew gingerly stepped in the boat, attempting to keep balance without spilling their coffees. Mo sat down too hard on one of the benches, when the boat rocked, causing the lid to pop off his coffee and spill hot liquid on his chest.

"FUCK!" He screamed and threw the cup in the air, causing it to spill half in the boat with the styrofoam cup landing overboard. It bobbed up and down like a bathtub toy, while the men cracked up with laughter.

"Little ducky, you're so fun, little ducky you're the one," Oly sang.

Montero stood up in the boat, keeping his balance perfectly as he held the drill gun in his hand. He was not happy. "You bitches want to scrape some moulding today? I got a monster job waiting for you on Rocky Neck. High dormers and all. You want it?" The boat went silent, except for Mo who was reaching over the starboard gunnel, trying to grab the cup as it floated out of reach. Montero walked over the bench seats and grabbed him by the rear of his pants by the belt, yanking him back into the boat. Mo fell into the hull, getting soaked from a puddle of residual green rainwater that sloshed around him.

"Shit!" he yelled, looking down at his soaked pant leg.

"Oh, yeah, I almost forgot," Montero said, throwing the top half of a detergent bottle at him that was used as a bailer. "There's some water in there that may slow us down. We should probably take care of that." Mo didn't move, but grabbed the handle of the bottle and bailed the water around him. "Now that we're done screwing around, everyone take a seat, adjust your footboards with this here gun if you can handle it, and grab an oar. We got one hour on the water before the next crew. And from now on, you can enjoy your liquid refreshment outside of the boat."

Oly whispered to Mo, "He's fucking Ahab. All he needs is an eye patch." Mo stifled a laugh and taped a pillow to his seat with duct tape. Oly grabbed one of the wooden oars resting on the pier. It was ten times heavier than the fiberglass Dreissigacker oars he had grown accustomed to in college. Someone had stupidly hash-marked the handgrip with a knife, thinking it would offer an advantage. The only advantage to Oly was that it would efficiently rip all of the skin off his hands. He placed it between the thole pins and laughed, moving it back and forth. "I always wanted to be a Viking," he said to Mo, whose jeans made a squishing sound as he sat on the bench in front of him.

They slowly pulled away from the dock, Montero perched high on the stern with an enormous rudder that dipped in the water like a Venetian gondolier. He looked so proud, his face tilted towards the sun and the inner harbor. His hair, usually held in place by a generous layer of Brylcreem, flopped freely in the wind. He looked ten years younger.

When the oars cleared the dock and floated in the calm waters of the inner harbor, Montero looked around for other boats and held up one hand while the other stayed on the rudder. "Not bad for a bunch of stiffs. Sit up straight. When I hold my hand up like this, you get in the ready position. College boy, you should know what that means. Push forward until you can sniff the arse of the guy in front of you. Whoever is behind Mo, I give you an extra few inches. When I put my hand down, you take a stroke, nice and easy. On race day, you'll pull like it's your final hour, which it will be if we don't win."

Even though the gigantic boat with the cheese-grater grips and the wooden bench seats was as far as he could get from the sleek eight-man boats of college, Oly felt liberated. The pain combined with the singularity of their goal focused him. He couldn't think about anything but the sweaty back of Mo in front of him and Montero's screaming as he kept the cadence and controlled the rudder. He couldn't think about settling down with Samantha or his uncertain life on the road with Jeff. The only noise they could hear besides Montero's voice was the ka-thunk, ka-thunk of the oars as they rocked between the thole pins. After a half-hour, they reached the choppy entrance to the harbor and Bobby made them stop.

"Boys, this is it," he said, as they bobbed up and down on the swells, their oars slapping the water. "Nothing else matters in your life. Not your money problems, your girlfriend problems, your drinking problems, your life problems. That's all over there," he yelled, pointing to the shore. "There's nothing you can do about that when you are in this boat. What matters in this boat is the guy in front of you and the guy behind you. That is it. You are not one individual when you step into this boat. You are part of something bigger than that. If you understand that, this boat will reward you. It will speak to you. It will sing. You will feel it when we cross the finish. Now let's turn this thing around."

Oly felt at peace with Montero's blessing. His mind was totally uncluttered for the first time in months. He had a purpose. It made him think about his relationship with his brothers and parents and why it was so hard to reconnect. He didn't feel like he had to be something else in the boat, and it brought him a calmness he hadn't experienced when he felt like he had to be a brother or a son who hadn't changed. Without saying a word, the men turned the boat around and lifted it, in unison, across the water when Montero put his hand down for the return trip.

After the final of six days of practice, Oly and the crew met at St. Peter's Club, a windowless cinderblock building on Gloucester's waterfront. The Fiesta was the one time of year that non-Italians could enter, bypassing the retired cigar-smoking fishermen posted on benches outside like sidewalk gargoyles. The inside was brown, dimly lit and grim, littered with cheap tables and yard-sale chairs. It stank of stale beer and cigarettes. A cardboard tray filled with forty Meister Bräus arrived without even being ordered. Mo, Paul, and Oly drank until they couldn't see, while Bobby nursed a coke, watching with disapproval. The camaraderie made Oly feel dangerous and primitive. He wiped his face on his sleeve and belched. He grabbed his crotch and put an arm around Paul, telling him how he kicked ass on the water. Oly felt the primitive, live-for-the-moment side of him that he recalled from *La Chasse,* and instantly thought of Jeff, imagining him in the boat. One important lesson that moved with him from Tchamba was that life was so unpredictable, short, and difficult. His mind gravitated towards heading to Georgia as soon as the race was over.

As the trays arrived and the smoky room began to fill with the stench of sweat, Oly joined his teammates in a drunken dance of back slaps, hugs, and slurred profanity. "I fucking can't fucking wait until tomorrow," Oly spat at Mo and Paul. "This is gonna be the best friggin' race of our friggin' lives."

They clinked cans and spilled Meister Bräu all over the cheap card table. There was no small talk. Each man drank, swore, and looked about the room, staking his territory before the big day. Montero's efforts to get them to slow down went unnoticed, as he sipped one Coke after another, watching his team get hammered. He was forced to accept the rationalization that the bonding ritual might outweigh the responsible choice to stop and go home.

Oly half expected someone to urinate next to their table, marking the space like a timber wolf. Two hours into the revelry, the sound in the room shifted from a steady banter to a pocket of silence, followed by outbursts of profanity and violence. Amidst a flurry of *what the fucks* from around the room, the crowd turned their heads toward the violence. Oly caught a glimpse of Bobby Montero's head of spiky hair getting shoved by an over-tanned electrician wearing a fluorescent-pink tank top. Before Oly could assess what was happening, his entire table had cleared, knocking chairs to the floor. Unable to think clearly, his mind dulled to a blur with alcohol, Oly followed the bodies and found himself swinging at sweaty shoulders and faces with bulging eyeballs. Paul and Mo stood side by side, taking punches at the electrician with ham fists. Blood spattered on the man's fluorescent shirt and Oly could hear him wheezing. The sight, mixed with a nauseating scent of sweat, cigarettes, and alcohol, made Oly dry heave. He caught the wild eye of a smaller guy from a crew nicknamed 'Determination' who looked as though he was going to jump Bobby from behind. Oly jumped on his back and the man crumpled to the floor. The slaps and thuds of men hitting one another with bare fists was nothing like the movies, and it was sickening. Oly felt the numbness of the alcohol wearing off, replaced by the alertness of an adrenaline rush. His heart raced as he felt his body pushed against its will from side to side. He felt strangely aroused by the complete submission to primitive instincts he hadn't felt since *La chasse*.

A large body rolled behind Oly's knees and he fell backwards, hitting his head on the wooden floor. Dazed with the sensation of losing consciousness, Oly heard the barking sounds of more reasonable men, calling for an end to the fight. A strong hand grabbed Oly's shirt and jerked him to his feet like a rag doll. It was Bobby. A trickle of blood stained the corner of his mouth and he had several scratches on his neck.

The distant, angry sounds of approaching police sirens changed the dynamic in the room. Everyone shifted their attention to getting the hell out. The pugilists, now exhausted and a little less drunk, assisted one another in an orderly escape out the emergency exit. The electrician, his fluorescent tank in tatters and splattered with blood, held the door, signaling for everyone to get out. He patted Bobby on the shoulder, as he helped them out the door. "You got in a couple good ones for an old man," he said, as Bobby walked by.

"You know that guy?" Oly asked, squeezing through the narrow passage to the exit. "Shit, yeah, he does jobs for us sometimes. Good guy."

Oly and Bobby followed a small group of the men down the street. He noticed Mo and Buddy in the middle of the pack talking to two men, as they lit cigarettes and mimicked their punches. Oly's head was pounding and he felt like vomiting again. The shift from violence to camaraderie confused him as he struggled to contain the alcohol-fueled emotions of a few minutes ago. The police lights reflected off the surrounding brick buildings, as the cars screeched to an abrupt halt. Bobby turned his head while they headed down Rogers Street. "Don't look back, college boy. You think you took a few licks from these guys, wait until you get a nightstick over the head. Those are the real thugs. Keep walking."

A well-dressed couple leaving Captain's Courageous stared at the men, as the cops ran into St. Peter's to prey on the poor bastards who didn't get out in time. The crowd who got out hustled into The Old Timer's, patting one another on the back as they entered, friend and foe now united in their mutual escape from the police. Mo came up behind Oly and put him in a headlock, pretending to tomahawk him in the head with punches. The men laughed and ordered a round of beers. It was almost midnight.

Oly couldn't believe that the men who were moments ago trying to kill one another were now re-enacting their punches and putting their arms around one another, like staged enemies in a world wrestling match. Bobby stood off to the side, looking concerned, and checking his watch. "The missus is not going to like this," he said to Mo, as he held out his tattered shirt.

"Well, think of the bright side," Mo said, putting his arm around him. "You didn't get drunk or arrested. That's a plus."

After a bizarre ritual of hugs with the electrician who tried to take his head off, Oly and Bobby made their way back to the pier and drove home, not talking as Bobby prepared himself for an awkward entrance.

CHAPTER 41

VIVA SAN PIEDRO

———◆———

ON RACE DAY, THE HARBOR slept quietly and flat as if she, too, were hung-over from the prior evening. The team met at the docks and worked in silent appreciation of a waveless ocean. The men taped their oars and adjusted their footboards with cordless drills. The St. Peter's Club President, Frank DeNucci, dropped by and he wasn't happy. He had a stilted walk from a replaced hip due to decades hauling nets and wore a 'Good Harbor Fillet' hat that was perched lightly on top of his head, as though someone had placed it there.

Frank had directed the festival for twenty years and he didn't like bad publicity, not to mention the ration of shit he'd gotten from his brother-in-law, the police chief. Six arrests. Two resisted. Three assaults on officers, one of whom had to be hospitalized. "Gentlemen. A little bruised today, are we? I heard there were some extra-curriculars at our club last night." He paused, taking in the expressions of the quiet crew. "Huh, Bobby, you know better than that, no? I had the chief on the phone this morning, promising we weren't going to have any problems today for the cameras. I gotta cancel the race today Bobby or what, you dumb shit?"

Bobby looked up from a roll of hockey tape he was unwinding. "Do what you gotta do, Frank. The Portagees started it."

"Hey Bobby, look at me, you sonofabitch. My mother's a fucking Portagee. You wanna do something about that?"

The rest of the crew stopped fidgeting with the footboards and looked up. Bobby had used up his penance dealing with an inconsolable

Em, with his torn shirt and reassurances that he had not been drinking. Frank had fished the waters off Gloucester his whole life and had the scars to prove it. He did not like to be embarrassed in the newspapers as the overseer of a drunkfest. It didn't help that the electrician in the fluorescent shirt was his nephew. Oly could see Bobby's hand tightening on the rudder handle, as he took the humiliating tongue lashing in front of his crew.

"You're painting houses because of your attitude, Bobby. You and your boatful of drunks. You got no chance in this race, just like you had no chance of being captain of the *Duchess* when you drank like a fish rather than catching 'em."

Bobby's faced changed. For just a moment, he had a hurt look on his face, an expression Oly had never seen and hoped that no one else had picked up on it. Frank had stepped over the line, but didn't seem to care.

"Why don't you start the race and shut the fuck up." The words came out of Oly's mouth before he knew they were there. He was hung-over and angry, still not thinking straight. Bobby's head whipped around with surprised eyes, along with the rest of the crew. They could feel the air leave the boat as they braced for the worst: elimination from the race.

Frank tilted his hat back on his head and put his hands on his hips, putting his foot on the gunwale of the boat, as he stood over them from the dock. No one said a word as Frank glared at a face he didn't recognize.

He squinted his eyes and peered at Oly. "What did you say, kid?"

Oly could feel Bobby's eyes peering at the side of his head. In the wooziness of his headache, he somehow rallied enough strength to be reasonable and salvage the race. "I said, we disgraced the honor of St. Peter last evening and hope to restore honor to his name." Oly smiled at the end.

"You smartalec sonofabitch," Frank laughed, exposing a mouth full of missing teeth and gold fillings. "No shit. Where the hell you from, Beverly Farms?" He shook his head, laughing as he walked away. "Restore honor to his name," he said, repeating Oly. "You assholes got no chance," he yelled over his shoulder. "See you in the loser's circle with your loser captain."

Oly shrugged his shoulders and smiled at Montero and the rest of the crew. "I guess we gotta win now."

No one said a word as they finished taping, adjusting, and settling. They rowed out to the inner harbor in perfect unison, while Bobby gently steered them to the start at Niles Beach. Oly caught him looking down and cracked a smile before pulling back on his oar. Twenty minutes later, in the middle of a huge crowd at Niles Beach, DeNucci stood waist-deep in the water, directing the three boats to line up. Parting the crowds on the banks of the Niles like a pharaoh descending for a royal baptism, Frank always made a dramatic and last-minute entrance. No one knew why he waded out into the water, soaking his jeans, to start the race. He just did. He waved the crews of the Santa Maria and the Nina to pull up next to Montero's crew in the Pinta. Oly recognized several from the fight, their faces bruised. One had a full bandage over his nose. Bobby spoke for the first time since the confrontation with Frank at the dock to warn them to look straight ahead and not catch any glimpses of the other crews. "We're gonna shock 'em today, boys," he yelled. "We're the fuckin' SHOCKIHS. You got that, SHOCKIHS!" Everyone gripped their oars a little tighter, as they backed into position.

Montero knew that Frank was going to try to screw them and stared at their oars to try to catch them paddling backwards into position so they'd be slow off the start. He held the starting rope like a starting girl at a drag race and thrived off the attention. Often times, he'd send all three boats to row back and forward until it was just right, like a ref calling off hockey players at a face-off. The Nina banged oars with the Pinta, as a few swells from the harbor pushed the boats askew. Bobby's gaze on Frank was intense as they played a chess match at the start, a game of wills to see who would flinch. Frank could sense the restlessness of the crowd behind him, but held them off. Bobby watched Frank's left arm grip the starting rope as his right arm started to move, a gesture that meant he was going for his hat to start the race. "Ready boys," he barked. "Eyes in the boat. Stop looking around. Eyes in the boat. Here it comes."

The tension was unbearable as boat horns flared in the distance and the smell of sweat and tanning lotion wafted through the air. As crowds of tourists lined Stacy Boulevard, Oly heard the voices of some of the Determination crew members trying to get his team's attention. "Hey, pussies, you gonna taste some sweet eye-talian sausage today. Hey, you fucks. Yeah, you. You lissenin to me?"

Right as the rope started to drop and Frank lifted his hat to signal go, Bobby thrusted his upper torso forward and screamed, "NOOWWW!" What happened next was like slow motion for Oly. Everything in his life floated before him at once, in a blurry haze. Samantha, Bawendi. Tchamba. Jeff. Chalim. Gunning. He felt that moment of ultra calmness that people experience just before they are about to die. Then he flashed back to the present. The boat felt like it was on land, it was so heavy. He pulled back so hard he nearly fell back into the boat. The crowd erupted as the other boats thrashed next to them, a frantic unleashing of energy that was now out of Frank's control. The speed with which they stroked felt twice as fast as what they had practiced and Oly could barely keep up.

From his crew days at college, Oly knew the importance of controlling rhythm and heart rate, and he did his best to keep both in check. But circumstances quickly spun out of his control as Montero spewed saliva on them with his wild-eyed yells of "Stroooke!" and the ferocious pace got the best of him. The pace was way too fast. Mo's back came at Oly faster than he could move his twelve-foot oar on the return and he caught Mo's shoulder blades several times. Oly could hear Mo's "FUCKS!" over the thrashing sequence, but he was powerless to stop it. Barely able to keep stride, Oly committed the cardinal sin of rowing—looking at the competition.

The Santa Maria was pulling ahead next to them, so close that Oly could hear their grunts. Oly knew they were experiencing the same chaos and pain, but that it could only be felt in the boat. The distraction caused him to lose his rhythm and he panicked to catch up, sacrificing the force in his stroke. The Pinta was losing ground. Once this happened with the enormous barges, it was nearly impossible to catch up. It had become a two-boat race.

A blur of pleasure boats, kayaks and lobster boats filled with spectators passed by the periphery of Oly's vision. They neared the half-mile marker anchored off Ten Pound Island, but the backward facing rowers could only tell the proximity by Montero's reactions. He swiveled forward at the hip and leaned forward on each stroke, urging the boat forward while screaming at the top of his lungs. Oly tried not to glance up, but could not resist reading Montero's face with its eyes darting ahead to the approaching marker and side to side as he assessed the Santa Maria. Oly's mind started wandering, a survival instinct to distract him from the pain. Thoughts of Samantha made him feel weak, so he flipped to Jeff and then Chalim, which helped him to focus. Chalim and Jeff were chanting for him, side by side, arms around each other like European footballers before a big match. He imagined Bawendi for a moment, making a rowing motion with his arms and laughing.

Montero's eyes grew wide. They could sense the boat was approaching the marker. He started pulling back on the rudder handle and gritted his teeth. "Starboard oars ease off, port shorten stroke and dig it in!" he ordered, as they started the turn. It was all Oly could do to keep his oar off Mo's back, as his muscles seemed to move in slow motion. They could see Determination pull a half-boat length ahead as they sped into the turn without losing momentum.

"Shorten that stroke port!" he yelled, with a tinge of panic. They rubbed the orange flotation marker and several oars banged off the top of it. The boat started to lose control and slow down.

"Fuck!" Buddy screamed, as his oar popped out of the thole pins. Montero pulled the boat around the marker, nearly breaking the rudder by leaning his entire weight on pulling the handle back. Buddy put his oar back into place as they finished the turn with the bow headed straight towards the finish. The stern of Determination was starting to crawl past their periphery and pull ahead. Oly was in so much pain that he started to feel numb, moving back and forth barely keeping pace with the oar behind him. He couldn't get enough oxygen.

Then Montero's eyes lit up. He looked to the side and noticed one of the oars of Determination straight up in the air. "They broke a pin! They broke a pin! Gimme TEN, Gimme TEN NOW! Stroke ONE, Stroke TWO, Stroke THREE, Stroke FOUR…!" He went wild and the boat lurched forward. The stern of the Determination came back into view as they could now see that only half of the oars were moving, as they tried to replace the broken pin.

"Tits on the beach!" Mo yelled, which caused the boat to lift into the final strokes of the power ten. They started to pass Determination, one seat at a time. It reminded Oly of the Head of the Rideau from university when they had a similar upset against a talented crew from Queen's. The boat started to settle down once they could see the full boat of Determination passing behind them. They could start to hear the roaring crowd and the excited voice of the loudspeaker projecting from in front of the old Birdseye factory.

"Shockis pulling ahead! Shockizz pulling ahead in the Pinta!" the announcer yelled. Oly pictured Frank DeNuccci throwing his Good Harbor Fillet hat down in the sand.

Montero's voice had gone into a hoarse plea/chant, replacing "STROKE, STROKE" with "SHOCK…IIZZZZ, SHOCK…IZZZ, SHOCK…IZZZZ." Two jet skis with harbor patrol pulled up alongside of them like the motorcycle escorts in the Tour de France. One of the officers nodded his head up and down acknowledging that they had this. The noise of the crowd grew louder, as the spectator boats anchored along the course started to get more dense. Oly felt a warm wetness on his palms and knew it was blood. The pillow taped to his seat had shifted to the edge and he could feel a burning where the hard seat had begun to drill a hole through his shorts. Mo began to lose stroke behind him and rammed his back. The thud felt like a baseball bat. He couldn't breathe. The finish line was near. Thrashing the waves and the rocking motion of the boat, several of the guys began to pick up the pace as the burning in Oly's throat felt like a hot air dryer. He glared at Bobby like a rabid animal, as he called for one last power ten to take them onto the beach.

The white hull lurched forward in one last stubborn surge. An air horn blew. It was over. Montero jumped off the stern into the water and started thrashing the waves with his arms, as spectators ran to surround them and hoist him above their shoulders. Mo and Buddy started vomiting on their footrests and Oly threw his oar into the water. Oly watched as the crowd carried Bobby Montero across the beach on their shoulders to chants of "Viva San Piedro." As the sweaty bodies hugged one another and women in white capri pants took photos of their boyfriends who tried to hoist them into the water in celebration, Oly looked at the dejected crews of the Nina and Santa Maria, still sitting in their seats, many holding onto their oars, stunned by the fact that it was over and they had nothing to show for it. He trodded over to the Nina, sinking in the sand, his tired legs barely able to move, and looked over at the men, some of whom he recognized from the fight. Several Gatorade bottles floated in the dirty seawater that filled the bottom of the bilge. Oly put his hand on one of the tanned shoulders of the men who were slumping in their seats. "You guys got nothing to be ashamed of. You gave it everything today. We just got lucky."

"Fuckin' shockers. You shocked us, that's for sure," the man with the tanned shoulders said, dropping his oar and pulling his feet out of the foot rests. Oly looked over the rest of their crew and sized them up, as several cracked open cans of Coors Light handed to them by their friends. They were really taking it hard. None of them were moving.

One of them downed the beer in several gulps and crushed the can in his hand, throwing it into the water. He wiped his mouth with his forearm. "Get back to your party, buddy. Not every day you win on Saturday. I been doin' this shit for almost a decade and never won. Maybe next year. Thanks for comin' over."

Oly turned to face the crew. They were still hugging and pouring beer over one another, while a group of photographers took snapshots.

The crowd parted while two of the crew took over hoisting Montero in the air and paraded him up the beach to get their trophy. "The SHOCKIHS, ladies and gentlemen," a man said over the loudspeaker that was set up on the beach. "Let 'em through people. The SHOCKIHS, let 'em through."

Frank DeNucci was nowhere to be seen.

CHAPTER 42
Au Secours

———◆———

As HE WALKED UP THE beach, holding a cold can of beer that one of the spectators had given him, Oly felt completely in control for one of the first times since leaving Togo. He didn't question why he was doing what he was doing. He had bonded with a group of men focused on a single goal, which had filled him with restored confidence in the future. *Just get on with it* he thought to himself, shuddering at the thought of clinging to the past like the RPCVs at the Cotter's party.

When he got back to Montero's house later that night after a celebratory meal at the Gloucester House, he pulled out a leather pouch filled with African mementos and unwrapped the two rings that Bawendi had given him, placing one on his thumb and one on his index finger as he'd been shown. As he softly clicked the rings together, making a ding ding sound that, according to Bawendi, summoned spirits, he looked around the room, waiting for something to happen. Togo tugged at the edge of his life in America. While all of the men savored the rowing victory surrounded with friends and family, he had instinctively looked for a familiar face and saw none. He clicked the thumb and index finger together. *Click, click, click.* Why didn't he even tell his family about the race? He was starting to hate being a stranger in his backyard, yet he couldn't bring himself to reconnect with his old life. He had secretly hoped that Jeff and Samantha would have somehow appeared. But the race, in its painful way, had given Oly the momentum he needed to move on, to make decisions about his future. To readjust.

Montero came into the room and leaned on the door jamb. "Nice job today, kid. I didn't think you had it in you. What's the clicking?"

Oly held his hand up. "Oh, nothing, just something I picked up in Togo."

"Which reminds me, son," he said, calling him that for the first time. "Now that you won the race of races, what's next?" He folded his arms and looked down at Oly.

"Yeah, I was thinking about that. Not really sure where to start. I feel like I should have just stayed over there."

"Africa?"

"Sort of."

"You gotta keep moving forward, pal, not backwards. You know that. What the hell happened to that girl? You gonna hunt her down? That should give you some focus for a while." Montero reached for a phone that was on the bedside table and picked it up by the lip on the back, holding the base and handing Oly the receiver. "You ain't paintin' houses for me much longer. Decision time."

Oly hadn't memorized Samantha's parents' number in Chicago, but he remembered the town and called information. Seconds later, Samantha's mother answered the phone with a polite *Hello?* When Oly responded, her voice instantly jumped an octave. "Oly! Samantha has been trying to contact you! I'll get her right away."

He heard a clunking sound as the receiver was put down on a table and the sounds of muffled but excited voices filled the background. Montero shifted himself in the doorway and stood straight, smiling as he turned to walk away.

"Oly?"

"*Oui, c'est moi.*"

"What the hell? I've called your brother's several times and left messages! What is going on? Where are you?"

"Shit," Oly said to himself. Andy didn't exactly know how to reach him at Montero's, though he questioned how hard he tried. "I'm really sorry. I'm not at my brother's and I don't think I exactly told him where

I was. I'm crashing at a friend's place." Oly could tell by her quivering voice that she was getting upset.

"I got a fellowship to Chicago and couldn't pass it up. I wanted to run it by you to see what you thought, but I this is a really good opportunity for a poor RPCV."

Oly gripped the receiver as hard as he could and held it away from his head. He was tempted to smash it on the wall and held it out for several seconds.

"Hello?" she said, her words floating into the air. "Hello?"

He put the receiver immediately back onto his ear, trying not to sound angry. Montero glared at him not to screw up the conversation. "I think you should go for it," he answered, finally, trying not to sound upset.

"You do?"

"Yes," he said, trying to sound supportive.

"No you don't. I can tell you're disappointed."

"No, I'm not. I'm not disappointed. I just don't know where this puts us."

"It puts us in the future, Oly. I'm trying to prepare for that. I'm working on the long game."

"Yeah, I know that. But things change. You'll meet some dude at law school and I'll never hear from you again."

"That is a possibility," she said. "So, maybe you should come out here and carry my books for me so it doesn't happen."

Oly held the receiver again in his hand, unsure if it was an offer or just a challenge.

Montero glared at Oly, sensing that the conversation was getting tense. Oly looked up at him before answering. He didn't know whether it was the new confidence he had gained from the race or the reluctance of attaching himself to Samantha's dream just to be with her, but he didn't feel desperate as he had before. Oly nodded to Montero, indicating things were fine and that he could go. The moment Montero left, Oly focused back on the conversation.

"Why don't you find someone to carry your books and tell him all about how much you miss me?" he answered. Oly couldn't tell if she was surprised by his response, but knew that he had no chance of keeping her if he went, pathetic and unemployed. "I think I'm going to join the project in Georgia," he added.

"Wow, that sounds exciting," she said, sounding disappointed.

"You don't seem excited."

"I am, Oly. It's just that I hope you know what you're getting into. Please don't take this the wrong way, but it sounds like you're trying to re-create something."

"What?"

"I don't know. It's hard to explain. I don't want to make you upset." Oly felt anger growing in his chest, but tried hard not to react. "Where is this going to take you, Oly? Is this something that will help you move on? You could get a job in Chicago; I was only kidding about the book holding."

He paused, reflecting on the option. "No, I'd be in the way. You need to focus on this and I need to get my shit together."

Samantha didn't object to the *get his shit together* part as he had hoped. "Well, we'll see," Oly said, filling the awkward silence. "Maybe I'll need a good lawyer if it doesn't go well."

She laughed. "You might be waiting a couple of years."

"Yeah, I might," he said, feeling like he took some power back. The conversation ended with promises to stay safe and keep in touch, neither one knowing exactly where they stood, but knowing that their relationship was either going to stand the test of time or drift into a nostalgic memory.

When they hung up, Oly turned on Montero's computer and opened Gunning's email. *Send me the information about getting tickets when you can,* Oly typed.

Bobby and Em had already sat down to eat. A place was set for Oly. "I take it went well?" Bobby said, looking up from his soup.

Oly stood over the table and looked at the two, thinking briefly of his own parents but then of the decision he'd just made. "There's an expression I learned when I was in Togo. Man proposes, God disposes."

"She's God now, huh?" Montero joked, glancing over at Em. "Go wash your hands before you sit down, college boy. You got a big day of work ahead of you."

CHAPTER 43

Au Service, II

———

Summer, 1993

It had been over a week since Montero's crew had touched a paintbrush. It was a mixed blessing to get back to the simplicity of working the old routine for a paycheck. The girl and sports talk were overshadowed by the race for an entire week. Bobby was in such a good mood that he sprang for lunch two days in a row and let the crew off early a couple of days. Oly's status even changed. On a brutally hot day, where one of the high, sun-facing peaks was usually left for the new kid, Mo stepped in and grabbed the ladder. "I got it, kid," he said, pointing for him to do an area that was in the shade and didn't require a ladder.

Oly spent almost the entire day wondering if he and Samantha had kicked off a slow breakup. He knew that she was going to start a new life and that there was little chance she'd move out east. As he brushed back and forth in long, even strokes so as not to splatter the paint on the foundation or the flowers lining the outside of the garage, he obsessed over her comments about re-creating something. He knew exactly what she meant. He was falling into the old RPCV trap. Many returned volunteers ended up in Washington, clinging to the mother ship (Peace Corps HQ), roaming the streets of the nation's capitol in native dress, filling the watering holes patronized by immigrants from their respective countries.

Oly began to feel that things were starting to wear thin with Montero. The afterglow from the victory had catapulted him into at least another month's stay, but he sensed that Bobby and Em wanted their private lives back. There were times when he felt he was walking in on conversation and it made for awkwardness in the workplace where Montero knew that if he lost his patience that it would make for an awkward dinner.

Oly finished the section of the garage and looked up at Mo, who was sweating profusely on the dormer peak. He was not in very good shape and Oly didn't want to see him faint and fall to his death, so he scrambled up the ladder and told him to work on another part. "I got this, dude," Oly said, jumping onto the hot roof. "Thanks for the effort, though."

"Fucking hot up here," Mo said, wiping his brow and working his way down to the ladder without protest.

As Mo descended and Oly turned to finish the dormer, he accidentally kicked over a full can of white paint that Mo had stupidly left resting on the tilted roof. Montero had cussed at them a million times for bringing a full can up on a roof and they knew why. Oly watched the can roll in slow motion over the black roof, paint sloshing out the top as it bounced over where the handle was attached to the side. Before he could yell, it hit the top of the ladder, spilling paint all over Mo. His unfortunate reaction was to let go of the ladder and throw his arms up, while the can bounced off him and splattered more paint on his face.

"Fuuuuuck!" Oly heard Bobby scream, as he watched from below. Mo lost his balance, jumping from his position on the ladder, about twenty rungs from the ground and crashed onto the ground, while the ladder smashed onto the patio next to him. Oly could see nothing but the top of the ladder separate from the house, followed by yelling and crashing noises. Without thinking, he ran down the roof, momentum taking him forward too fast to see if Mo was alright. As a result, Oly had lost the focus on his own balance and stood on the edge of the gutter, waving his arms to gain back his center, but it was too late. Thirty feet above the ground below, all he could do was lean over and grab the gutter as his body pushed him forward towards a fall. With his heart beating out of his chest and the white paint dripping onto his hands and off the roof, Oly hung from the gutter and felt his shoulders burning with pain.

The homeowner, a thin, attractive woman in her forties, had come out of the house to see what all the noise was about. She was holding a small child and screamed when she saw Oly hanging from the gutter. The guys all jumped from their ladders and gathered below Oly, unsure what to do. Oly was paralyzed by the fear and pain, unable to do anything else but hold on. The woman ran into the house, screaming that she was going to call 911, while the men debated what to do next.

"Jump? What the fuck? He'll break his fucking legs on the driveway."

Mo had sprained an ankle in the fall, but grabbed a ladder and moved it underneath him but it was short. Oly moaned, shaking his head from the paint that was dripping on his forehead. "Shit," Mo said to himself when he realized the ladder wasn't big enough. Oly's legs began to feel like cement poles, pulling his shoulders down so that he could barely hold on. When he glanced over his left shoulder to alleviate some of the pain and keep the paint out of his eyes while the guys tried to rig up a ladder, he saw a mail truck pulling up to the house. *Life just goes on*, he thought to himself.

"Hang on!" Bobby yelled, as they stabilized a ladder against the house. Oly adjusted his grip and felt his sweaty fingers gaining a little strength from the encouragement. The wailing of fire engine sirens filled the distance, like a worried mother coming for her child.

The woman peaked her head out of the house. "They're coming! I told them to hurry!"

"They're not going to get here in time," Mo said, looking over at Bobby. "He's going to fucking fall." Oly could hear Mo's heavy breathing as he scrambled up the ladder. Mo grabbed Oly's legs, causing Oly to want to let go. "Don't let go yet," Mo sputtered in heaving breaths. He then moved up the ladder next to Oly and put his arms around Oly's waist, lifting his weight up so Oly felt relief on his hands. "Okay buddy, let go easy," he said, hugging Oly. "I got you. Anything to get out of fucking work, huh? You got paint all over my favorite shirt." Oly felt like he was going to pass out as he let go of the gutter and Mo held onto him. His shoulders hurt so badly, he thought both arms were dislocated.

The sirens were now accompanied by the roar of accelerating diesel engines as they turned onto the street. Oly's body started to ignore his brain's orders. He couldn't move his arms and relied on Mo to hold onto him and carry him down the ladder, holding onto him with a strong grip. Oly could hear Bobby giving orders to Mo as he lowered him but felt a wave of unconsciousness overcoming him.

The hydraulic brakes of the fire engines made a loud hissing noise, accompanied by the loudspeakers of the two-way dispatch radio. Before things went black, Oly felt Bobby assist Mo in taking him from the ladder and putting him on the soft grass. A number of voices and noises surrounded Oly as he lay on the ground, smelling the sweetness of the lawn as the EMTs tended to him. He slipped into unconsciousness.

When Oly opened his eyes, several minutes later, all he could see were shadowy round figures like balloons bobbing above him, blocking out the sun. He could not move his arms from the pain and wanted to pass out again. A man in a uniform was mouthing for him to stay still, but he did not hear the words. Everything seemed to be moving in slow motion around Oly as he tried to get up. The blurs started to come into focus and he could hear Montero's voice. He was holding up a bottle of water for Oly to drink. Most of the water dribbled down Oly's front. A set of hands pushed him up from behind so that he could sit up. Mo. Oly started to remember, but could not comprehend how or why he got there. "Roof?" was all he could manage to say to Montero, who was smiling as he held the water bottle up to Oly's lips like a newborn baby.

The ambulance, fire engines and police cars were lined up along the curb by the street. Mo held the bottle to his lips, and Oly started to recall what had happened. He started to feel embarrassed by all the fuss and could hear the squawking of the loudspeakers from the fire truck while the diesel engines idled. Neighbors had started coming out of their houses to see what was happening. He tried to get up and the EMT, along with Bobby, held him down. "Not so fast, big boy. They're gonna check you out before you go anywhere."

Oly spotted a gurney coming in his direction, pushed by two EMTs. His arms were in a lot of pain, but he started to panic at the thought of going to the hospital. His Peace Corps insurance had run out and he didn't want to burden anyone with an unsightly bill. "I'm good," he started to wave his arm, causing a flare up of pain through his shoulder.

Mo put the bottle down. "Chill out, man, they're trying to help."

The EMTs started to move around Oly to get into position to put him in the gurney but Oly waved them off. "It's okay. I'm okay. I just can't move my arms, but I'll be okay."

Montero, who had come into focus, frowned at Oly. "You might have some broken bones, come on, let's get you checked out." He waved at the EMTs to continue.

"No, I'm good," Oly said, trying to stand up. "I'm good, please, Bobby. It's going to be okay. I don't need to go to the hospital." The thought of his parents finding out and all the drama that would ensue without insurance being the least of his problems was worth the price of dealing with sore shoulders for a few weeks.

One of the EMTs stood with his hands on his hips, as Oly staggered to his feet. His biceps were enormous and he flexed as he spoke. "Well, we can't force him and we can't stay here all day." He gestured for one of the EMTs with the gurney to hand him a clipboard and then reached for the Walkie-Talkie mouth piece that was attached to his shoulder, telling the fire engines that they could leave. "We'll do a final check on you to make sure you're not dyin' and then you can sign this and off you go." Oly nodded slowly and took a pen from one of the EMTs. He gestured for the EMT to hold the clipboard at waist level because he couldn't move his arm any higher.

"You sure about this?" Mo asked, looking concerned for the first time since Oly had known him.

"Just get me a beer out of Bobby's truck and get on with it."

The EMT with the biceps circled with his index finger in the air, signaling that it was time to wrap up. Oly signed the form at waist level with a shaky hand and the fire engines cut their lights before backing into the driveway to leave. Most of the neighbors returned to their houses.

Mo went to retrieve a beer from Montero's truck. When the last police car left with the EMTs behind, everything became quiet again, as though nothing had happened. "There's an extra set of clothes in the tuff box, grab those while you're over there," Bobby yelled to Mo. When Mo returned from the truck, he juggled several beers from a cooler along with a pair of jeans and a black t-shirt for Oly. Mo threw the clothes on the grass next to Oly and popped open a can for him. When Oly tried to reach for it, he winced in pain.

"Here you go, Oly, down the hatch," Jeff said, as he held the beer to Oly's lips, causing most of it to dribble down his shirt to the delight of the crew.

"What a disaster," Bobby said, looking up at the roof covered with paint and the bent gutter. Out of the corner of his eye, he saw the homeowner walking towards them.

"Bad news," she said, holding a wireless receiver in her hand. "I just got off the phone with my insurance guy and he said you guys are probably going to have to pay."

"Don't worry about it, lady," Bobby snapped. "I'll fix your roof."

She walked away shaking her head, as Mo crushed a beer can and threw it on the lawn.

CHAPTER 44
FACE À FACE

———◆———

MO AND BOBBY CARRIED OLY to Bobby's truck and laid him in the back of the cab on top of some old clothing. His shoulders hurt so badly that all he could do was sit up against the inside of the truck rather than lie down. Through the blur of pain and numbness of alcohol, Oly thought about his parents and wanted to go home and be taken care of. He couldn't imagine how he'd explain that he fell off a ladder while painting the side of a house for some guys they didn't even know existed.

When they pulled up to Montero's house, Bobby helped Oly out of the truck and into the house. Em had eaten already and left two plates on the table, covered in aluminum foil. Oly could smell the remains of the cooking: a combination of squash and chicken pot pie. Montero helped Oly onto a chair and went into a bathroom off the kitchen to get cleaned up. Oly could barely move his arms as he tried to peel back the foil and watch the condensation run down the inside and drip onto the warm food. He could hear the distant muffled noise of a television. He had forgotten to wait and was halfway through the meal when Bobby came in the room, drying his hands with a small towel. "Hey kid, how ya holdin' up? I see your appetite survived. You don't look too good," he said, as he watched Oly slowly move his arms to eat. "Want me to feed you?" he joked, holding up a spoon. Oly could tell Bobby was filling the space with awkward small talk, as if he had rehearsed with Em how it was going to go and was waiting to get started. Bobby stayed standing, making Oly feel unwelcome and self-conscious as Oly ate with his left arm dangling by his side. "You need some aspirin or something?"

"No, thanks, I'm good."

"Could you sit down, please? You're making me nervous," Oly said. Oly shoved a large spoonful of chicken pie in his mouth, while Bobby took a seat.

"I am going to save you a speech," Oly said, wincing in pain. "I know that this can't continue. I know you've been great and I know that I almost cost you your company today because I'm probably not cleared for your insurance yet. You've been great to me. I know all that. And now it's my turn to tell you I need to move on because this isn't working."

"What about your family?" Bobby said.

"I just left my brother's and my parents would freak out if I landed back with them like this. I can just hear my mother weeping in the kitchen as I lay on the couch trying to get the feeling back in my arms."

Bobby folded his arms and leaned back in the chair, looking at Oly with disappointment.

CHAPTER 45
LE PROMIS

———

OLY WOKE UP EARLY, HARDLY able to move his arms. He forced himself to get up and find some Tylenol in the bathroom. The house was quiet. He figured that Montero had already gone to work. When he went downstairs, Em sat at the table wearing a blue blouse and jeans, sipping coffee. She looked up and smiled. Her hair was in a clip with several strands hanging down by her face. She looked up at Oly when he carried his heavy bag through the doorway to the kitchen with his left arm dangling.

"Oh my, can I help you?"

"No, I got it," he said, plopping the bag down by the front door.

"Sorry that Bobby had to get up and leave early. He left a note for you." Oly picked it up and glanced at the bread and jam on the table. *Good luck. Stay focused and keep away from roofs. I'll tell the crew that you joined a professional rowing team.*

"Sit down and have some breakfast. I can call you a cab when you're ready. Do what you need to do." She read the expression on his face and stood up to refill her coffee and offered him some. She handed him a full cup from a heavy mug that had *St. Peter's Fiesta, 1989* printed on the side and caught Oly looking at the number written on his arm. She had her back turned to him as she emptied the dishwasher. "Don't be afraid, Oly. You're young. You'll figure things out. I have a couple of appointments to make, but you can stay as long as you want and use the phone."

They sat quietly, eating bread and jam, sipping coffee for several minutes. His shoulder throbbed with dull pain, which distracted his thoughts. Realizing that Jeff was likely his only option did not help the pain. Em stood up, consumed with her own thoughts about the day and gulped the last of the coffee. "Even though I'm upset with Bobby for the whole rowing melee, what you did meant a lot to him. There was a reason for all of this. You'll figure it out someday." She turned to grab her keys off a hook by the front door and put her hand on the brass knob. "Just push the button on the lock when you go, okay? Take care, Oly, and keep us informed on how you do." She winked at him as she softly closed the door, leaving Oly alone in the house.

Oly sat in silence. An antique clock ticked in the other room, causing him to feel anxious. *Time marches on,* he thought to himself. He imagined Bobby and the crew setting up on another site, Samantha going to her first classes, meeting guys, Jeff doing who knows what. Things just kept moving, whether or not he was in the game. He looked around the kitchen at the stacks of bills, the worn countertop, the stainless steel appliances. The curling photographs of family tacked to various cabinets. Everything that reflected a settled life. Contentment. He wondered if he'd ever live in such a place and accumulate the artifacts of normal life. He imagined how happy Samantha must be, settling into her new life in Chicago with clarity and focus.

He scribbled down several scenarios on a piece of paper and stared at the phone. He had forgotten how much fun it was to turn the dial and the noise it made each time. It almost made him laugh. Eleven times before the ring started. What a simpler life. When it started to ring his mind raced for things to say. *House burned down. Won the lottery and starting an around-the-world trip. Fell off a roof and homeless again.*

"Hello?" Samantha answered after only a couple of rings. He wasn't ready and didn't answer right away.

"Oly?"

"How'd you know?" he finally responded.

"Who else do I leave speechless? I was wondering when I was going to hear from you. I start classes in a few days."

He paused for a few seconds, the *tick tock* of the grandfather clock filling the silence like an impatient observer. "Yeah, I'm sorry. I've been busy planning for the Georgia trip."

It was Samantha's turn to pause. "Please be careful," she said. "I'm going to be really busy too, but we need to stay in touch." He felt a flash of anger, wanting to call her out on the non-committal tone of 'staying in touch.' It reminded him of the girls in college who wanted to 'stay friends.' "What are you going to do when you're down there?" she asked.

"I'm not exactly sure, to be honest. When I connected again with that professor from Howard, he seemed like I could help them do some research or something."

"What does that have to do with you?"

"He mentioned to me that the people on the island were descendants of slaves from Togo."

"Wow. That sounds interesting."

Another pause.

"So, I can visit during my next break in a few weeks. You think you'll be around?"

"I might," he said, trying unsuccessfully to sound neutral.

"Stop it, Oly. I'm not playing that."

"Playing what?"

"You know, you may or may not be around."

"*Si tu sors, je sors*," he said

"*Si tu sors, je sors*," she answered. "I'm going to miss you. Send me a note when you get down there and let me know how things go. Have you heard from Jeff?"

Oly squeezed the receiver a bit tighter. "No, he hasn't really been in touch. He moves around a lot. The last time we spoke, he said he had to straighten some shit out. Don't we all. He'll pop up again."

"I'm really impressed with what you're doing, Oly."

He was surprised at her comment because it seemed less of a choice to him and more of an act of desperation. "Why?"

"I don't know. Maybe because I'm starting to put all that behind me and adjust back to the life I was expected to lead." Her honesty made Oly feel alive, like he wanted to be with her immediately.

"Well, at least you're doing something for the future. I have no idea what's going to come out of this."

"Don't worry about the future, Oly. Just make sure I can be a part of it."

Oly felt confused, a wave of emotion welling up inside that he knew might be a mistake to express. She wanted to be with him, but flew halfway across the country?

"Be careful down there and let me know how things go. I'll be thinking of you. Take care." Oly held the receiver to his ear until he heard Samantha hang up and the line go dead. He reached into his pocket, pulled out Gunning's number, and stared at it.

CHAPTER 46
CERTAINES CHOSES

———◆———

OLY TOOK SEVERAL MINUTES TO write a note to Bobby Montero. He didn't want to disappoint, sound shallow, or indecisive. He decided to be truthful, as he knew that Bobby would never buy some fabricated story about finding work and settling down.

> *Thanks for everything Bobby. You have been too kind to me, and apologies for the accident and the mayhem at the fiesta. I learned a lot working for you and hope that the Shockers will live forever. I am planning to head to a place called Sapelo Island in Georgia to relive my Peace Corps years (just kidding, sort of). It could be dicey so send the Marines if it goes to shit. (Just kidding).*
> *Save the Whales,*
> *Oly*

A light rain had started as Oly crossed the sidewalk outside of Montero's house. It wasn't as hard as he thought it would be to say goodbye to Em, and he was relieved that Bobby wasn't around to complicate things. He looked down at the hockey bag, feeling as though it were speaking to him. *Again? What the hell's your problem?* He kicked it in the bread basket. No response. He walked the two miles to the commuter rail and spent the entire ride to Boston staring out the window. It felt strangely good to be anonymous again, like a reset button.

When the train pulled into North Station, it was still drizzling as he crossed Causeway Street to a small neighborhood library. He glanced in the direction of the Peace Corps recruiting office down the street at the Tip O'Neill building and smiled. *Full circle,* he thought to himself, strangely at peace. Being focused on actually doing something made him feel good, even if Sapelo was a fool's errand.

When he dragged the hockey bag through the front entrance, an attractive twenty-something librarian with long brown hair and a tight brown skirt stood in front of him, hands on her hips. She looked at him over the top of her glasses, a flirtation he hadn't expected. "Ahem, sorry, but the Garden is across the street.

"Ha! Hockey joke!" Oly said, wiping a strand of wet hair from his face. "Didn't expect that!"

She smiled, making him wonder how boring her job must be that she was actually talking to him. "Sorry, let me unpack your overdue books. I think you've broken the record for amnesty week." She reached down for one of the straps on the bag, as a flowery waft of her perfume settled over him. He struggled to maintain his composure and looked over her shoulder at the dankness of the library, wondering what such a perky, attractive girl was doing in such a grim setting.

"I wouldn't open that if I were you, and those are definitely not overdue books."

"Hmmm, well what can I help you with then?"

"I need to use a payphone and I'm looking for information on a place called Sapelo, Georgia."

"Peachy," she smiled again, turning her back on Oly so that her hair swished behind her. Walking away, she pointed. "Microfiche and film over here and payphone over there. And you can leave the hockey stuff or the books or the body or whatever by the coat rack over there."

It took Oly a few minutes to dig through the bag and find a few coins for the phone. He dug through his wallet for the wrinkled paper with Gunning's number on it and stared at it again before dialing. Gunning's secretary picked up. When she put him through to Gunning, Oly stared down at the paper and smoothed it out.

"Professor Gunning here."

"Hello, Professor."

"Young Richard! So nice to hear from you! We were actually making plans without you but your timing is well placed. There are a number of important hearings coming up and although we are working to find legal representation, there is a demand for a fairly significant amount of research and leg work that needs to be done."

Oly explained the visit to the library, left out the details of the roof incident, and finished with an offer to join the mission.

"Unfortunately for me, the chancellor here has me tied up in some committee work and I don't know that I can join you on the journey. However, I remain hesitant that this is something you should venture into."

"Why?' Oly asked, somewhat alarmed by Gunning's change of heart.

"The situation is getting a bit tense. I've received some threats and am wondering if it's all a bit too much."

"What kind of threats?"

"You know, the usual, meddling, stay-out-of-our-business threats. Nothing the Friends haven't heard before, but these are a bit more direct. The last one mentioned my address and workplace."

"Holy shit. Did you report it?"

There was a pause on the phone followed by an exasperated sigh. "Richard, I know you spent time in Africa and believe that there may be a different attitude in America towards such injustices, but reporting this sort of thing to the police only seems to generate more problems."

Oly paused, looking across the floor at the librarian who was shelving some books, making him think that maybe he should just hang up and fly to Chicago.

"Hello?" Gunning said, when Oly didn't say anything for several seconds.

Oly's mind began to wander. He looked down at the hockey bag, glanced again at the librarian, and started to feel the darkness of being alone. He thought of his parents, going to Chicago, and even what Jeff might have thought.

"I'm going to check it out," Oly finally said.

"What?" Gunning said, surprised.

"I don't know. I just need to go. I don't see a range of options here, Professor. Looks like you're dropping the whole thing if I don't take a shot."

Gunning paused. "I don't think this is appropriate for you, Richard. A lot has changed there since you and I met for lunch. I believe that we should keep in touch, but this is not the best time."

Oly could hear the worry in his voice, but felt for the first time since he signed the agreement to join Peace Corps several years earlier that he had to do it.

"Sorry, Professor. I'm going. Put me on the list and I'll be at the docks in a few days." Oly could hear a muffling noise on the receiver, as though Gunning put his hand over the phone. Gunning was talking to someone else in his office and Oly could not make it out. "Hello?" Oly said. "Hello?" Gunning didn't respond for several seconds.

"Okay." Gunning finally answered.

"Okay, what?" Oly asked.

"Okay, we'll sponsor you. You can do some research for us, maybe attend a hearing. But that's all. I don't want you doing any more. It's not safe and I'm not going to be there with you." "Thanks, Professor. I survived a couple of years in Tchamba, didn't I?"

"No comparison," Gunning said, lowering his voice. "You were giving people something there, not trying to take it away. There's a big difference. I will reimburse you for a bus ticket after you return and we will put your name in for the ferry. You need to have identification, as it's by invitation only to the island."

"Bus?" Oly responded, surprised. "Yes, my friend. Bus. We are a non-profit after all. I thought you said you were Peace Corps, yes?"

"*Was*, Professor. That's in the past."

"Well, the trip will be a good warm up for Sapelo. Let us know when you arrive," he finished before hanging up.

When Oly turned back to the librarian, she was sitting at a microfilm desk, attaching a reel and spinning it through. She smiled when he walked over. "My hockey coach," he said, pulling up a chair next to her. "I told him I was going to be late to the game tonight."

"Well, I'm sure that researching microfilm of Sapelo was a valid excuse." She paused to look at him. "Who are you?"

"My name is Oly. Hi. I'm actually not a hockey player." She examined him, picking up on the fact that he seemed unsettled. Oly still looked like the average guy from Boston, with his Irish-English features, but something was off that intrigued her.

"Thank you for clarifying that. My name is Erin. I'm actually not a librarian."

"Really? What are you?"

"A frustrated artist."

"You don't look frustrated to me."

"You should see my work," she said, looking up at the ceiling with exasperation. She brushed her hair away from her shoulders and looked intently at the screen.

"So, Oly, not a hockey player, what brings you here looking for news about this Sapelo place?"

"I don't know what kind of an answer would make sense. I was living overseas for a while and then came back and fell off a roof. I'm looking for someplace a little closer to sea level."

"Boston is at sea level."

"Good one. Sea level, but a little more exotic. I grew up here."

"Lost treasure?"

"I hadn't thought of it like that. Maybe. And maybe mix in a little danger if the pirates who put it there come looking."

"What were you doing overseas?"

"Peace Corps."

"Really? Oh, I always wanted to do that. I chickened out. How was it?"

"Hot."

"Anything else?"

"Yes, things happened to my body that I never experienced before. I probably shouldn't say."

"Hmm. That sounds gross." She turned her attention back to the microfilm knobs and zoomed through half a roll and stopped on one section.

"Well, there are two major themes on your little island. Freed slaves and casinos, with R.J. Reynolds as a sidebar. A lot of history for a sandbar."

Oly leaned over, getting a whiff of a perfume that made him want to kiss her neck. He thought of Samantha and felt frustrated. She stopped a frame on a newspaper photo from the 1920s of a group of black workers in overalls leaning on shovels over a half-built foundation in the jungle. "That's the Reynolds' mansion when they were building it. Looks like he finished it a couple of years later and had some big-shot visitors. Carnegie, Roosevelt, even Jimmy Carter went there when he was president. Of course, R.J. was dead by that time." She then flipped through to another article in the Sentinel Times about how the Sea Islands were granted to freedmen. "Look, here's a place called 'Hog Hammock.' Maybe you should stop there when you visit."

Oly squinted his eyes. "Hog Hammock. Pig in a blanket. Sounds cozy." She then stood up behind him, causing a flash of desperation in him that made him want to ask her to stay.

"I'll leave you to it, then. Good luck, treasure hunter," she said, before walking away, flipping her hair. "Don't be late to your hockey game."

That's it? he thought to himself. He watched her walk away, trying to visualize Samantha and feeling desperate and distracted from the task at hand.

The black and grey slide had a gentle glow from the bulb that was behind it on the screen. He used the knob to gently turn through an article from 1934.

RJ Reynolds, tobacco magnate, purchases Sapelo Island from Howard Coffin. Originally settled by the Spanish and French in the 17th and 18th centuries, the area was owned and developed by Georgia Legislator and plantation owner Thomas Spalding, whose slaves are mostly the ancestors of the current residents of Hog Hammock.

The article described how Reynolds was seeking to enlarge the sugar plantations and use the island as his retreat. The irony of a tobacco plantation owner buying an island occupied by descendants of slaves did not escape Oly. He imagined the possibility of how many came from Togo, known at one time as the Slave Coast.

He skipped ahead and found more current articles on the University of Georgia's Marine Institute on the island, the ebbs and flows of land ownership, and Jimmy Carter's visit in 1979. The articles skipped years in chunks, as most forgotten places do. He then stopped on a series of articles written more recently by the *Sentinel, Chicago Tribune,* and *Washington Post,* all on the same topic, a disputed land deal between an Atlanta-based gambling operation and the Friends of Sapelo. That was it. Oly had to change the reel to find more recent articles, but a number of them quoted Gunning and cited a lawsuit filed in 1976 by a Maryanne O'Brien Reynolds, a Hollywood starlet in the 1940s, who agreed to give up her career and move to Sapelo with R.J. in exchange for a pre-nuptial agreement (in R.J.'s handwriting), that turned over the entire 16,000 acres of Sapelo Plantation, Inc., to her as collateral.

Oly scanned a small piece written in the Georgia Law Review. It quoted the daughter of Mrs. O'Brien Reynolds as filing a new lawsuit backed by an Atlanta-based gambling company that was trying to circumvent the ban on land-based gambling operations in Georgia by using the land allegedly bequeathed to her mother as the site for a casino. It cited a number of reasons why the 16,000 acres should be exempt from the laws and referenced a recently submitted counter lawsuit by the Friends of Sapelo. Oly looked quickly at the clock and back towards the librarian who had put her glasses on and was sorting books. He watched her without her noticing and wondered if she was thinking about him. She looked up when he stood and smiled. "Find what you were looking for?"

He wanted to say something cheesy about her but stopped short, trying to read her flirty eyes for authentic interest or whether she was just playing out of boredom. "Yeah, I did. It might get me in trouble, but I've got nothing to lose."

She walked over to the machine that Oly was working on and looked over the top of her glasses. "I'll make a copy of this for you so that you can read it later."

When she came back to him with the copy, she held onto it just long enough for him to have to pull it out of her hand.

"I hope whatever you're up to works out," she said, intrigued by the air of mystery around Oly.

"And I hope the art thing works out for you," Oly smiled, wishing he could have spent more time with her to explore the question. He winced from the lingering pain in his shoulder, as he lifted the bag.

"Are you okay?" she asked, coming closer to help him.

"Yeah, I'm good. I've been carrying this baggage for a while."

Oly shuffled across the street, balancing the weight of the bag on his hips as he thought about Erin and what would become of her. He had refrained from asking her for her number, but had started to wonder how long he was going to pretend that Samantha was going to come back into his life.

CHAPTER 47

LE VOYAGE

———◆———

WITH NO PLACE TO STAY and the remains of his painting money and read-justment allowance wearing thin, Oly went to the Greyhound terminal at South Station and bought a one-way ticket for less than a hundred dollars. He grimaced at the twenty-hour trip, but knew there was no choice with his budget limitations. The thought of calling Andy for a loan crossed him mind, but then he'd have to fill him in on the whole Sapelo thing and it would likely get back to his parents. He considered calling them from the bus station but squelched the idea, choosing to leave them with the belief that he was still painting houses or temping somewhere.

Oly thought about the half days he used to spend in Togo, waiting under tree cover for several hours for buses to fill up prior to departure. The good news was that the bus was leaving that evening, full or not, sparing him the expense of a hotel room. He bought three sandwiches, a large bottle of water, a couple of newspapers and a half-priced copy of a Robert Ludlum novel at a nearby 7-Eleven.

Oly sat on a bench near the bus bay as passengers gradually started showing up, and ate one of the sandwiches, a stale ham and cheese that was more filler than food. By the time the bus driver showed up, around 6:30pm, Oly noticed from the other passengers that he was one of only two white people waiting. After shoving the hockey bag in the under-neath storage, Oly showed the driver his ticket and boarded, sitting next to a large middle-aged black man wearing a light-blue button down shirt.

Oly laughed and the man looked over the top of his reading glasses with scorn.

"Oh, sorry," Oly said. "It's not you. Well it is, sort of. You remind me of a guy I sat next to a long time ago on a plane."

The man smiled. "Well this isn't a plane, son, and he must have been a good lookin' fellow."

Oly put his hand out. "Reasonably," Oly smiled, taking the man's hand in his grip and sitting down.

"Why you taking the bus all the way to Georgia?" the man asked.

"You mean why aren't I flying like the other whites?"

The man chuckled, removing his glasses as his belly gyrated up and down from the laughing. "Yeah, like the other whites. You get right to it, don't you? Name's Benjamin. Originally from Philly and splitting time now with family in Atlanta and Boston."

"And I'm Oly. Originally from Boston area and now splitting my time between where I last stayed and where I'm going to next."

"Ah, to be young and free," Benjamin said, as he placed the glasses on his forehead and leaned his head back on the headrest. "Enjoy it while you can, brother. Enjoy it while you can." Benjamin took a white kerchief out of the front pocket in his shirt and wiped the glistening sweat from his brow. He looked over the top of the seat to see if the driver was getting ready to leave. "No toilet on this one," he said, looking around. "You better go while you can. I think he only stops a couple of times."

An hour later, and with the bus only half full, the driver mounted and yelled out before taking his seat. "Last chance for toilet before New York folks!"

"Told you," Benjamin said, smiling before he leaned back.

Oly hadn't expected to feel so lonely during the trip. Benjamin snored most of the way, with a *Wall Street Journal* splayed out on his belly. Oly tried to read his book, but found it was making him nauseous. He thought about the painful eight-hour journeys he used to take from Tchamba to Lomé, wondering how he had survived with similar boredom and half as much sitting space. The rest of the passengers seemed to melt into a zombie-like state, almost a suspended animation, like you read about in those deep space travel books. Over the top of the seats, Oly spotted a headphone set resting on top of the moppy hair of the other white person on board and was jealous. *Gotta get a Walkman,* he thought to himself.

By nightfall, they had arrived in New York, then passed through Jersey and Pennsylvania, and stopped twelve hours into the ride at a rest stop in Virginia. It was summertime and hot. The air-conditioning on the bus made it that much more difficult to adjust. Oly nudged Benjamin. "Halfway there," he said. Benjamin came to and looked around, his eyes bloodshot.

They ordered fast food at a Popeye's and sat together at a booth that was so small that Benjamin's stomach pressed against the table. "Gotta lose some weight," he joked, as he took a large bite of fried chicken.

"How many times have you said that?" Oly joked.

Benjamin wiped the grease from his mouth with a napkin and stared at Oly. "So, tell me again, son, why are you going to Georgia?"

Oly smiled. "I don't think I told you the first time."

"Yes, that's true. So, tell me the first time."

"Believe it or not, I'm a former Peace Corps Volunteer and I've been asked by an organization to help them reclaim land in a dispute that is being threatened by a casino. Benjamin frowned and put his chicken down. He picked up a napkin and slowly wiped his mouth, not taking his gaze off Oly.

"Son, you ever been to Georgia?"

"No."

"I didn't think so."

"You have any idea what could happen to you going down there and stirring up trouble?"

"Who said I was going to stir up trouble?"

Benjamin laughed, his belly pressing against the table as he leaned forward and reached into his back pocket, pulling out his wallet. He squinted his eyes as he pulled out a ratty card and handed it to Oly.

"Name's Ben Jarvis. Retired detective, Philadelphia P.D. I know a few things about reading people." Oly studied the card before sticking it in his pocket. He looked up at the driver waving for everyone to get back on the bus.

CHAPTER 48

COPAIN, COPINE

———

WHEN THEY SETTLED BACK IN the bus for the second half of the trip, Oly thought about whether or not having Jeff would have helped. His mind then started drifting over the last several months of his life: Samantha, the RPCV party, Andy, Brett, his parents, Montero. A kaleidoscope of images that had culminated with him being on a busload of strangers, heading into a potentially dangerous situation, with few people knowing where he was going or what might happen. Despite the loneliness, he decided that Jeff would have made it worse. Oly settled in and out of sleep as the bus rocked back and forth over the excruciating boredom of the route from Virginia and North Carolina, west towards Atlanta. He pulled out the printouts from the library and started reading over the history of Sapelo and the land sales from one generation of white owners to the next. Spalding, Swarbreck, Coffin, Reynolds. Like most of history, the disenfranchised had virtually no records, so there was hardly any mention of the freedmen ownership of land from places like Hog Hammock to Raccoon Bluff. Now it was all being disputed and questioned.

As Oly looked through the paperwork, Ben glanced over. "Sea Islands. Beautiful part of the world. Direct descendants of slaves, you know."

"Yeah, I've heard," Oly said, not sure how he felt about Ben weighing in again.

"You got an invitation to where your going?" he asked. "A lot of those places you can't get on without invitation."

"Yeah, I think so," Oly said. "The group that called me up said there'd be one waiting for me at the dock."

"All right then," Ben said, resting his head back. "All right then." Oly could tell Ben wanted to say more but didn't.

The arrival in Atlanta was uneventful. The passengers exited the bus as though it were just a trip down the street, and headed in opposite directions without the fanfare of rushing into people's arms. Oly exited with Ben and shook his hand one last time with his hockey bag at his side. Ben, who was nearly the same height as Oly, took out his kerchief again and wiped his brow before reaching out to shake Oly's hand. "You be careful, son. And don't be afraid to give me a shout. I know a few people down here if you get in a pickle." Oly tried to dismiss the offer as though it weren't necessary, but felt a chill as he watched Ben turn away, waving to a taxi.

It was nearly six a.m. and the humidity was sweltering. After another five-hour bus ride through Savannah and finally to the Meridian docks, Oly looked out onto the open Atlantic Ocean. He remembered reading somewhere that the Sea Islands were about the closest one could get to West Africa from the U.S. without getting wet.

With the exception of a pudgy white man dressed in sweat blotched khaki and a Panama hat, everyone who lined up to board the ferry was black. Not African-American black, but Togo black. Oly couldn't help stare, as many of them reminded him of people he knew from Tchamba. They carried cardboard boxes of supplies, propane tanks, bags of various shapes and sizes, large jugs of drinking water and coolers. With no grocery store on the island, save for a tiny market with canned goods and occasional produce, residents were on their own to bring in everything they'd need to survive, except for electricity, which ran for six hours a day (when the generator wasn't broken by storms or poor maintenance) and water, which was good for cleaning and cooking but not recommended for drinking.

Oly hadn't slept well on the bus and was exhausted from the travel. He lined up behind three boys, who walked on with hardly a nod of recognition from a woman wearing a blue Department of Natural Resources shirt and holding a clipboard. She knew the locals well. When Oly approached her, she looked him both up and down, her gaze resting on Oly's bag of clothes before looking him in the eye like a trained customs officer. "And what can I help you with?" she asked, frowning down at her list.

Oly glanced at the clipboard. "Richard Olymeyer with Friends of Sapelo." She scanned the list with her finger to the bottom and then flipped the page, still frowning. Then her face lit up.

"Well, I'll be," she said, breaking into a smile. "That you are. Well I'm Jocie Beauchamps and I'm a lifelong resident of Hog Hammock. Got you right here. Professor Gunning called yesterday."

Her expression completely changed, making him no longer feel like he was making a big mistake. "Libeth is going to meet you on the other side. Welcome aboard," she said, before turning back to the line. Oly practically danced down the gangplank to the boat when she waved him through.

When he got on board, Oly caught the eye of the boys and waved, giving them a half salute. The three smiled and waved back. Oly leaned on one of the railings to watch the rest of the passengers boarding, relaxing fully for the first time since he left Boston. He caught the man in the Panama hat staring at him and felt immediately self-conscious, checking his pocket for Ben's card. He recalled the sensation of standing out in a crowd as a minority in Togo. Jocie's expression had changed as the man next in line approached her at the gangplank. She reached down to her belt and unclipped her Walkie Talkie and spoke into it, looking the man up and down with a frown as she spoke. She clicked on and off several times, having a back-and-forth with someone on the other end. After several seconds, she checked the man off the list unceremoniously and waved him through. *What the hell,* Oly thought to himself. Jocie looked quickly up at Oly on the railing before turning back to the line to board the rest of the guests. It was as if she didn't want Oly to catch her looking afraid.

During the half-hour ferry trip that wound through chocolate-brown river channels that opened into a wider channel of deep blue water, Oly absorbed the smells of the landscape and observed fellow travelers. He began to feel self-conscious. He hadn't felt this white since he left Togo. Over the stern of the boat, he watched two small children pointing at the water where two harbor porpoises emerged and dived seamlessly through their wake in a playful exercise. He couldn't stop thinking about the man in the hat who had disappeared to the air-conditioned interior of the ferry. As they headed into more open water, the ferry picked up speed and cooled them off.

Libeth Watkins was waiting for Oly at the Sapelo dock in a 1980 Ford Country Squire wagon, with peeling faux-wood paneling and no windshield. A large piece of the paneling hung off on the side, like peeling paint on an old house, and dragged on the road. Oly was curious as to why someone hadn't peeled it off. The other passengers walked down the one dusty road leading to the dock, some carrying packages on their heads or piling into rusty pickups. Libeth smiled and waved in recognition at the younger of the two white strangers.

When the sea breeze wasn't blowing, the humidity was unbearable. Sweat poured down Oly's forehead, and his shirt immediately clung to his chest. He threw his plastic bag in the back of the wagon next to boxes of tools, books, various clothing, broken fishing poles, and a distinct smell of gasoline. It looked like someone's garage from 1972. Oly noticed Libeth giving the man in the Panama hat a sideways glance that she hoped Oly hadn't noticed, but he did.

After exchanging pleasantries about the trip, Libeth headed down a long, semi-paved road, one of only two on the island. The idle on the car was so high that she didn't even push the pedal; the engine just whirred and pushed them along. As they bumped along, a hot breeze blowing through the glass-less windshield, Oly reviewed the events of the last twenty-four hours, and started to feel a wave of anxiety for making a huge mistake. He should have been lying next to Samantha, watching her sleep in the early dawn hours, considering a run to the local coffee shop. A giant palmetto bug flew through the opening and nearly hit him in the eye. "What the f..." he said, swatting it to the side so it landed in the back, making a loud racket like a landing helicopter. Libeth laughed and chastised him for the vulgarity. "Sorry, ma'am," Oly said, surprising himself with his first 'ma'am' since he'd been in the South.

They passed a woman who walked by, balancing a large jug on her head. Libeth greeted her through the windshield as they passed and the woman grunted in a reciprocal echo, exactly as they did in Togo. "Did you hear that?" Oly said. "What did you just say?" he said, leaning forward to Libeth.

"Nothing, honey, just hello. Whatchya so riled up about?"

"Did you know that's how people greeted one another in West Africa, where I lived?"

"No I didn't, sweetie, but it wouldn't surprise me. You know who we are, right honey?"

After a mile of on-again off-again pavement on the washed-out road, Libeth turned and stopped at a brown trailer home shaded by a grove of gigantic palm trees with a number of rotting coconuts at their base. "What do you do when it rains?" Oly asked, when they pulled up. In addition to no windshield, the car didn't have a key. Libeth reached underneath the steering column and touched something to cut the motor.

"Drive like hell," she said. "Sometimes you make it, sometimes you don't. Used to have a plastic bag I could throw over 'til the storm passed. Don't know what happened to it."

"You know, when I was a little girl, there was no roads at all. Reynolds paved all these when I was a little girl. I still remember all those big trucks coming over on a barge. Whole village came out to watch. Hasn't been touched since, as you can tell. Sapelo's takin' 'em back, just like it should, just like the Friends." Her words, smooth as buttermilk, hung in the air. A mangy yellow dog pulled itself from underneath the trailer and came to greet them. "Sweeeetie," Libeth purred. "Hey baby, this is my friend," she said, stepping out of the car and holding Sweetie's head in her hands. "You need some water, Sweetie?" Sweetie wagged her tail and led Libeth to her water dish next to the front door.

Oly had never been in a trailer home before. His family owned a Coleman camper when he was young, but it was for trips to New Hampshire in July, not living. Libeth opened the squeaky, rusty screen door and held it on her hip while she reached into her pocket for a key to open the front. "You lock it?" Oly asked, looking around.

"Lately, yes. Not like it used to be."

"How's that?"

"We can talk about that later. We gotta eat."

A wave of fresh, dry, conditioned air greeted them when they stepped in the trailer. Oly instantly felt the sweat from his matted shirt starting to evaporate.

"You have electricity?"

"Yup, one of the few. Ain't cheap, but you can't live here without it. Goes out a lot, though. And more frequently lately, which I believe in my heart is not by chance."

"What?"

"Professor Gunning briefed you on what's going on, right?" she said, looking exasperated.

"I thought we were going to eat first," Oly joked.

She laughed. "Oh yeah, that's right. I'm getting all serious on you and you must be starving!"

How Libeth made a home in such a harsh environment reminded Oly of Tchamba. When he'd visit Bawendi or other friends at their houses after a hot, dusty ride through a parched landscape, he was amazed at how cool and clean it was inside, thanks to thick clay walls and women who constantly kept the dirt out.

A narrow hall down the middle of Libeth's trailer led to a bay window, beneath which sat a small worn leather couch. The air conditioner hummed as they sat at a table in a tiny but well-organized kitchen. Oly looked at the framed photographs of Libeth's relatives on the wall, several of them black and white and stained with age. Libeth caught him looking while she placed a large bowl of peaches in front of him. He felt at peace, in spite of the anxiety of what lie ahead.

"Ha, you remember that greeting from Yianne? That second picture of the two gentlemen is where I learned it. That's my granddad. He was the youngest son of my great granddad, who came over from Georgia. He worked on Mr. Spalding's plantation before Reynolds got here. His place is rotting in the woods on the other side of the island. You'll see later," she said, pointing towards the opposite wall of the trailer. "This land's been in my family as long as I can remember."

Oly grabbed a peach and took a huge bite. He hadn't eaten since the mainland and was starving. Juice ran down his chin while Libeth reached for a tray of biscuits and laughed. "Whooee. I tell you what. People'd swim from the mainland to get their hands on my peaches and biscuits." They sat in silence for a few minutes while Oly ate the peach down to the pit.

An old man riding a rusty orange Schwinn with a torn basket on the front rode past the trailer, looking over as he passed. Sweetie went over and trotted with him while he passed, wagging her tail.

"Who's that?" Oly asked.

"Don't mind him. That's Bobson. He's harmless. Likes to check on me from time to time. Good man he is. Looks after me." When Bobson passed, Sweetie went back to her place under the trailer. Libeth left the table and pulled a scrapbook from a shelf, before sitting at a wraparound couch at the far end of the trailer.

Oly grabbed a second peach and went over to sit on the couch. "Here it is," she said, holding an old, stained book out to him. "Here's my family, going way back." A musty smell wafted out from within the warped, tan cover as Oly gently turned one of the plastic pages that protected the photos. One of them, an ancient daguerreotype, showed a black couple in ragged clothes standing in front of a dilapidated, sagging shack.

"That's them," said Libeth. "Slaves. From Africa to Sapelo, my great-great-grandparents. On the left is James and the lady is Ma Peppers. They were separated to different plantations in Georgia and by the grace of God found one another after the war, re-located to Sapelo with Mr. Spalding. They were later on Freedmen's Bureau land that was later swindled with some fancy paperwork. Being illiterate an' all, they had no idea what they were signing, and the only thing on record is some barely readable deed with a scrawled 'X' on it. Just like the Indians. No offense, Oly, but you white men know how to steal."

She flipped a page in the book and sat back, exasperated. "I have a Freedmen's Bureau document that granted thirty acres of land not too far from where I picked you up at the ferry. There's no evidence that it was ever rescinded, except for this here scrawl. Could have been anybody that signed that. Now you know why they didn't want my people to read and write. And there you have it. None of it would have mattered if these fellas from Carolina, or wherever they from, left well enough alone. But now they're after us again, and damned if I'm leavin' now. Too old for that. Too old."

Oly thought of the man in the Panama hat and started to say something, but stopped himself. He already knew the answer.

"C'mon, grab a biscuit and let's go for a ride," Libeth said, closing the album. "This all can wait. I got some people for you to meet. Take some peaches if you want," she said when she caught Oly staring at the bowl.

When they headed back on the road, they passed the three boys from the ferry, who stopped to stare. Libeth laughed and waved at them. "Can't say if I ever had white people in my car. "Excuse me, boys," she said, yelling through the windshield. "You know which way to the Reynolds' mansion? I got a lost boy here." The boys laughed and waved back to Libeth.

"I think it's the other way," one of them said.

Turning past what appeared to be an overgrown field, Oly asked what it was. "Tobacco," Libeth responded from the front. "Mr. Reynolds' tobacco."

Oly remembered some of the research he had done at the library, which now seemed so long ago. "He bought it from Coffin in the 1930s, right?"

"You got that right," Libeth said, tilting her head at the invisible rearview. "All his. Gotta give him some credit though. He turned a lot of the undisputed land over to the state and DNR, so a lot of it's protected. We'll go see his house later if you want."

"Here we are," Libeth said, turning left onto a narrow pathway that seemed more suited for two wheels than four. They came to a stop next to the remains of a barely noticeable wooden structure no larger than a garden shed that had all but disintegrated into the earth. When Libeth cut the engine, the whirring sound of old fan belts gave way to the chirping sounds of cicada. The roof of the structure, mostly rotted, had bowed down to the ground at one corner, like a man tipping his hat. As they walked around what was left of the walls, Oly peered inside through a glassless window. The floors, now completely dirt, had given way to weeds. Kudzu poured over the rotted walls like living wallpaper. Libeth gave him a moment to look around before speaking. "You 'member that photograph I showed you? Welcome to the house of James and Ma Peppers."

"No shit," Oly said, examining the remains.

"This is it, baby. No history book. These were real people. Slaves and descendants of slaves, right here on this ground," she said, holding her arms out. "And this was their land, all theirs right after the war. My grandparents worked for Coffin and Spalding and then stayed in it until around the time Mr. Reynolds took over."

"Why did they abandon it?" Oly asked.

"After Mr. Reynolds died, his family stopped using this as a plantation and turned it over to the state as a nature preserve. The family moved to where my trailer is now. The problem is that where the preserve begins and ends is in dispute. Now this here shack is the only claim I have to this property. It's all I got to prove that they existed and lived here where those boys want to put their casino. I don't know what the good professor has told you, but it's getting ugly. Why Reynolds never tore it down is beyond me. Probably thought it didn't matter since there never was anything legally that gave my James and Ma Peppers any land."

"The dude in the Panama hat," Oly said, as they headed back to the car.

"What's that?" Libeth said.

"Some white dude in a Panama hat got on the ferry with us. They gave him a hard time at the ferry but he got permission to come over anyway.

"Sounds about right. They comin'," she said, slamming the heavy door to the car. "They comin.'"

When they pulled out of the dusty field, Oly looked back at the rotting remains of the house and thought of Samantha. "Shit," he whispered under his breath.

They retraced the road and eventually turned into a cleared space on neatly trimmed green grass anchored by a white, one-story structure in the middle. Libeth stopped. "Our church. Our preacher, Brother Samuel. He will put you up. We have a day tomorrow, so get some rest." It occurred to Oly that they hadn't really discussed any sort of plan, that Libeth was just leading them from one thing to another. Whatever was happening was unfolding rather than planning.

The familiar sense of loss of control from Peace Corps was returning, along with a nostalgic desire to be back with Montero and the crew, painting houses. That was why he loved painting so much. Predictable. That was, until he fell off the roof. When they got out of the car, Oly noticed that the white walls of the church were not exactly cement but more like dried granola. "What is this?" Oly asked Libeth, as he put his hand on the bumpy surface.

"Shells," Libeth said. "Not much in the way of rock on Sapelo. We use what Mother Nature gives us. Mixes well with cement and lasts forever." Brother Samuel burst out the front door right as Libeth started to knock. They exchanged pleasantries while Samuel looked over at Oly with a relaxed expression that seemed to already comprehend why he was there. He wore a clean white button-down shirt and a bolo tie with a malachite inset.

"Wellllcome to Sapelooo!" he announced in an accented baritone accustomed to echoing the word of God. "Please, come in," he said, gesturing to the tiny entrance.

Libeth whispered to Oly, "He's Nigerian. Came to us several years ago. Very nice man. Says it's like being back home here, minus the armed soldiers looking for handouts."

Although it was small inside, the interior coolness was a welcome contrast to the thick, humid air outdoors. Facing the front of the room were six pews, three on each side, with an unfinished appearance, as though they'd been made in a high-school shop class. A simple cross was nailed to the front wall over a wooden chair placed in front of a cloth-covered table. "The Lord is in this house," Brother Samuel said. Then added, "He welcomes you."

"Yes," Libeth interjected. "Brother Samuel has volunteered to shelter you during your stay. You will be in the Lord's hands here." Brother Samuel pointed to a square, brick enclosure on the edge of the grass.

"There's an outdoor bucket shower over there with a latrine next to it. I'll get you some towels and we keep the buckets filled, so you don't worry about that. You ever use a latrine?"

Oly smiled. "Yes, Brother Samuel, I am familiar with the ways of pre-plumbing toiletry."

"And as long as you are a guest of the church," he continued, "no harm shall come." Oly felt uneasy at Samuel's reassurance of divine protection. "And just in case God is busy, I'll have one of our brothers keeping a watch outside at night so you can rest. Now let me straighten up a bit while you go get somethin' to eat, it must have been a long trip."

Libeth made plans for them to eat at the only restaurant in town, which was neither a conventional restaurant nor in a town. Rather, it was the tidy single-wide trailer of a woman named Lulu who had done quite well for herself running a popular soul food bistro in Atlanta and decided to retire to Sapelo. Visitors to Sapelo would never know the trailer was a restaurant unless someone they knew brought them there. There was no sign, no handicapped parking, and no menus. But inside, Lulu had transformed her trailer, just as Libeth had done, into a comfortable, home-style eating establishment complete with neat tables, a sofa, and a full-sized oven.

Cool, clean air floated in from an air conditioner that was connected to a gas generator in the driveway. Platters of fried okra, chicken with gravy and biscuits, and her specialty turtle soup awaited them. Oly looked over at the tiny kitchen trying to imagine how such a feast could be produced in such a space. Lulu and Libeth went over and sat on the couch, speaking softly while Oly ate. He looked over and noticed Libeth's face taking on a serious expression as Lulu spoke. When her eyes caught his, she changed quickly to smile. Oly started to feel the same separation between him and his hosts that he experienced in Togo. Always the yovo, on the outside of something swirling around him, but often at the center of the conversation.

As dinner turned to dessert, Lulu placed a peach cobbler in front of them. "Now, where's that gonna go, Miss Lulu?" Oly tried in a bad Southern accent. "Fatten' me up for slaughter?" Libeth and Lulu laughed a little too hard for the joke, wondering nervously if Oly was reading their minds. Libeth looked at Lulu before reaching into her bag and pulled out a legal-size, brown envelope that she handed to Oly. It contained a letter.

"Go ahead now, read it" Libeth insisted.

"Ladies and Gentlemen," Oly began. "On behalf of the Friends of Sapelo, the descendants of freed slaves whom for centuries have struggled for prosperity and peace that are righteously theirs, and by the grace of God stand before you today, we thank you for your trust, your support, and your participation in this cause." Oly gently pulled a plastic sleeve out of the envelope that contained one sheet of stationery filled with several sentences in flowery cursive handwriting. It was slightly browned with age and dated at the top. October 20, 1945. The name R.J. Reynolds, Jr. was embossed at the top in simple red block letters. Oly read it to himself, then out loud.

I, R.J. Reynolds, Jr., principal owner of Sapelo Plantation, Inc., hereby transfer said estate of 16,000 acres and its relevant properties, titles, and settlements, to Ms. Marianne O'Brien.
Signed Richard Joshua Reynolds, Jr.

"What's this?" Oly said, looking up. "Who was Marianne O'Brien?"

"His second wife," Lulu responded. "She knew R.J.'s track record with women and didn't want to leave her Hollywood career unless she knew something was in it for her. He promised but didn't deliver the goods on this pre-nup."

"What do you mean he didn't deliver?"

"There's no legal record of the transfer. We did some digging with our friends in the archives and found nothing to indicate this ever happened, unbeknownst to poor Marianne. The land was since sold after he died and has been divided up, some of it under private holdings we don't have access to and some by the state. In other words, some very powerful people stand to make a lot of money from this deal. This letter stands between that.

"How do you know?" Oly asked.

"Because one of R.J. and Marianne's children, Patrick, became an ardent environmentalist and took interest in the property a few years ago, so we're told. He's our only hope right now, but we don't know where he is to get this to him."

"What do you need me for? Just hire a P.I. and mail him the letter."

"Oh, I see, how long you been in the South? So, a group of black folks from the Sea Islands lookin' for the grandson of R.J. Reynolds in the middle of a multi-million-dollar land deal that has been publicized throughout the state. No, word won't get out on that. I'm old, but not old enough for a burial at sea just yet."

"So, what do you want from me?" Oly asked.

Libeth and Lulu looked at one another. "If, by a miracle of God we were able to contact this man, we don't know his intention. Say we got him the letter and he just turned around and was part of the land deal. There goes the land and we're toast as well."

Oly jumped ahead of their thinking. "So, you need some bait to get him out to see what he wants without letting on you have the letter. White bait."

Libeth and Lulu looked at one another, while Oly sat forward on his seat, picturing himself attached to a large hook.

Oly picked up the letter resting on the table and held it. "I just cannot believe how much power these people had to affect so many lives just because they felt like it."

Libeth turned the subject. "What did you do in Africa?"

"How did you know I was in Africa?"

"Gunning filled me in. Just before you came down, I told him we needed more than just a white man. He mentioned your experience in Togo and how you met." She laughed. "He must have really seen something in you. I still don't get how that qualifies you to do a land hearing, but he must have thought something about you to do all this."

"Because I'm cheap?"

Libeth and Lulu cracked up laughing, slapping their knees and rocking forwards. "That must be it!" Lulu laughed. "That must be it. White and cheap!"

When they calmed down from laughing, Libeth spoke again in a more serious tone. "My daddy worked for Mr. Reynolds for a while. I actually saw him once or twice when I was a little girl. Or should I say, I saw his Cadillac fly by. Sure was strange seeing such a fancy car bumping along these roads. Seemed out of place. He never ventured off the estate when he was in Sapelo and he came here only to have parties and entertain guests at the big house. You could always tell when he was here 'cause he employed half the island when in town and everyone would be running around trucking in supplies and sprucing up the place. Around the time that Mr. Reynolds died, my daddy was helping move furniture out of the estate. He found the letter in one of the desk drawers. Don't know why he kept it. Probably thought a day like this would come. He kept it in his bureau for years and it was passed onto me when he died. It's been calling at me to do something with it ever since."

Lulu got up and started cleaning up the kitchen area. "You want some biscuits to snack on at the church?" she asked, wrapping several in a cloth.

"You don't have to ask that twice," Oly said, holding his hands out.

When they got up to leave, it was long past dark. Oly was thinking about all that had been talked about. The letter. The land. The history he didn't share with his hosts. The yovo. Lulu and Libeth gave one another hugs and promised to talk the next day. Libeth turned to Oly. "C'mon now, you gotta get some rest. I'll take you back to the church."

CHAPTER 49

LES PETITS PROBLÈMES

———◆———

LIBETH SAID NOTHING FOR SEVERAL minutes as the car rumbled along, a hot breeze blowing through the space where the windshield used to be. "What you thinking about, young man?" she asked, as they headed around a bend towards the church. Oly revisited the feelings he had when he drove up on the Howard students in his Yamaha, his boubou flapping in the breeze. *Here I am, fellow Americans! We share a country, but not a heritage and here I am pretending to share your experience! Let's party!*

"I was just wondering if I should be here or not, to be honest." It was too dark for Oly to see the expression on her face, but he could tell by the lack of an immediate reaction that she wondered the same. He thought back on the foolishness of driving up on the Howard students on his Yamaha, his boubou waving in the breeze like a white savior. "Things were complicated in Togo. When I met Professor Gunning, I stupidly thought they'd embrace me, but they didn't. They actually seemed angry. And here I am, doing what? Looking for redemption?" Libeth said nothing. The whirring of the fan belt was accompanied by the song of chirping frogs, as they drove the rest of the way to the church in silence.

The windows of the church were lit up like the eyes of a candle-lit pumpkin, as they pulled up in front. "Looks homey," Oly said, as Libeth cut the engine. A hurricane lamp burned inside the church, casting an orange hue on the inside walls as though it were on fire. It was almost the exact model of the lamp Oly had in Togo. "I can clean a wick and light these things with my eyes closed." He held the lamp up by his head and swung it back and forth as he bent over, pretending to be a night watch. In a witch voice, he crackled, "Who goes there? Yovo, is it you? Come to take our land, my little yovo?"

A pew had been made up for him to sleep on, along with pillows. A note was resting on one of them. "Oh look, a little note," Oly said, picking it up. "I wonder if it's the breakfast menu." In scrawling block lettering was written one word: *LEAVE.*

He stared at the note and turned it over a couple of times, looking towards the window as if he could spot the person who wrote it lurking outside. *You're in God's house,* he said to himself.

"Gimme that," Libeth said, snatching it out of Oly's hand. She peered at the note and turned it over to see if anything else had been written, then crumbled it up and threw it down on the floor. "Sons a bitches," she said out loud, gesturing so that Oly looked at the gigantic shadows she cast on the wall behind her.

"Guess it's not too difficult to find the other white people on the island," Oly said, trying to find levity in the moment.

Libeth laughed, breaking her anger. "You got that right!" she said, turning towards the altar and blessing herself for her transgression. Libeth paced around the pews, contemplating what to do. "Can't leave you here alone," she said. "You gotta come with me."

"No." Oly answered, without thinking.

"What?"

"I said *no,* I'm not going to go."

Libeth folded her arms, considering his intention. "You gettin' all brave on me, now?" she said, questioning Oly's sudden resolve.

"No, not really. I'm just not giving them what they want. We run scared now, we run scared right off the island."

Libeth peered up at Oly, her eyes taking him in as she measured his face. She could tell he was terrified, but was trying not to show it. She decided to back off. "Well, alright. If that's how it's gonna be. But there ain't no phone out here. You know that if they come, you on your own. You okay with that?"

"No, I'm not," Oly said. "But it's the choice I'm making."

They both stood, quietly considering their next move. Libeth figured she probably could have convinced Oly to come with her, but quickly calculated that if he did in fact make it through the night at the church that he'd be ready for whatever may come after that. She smiled. "Alright, young man. You stay right here. God keep an eye on you. You just stay right here," she finished, tapping one of the pews gently, as she headed to the door.

Oly stood outside the church, as Libeth got into the car. He waved to her and waited until he could no longer hear the whirring fan belt in the distance. The chirping tree frogs took over from the mechanized sound, making him feel lonely and strangely comforted at the same time. He stood in the stillness for several minutes, feeling the sweat building up on his skin despite a gentle warm breeze. The rhythmic chirping brought him a sense of calm in the darkness. *Wouldn't they stop if someone were lurking around?* he thought. The cloudless sky was filled with speckled stars, reminding him of Togo, where the lack of light pollution allowed Mother Nature to shine, literally.

Oly's parents and brothers didn't know where he was. Jeff and Samantha knew, but had no idea what he was doing or where he was staying. Bawendi and Chalim had no idea, but probably would have laughed at the stupid yovo who went back to America and then tried to find himself in Togo again. He thought about the countless nights when he lay alone, sweating in his hammock, looking at the same inky darkness and glittering night sky, wondering where life would take him. He thought of Bobby and the crew, wondering if they just went back to their old routine and forgot about him. *What would happen if I just disappeared?* he thought to himself. "Shut up!" he yelled to the darkness. "Just shut the hell up!" he yelled again.

The chirping paused. He started laughing and sat down on a grassy patch in front of the church, staring up at the stars. *If Bawendi and Chalim could see me now,* he thought. *Bobby and the boys. Andy and Brett. Samantha.*

Jeff. Mom and Dad. He pictured them all lined up, standing across from him in the darkness, chatting with one another, comparing notes on his life. Even though his parents would seem confused at times, Bobby and Tchalim and Jeff would probably all come to agreement on his current situation. Samantha would chime in, telling his mother that he needed to get whatever it was that brought him to Sapelo out of his system.

Oly went back inside, where it was noticeably warmer, and tried to rest on the pew. He found himself starting to pray, a deep sense of calmness washing over him. The corrugated metal roof creaked as it contracted from the heat of day to the coolness of night. Oly bowed his head, his hands clasped together, and felt for the first time in a very long time, at peace.

The creaking of the tin roof, coming back to life from the heat of a new day, caused Oly to wake from a fitful sleep on the pew. He sat up, disoriented, and looked around. His t-shirt was drenched with sweat. He thought about the night. The frogs had gone silent. He thought about the note, wondering if anyone had come by during the night without him knowing. The door was locked shut and the air inside was stagnant and thick, with the faint scent of wood.

The familiar whirring sound of Libeth's car preceded the sound of bald tires on gravel until she came to a stop in front of the church. "You still alive?" she yelled through the open windshield. Oly opened the door slowly and held a hand to his chest with one hand outreached towards her. Libeth's eyes bulged out and she screamed. Oly stumbled down the front step, letting go of his chest and laughing, resting his hands on his knees. Libeth parked the car and jumped out, waving her finger at Oly. "You damn white boy. Whatchyou tryin' to do, give me a heart attack?"

Libeth was wearing a peach-colored dress that made her look her Sunday best. She clutched a brown paper bag in one hand with small grease stains on the bottom and was sweating profusely, her chest heaving up and down. Oly felt bad and stopped laughing. "I'm really sorry," he said.

"These biscuits are going to the needy you pull somethin' like that again," she said, calming down as she held the bag away from Oly.

"I am the needy," Oly replied, reaching out. He was starving and shoved a warm biscuit in his mouth.

"Glad you made it through the night," she said, watching him scarf the biscuits. "Couple people from town came out during the evening to check on you, so I knew you were alive, but damn you gave me a scare. C'mon we got a big day ahead of us, so put a dry shirt on and let's get going."

The vinyl car seats were already warm from the morning sun, as Libeth drove slower than usual, gliding on the idle speed without accelerating, as if she didn't want to reach the destination. They passed through a densely wooded area that blocked out most of the sun, and came to a clearing a few minutes later. A large, unkempt and strangely out of place circular driveway curved around to meet them. It was like the entrance to an ancient temple. At the top of the semicircle was the whitewashed mansion of R.J. Reynolds, born out of the jungle and barely winning its battle against entropy. The bottom half of the outside walls were a greenish brown from years of heavy rain and rot, vines climbed up the multiple chimneys, and several of the large windows were covered with plywood.

Libeth was quiet as they pulled to the top of the drive and she cut the engine. "This is the summer cottage. You should see his real homes in North Carolina and Paris. His wives refused to come because they didn't like all the bugs and the heat. I guess you could say it was his man cave." Oly said nothing as he tried to put the estate into context with its surroundings. The sprawling, crumbling structure reminded Oly of the Lomé palace of former Togo President Sylvanus Olympio that Eyadema left to rot as a reminder that he was the boss after Olympio was killed in a coup in 1963. The ornateness of the place completely mismatched its primordial surroundings, similar to the air-conditioned mansions constructed outside of Sokodé for Eyadema's cronies.

In the center of the circular drive was an empty in-ground swimming pool in the shape of a cross, surrounded by marble winged cherubs. A set of marble stairs led into the pool, like a Roman temple. The statuettes were covered with moss and grass grew between cracks in the surrounding patio. Oly envisioned 'flappers' of the 1920s dancing around, spilling champagne and giggling as they dived into the pool with their clothes on. Libeth waited for Oly under a gigantic column supporting the front veranda, next to a sign describing the hours and history. *Built in 1924, summer home of Mr. R.J. Reynolds, visited by President Carter in 1979.*

Libeth explained to Oly that up until the mid-eighties, before the estate fell into disrepair, it was often used for fancy political gatherings and celebrations. She reached into her purse and produced a key for a heavy front door that was etched with ornate carvings of what appeared to be grapevines. The raised cathedral ceiling in the foyer was lined with ceramic tiles, which, though now decayed and moldy, were painted with colorful tropical scenes of broad-leaved plants and parrots. She led Oly up a marble-floored hallway to what she called the 'circus room.' In place of a ceiling, a huge canvas enveloped the top of the room, with colors alternating between a faded red and yellow. The walls were painted with cartoon-like images of monkeys, elephants, and circus performers.

"Holy shit," Jeff said, pointed at the ceiling. "Did you ever read *The Great Gatsby?*"

Libeth smiled. "Imagine what happened in here while my folks were resting up for another day of picking. My grandfather used to cook for Mr. Reynolds. Yes, he knew how to party. He used to ship low country affairs right from the mainland, champagne and all. My grandfather and his brothers would be catching shrimp for days in advance to get ready." She led Oly down a winding staircase to the basement. She flicked on a single light, revealing a full-sized bowling alley. Next to it was a full bar. Beside a bathroom door was a life-sized mural of a flapper bending over to fix one of her shoes. The decadence was fascinating and incomprehensible. The juxtaposition of decadence and poverty in Sapelo reminded Oly of his visits to the homes of American Embassy employees whose houses had perfect green lawns, dishwashers, and wall-to-wall carpeting in the midst of grinding poverty. He remembered one USAID employee in particular whom he had visited in Niamey, Niger who had a room full of pinball machines that were running off a generator.

Oly couldn't stop thinking of the threatening 'leave' note and the motivation for writing it. Seeing the old estate reinforced what they were up against. When they exited back to the oppressive humidity of mid-morning, Libeth closed the doors and sighed, "Gets me every time I go in there. I think of all my people who built this for nothing. All we got to show for it is that rotting shack on the other side of this field."

They went back to the car and drove away, with only the sound of the fan belt to carry on their whining conversation. The ancient smells of a rotting, growing jungle drifted through the open windshield. Oly pictured Togolese women on the roadside with babies strapped to their backs and gigantic bowls of yams on their heads. He stared out the window, uncomfortable on the hot vinyl seat, wondering what Bawendi would make of the mansion. He recalled Bawendi's anger when he stayed with him in the village. The pained expression on his face when he lectured Oly about Dixcove reminded him that enduring the past did not mean that they accepted it.

"Libeth, what makes you think some white boy with good intentions is simply going to undo all the evil that other white people did before us?"

Libeth didn't answer, as they turned onto an unfamiliar road past the church. She looked up at an invisible rearview. "Not asking you to undo. Not asking you to do anything you can't. Just asking you to be there. Show up's all you gotta do. We do the rest. You ain't up for it, I bring you back to the docks and we find someone else."

Several minutes later, they turned onto a road unfamiliar to Oly past a small wooden church on the edge of the settlement. Two rusty bicycles were leaning against it and the door was open. "Welcome to St. Luke's," Libeth said. "We came here when I was a little girl. We'd get all dressed up, no matter how hot it was. I rode a mule buggy with my daddy. We'd sing, and smile and sometimes have a basket of peaches next to us. Not a care in the world, just going to say hello to God. It was so simple. I don't remember when I learned all the things I know now, but sometimes I wish I was ignorant of it all, and just had that basket of peaches next to me."

CHAPTER 50

DOUCEMENT, YOVO

———

"WELL, LOOK WHO IT IS," Libeth said, walking in and acting surprised for Oly's benefit, even though she knew full well who was going to be there. Oly fluttered his sweaty shirt at the relatively cool, drier air of the interior. Two black men in white button down shirts and dress pants were sitting at an old wooden table covered with papers and looked up. A large jug of water and a bowl of peaches were between them. It appeared as though they had been there for a while.

Libeth grabbed a peach, while the men stood up. "I'd like to introduce you to two of the Friends' founding members, Dr. Myles Hall, a descendant of original settlers of Hog Hammock and good friend of our Professor Gunning, and Mr. Charles Walker III from the South End." She held a hand to the side of her mouth. "House negro." The men laughed and pointed at Oly's look of shock.

Mr. Walker reached his hand out to Oly. "That's a good sign if we can make those jokes in front of you. Professor Gunning spoke highly of you and his visit to your village in Tchamba." Oly was surprised they seemed to know details about him and looked at the papers spread out on the desk, as he shook Walker's hand.

They sat down, offering chairs to Libeth and Oly, along with a cup of water. Oly took a sip as the three watched him. Oly looked at the well-dressed Mr. Walker and started to feel out of his element. In spite of the heat and rural setting, he was dressed in a white business shirt and green bow tie, as if he were at a law firm in Atlanta. Dr. Hall was wearing an equally business-like shirt, except his was blue and short sleeved. He didn't wear a tie, but looked over the top of his bifocals when he spoke to Oly. "You look a bit in shock, young man."

Oly glanced at Libeth, who was finishing up her peach. Hall continued. "We were expecting Professor Gunning and that is not meant as a slight, but he spoke of your interest in the descendants of the Togolese people, many of whom could very well be here in Sapelo. I wouldn't be even surprised if there are connections to the village in which you stayed. What was the name of it again?"

"Tchamba," Oly answered.

"Yes. The old man," Hall responded, smiling at Oly's astonishment that he knew the translation.

Hall turned his attention to Libeth. "Libeth showed you a letter from a ways back. Well, that's the tip of the iceberg for us. You know we've been fighting the development of this island since Mr. Spalding first turned it into a plantation and then Reynolds and those that followed. It's one of the last frontiers of land ownership that we can actually lay claim to. Everywhere else we'd get laughed out of the court, just like our Indian friends."

Walker picked up the thread, looking at Hall to finish, as though they had rehearsed their lines. "Around the time when you arrived on the ferry, a truck with several white men we didn't recognize came through. We know they weren't the usual fish and game wardens and no one from the DNR knew them. They signed the register as consultants and were invited by members of the old Durant family, who happen to claim ownership to a large part of the land we're disputing."

"So, maybe they're just on a fishing trip," Oly said, grabbing a peach and taking a big bite.

Walker laughed. "They are, son, but this ain't catch and release. It's for keeps," he said, laughing at the analogy.

Libeth looked over at the papers on the table. "All deeds and contracts," she interrupted, annoyed at the joking. "Goes all the way back to Reconstruction. Some of it original, like our favorite love letter.

Mr. Walker and Dr. Hall spent a few weeks in the state archives and Registrar of Deeds' office in Savannah. Unbelievable what they had in boxes." She picked up one of the papers, yellowed with age. "This is an original deed from the Freedmen's Bureau about Hog Hammock and signed by Dr. Hall's great, great grandfather. Land that was later taken away by Mr. Spalding, but there's no evidence of purchase or anything. Just taken. It's all right here."

"How did you get them out of the archives?" Oly asked. Hall and Walker looked at one another. "Okay, you don't have to answer that."

"So, as you can tell," Libeth continued, "there's significant interest in this place right now with the casino developers and anyone who stands in the way. *Significant interest*," she said, slowing her words.

"Does anyone know about the letter Libeth?"

Hall jumped in. "Know about it? From what we can gather, yes. Know that she has it? She wouldn't be here right now if that was the case. The whole thing blows open if that comes to light. The whole thing."

"So what do we do?" Oly asked, starting to sweat profusely in spite of the relative coolness of the church.

"One thing at a time. We got a hearing in a couple of weeks. Zoning board in Savannah. Low-level stuff. They have no idea what's coming. We're pretending it's about permission to build a dock, but it's going to be this whole case. We're asking some of our friends in the press who've been covering the story to go, but we're not telling them the details, just to be there. You don't have to say anything other than provide us with some research help and maybe say a few words about your knowledge of the descendents from Togo, for historic perspective. And being white will really throw them off."

Oly sunk his teeth into a peach. "I'm gonna need a suit."

For the remainder of the morning, as the heat index started to skyrocket in the church, the group guzzled water and pored over the documents, building a fact pattern for the hearing. Oly's head started to swim in the heat and he began to think of where it was all going to go.

A man rode by on a bicycle with a large basket filled with pies, fruit, and sandwiches for the team. Oly looked up through the open church door, surprised. "How did he know we were here?"

"Honey, everyone know we're here," Libeth said, getting up to thank the man and take the basket. "Everyone," she said, when she returned to the church, looking up at the sky.

He felt a wave of guilt for not keeping in better touch with his parents and how things were left with Andy. He tried not to think about Jeff, but imagined him tending bar. Samantha was probably having coffee with friends in cool, safe Chicago. Maybe even with another guy. Unable to get the last image out of his mind, it struck Oly that there was a good chance she was looking past him. He tried to keep the thoughts out of his head by focusing on the research papers in front of him. He noticed that Dr. Hall and Mr. Walker hardly spoke as they read and took notes. Libeth took a break from time to time and would sit back, closing her eyes. Oly looked through a large brown binder labeled 'historic context.' Inside were transcripts, newsletters, and old copies of diaries that locals had written. He picked up one page that appeared to have Arabic writing on it. "What's this?" he asked the group, holding it up.

Mr. Walker looked over the top of his glasses from his seat at a small table. "That's the Ben Ali diary."

"Who?"

"Bilali Mohammed. He was Spalding's head slave. Word is that he ran over five hundred slaves and even helped fight off the Brits in the War of 1812. Imagine that. A Muslim slave fighting for America." He pointed at the paper in Oly's hand. "What you have there is the first Islamic text written on American soil." Oly studied the copy of the smudged handwriting.

"You know Tchamba was Muslim." Oly said.

"Yes, I know," Walker said, taking the glasses off his head. "I told you that this island was settled by people from your area. I believe Bilali was originally from Sierra Leone, but the whole region had pockets of Muslims. Lots of migrations throughout West Africa."

A slight breeze picked up and blew through the open front door of the church, causing it to swing. Oly could see dark storm clouds rolling in against the oppressive heat of the day. "Storm's comin'," Mr. Walker said, as he looked towards the door.

They took a break to eat the food that the man had brought them. "I'm starving," Oly said, getting up to take one of the peach pies from the basket.

Libeth looked up and smiled, "We been at it some time." She looked at a pile of papers labeled 'deed stuff' and another labeled 'evidence.' Hall had drawn a family tree of sorts to assist them with the various connections to the land and had tacked it to the wall next to one of the stations of the cross. The three of them ate in silence, each lost in their own thoughts.

"I left America because I starting getting restless when I saw my whole future lay out in front of me," Oly said after taking a last bite of pie. "After college, it was all right there. Work. Family. Suburbs." Libeth looked over at Walker and Hall. "Then I went to Togo and didn't see anyone with a future in front of them. Everything got smaller, like it was just day to day. Now I'm back here and realize that what I left was what most people would give anything to have."

Dr. Hall laughed and poured himself a glass of water. "Son, I think you've got a healthy case of white man's disease."

Oly smiled. "No one understood what I was doing in Togo. They'd say, 'You live in America, what are you doing here?' I started to question myself. Even people in America weren't sure why I wanted to go to Africa. It didn't add up. Now, I'm back here and it's starting to make sense."

"How so?" Libeth asked, wiping her mouth from eating a sandwich. As she did so, the inside of the church had begun to darken, as rain-bloated clouds floated overhead.

"They called me 'yovo' and I couldn't stand it. There was always a line, even though I ate the food, wore the clothes, and tried to speak the language."

"Of course there was a line," she said. "You were the only white man in the entire town. What did you think?"

"It was more than that," Oly said. "I couldn't stand it because I thought it would solve the things I was running away from in America. The funny part was that I came close. Then, I ran into those students with Professor Gunning and felt ashamed for being such a fraud."

"A fraud?" Walker spoke up. "How do you mean?"

"I pulled up in my African clothes on my motorcycle and assumed they'd be glad to see me, which they were not."

"Understandable," Walker replied.

"Yeah, I know," Oly said. "It was awkward."

"So where does that put you now?" Hall asked, looking intently at Oly. A cool breeze floated through the front door accompanied by a large thunderclap in the distance.

Libeth jumped up. "Oh dear, gotta cover that windshield. Be right back." Oly smiled, turning his head towards the coolness and the sound of heavy rain approaching, as he watched Libeth pulling a large piece of plastic out of the back seat and securing it over the open windshield, her dress fluttering in the breeze as she scooted around the front of the car.

"It puts me right where I'm supposed to be," he said, smiling at Hall and Walker, as Libeth came running back inside, seconds before the skies opened up.

The inside of the church became darker. While the rain thrashed the tin roof, blocking out any possibility of conversation, the four flipped through documents, each lost in their own worlds. Walker picked up a lantern that was next to one of the pews and lit it, causing their movements to be cast as shadows on the walls behind them. The four sat quietly for nearly an hour until the rain began to subside. Dr. Hall finally spoke. "When you were in Togo, how did you connect with the people?"

Oly considered the question, the faces of dozens of people flashing through his mind.

"Mostly in French," he joked. Walker and Libeth laughed. "It was not easy to connect at first, because everyone kept calling me 'yovo' and asking me for things. But then as I went to the market everyday and got to know people, it got easier. I started getting dinner invites and the word got out that I was sticking around."

"And now, here you are in Sapelo. Does your family know you're here?"

"Not really."

"So, why are you doing this work?" Libeth cast a glance over to Hall, wondering if he was planting doubt in Oly.

Oly smiled at Libeth, noticing her concern. "When I left Peace Corps and came back, I actually felt worse than when I entered. I didn't expect that. People thought I was the same, that I just disappeared for a couple of years, but I wasn't. Everything changed with me, but I just didn't connect anymore like I thought I would. It was the same feelings I had when I joined Peace Corps after college, but then it got a lot worse when I came home."

The rain had started to subside, allowing them to hear one another better. Libeth got up and opened the doors again so that a breeze could come through. Hall kept his attention on Oly.

"So, how is coming here helping that?"

"Dr. Hall, take it easy on the young man," Libeth cut in, feeling defensive for Oly.

"That's okay, Libeth, I need to answer his question. He's got a right to ask it." Oly looked at the shadows on the wall behind Libeth, Hall and Walker. None of the black shapes were moving against the white wall. He looked behind himself at a similar black shape cast by the lantern. "The light doesn't care what color we are. Look at our shadows. But, for us, it makes a big difference." He paused as the rain came to a stop, the church falling completely silent as the three looked at him. Oly became nervous, not sure of his words, but knowing that he had to explain himself. "I don't know if coming here is actually going to help with anything. I doubt I'll be any more accepted here than I was back home when I got back from Togo. But when Professor Gunning visited my village and then when we later connected, I knew there was something more to being 'yovo' than just building a bridge or making some friends."

"Is this your white-guilt part speaking?"

Oly laughed. "Yes, I guess it is. But I didn't come for just that. Did you ever hear the expression *homme propose, dieu dispose*? It's French."

"Yes, I recognize the language," Hall said, somewhat defensively. "I saw it a lot in Togo written on buses, buildings, restaurants."

"Then you know it pretty much means that whatever man creates, God decides if it's going to stick around or not."

"Yes, I got that." Hall smiled.

"Well, from where I come from, we propose a lot. We're always proposing, trying to shape the circumstances around us. Improve it. Control it. That's the same feeling I took with me to Togo when I tried against all odds to build a bridge. Then I realized I was putting my energy in the wrong direction. I was really being a yovo and it made me angry with myself for not literally seeing the signs before me."

"Aren't you trying to do the same thing here? Improve things? Control them? Propose?"

"I'm not proposing anything. I'm helping you do that. We'll see if God disposes or not."

Libeth and Walker laughed. "The humbled yovo," Hall smiled.

Oly's emotions started to catch him. "I learned a lot from telling people what I thought was good for them. This is different."

Libeth stood up, stretching her legs. "Okay, gentlemen. That has been a very philosophical journey and I've learned enough to make me hungry. I'm gonna see what Lulu has for us tonight. Anyone want to join?"

"I'm in," Oly said, anxious to get some air after a long day of sitting and reading. When they stepped outside the church, the rain had left a sweet tropical smell that Oly breathed in deeply. The night frogs were just beginning their song, as the heat of day began to cede to early evening.

"Can I drive?" Oly asked when they got to Libeth's car.

Libeth laughed. "You sure? She's no car, you know, she's got a mind of her own." Libeth reached under the steering column and started the engine. "Keep your foot on the brake and let go of it to accelerate. It's the opposite of what you'd think. Letting go of the brake pushes you forward."

The car pulled away from the church when Oly took his foot off the brake. The dead air became a warm breeze that flowed through the empty windshield opening. "Riding in this car is like this whole experience. Can't control the speed, can hardly control the direction," he laughed, laboring with a steering wheel that had long lost its power and fought against his efforts to turn.

"We got some work to do, but we made some progress today," Libeth said over the whirring fan belt. "You stick around for a few days until the hearing and you never know, maybe one of man's proposals will get accepted by God."

"It's not God I'm worried about," Oly said, as his arms strained against the stubborn steering wheel.

Lulu already had two boxes of food ready for them when they arrived. She helped load them into the car and had a quizzical look on her face. "How'd it go today?" she asked.

Libeth paused to wipe some sweat from her brow and put her hands on her hips. "We did some good work today, Lulu. Some good work. Couple more days and we'll be ready. Just a couple more days."

CHAPTER 51

LA CHASSE

———◆———

OLY AND LIBETH THOUGHT ABOUT what may lie ahead. Oly's mind wandered to *La Chasse*, the annual hunt sanctioned by the president that allowed Togolese to kill any wild animal that moved, so long as it was brought back to the Prefecture as an offering to the president. Oly made jokes at the time about how the president could possibly eat so much meat.

On a sweltering morning, late in the second year of Oly's stay, the harmonious purr of a Vespa, accompanied by the distinctive wail of a DT-100, disturbed the silence of a normally quiet morning in Tchamba with a sense of purpose. The DT entered Oly's compound first, making a huge racket that scattered a flock of chickens and literally scared the shit out of a goat, who had been peacefully sleeping under a small tree. It was Jeff, followed by Chalim. Samantha looked up from the washing bowl and groaned. She knew this would not end well for Oly. Chalim had a large basket strapped to the space between his legs on the Vespa and wasted no time in jumping off to make an announcement.

"*Patron, c'est La Chasse aujourd'hui, qu'est-ce que tu fait! Allons-y*" he yelled through Oly's window, hardly noticing Samantha in front of him.

"*La Chasse? Quelle chasse?*" Samantha asked, standing up and dumping the bowl of dirty water onto the ground. She had a meeting with a woman's business cooperative selling textiles outside Koussountou and had no time for *La Chasse*, whatever that was.

"Oh, yovo," Chalim clucked, mumbling something in local dialect and laughing. "*Les bets. Les animaux sauvages.*" He grabbed a stick that was in the basket and pretended to throw it. La Chasse was the one time of year when the ban on killing wild animals was lifted and people could hunt the animals that destroyed their crops and ate their chickens. President Eyadema's astonishing propaganda machine sold the hunt as a tribute to African hunting tradition, thereby keeping the people in the stone age, hunting with sticks and clubs, while soldiers stood by with automatic weapons to make sure no one broke any 'rules.' Entire swaths of forest were burned and gigantic plumes of smoke filled the sky, as villagers attempted to smoke out wild rabbits, antelope, snakes, and monkeys from the bush. It was exhilarating and frightening.

Samantha looked over at Jeff, who shrugged. "Did the crazy yovo make it home okay last night?" he asked.

Oly emerged from the house, his eyes bloodshot, rubbing his head. "Takes one to know one, *mon ami.*"

"C'mon, man, time's running out and you can't leave the hardest job you'll ever love without killing some endangered species with a stick."

"I feel like death," Oly said.

Chalim stared at Oly and patted the rear seat on his moto. He revved the throttle. Oly knew he had no choice.

"*Bonjour, madam,*" Chalim said, finally acknowledging Samantha.

"*Bonjour,*" she replied, in a skeptical tone. Oly was in no condition to leave the house, let alone throw sticks at wild animals. He went back into his house and emerged a few minutes later, wearing a traditional Tchamba shirt along with the type of straw hat that farmers wore in the fields. He had some sort of animal skin draped around his neck that he planned to use as a sack. *Or to vomit in*, Samantha thought.

"We'll take care of him," Jeff said towards Samantha, noticing the worried look on her face.

"That's exactly what I am afraid of. And I assume that I am not part of this tradition?"

"Oh, you are a very important part," Jeff answered, without hesitation. "Who's going to roast my wild boar?"

"Your boar was roasted a long time ago," Samantha answered, turning to Oly. "I guess if this is how you want to spend your last days in country, it's your choice. Just don't do anything stupid. I know the odds against that are slim."

Oly seriously considered not going, but was already mounting his motorcycle by the time he decided it was really a bad idea. Chalim and Jeff took off, leaving Oly little time to catch up.

"I guess I'll catch up with you later?" he said to Samantha, who frowned at him.

"Go do your caveman thing," she said. "Just remember that Rollings is not bailing you out of jail."

On the way to the villages where much of La Chasse took place, the three stopped at the local *medecin traditionel* to smear chicken fat on their faces for good luck. Chalim laughed as Oly reluctantly held a dollop of the foul stuff, wondering aloud if such medicament worked on white people. The *medecin* smiled a toothless grin, his smile stretching across a face like a dark shrunken apple, as Oly handed him a hundred francs for the 'treatment.' Several minutes later, they pulled up to a tiny village, where they could hear the frenzied beating of drums accompanying a large gathering.

The crowd moved as one to the beat, the men singing at the top of their lungs, with sticks raised above their heads. No one turned to notice the two white men arrive with Chalim. Jeff jumped off his motorcycle and joined the dancing frenzy, howling along. The sweet smell of burning bush, something like a fall day in New England, assaulted Oly's nostrils as gigantic plumes of smoke rose in the distance. Oly wished he had stayed behind with Samantha. His head was pounding. The drummers turned the dance into a march and led the hunters toward the rising smoke after a final quaff of tchouk from a gigantic gourd that was in the middle of them. Jeff was wild with anticipation along with Chalim. Oly was terrified. Chalim handed him a long stick and motioned for him to follow. A small boy began to cry at the white man covered in grease, and ran to hide his face in his mother's legs.

The only reassurance Oly felt, as he followed Chalim in a pack of tchouk-fueled hunters, was that he did not notice anyone with firearms. Otherwise, he was convinced that thousands would have died in the chaos. Already sweating profusely in the midday heat, Oly cursed himself for not bringing water, as the pungent smoke and dust burned his lungs. Astonished villagers who had never seen a white man on La Chasse pointed and muttered in local dialect. Oly looked at Chalim, who explained, "They say you like gri-gri. Magic. You bring them animals."

They came upon a gigantic bare kapok tree, with a crowd of hunters surrounding it on all sides, singing. A lone baboon clung to a branch, exposed and terrified. His expression looked human and it was unsettling. His eyebrows twitched and he looked rapidly from side to side following the men circle the base of the tree. Oly looked over at Jeff, who was jumping around, howling with Chalim with his stick raised, like a scene from Lord of the Flies.

The men, along with Jeff and Chalim, leaned back and hurled their sticks all at once from both sides, a swarm of sticks and clubs hurtling toward the tree. Most of the sticks bounced harmlessly off branches while the rest flew over the top, passing one another in mid-air and raining down upon the men on the opposite side. The hunters covered their heads for protection from their own weapons, and the baboon, sensing an opportunity, made a run for it. Scaling down the tree at full speed, he leapt off the trunk several feet from the ground, arms fully extended. He was headed directly for Oly, one of the few who did not throw his club at the tree. The scene unfolded like a movie in slow motion, plumes of smoke flowing across the plain, as the men regained their composure, grabbed sticks off the ground for the second wave of attack, and looked directly at Oly. Chalim's eyes went wild as they registered what was taking place, and he screamed for Oly to throw his weapon.

The baboon's distorted face became all mouth, as its red cavern full of white teeth sprinted at full speed toward Oly. It tried to change direction, but a flurry of sticks followed like arrows in a medieval battle. Oly made out the words *YOVO! YOVO!* fluttering above the monkey's screams. Several sticks bounced off his legs. Oly covered his head with his arms in a feeble attempt to hold off the flying clubs, but one (with a particularly large knot) caught him in the shoulder, knocking him to the ground. As he fell, the baboon tripped as well and landed next to him, exposing an underbelly of orange and white fur.

Oly hit the hard ground, dropping his club and grabbing his shoulder in pain. A savage death cry from the baboon rang in his ears next to him: a wounded comrade. Oly smelled the sweet stench of men's sweat mixed in with smoke and dust. The ground shook with the pattering of feet on the ground next to him, as a cheer exploded on all sides. The men were chanting a victory song; Oly felt himself fading out of consciousness. A heavy arm reached beneath him, helping him to his feet. *"Monsieur Oly, ça va? Monsieur Oly?"* Chalim's dark face blocked out the sun as Oly looked up at the blur. He could hear Jeff's voice behind him yelling something about air and water. The men all circled around Oly and Chalim, holding the limp body of the dead baboon above their heads, chanting and screaming. One of them held Oly's arm in the air and placed one of the baboon's hind legs in it. They all began jumping and cheering together. Patches of dirt stuck to the chicken fat on Oly's face. Chalim and Jeff held him up on either side to keep him from falling again.

The hunting party walked for what seemed like miles until they finally reached the village where they had started. Chalim whistled with joy, as he strapped the lifeless baboon to his Vespa for the drive to the prefecture. Oly sat under a tree to collect himself, while Jeff jumped on his motorcycle. "C'mon, man, we got to celebrate, yovo style."

Oly didn't move. "They look like baby's hands," he mumbled.

Jeff, getting impatient, dismounted his motorcycle and walked over, holding his helmet under his arm. "What are you talking about, man? Stop freaking out."

"The hands," Oly continued. "Did you see them? The monkey had hands like a baby."

"Yeah, I know, it's kinda gross, but what the fuck, this has been going on for thousands of years. A man's gotta eat, right?" Jeff realized as soon as he said the words that it would not make either of them feel better. The thought of eating baboon was more than either of them could take. The landscape started to swim before Oly's eyes and his shoulder felt like it had been dislocated. "C'mon, man, get up before the kids start coming over asking you for a nickel," Jeff pleaded, lifting Oly up by the armpit. Jeff gave Chalim a wave to go on without them, partly because he didn't want him to wait, but mostly because he wanted to keep the baboon hands as far away from Oly as possible.

After a dusty four-kilometer ride, Oly and Jeff pulled up to the prefecture where a crowd had already assembled. Chalim had already unstrapped the baboon and laid it down on a gigantic plastic mat, along with all of the other animals from La Chasse. Every animal imaginable was laid out, big and small, like a horrible massacre at a city zoo. Antelope, several species of bush rat, snake, monkey, a huge wild boar, even a baby hippo, were lying out in various states of bludgeoned trauma.

A plume of smoke floated above the white-washed prefecture building, as the pungent smell of burning hair assaulted Oly's nostrils. It was a smell he never got used to. Several soldiers were picking through the corpses, lifting up various limp and bloody heads and pointing to refrigerator trucks that were waiting nearby. The best meat was going to Lomé.

Jeff tapped Oly on the shoulder. "Were we expecting company?" he said, pointing over at another Peace Corps motorcycle.

"Shit," Oly said, recognizing Samantha's helmet. "She's not going to like this."

Oly tried to straighten himself up, but knew it was useless. He reeked of chicken fat, was covered in dirt, and knew there must be some blood mixed in. He dropped a hunting club that he was holding for some reason and approached Samantha, looking down with sadness at a dead baby gazelle laid out next to its dead mother.

"So," she said, before Oly had a chance. "You boys have fun? Kill anything?"

"Holy shit, you should have seen it," Jeff started before Oly put his hand up.

"No, actually, other than the burning bushes it was pretty uneventful."

Samantha gazed over at three armed soldiers struggling to hoist the baby hippo into one of the refrigerator trucks. "I see that one isn't going to the petting zoo."

Chalim came running over, the lifeless baboon thrown over his shoulder, like a father playing with a child at the park, the difference being that his 'child' had hairy legs, a bright blue and red bottom, and happened to be dead. Oly started vomiting as soon as Chalim was close enough for him to see the hands up close. Chalim held up one of the legs and pointed at Oly, who was hunched over, heaving. "*C'est lui, c'est lui!*" Chalim cried.

Samantha looked over at Jeff, who shrugged. "It wasn't quite like that," Jeff tried to explain. "He was more of a decoy."

She put her hand up. "I don't need to hear anymore. I think I'm going to puke, too."

"*On y va, non?*" Chalim gestured, using the baboon's hand to wave. He ran off to one of the large fires that was being used to burn the hair off the animals. Oly stood up and wiped his mouth on his shirt.

"I don't know what's making you puke more, the dead animals or the chicken fat smeared all over you," Samantha said, with a look of disgust on her face. "Listen, I'm out of here. I hope you boys enjoyed Oly's last day in country. JFK would have been proud."

"That was cold," Oly said, trying to wipe the chicken fat off on his shirt.

She reached for her motorcycle helmet. "What the hell are you trying to prove, Oly?" she asked, her eyes watering up as she put the helmet on.

"Where are you going?" Jeff asked.

"Oh, I don't know. I think there's some white guy leaving Togo tomorrow. He decided he wasn't yovo anymore, until reality hit him and he had to go home. I just was going to see if he remembered which direction that was." She straddled her motorcycle without waiting for a response and kick started the engine with anger. She looked directly at Oly, her eyes piercing through the opening in the helmet, while she revved the throttle. She didn't have to say a word. He knew what she was thinking. Was this how he wanted to end things? Was he happy now that he was 'accepted?'

Chalim put his own hand on Oly's shoulder. "*Tu viens, non? Le chef vous attends.*"

Oly shrugged.

"Go ahead, Tarzan," she said, revving the throttle. "You go party with the *chef*. I'm going to look for that white guy who's packing up his ideals."

Jeff shoved him in the back, while Chalim pulled him in the opposite direction. Before Oly could make up his mind, Samantha spun the tires and took off in the direction of Koussountou.

"Well, that went swimmingly," Jeff said. "You got no choice now. You have to party."

"*On y va!*" he yelled to Chalim, grabbing Oly and holding his arm up. "*Le chef nous attends!*"

CHAPTER 52

LES PETITS PROBLÈMES, II

———◆———

I'M GOING TO LOOK FOR the white guy who's packing up his ideals was all that Oly could think about, as Libeth drove back to the church. He revisited the primitive, carnal feelings at the time of *La Chasse* and felt some of the feelings returning, in addition to Samantha's disapproval. Libeth started humming as they bumped along the dirt road. Oly started to relax. "Did I ever tell you about the time I went on a hunt in Togo?"

"A what?" she said, laughing.

"A hunt. I was running around the bush on a hunt. The president declares one day a year for a hunt and everyone goes crazy. They burn half the countryside down to chase out the animals, it gets out of control, no guns are allowed, and people throw these crazy clubs all over the place. I almost got killed."

Libeth steered the resistant steering wheel towards the last curve before the church, snickering to herself. "Boy, you the strangest white man I ever met. Not that I met many. But you got one crazy story to tell. Hunting in Africa, unnh, unnnh," she said to herself, tssking as she did so.

When they got back to the church and started unloading the food, Oly noticed that something was wrong. One of the side windows was smashed and there was no one around. "Libeth, you stay here," Oly yelled, as he ran towards the house, unable to see Dr. Hall or Walker.

"Dr. Hall! Mr. Walker!" Oly yelled out, not thinking about what may be waiting for him as he burst through the door.

The two men hardly looked up when Oly entered. Oly couldn't see them from outside because they were both on their knees, picking up the broken glass that had been scattered throughout the room. A large rock leaned against one of the pews. "Had some company while you were gone," Walker said. "I would have called you to bring more food, but they didn't stay too long."

Oly wanted to laugh but could tell by their faces that they were still shaken. "Libeth, come on in," Oly yelled. "They're alright. It's just a broken window."

"Broken window, my ass!" Libeth yelled, as she entered the door behind Oly. "Dr. Hall. Mr. Walker, who did this? You see anyone? I'll march right on down to the DNR and use their phone for the sheriff's office. Did you see anyone? Tell me right now."

Hall and Walker looked at one another. "Couldn't tell exactly Libeth, but you probably have an idea who it might be."

Libeth picked up a shard of glass and held it up, then looked at the broken window. "They've been drivin' us around in fear for such a long time, don't they know we're numb to it all by now?" she started laughing. "Broken glass. Broken bones. Is there anything left?"

Oly went over and started to clean up the papers that were scattered. "Why don't we eat and then everyone needs some sleep. This is not going to be solved right now."

Hall and Walker agreed. They put the food out on a small table they cleared at the back of the church. Dr. Hall bowed his head and led the group in prayer. "Dear Lord, thank you for these bountiful gifts to nourish our bodies so that we may feed our minds. We thank you for looking over us as we seek what is right by your name dear Lord, Jesus Christ our Savior. Amen."

Oly looked over at Libeth, who continued to pray with her head down. He waited until Walker picked up a biscuit before he took a piece of chicken. The night frogs had started their song and the air hung heavy. Oly noticed that he was starting to smell very badly when he lifted one of his arms.

"Whoooeee," Libeth said. "You're riper than a rotten papaya." The four of them laughed harder than was necessary. The tension was broken. "I'll have someone fetch water for you. Nothing like a nice bucket shower."

Oly took a big bite out of a piece of chicken and swallowed. "You mean I came all the way back to America to have a bucket shower? What do you think I did for two years in Togo?" They laughed again.

"Boy comes to Sapelo and thinks he's in America," Hall remarked. "Not sure what to do with that." For several more minutes they ate quietly, revisiting some of the trauma of the evening, but reassuring themselves that if they stuck together it might be okay.

Well into the evening, after Bobson rode by on his bicycle and Libeth sent him off for water, Hall and Walker looked over at Libeth. "Mind if we get going, Libeth? We got a big couple of days in store." Hall then looked at Oly. "If you need, son, one of us can stay here with you."

Oly considered the gesture. "I think I'll be fine," he said, trying to sound confident. The three got up after they finished and wrapped up the trash to bring with them. They walked outside to say goodbye and Libeth gave Oly a hug.

"It's not the last time you're going to see me," he said to her, as she held him back to take a look at him.

She laughed. "You got that right. You got a hunt to attend to. A hunt!" she yelled, laughing as she pointed in the air.

Bobson rode up just as Walker, Hall and Libeth got into her car. He rode his bike with a large bucket of water balanced on his head. Libeth instructed him to leave it out back where Oly could wash himself. Bobson handed Oly a towel and a bar of soap with gnarled hands that had known a lifetime of hard labor. They reminded Oly of the villagers in Affem-Boussou.

Oly watched the car drive away, followed by Bobson on his rickety bicycle. Oly looked up at the stars, which filled the sky in the absence of any nearby city lights. He looked at the flickering light inside the church through the broken window and felt a well of emotion run through him. *Where's Bawendi when I need him?* He thought to himself. He looked at the treeline opposite the church and imagined Chalim bursting through on his Vespa, armed and ready. He imagined the villagers of Affem coming down the road, singing the yovo song and laughing. *Homme propose, dieu dispose!* they'd say over and over. He imagined Samantha and Jeff, standing next to one another, as the villagers passed them, shaking their heads at how their yovo friend got himself into another predicament. He imagined his parents with Andy and Brett, talking to one another and pointing at the broken glass. *What is he doing?* they'd say. *Has he gone mad? Do we need to call the police?*

Oly walked around to the back of the church where Bobson left the water, took off his clothes, and dipped a cup that was left nearby into the cool water. He closed his eyes as the water poured over him, feeling a sense of calm in spite of the uncertainty that awaited him.

Sleep came fast after the cool bath. Oly was not afraid, even as a breeze came through the open window, reminding him about what had happened.

When he awoke the following morning, Oly's back hurt from sleeping on the pew, but he felt refreshed. He stood up, stretched and walked over to the piles of papers. He picked up a handful and started reading. There were so many details and so many dots to connect that it felt overwhelming. He didn't understand much of the legal language on the deeds and wondered how Hall and Walker were going to put it together to build a case. He picked up one of the original deeds and held it carefully in his hand. He thought of Jeff and wondered if he would have stuck around. He imagined faxing the documents to Samantha in Chicago to get her help, laughing at her reaction as they came through the machine. Of course, there were no faxes on the island, but he smiled at the possibility of her reading his cover note.

Dear Samantha; I hope you are well. I'm on Sapelo now and I need your assistance in tying these letters to this land dispute that we are trying to resolve. Let me know what you think. I hope you are well.

He wondered how she'd react. The familiar whirring sound broke Oly's thoughts, as he put the deed down. He looked over at the source of the noise and Libeth's car was rambling down the road. He went outside the church and saw her waving through the windshield as she approached. He could tell she was happy to see him. Walker and Hall were in the back. They jumped out when the car pulled up. Hall was holding a greasy paper bag and Walker had a large basket of peaches. "I know what that is," Oly said.

"We are glad to see you!" Hall said. "I was telling Libeth on the way home yesterday that it was not a good idea to leave you alone out here, but you seem to have survived!"

Oly put a hand to his back. "I almost didn't survive the pew as my bed, but yes, I'm in one piece."

The four went inside, as the morning temperature started to climb. The church was cool inside, not yet broiled by the relentless sun. "Okay," Hall started, a biscuit in his mouth. "We got deeds to read!" They spent the entire morning, taking only the occasional break, reading through the piles of material that had to be deciphered and connected to the dispute. Hall had them organize into three piles: *historic context, legal documents, anecdotal.* Oly found himself reading more than sorting, but Hall kept him on track and made sure that he stayed focused. After several hours of the same routine, they'd take a break. Bobson always seemed to appear with food when they needed it the most, a cornucopia from Lulu's.

There were no more unexpected visits, as the four worked relentlessly for two more days. Libeth put in a report about the incident with the DNR, who assured her they'd follow up with the sheriff. She didn't share details about the case they were working on, but emphasized that what happened was more than likely intentional. (She retold the story several times to Hall, Walker and Oly, re-creating each time how she put the rock down on the table at the DNR as 'evidence.'

By day four, Hall and Walker felt that they had the makings of a case. Timelines were established, historic context, and the critical legal documents. They had done as much as they could. Oly was depleted from the exhaustion of working all day in the stifling church and sleeping on the pew, but felt energized by Hall's confidence. "This is about the best we can do for now," he said. "I'll head out to Savannah tomorrow, where Professor Gunning is supposed to meet us and we'll see if we can't present a case."

"Gunning's coming down?" Oly asked.

"Yes he is. You may get to meet him if you come over, but no obligation. He sent a telegram the other day that he wanted to be in Savannah for the hearing. We're excited to show him what we've put together."

"There's a ferry leaving today," Libeth said. "If you want to get a head start, maybe clean yourself up a bit, if you know what I mean," she said, laughing as she mimicked sniffing her underarms.

Oly had started to feel restless after the long days at the church and jumped at the opportunity, plus the chance to see Gunning and tell him what he knew to get ready for the hearing.

Oly packed up his belongings, and looked one more time at the three piles of documents they had put together. "Take care of that stuff," Oly said, as he shook Hall and Walker's hands. I hope to see you at the hearing. And if I don't, thank you for including me in this, it meant a lot.

"That was nothing, son," Walker said. "It was our pleasure. And on behalf of the Friends, we are eternally grateful."

Oly and Libeth got into the car and Oly looked back several times as they drove away, wondering if he'd ever see the place again. "I know what you're thinking, son," Libeth said, as she turned the car. "Don't you worry. We're gonna fix that window," she said, laughing.

"Yes, that's exactly what I was thinking. The window."

When they passed a large field that had once been a tobacco plantation, now overgrown, Oly spotted a man in khakis and a sweaty shirt standing in the field behind an object that appeared to be a tripod. "Man in the Panama hat. I wondered where he was hiding."

"What was that?" Libeth said, sounding somewhat alarmed.

"That's the dude from the ferry. Looks like he's taking pictures or something."

Libeth pushed on the brake to slow down, but it only caused the car to jerk forward, making a squealing noise that made the man turn and stare.

"That ain't picture taking. He's surveyin' the property, taking measurements," she said, her mind racing. She looked back to see if they should return to Hog Hammock. Not enough time. "This is the disputed land," she said, finally looking ahead while the man continued to stare them down as they passed. "It's part of the estate and is supposed to be off limits until after the hearing. This ain't good that he spotted us. He ain't supposed to be here and he knows it. Folks told me the other day he was staying over at the University of Georgia barracks they got over on the nature preserve on the other end of the island."

"Stop the car," Oly said.

"What are you talking about?" Libeth said. "You got a ferry to catch and the hearing is coming up. That's where we fight 'em."

"You know where that broken glass came from, right?" Oly asked. Libeth went silent. "And now they're surveying disputed land? You think they're paying much attention?"

Before Libeth could stop him, Oly jumped out of the slow moving car and walked quickly towards the man, who was still staring at them. The man's sweaty, red face started to come into view with more detail the closer he got. It was difficult to walk over the dried, stalky grass and the remains of an overgrown tobacco field. Just before he reached the man, Oly heard Libeth's engine rev back to life and speed off. He felt terrified, not certain that he had done something he could take back.

Before the man could speak, Oly kicked out one of the legs of the tripod and watched it tumble to the ground. The man's pungent body odor filled the air before either of them said anything. The man stepped back, nearly tripping on a clump of dried earth, his sweaty expression turning to anger.

"What the hell you doin'?" the man yelled, shocked at the attack, but emboldened now as he assessed the youth of his opponent. "You some do-gooder college kid lookin' for trouble? You know who I am, you sonofabitch?"

Oly's heart pounded in his chest uncontrollably, making it hard to breathe enough to get the words out without sounding panicked. He pointed at the fallen tripod and yelled, "You ain't no birdwatcher. I know that, you asshole!"

The two of them looked at one another for several seconds, assessing one another through heavy breaths before the man put his hands on his hips and laughed up at the sky, putting his arms out straight to expose large sweat patches under his arms. "You a long way from home, boy," he barked, in a confident, snarling tone, now that he had surmised that Oly wasn't representing any government agency or police. A dull, roaring sound grew in the distance as the man looked over Oly's shoulder and grinned, speaking softly and pointing directly at Oly's chest. "You a looonnng, way from home."

CHAPTER 53

HOMME NATUREL

———◆———

CASHEW FARM WAS ALL OLY could think of as he watched the manmade dirt devil heading towards him. It was going too fast to be Libeth's car and by the man's reaction, something told him it wasn't the police. Oly became paralyzed by fight or flight, glancing quickly back and forth between the man and the car approaching fast, now in view. Oly tried to compose himself as his heartbeat pounded in his chest. "You're a long way from home too, buddy," was all he could think to say. "You're nothing but another yovo, that's all."

The man looked at him, confused. "A yo-what?"

"You think you're going to just walk in here and take what you want? You realize it's not like that anymore? You realize you can't just take things because you want? You know what Mr. Reynolds left behind? You know what he did?" Oly feared he said too much, as the man squinted his eyes, measuring Oly again.

"Whatchyou mean by that, boy, huh?" he said, approaching Oly. "Whatchyou mean by that?"

The vehicle was coming closer and fast. Oly didn't want to continue the line of questioning and quickly calculated his options. He dashed for the camera and grabbed it out of the dirt, trying to wrangle it from the tripod. The man, moving much slower than Oly, yelled. "Hey, you can't do that! That's private property, boy! You gonna be in a world of hurt!" The man grabbed Oly with a sweaty arm, trying to pry the camera loose, but Oly shrugged him off easily.

"Fuck off," Oly snarled, holding the now detached camera in his arm. Oly could see the car clearly now, and there was more than one person in it.

The man laughed. "Yeah, that's right, boy. You gonna get your ass kicked. Now why don't you just hand that over and make it easier on yourself," the man said, holding his hand out.

Oly looked into the man's eyes and considered him as sweat poured from his brow. "*Homme propose, dieu dispose!*" Oly yelled, holding up the camera, before he turned his back and ran. The man started laughing. "That right, boy. You run. You run like hell. This here's my island, boy. You ain't gonna hide. You ain't..." he continued, his words trailing off into the thick air, as Oly stumbled as fast as he could in the opposite direction. Although he didn't look back, Oly could hear the car's engine revving high as it tried to cross the field, straining against the earth until it stalled and came to a stop. He could hear men's voices yelling, but he didn't stop running. A swampy, forested area bordered the edge of the field and Oly ran into it, soaking his legs up to his calves. The heavy organic scent of rotting vegetation assaulted his nostrils and he tore his pants on a prickly vine, opening a large gash on his left leg.

After tripping over the uneven ground and soaking himself from falling several times in the murky water, he began to slow down. The men's voices were absorbed by the heavy, humid air and he felt alone. A slightly cooler breeze joined by the distant sound of waves joined his pounding heart. Confident that no roads were nearby and the vehicle couldn't possibly follow him, Oly collapsed onto the sand, exhausted by the post-adrenaline rush. His leg ached and bled. Weary logic started to replace the instinctive impulse to run and survive. He hoped that Libeth got back safely and was able to alert Hall or Walker to help them or at least call for help. How would he let them know where he was? He looked through the trees and could smell the salt air that accompanied the sound of waves. He was desperate with thirst, his mouth covered with a dust that he couldn't wash out. He looked down at the swampy water at his feet and was tempted but realized it would make things worse.

He walked toward the wave sounds until the trees opened up onto a beach, exposing him to the refreshing joy of open ocean. The breeze dried his shirt and made him feel alive. He thought about continuing along the shore until he could get help but the pain in his leg caused him to nearly pass out. Distracted by pain, hunger and thirst, his weary logic decided that he had just as good a chance of stumbling into the wrong hands and he did getting found by the right ones. He decided to stay put until he could at least get some rest and deal with the pain. He held the camera out and looked it over, brushing off some of the sand. It was an older model of a Pentax 35 mm and it was heavy.

A large dune served to protect him from the wind, as Oly fell asleep almost as soon as he lay down in the sandy refuge. After what had seemed like just several minutes turned out to be several hours, as the adrenaline rush in Oly turned to fatigue. He opened his eyes to early evening, awoken by the complete sounds of the night symphony, as the night sky had taken over with millions of stars that shined indifferently.

Although the bleeding had subsided, his leg ached with a dull pain. He stumbled down to the water's edge and washed off the cut. The salt water felt good on the wound as he splashed water on it. He swatted several flies from the matted blood and sat back, looking up at the same sky he had stared at so many times with Bawendi and Chalim. "*Homme propose, dieu dispose,*" he said to himself. *What the hell happens now?* He was back in the Aledjo tunnel in the darkness, helpless, the noises of nature screaming at him just as the other passengers screamed out of fear that a truck was coming the other way down to collide head on. His emotions started to take over, opening up a well of thoughts and images that pushed him down in the dune, causing him to sob uncontrollably as his mind processed what had just happened. When he cried about as much as he could, opening his eyes to the dark grey stain of his tears in the sand, he looked at the camera and felt resolve. He was not going to give into the fear or the helplessness that he felt when they passed through Aledjo. He was going to come out the other side, into the light, and finish what he started. He was starving, but settled down into a deep sleep for the rest of the night.

Shortly after dawn, the sun peeked over the horizon and instantly heated the humid earth around him. The orchestra was getting ready to rest, the prelude to another day on earth nearly complete. Oly came to, sweating and parched, his leg pulsating with pain. *What would Montero and the boys be saying about this?* He imagined them laughing their heads off when he kicked the tripod out. *What are you going to do now, college boy?* He was back at the St. Peter's fight and how they all had one another's back. Bawendi and Chalim, what would they think? He imagined the two laughing at Oly going all the way back to the comforts of America, only to get in trouble in a place that resembled Africa. There had to be some expression for that. He couldn't reconcile whether Samantha would be bemused or disappointed in how things had turned out. At least he caused the mess and she couldn't say he was Jeff's lackey. *Shit,* he thought, his mind thinking logically again now that the emotion started to subside. Libeth.

Oly pushed himself up on all fours, breathing in to control the pain in his leg. His still weak shoulder buckled under the weight, so he used one leg and the other half of his body to stand. *Piece of work,* he thought to himself. He stood up, slowly, holding his injured leg out as he tried to cover his sleeping spot with the other. No use, it just made more marks. He tried to lick his dried lips with a tongue that felt like a piece of bark in his mouth. He hadn't eaten or had anything to drink in over twenty-four hours and it was starting to cloud his thinking.

He started to replay the events of the evening and wondered why he ran. What were they going to do? This was America, right? The sound of the car engine replayed in his head. It was a violent, angry sound, just like the military trucks in the cashew field that triggered the same impulse to move quickly. "Fuck," he said to himself, wincing from the pain as he started limping. He stared at the camera and wanted to smash it. *What the hell did I think I was going to do? Talk sense into that guy? Why did I have to confront him? Why couldn't I just wait?* Oly tried to force himself not to think that he could have blown up the whole hearing. He started to feel foolish for allowing himself to fall into the yovo trap that he could just confront things and they'd work out. *Just who the hell do you think you are? Some kind of superhero?* He turned the camera in his hand and held it up as though taking a picture. "Yeah, that's right," he said. "Pose for the superhero. Yovoman."

The sound of the ocean nearby reassured Oly and kept him from losing his focus completely. It was hard to imagine that ships came from these shores all the way to Togo and back, filled with the ancestors of Bawendi and Chalim, chained, scared, dying, forever changed if they survived. "The closest you can get to Africa without getting wet," he said to himself, looking over at the incoming tide. He wished that Chalim and Bawendi were there with him, and imagined trying to swim back to Togo. Would they want to go back with him? He wondered at the irony of them deciding to take a chance on life in America, while he preferred to go. He could eat fish along the way and ride on dolphins until they dropped him off in the Bay of Benin. How long could it take? And then he could disappear, stay forever where he belonged, the African Colonel Kurtz, surrounded by people who would take care of him and maybe even understand him.

The beach eventually led to a path through the thick brush, back into the dark unknown and away from the calming sea. He stared down it, and then back along the coast. *Escape or reality*, he thought. He wasn't going back to Togo on the backs of dolphins and there was no escape. "Escape to reality," he said aloud, putting the words together and heading slowly down the path, which led to a two-track road that wound near an overgrown cotton field. As the coolness of the ocean air gave way to the stagnant humidity of inland, Oly's steps became heavy and deliberate. "Escape to fucking reality," he said again, aloud.

A man appeared from nowhere, passing him on a black bicycle, and looked up at Oly's voice, giving him a startled look. It was Bobson. He put his leg down to stop the bike and looked up under a torn, twisted straw hat, just like the farmers wore in Togo. His face was lined from years of hard manual labor in the hot sun and his hands, lean and strong, lifted up from their grip on the handlebars. "You must be the fellow they're lookin' for. You gotta go, young man. Caused quite a stir, yes you did. You gotta go. They looking for you."

Oly's heart started pounding again, as he re-entered reality and the trauma of the night before. "Who? Who's looking for me? What's going on?"

He frowned at Oly, looking around. "Ms. Libeth, she gone. They all gone," he said, waving a pointed finger off toward the coastline. He got off the bike and looked toward the tree line, sweat pouring down a salt and pepper beard. "They come last night. Men in trucks. They burn the wooden church. They burned it all."

"What do you mean they burned it all?" Oly yelled, causing Bobson's eyes to widen. He moved his bicycle off the road, closer to the tree line in case anybody came down the road, and lowered his voice. "It's all gone. Now you gotta go. Go on, mistah, you gotta go."

Oly felt faint, as the blood left his head and his heart began to race. His leg ached in pain again and, for the first time since the cashew field, he felt like his life was in real danger. Without offering any more advice as to where he should go or God forbid find help, Bobson mounted his bike as if to separate himself from Oly as soon as possible, pushing the pedals with his wobbly knees outward.

CHAPTER 54
YOVO PART

———

THE WINDING ROAD TURNED INTO crumbling pavement, a sign that he was approaching Reynolds' mansion. Oly spotted the faint glow of interior lights. The same feeling that had visited him on countless nights in Tchamba came back to him - an outsider in a culture, wondering where he belonged. He walked along the tree line and noticed that more lights than usual seemed to be on in the sleepy mansion. Two vehicles were parked outside, one resembling the car that pursued him across the field. The faint odor of cigarette smoke reached him. He left the road and struggled through the thick under brush.

Already dripping with sweat in the early morning heat, he started to feel woozy. The sooty smell of a burned-out fire triggered Oly's senses when he got back on the road, a disturbing combination of melting plastic and building materials, not the pleasant cooking fire smell he had become used to on the island. A group of islanders Oly didn't recognize was gathered in front of the smoldering remains of St. Luke's, where Oly had spent several nights in what now seemed an eternity ago. They were hugging and crying, as the pastor tried to console the small gathering. Before he had a chance to react, a young man who had been standing by himself noticed Oly and tapped the shoulder of one of the people in the group, pointing in his direction. They turned in unison at the arrival of the white stranger and the sobbing ceased, followed by dead silence. Oly was in too much pain to run and could not find the words to explain how he was there to help. Before Oly could say anything, they laid upon him, faces twisted in anger, lips curled up with white teeth, chattering at him all at once. They surrounded him on all sides, assaulting him with their words, saliva spraying into the air. Charred papers that he had been studying only hours before fluttered through the air around them were destroyed forever, left in a heap of ash. "You goddam newspaperman!" they yelled, pointing at his camera. One man tried to grab it from him. "What you doin' here? There ain't nothing here to see. You need to go away from here!"

Oly looked down at the camera and almost started laughing at the misunderstanding. "I'm not a newspaperman. I was here in the church." He looked straight ahead at the pile of burned rubble and started to walk towards it, afraid no longer. Lying under a large half-burned beam that formerly held up the church roof, Oly spotted his hockey bag, twisted and melting, but still recognizable. The group, puzzled by his non-reaction to their anger and curious as to why he walked towards and not away from the disaster, parted and watched. He climbed across the smoky, still-hot ruins and lifted the edge of his bag up, looking back at the group, as pieces of his charred clothing spilled out of it. "This is mine."

The group considered what he had said for several seconds until a tall man with sinewy arms and torn overalls stepped forward in anger. He pointed over to something on the edge of Oly's vision, lying in the grass about fifty yards from the old church ruins. Three people were kneeling down over the lumps, blocking his view. When he quickly scanned the scene, he recognized a pair of legs, barely covered by the remains of torn pants and with one shoe missing. It was Hall. Oly limped over to him, pushing a man who tried to block his way. "I know him!" he yelled. "Let me go!" When Oly got to Hall, he was not prepared for what he saw.

Although he was still alive, barely, he was badly burned and moaned in a semi-conscious state of pain. The three people tending him were crying and hardly noticed Oly, one of them holding Hall's badly burned hand. Oly looked up past the trees in panic, as if he expected to hear sirens coming to the rescue. "Shit," he muttered, turning his head aside while he tried to kneel next to Hall. The sight of this nearly unrecognizable figure and the nauseating smell of burned flesh triggered a vomit reaction that Oly could barely suppress.

The man with the sinewy arms had walked up behind Oly and yelled in his ear. "You have ruined everything! You must leave Sapelo now! You cannot be here!"

You cannot be here. The words drilled into Oly's head and he started to feel woozy, as if he were going to pass out. Images of Jeff, the bridge project, falling on the roof, leaving Andy's, all flooded his brain all at once. *You cannot be here.* "Goddamn it, yes I can," he yelled, startling the group. "I can be here. I can! This camera has evidence that these people want to take your land," he said, holding it up. "And I'm not leaving until this is over." The group silenced, taken aback by Oly's resolve and anger. "Libeth," he whispered after a minute of silence, his subconscious saving him from hopelessness.

"What?" the man with the sinewy arms asked, surprised.

"Libeth."

The man held his hand out to the group behind him without turning, still facing Oly. "She gone, white man. You see that man dyin' over there? You best be gone, too, if you know what's good for you. You best be gone, too." And without another word, the group became silent again, staring at him with a pitiless contempt that left him cold.

Distracted by the pain in his leg, the thirst competing with hunger for attention, the burning building and the dying Hall all providing more than enough reason to give up, he stood. "I told you, I'm not leaving." Oly stood, taking one last look at Hall as he moaned again in pain and back at the church where several people poured buckets of water on the burning pile. "There was another man," he said. "Mr. Walker. What happened to him?"

"Don't know about him. Maybe he's underneath all that. This the only man we found when we got here. How do you know Libeth?"

Oly didn't answer the man but stood up and started limping past him, along a path that skirted Hog Hammock, leaving the chaotic scene at which he could no longer be.

The first thing Oly noticed as he approached the worn two-track through the cool passageway of overhanging trees, was that the Country Squire was missing. The second was that her dog, Sweetie, didn't come out to greet him. Oly called her name, but was greeted only by the heavy silence of late-morning heat and humidity. Nothing appeared to have been disturbed except that front screen door hung open, swinging listlessly. Oly knocked. Nothing. When he leaned over to peer in a window, the muffled drone of car tires on gravel came into earshot. Straining to hear if it was the whirring of Libeth's car, Oly decided not to take the chance and hurried around to the back of the trailer.

He crouched on all fours to look under the trailer at the approaching car and noticed the new tires of a vehicle that was not Libeth's. He hoped it was police and but didn't dare look out to confirm. The engine halted, followed by the slamming of the passenger and driver side doors. Oly heard the murmuring of men's voices, as the scent of cigarette smoke reached him. Though he could not make out all of the exact words, the conversation sounded cautious and tense, not helpful or concerned. "She can't go too far," one of the men said, eventually. "We'll get that fucking camera back."

Oly peered out just enough to see that it was the car that chased him. The men didn't go inside the trailer, but rather seemed to be waiting. Had they already been in? Where did Libeth go? Eventually, the men drove away, leaving behind the faint smell of cigarettes and exhaust. Oly didn't come out until he could no longer hear the sound of tires on gravel. He went around to the front and walked through the open screen door, greeted by a stench that made him pull back. He held his nose shut, resisting the urge to vomit, the coolness of air-conditioning absent and replaced by stifling humidity. Oly's eyes opened wide, as he couldn't believe the scene before him. A cloud of flies buzzed in the kitchenette that was now emptied of its contents, everything scattered and broken. He grabbed a jug of water and gulped nearly all of it before snagging a handful of crackers that had been spilled on the counter and stuffed his face, without hardly chewing. When he looked around the trailer the stench overwhelmed him again, as he waved the flies off and picked up an overturned chair. Clothes were strewn about the floor and drawers were left open, the insides spilling out. When he looked down, with sweat beginning to drip down his brow, Oly stepped on something that slid under his foot, causing him to reach for a table to keep his balance. Feces. The linoleum floor was covered with it. He hurried to the living room, as a gag reflex forced the crackers back into his throat. Though the smell was less pungent in the other room, the mess was not. Cushions had been strewn about, lamps on their side, and on the ground, broken glass. As he looked around, glass crunching under foot, Oly found a broken frame that had been handed to him only several days before, under very different circumstances. He picked up the photograph of Libeth's ancestors standing in front of their humble shack and began to tremble with anger, a stinging sensation growing in the back of his throat. In it, the faces of Bawendi, Chalim and all the people he had known in Togo began to appear. *You cannot be here,* rang in his head again, causing him a flash of anger. He pounded his fist on a wooden cabinet, causing it to crack and then folded the photo, putting it in his pocket. He sat in the silence for a minute and then got up to escape the stench, when he heard a whimper. Sweetie. She came out from under Libeth's bed at the end of the trailer and was covered in her own feces, her body shaking with fear and hunger. She looked up at Oly with a faint look of recognition. Despite the stench and dirt, Oly reached down, taking her face in his hands. "It's alright, Sweetie. I'll take care of you. It's alright, Sweetie. It's alright." Cleaning the dog gave Oly a new sense of control and hope that he desperately needed. He shared with her some of the food that had been left behind and looked around outside, trying to figure out what his next move was going to be. If only Sweetie could talk. He grabbed as much of the spilled food as he could find, and filled two plastic bags with everything from bread to fruit and biscuits. They exited the trailer and looked around. Sweetie wagged her tail, as if to signal to Oly that Libeth was out there somewhere and it was okay. On the sandy road leading to the trailer, he noticed several sets of car tracks. *Bastards,* he thought to himself, clutching the camera as he gave Sweetie a pat on the head.

CHAPTER 55

AU SECOURS, II

EMBOLDENED BY SWEETIE'S COMPANY, OLY followed the two-track. She led him along the twisty roads she had walked a million times before, quietly making their way toward the one direction as generations before them did whenever there was trouble on Sapelo: the ocean. She led Oly from a break in the road onto a worn path that led through a grove of trees and looked up at Oly with an *are you coming?* face as she walked ahead, her head bobbing up and down. Oly was astonished that Sweetie knew they were in trouble, but knew where to take him. As Oly followed through the grove and then onto a salt marsh, he felt a change in the wind and temperature and knew they were close to the sea. With quiet determination, Sweetie kept walking, the gravel under their feet gradually turning to sand, the air filled with a briny scent of organic decomposition.

When they reached a muddy embankment, Oly spotted the destination that Sweetie had in mind: a river bend that led around the outer edge of the island, hidden from the deep water approach to the landing. When they made their way down the embankment to the water's edge, a small flotilla of boats, several in disrepair and turned over on their sides, awaited them. Spotting a grey, wooden skiff with a set of oars inside, Oly quickly understood what she was telling him. Libeth was not on the island. *How did she know? How was that possible?* She scratched in the sand, assuring Oly that she knew what she was talking about.

"Nice job, Sweetie," Oly said, as he picked her up, placing her gently in the boat. "Nice job." He took the camera and pretended to take a picture of her. She looked at him as if to say, "Really? Is this the time for this?" He laughed at her face and sat in the boat, feeling as comfortable as a child getting on a bicycle. Pulling away from the land and tightly gripping the oars, Oly headed into the wind, staying alongside the banks of the river so as not to be noticed. Sweetie collapsed on the bottom of the boat, curled into a ball and shut her eyes. Her work was done. She couldn't track on the water, anyways. It was up to him. Despite a fatigue that threatened once again to defeat him, partnering with the pain in his leg and the dull ache of his shoulder, Oly pulled back as hard as he could, fighting an incoming current.

"Shockizzzzz, shockizzzzzzz," he began to chant. Montero was there, balancing on the stern, screaming at him. The power of his stroke on the oar-locks created a rhythmic banging that put him into a hypnotic trance, erasing the pain and driving Oly forward. A great heron, surprised by the noise, launched itself from the green banks, giant white wings spread in its wake. A gentle breeze picked up and Oly could feel the sweat drying on his back. The pain is his leg was a distraction, but he couldn't stop rowing. It was the one thing in the past months that he wanted to do without stopping. The inlet led to the open river where the current picked up and the fresh sea air filled his senses.

"Shockizzzz, shockizzzzz" he kept saying to himself, each time causing Sweetie's ears to prick up on cue. In spite of the current, his strength grew, as he left the smothering humid air of Sapelo.

After about an hour of rowing, a low, rumbling sound broke his trance and brought Sweetie to attention. She sat up in the boat and looked in the direction of the noise. "Hey, girl, what is it? Is that a boat?" She shook her tail, standing up on all fours. Oly looked at a small trail of smoke over the top of the marsh. It wasn't going fast and seemed big. The ferry or a barge. Could be looking for him, could be hired by those who'd rather not see him make the mainland. Who would know what had happened to him in this tangle of rivers and tidal inlets? He'd never be heard from again. Sweetie looked back at Oly with uncertainty. *Homme propose, dieu dispose.*

He crossed the current and directed the boat toward the banks. They entered a small indentation along the shore, becoming all but invisible in the high, muddy banks of the river. Oly eased the skiff against the soft mud, as the rumbling sound became louder and the superstructure came into view. The ferry. He lay down in the bottom of the skiff, lying on top of the oars so as not to get soaked by the water sloshing around in the ballast. He held onto Sweetie so she didn't look out.

As it passed, he could smell the fumes from the engine and hear the voice of the man he confronted in the field. He was tempted to sit up with the camera and take the man's picture. Instead, he looked at Sweetie curled up and smiled. "Yeah, I know. The long game. Play the long game," he said to her, causing her ears to twitch. The ferry passed, its speed against the current creating a frothy wake that caused the skiff to bounce up and down. Within minutes, it was quiet again, the noise absorbed by the marsh and the ferry obstructed by the high grasses of the river banks.

When he felt it safe to sit up again, Oly felt the folded picture that he had forgotten about jabbing into his leg. He pulled it out and stared at the picture of Libeth's family. His attention was drawn immediately to their eyes, where he saw the fatigue of a life lived in fear and pain. Bobson was right. Togo was right. They were all right. He was a yovo and he would always be. Who did he think he was? He was a fool to think he could make a difference when the only thing he'd ever be was a stranger. And now, here he was, a stranger in his own country, a foolish yovo trying to re-live something that gave him the fleeting satisfaction that he was doing some good in the world, but in reality was only making it more complicated. The fear and fatigue in Libeth's family's eyes was real; his was manufactured by a set of stupid decisions and circumstances that he could have (and possibly should have) avoided. It may have even cost lives. He thought of Hall, wondering if he lived, and of Libeth, if she was even alive on the other side of the river. His mind wandered desperately to Samantha, wishing that she were there to give him strength.

A shock of guilt and anxiety flowed through him as he put the picture away and shoved the oars back in their locks. He started rowing again, now against a current that was reaching its full incoming tide strength. It was becoming hopeless. *Shockizzz. Shockizzz.* He tried one more time. His hands were starting to bleed and the image of Montero started to fade, replaced now by the image of Samantha working on a paper in a cozy café, a mug of hot coffee next to her. What a complete fuck up, he started to say to himself, chanting, "Fuuuuck up, fuuuuuck up" instead of "Shockizzz."

He started to cry, the pain returning to his shoulder, his leg, his body. He looked back at Sweetie. whose ears lay flat on her head, mimicking his determination. Oly rowed harder, the adrenaline pushing him as he thought of Libeth's family, his own family, and the fact that no one in the world knew where he was. "Toughest fucking job you'll ever love!" he screamed. "Toughest fucking job!" he screamed again, rowing so hard that he almost fell backwards in the boat. He rowed until he was completely exhausted and had to take a break. He put the oars inside the boat and turned in the seat. Sweetie was looking at him with her ears raised, as if to say, "that's it?"

He leaned over in the boat, getting down on all fours despite his pain and put his head against Sweetie's body, listening to her heart beat along with the smell of wet fur that rubbed against his face. She stayed still for a minute, but seemed to become restless with the backwards direction of the boat and squirmed out of his arms. She pulled herself up on the bow, her ears flapping in the wind, listening. *Maybe you're giving up, but not me.* She started to lean forward, putting her front legs over the bow so that Oly had to move forward to keep her from jumping out. "What is it girl?" he said, trying to see what Sweetie was looking towards.

Every few seconds, through breaks in the high grass along the banks, he saw what appeared to be a blue flash. Lightning? He followed it. No, it was consistent and moving fast, heading in his direction. Then, seconds later, the noise that Sweetie heard well before he did, the distinctive whine of high-powered outboard engines at full throttle.

The sound got louder as it came closer, and Oly began to row as hard as he could to get into the open water to be noticed. He looked down at his hands, covered in blood from the oars ripping the skin from his wet hands and started to feel faint, his energy draining away. When the boat came into view, Sweetie started to bark with excitement, competing with the roar of the engines accompanied by the urgent wail of a siren. No longer able to row, Oly slumped in the boat and started to feel the dull sensation of losing consciousness wash over him.

The boat, a twenty-five foot Zodiac with the distinctive orange markings of the U.S. Coast Guard, made a wide sweep around Oly, cutting the wailing siren as it came to rest and making a huge wake that sloshed up against the river banks. A loudspeaker crackled over the water with the crisp, clear voice of someone in charge as the engines slowed to a rumble. The blue lights flashed over Oly's boat as the man spoke, his crew looking on with caution through their dark sunglasses. They were all armed.

"Please identify yourself immediately. This is the United States Coast Guard. Please identify yourself." The loudspeaker clicked off. Oly whispered his name, hardly loud enough for Sweetie to hear. She looked down at him sitting at the bottom of the boat and then turned back to the Zodiac, barking. Oly put one bloody hand over the gunnels and tried to say his name, but could only emit another whisper. He put the other bloody hand up and waved. He couldn't lift his head to see the Zodiac, but heard the engines getting closer. "Please identify yourself," the commanding voice said. "If you do not do so, we take permission to board. Do you copy?" A cloud of exhaust fumes washed over the skiff while the Zodiac drifted closer. Sweetie started barking and climbed back into the boat to signal that someone was below. Oly tried to wave Sweetie off as she licked his face. She was happy for a reason she wouldn't understand until later. The last thing he remembered was the skiff tilting, as though someone stepped on the gunnel.

When the vessel pulled up and saw the unconscious man lying in a puddle of bloody sea water, the crew quickly tied alongside and moved fast. They wrapped his leg, secured him in the Zodiac, called the chopper that was waiting on the mainland, and put Sweetie in a prominent place on the bow, as they sped to the dock.

As Oly floated in and out of consciousness, he felt the tightness of straps securing him and the chatter of people who were now in charge of whatever would happen to him next. *Red bird one, red bird one, this is seadog, repeat red bird one, this is sea dog, standby for an E.T.A. of nine minutes. Coordinates 56.5 degrees north by 74.45 east, Sapelo Island landing. I have a white male, losing consciousness, loss of blood, severely dehydrated, possible sunstroke. Assumed, but not confirmed as Mr. Richard Olymeyer. Repeat, assumed, but not confirmed as Mr. Richard Olymeyer.*

Captain Raymond Petitmon of the U.S. Coast Guard, the nephew of one Libeth, stood at the wheel, throttle on full speed, occasionally looking back at the crew as they tended to Oly. Sweetie stood facing the breeze with her ears blown back, knowing exactly where they were going. When they got closer to shore and started to slow, Oly came to and tried to put his head up. A large Coast Guard helicopter waited on the landing next to a bank of brown Georgia State Police cars, white media trucks, and a dark-skinned woman who paced back and forth.

Petitmon pulled back on the throttle, the vessel resting into the backwash of its wake, as the Zodiac crew prepared to land at the dock that Oly had departed from only several days earlier. Oly could barely keep his eyes open as one EMT pricked his arm for an I.V. "Sweetie," he whispered, trying to turn his head towards the landing.

"Aww," the EMT responded. "That's the first time anyone has said that after I pricked 'em. You're sweet, too."

"I think he was talking to me," Libeth interrupted. Oly was too woozy to respond as the I.V., a combination of sedatives and saline, started to flow into him. Libeth came over and was standing over Oly, going in and out of focus, her mouth moving without words attached to them. It was the last thing he remembered, along with the sounds of the helicopter revving its engines for the flight to St. Jude's in Savannah.

"Wanna join him, Aunt Libeth?" Petitmon asked, as he walked up behind her. "There's plenty of room," he said, holding a helmet toward her. While Oly's limp body was being hoisted into the cargo bay, she grabbed the orange and white helmet and pulled the visor down, giving her nephew a thumbs up signal and waving to the cameras that were pointed at them. The pilot pushed the throttle forward and gave the crew on the ground a nod, while the engines roaring back into life from their neutral landing position. Within seconds, the sound drowned out all noise until the rotors became a blur and lifted the heavy craft from the ground. Libeth looked out onto the swarm of vehicles that had arrived, lights still flashing, and waved at the media trucks below. She was holding Sweetie in both of her arms and had a huge smile on her face as the copter banked away from them and toward the open ocean. A few seconds later, when the helicopter ended its ascent and leveled out, Libeth looked out the window of the cargo door toward the direction of Sapelo. The chaos of the last few minutes settled into a rattling hum as they reached cruising altitude and started moving forward. She pulled the picture from Oly's pant leg and started to cry. She then looked at the camera that one of guardsmen had placed next to Oly and smiled, remembering the confrontation in the field. "Well I'll be damned," she said. "What do we have here?"

She stared out the window through the tinted visor and looked down at the middle of the winding river that led to the island. Her eyes fixed on a tiny speck, the abandoned skiff that once held Oly and Sweetie. It was riding the current toward the mouth of the river leading to open ocean, in the direction of the coast of Africa.

Several hours later, at the intensive care unit of St. Jude's, Oly slowly gained consciousness and squinted his eyes in the blinding light of the room. His brain could not make sense of what was happening, but returned to where he had left off twelve hours earlier. Several shapes floated above his bed, like unfocused balloons and he could hear voices in varying tones of familiarity. Libeth. Walker.

"Sweetie," Oly managed.

Libeth stood over him, holding his hand. "Right here," she said, squeezing it. Oly could smell Libeth's fragrant soapy smell, but her face didn't come into focus. "You done good. Sweetie just fine. And Hall in the next room. He's in rough shape, but he'll live. This here camera could be blow the cover off this whole thing. You did something, young man. You did something."

Oly looked down at the throbbing mitts that used to be his hands and turned to the attention of his aching body. "Shit, everything hurts," he said, groaning.

"It won't for long, honey," the nurse said, adjusting his I.V. Once I get the drip in, you'll get all the relief you need. Just relax."

He looked up at Libeth. "What happened?" he asked.

Libeth sighed. "After you run off, I lost you and that night they come. First they stop by the community center looking for y'all. You weren't there, so they come 'round my place. Whole bunch of 'em. That's when it was time to go. Wasn't thinkin' when I left Sweetie, but I didn't think they'd go inside if they knew I wasn't there."

"Who were they?" Oly asked, as he tried to sit up and take a gulp of water.

"Goons from the casino group. A friend of mine got back across by flatboat like you did. He says they come from those guys trying to buy up the land before the hearing. They off and headed back to Hog Hammock. No way to warn Walker and Hall, who were still there. Walker escaped with some of the originals, but they got Hall inside, nearly killing him when they burned it." Oly's mind flashed to when he came upon the scene. "So we finally get to the ferry and got the hell out of there," Libeth finished. "And I called my nephew and Professor Gunning."

CHAPTER 56
ENTRE LES DEUX

———◆———

FOR TWO FULL MINUTES, NO one said a word; the trauma of the past twenty-four hours sinking in, broken only by the periodic beep, beep of the machines monitoring Oly's vitals.

Oly looked at Libeth. "What now?"

"What now?" Libeth laughed. "What now?" she said, shaking her head, tssking just like the women in the Tchamba market did when he tried to haggle. "You in it now," she wagged her finger in his direction. "You in it now. The Feds are gonna be all over those boys and we're filin' in court tomorrow mornin' once I can pull some papers out of the car. Course, as you well know, there's not gonna be a hearing. We're goin' right up the ladder on this one. Yes sir. I got the Attorney General's office on it and I'm even expectin' a call from a couple of TV stations we met at the dock. They're all fightin' over this story. So that's what now, that's what now. And once I develop the film from that camera, oh boy, we're gonna be eatin' peach pie, white boy. Peach pie!"

She pulled out the picture of her family that Oly saved from her home. Tears started rolling down her face as she considered it.

"I'm sorry," Oly said. "I tried to save it, but the frame was smashed and your place was ... uh ... it was turned over." As she stared at the ramshackle hut with the family standing out front, dignity their only possession, Oly's eyes began to water.

"Never thought a reckoning would come," she said, tears rolling down her cheeks. "Never thought it would come." She looked at her purse and reached inside. "I managed to save somethin' else, too," she said, her eyes gleaming as she pulled out the original Reynolds letter.

THE HEARING TOOK PLACE AT the U. S. District Court in Atlanta. All of the major networks broke into regular news to show the opening proceedings live. The Peace Corps Director made a statement to the press, effectively distancing Oly's actions from the agency of the Peace Corps, while admiring his 'courage', as she called it. Libeth was dressed in a lavender business suit and pushed Hall, who was still recovering, in a wheelchair. Sweetie tagged alongside, somewhat overwhelmed, her tongue wagging as she tried to keep up. Oly walked on his own, limping next to Libeth, giving half smiles to the cameras as they flashed in his face. A CNN reporter, whom he recognized from television, put a microphone in front of him. "Mr. Olymeyer," she said. "How are you feeling? What brought you here?"

"I'm feeling great and Miss Libeth brought me here."

"Miss who?" she said, pausing to look down at her notes. Oly limped past her and caught the eye of Professor Gunning, who was wearing a dark suit and headed directly towards him. The cameras followed and blinded both of them by flashes as they hugged.

"Mr. Oly, I never thought it would turn out like this. We developed those pictures from the camera and have the district attorney's attention. Even though we lost much from the fire, we have enough to really make a case. I cannot thank you enough for your service. You truly did something we did not expect."

Oly smiled and looked at the cameras following his every move. "I've never had anyone tell me that. Thank you."

When they went inside, the court was packed. Libeth put her hand on Dr. Hall's shoulder and squeezed. She had a seat near the front, next to Oly. "Sweetie had to stay outside," she whispered.

Oly stared at the back of the man whom he confronted with the camera. He looked up at the grim-faced judge, who pounded his gavel, silencing the court. Libeth looked up at Oly. "*Homme propose,*" Oly said. "*Homme propose.*"

Two weeks later, after the court decided in favor of the Friends and put an injunction on future developments, Oly flew back to Boston to explain to his family how he ended up on CNN, found Jeff who was bartending on the Cape, and contacted Montero and the crew who took him out for a big night in Saugus. After a week of re-connecting, he got dropped off at Logan Airport by Andy and Brett. "Don't know where the hell you came from, brother," Andy said. "First thing, you're sleeping on my couch, chasing Internet creeps. Next thing, you're on CNN."

Brett poked him in the ribs. "You ever going to chill?"

Oly laughed and looked down at his ticket to Chicago. "Yeah, I'm going to chill. In about five hours, my friend. I'm going to chill."

—————◆—————

Started on a napkin in the Cantab Lounge in Cambridge in the summer of 1998.
Finished first draft on July 10, 2009 in Quebec City at the Palais de Congres.
Revised in Leysin, Switzerland from 2009-13.
Finished final draft at the Willowrest in Annisquam on August 4, 2014
Completed edits of final draft at Bushman on Tioman Island, Malaysia, April 13, 2016

www.ingramcontent.com/pod-product-compliance
Lightning Source LLC
Chambersburg PA
CBHW030628020726
47493CB00006B/1618